SAVE
YOUR
BREATH

ALSO BY MELINDA LEIGH

MORGAN DANE NOVELS

Say You're Sorry

Her Last Goodbye

Bones Don't Lie

What I've Done

Secrets Never Die

SCARLET FALLS NOVELS

Hour of Need

Minutes to Kill

Seconds to Live

SHE CAN SERIES

She Can Run

She Can Tell

She Can Scream

She Can Hide

"He Can Fall" (A Short Story)

She Can Kill

MIDNIGHT NOVELS

Midnight Exposure

Midnight Sacrifice

Midnight Betrayal

Midnight Obsession

THE ROGUE SERIES NOVELLAS

Gone to Her Grave (Rogue River)

Walking on Her Grave (Rogue River)

Tracks of Her Tears (Rogue Winter)

Burned by Her Devotion (Rogue Vows)

Twisted Truth (Rogue Justice)

THE WIDOW'S ISLAND NOVELLA SERIES

A Bone to Pick

SAVE YOUR BREATH

MELINDA LEIGH

Montlake
Romance

Published by Montlake Romance, Seattle

www.apub.com

Amazon, the Amazon logo, and Montlake Romance are trademarks of Amazon.com, Inc., or its affiliates.

ISBN-13: 9781542092838
ISBN-10: 1542092833

Cover design by Caroline Teagle Johnson

Printed in the United States of America

For Charlie, Annie, and Tom—
you are my world.

Chapter One

Where is she?

Hiding in the shadows outside Olivia Cruz's small white bungalow, he checked his watch. It was nearly ten o'clock. For the past few weeks, Olivia had left her house on Thursday evenings around five o'clock and returned by nine thirty. She should be home by now. Unless she'd changed her routine.

He crossed his arms and tapped his chin with a forefinger.

Maybe she wasn't coming home at all tonight. She occasionally spent the night at her boyfriend's house. Sometimes, the boyfriend slept here, but that hadn't happened on a Thursday night.

He'd give her another twenty minutes. If she didn't show up, he'd return to his van. He'd left the vehicle at a park about a mile away and jogged to Olivia's house. For now, he was comfortable and in a good position near her garage. A six-foot section of fencing at the front corner of the bungalow shielded the garbage can from passersby and provided him with an excellent hiding place. The September night had a pleasant snap. He peered around the wooden panel and scanned the street. The suburban neighborhood was quiet enough to hear the soft sounds of the night. A breeze rustled dead leaves on the grass, and a dog barked in the distance.

Headlights swept across blacktop as a car turned onto the street. Excitement and nerves warmed his blood.

Is it her?

He took a long, deep breath of woodsmoke-scented air and controlled his heart rate. He'd studied his target and planned the night with meticulous precision. Yesterday, he'd collected the surveillance cameras he'd planted several weeks before. Designed to catch thieves stealing packages from doorsteps, they looked like landscape rocks. With sixty days of battery life and cellular transmission, the cameras had allowed him to monitor Olivia's activity remotely. The cameras—and plenty of good old-fashioned surveillance from his van and the shed of a vacant house behind hers—had enabled him to paint an accurate picture of her daily routine.

He would take no chances.

The vehicle approached. A white Prius. Olivia's car. She was home.

It was on.

He cracked his neck and pulled the gloves from his pocket. After tugging them on, he opened his lightweight running backpack in which he carried a roll of duct tape, a length of rope, a mask, and a knife. His fingers traced the outline of a capped syringe in the chest pocket of his jacket.

He had everything he needed.

He pulled the mask from his backpack and put it on. In the unlikely event he was unsuccessful, his identity had to be protected. He'd prepared for every possible *what-if.* Having a Plan B was just as important as a Plan A. He could not get caught.

The garage door rolled up, and the interior brightened. The Prius turned into the driveway of Olivia's bungalow and drove into the garage. Listening, he poised on the balls of his feet and waited.

Timing was key.

Inside the garage, a car door opened, then closed. Olivia's heels clicked on the concrete. He pictured her crossing the floor to the door that led into the house and then simultaneously opening the door and reaching for the button on the wall. Mounted to the ceiling, the garage door opener clicked and hummed. A moment later, the door began to roll down. He heard the interior door close. Like most people, Olivia went inside before the garage door fully closed.

As it lowered, he ducked and stepped over the red-eye sensor into the garage. He had no time to waste. Olivia would have disarmed her security system using her fob from the car before she entered the house. From his surveillance over the past few weeks, he knew she would go into the kitchen, set down her purse, and remove her jacket and shoes before digging the fob out of her pocket. He had at least sixty seconds to get in before she reactivated the system—with him already inside the house. Olivia sometimes woke and paced her house in the middle of the night, so he knew she didn't use motion detectors when she was at home.

Counting off the seconds, he strode toward the door, his running shoes silent on the floor. His fingers closed around the knob, and he gave it a gentle twist. He pushed lightly and opened the door an inch. Pressing his eye to the crack, he looked inside. The laundry room was empty, with only dim light bleeding in from the adjoining kitchen. This was the part he hadn't been able to plan. He'd never been inside her house before. He knew only the basic layout of the rooms from what he could see through the windows.

Pushing the door farther, he slid through the opening, then closed it soundlessly behind him, making sure to release the knob slowly. Then he stood and listened. A doorway led from the laundry room into the kitchen. The white-paneled door between the rooms stood open. A few breaths later, a soft beep signaled the reactivation of the alarm system, and he heard Olivia moving around in the kitchen. Footsteps approached, and sweat broke out under his arms. He glanced around, looking for a place to hide. There was a closet across the room, but he wouldn't make it in time. His heartbeat thudded in his ears as he slid behind the open laundry room door and then pressed his back to the wall.

Then he waited.

He could overpower her here if necessary, but that wasn't ideal. Olivia looked like a scrapper. She'd fight him. He preferred quick and easy.

Her shadow passed across the doorway, and her steps retreated again. He heard the sound of the refrigerator opening and closing.

He exhaled.

Another door opened farther back in the house. Olivia was going into her bedroom. He crossed the tile in a few strides and opened the closet door. It was full of heavy winter boots and coats. Perfect. She wouldn't be opening it tonight.

He slid inside to wait for the house to become quiet again.

For Olivia to go to sleep.

For the perfect time to execute his plan.

Chapter Two

Olivia Cruz stared at her open closet. She'd spent the last hour rearranging her clothes for autumn. Technically, mid-September was still summer, but the weather in upstate New York had turned cool over the past week. The leaves were changing color and beginning to fall. Last week, she'd broken out her flannel pajamas. Tonight, she'd moved her sandals to a rear shelf and lined up a few pairs of ankle boots in front.

Now what? She could separate her blouses by color.

This is stupid.

Her closet was already ridiculously, ruthlessly organized.

She had an important decision to make, and she'd been procrastinating for days. She backed out of the walk-in closet and firmly closed the door. Sleep would help. But she'd managed little of that lately, and she dreaded lying in bed, staring at the ceiling for yet another night. She rubbed a lump of indigestion behind her breastbone and padded to the bathroom in search of an antacid.

Her weekly dinner with her family had distracted her earlier in the evening. Her mother had served frijoles negros, Olivia's favorite traditional Cuban dish. Olivia had overindulged, and the minute she'd left her parents' house in Albany to make the hour drive back to Scarlet

Falls, her true crime research had flashed right back into her mind and unsettled her stomach.

Chewing an antacid, she mulled over her stunning discovery. The implications of what she'd learned further stirred the black beans and rice in her belly. As a journalist, her job was to seek the truth, not play judge or jury. But should she choose to pursue and publish *this* truth, other people could pay the price for her revelation—possibly with their lives.

Her new book proposal was overdue, but Olivia's predicament felt like a no-win situation. Ignoring the truth went against all her principles. Then again, so did putting other people in danger.

But how much risk was involved? Could she live with being responsible for even a single innocent person's death?

Obsessing about her research had translated into three consecutive nights of insomnia. Enough was enough. She didn't need to make this decision alone. What she needed was outside perspective. She brought the antacids with her into the bedroom, picked up her phone from the nightstand, and checked the time. Eleven o'clock. She sent a CALL ME IF UR UP text message to Lincoln Sharp, her . . .

The word *boyfriend* seemed silly at their ages. She was forty-eight. Lincoln was fifty-three. They'd been dating for several months, and they spent the night together once or twice a week. She assumed their relationship was exclusive, although they hadn't specifically discussed it.

Labels weren't important to either of them, but when she saw him or he called unexpectedly, the stirrings of excitement and joy in her blood made her feel like a teenager. Beyond her attraction to him, she respected him both personally and professionally.

So why had she been stewing over her decision instead of asking for his opinion?

Lincoln owned and operated a private investigation firm. As a retired police detective, his practical experience with the legal system— and his knowledge of criminal behavior—exceeded hers. She valued his insight and trusted him to keep her research confidential. If she decided to pursue the story, she would hire his firm to help with the investigative legwork anyway. She may as well bring him on board now.

She burped. Her indigestion began to burn its way up her esophagus. She chewed a second antacid, the chalky taste coating her mouth. She reached for the glass of water on her nightstand and sipped.

A few seconds later, her phone rang, and she pressed "Answer."

"Is everything OK?" Lincoln asked in a worried tone. Her late-night text was unusual.

"Yes," Olivia assured him.

"I'm sorry I missed dinner with your parents again," he said. "I wrapped up my case tonight. I should be able to make dinner next week."

He didn't talk much about work, which was fine. She understood his professionalism and appreciated his need to maintain client confidentiality. But he had mentioned the case had involved a great deal of evening surveillance.

"They understand," she said. "I called because I'm stuck in my research, and I'd like your opinion. Are you free sometime tomorrow afternoon? I can come to your office."

"Sure." Interest brightened his voice. "How much time do you want me to block out?"

"An hour should do." She considered his associates. Lincoln's business partner, PI Lance Kruger, and Lance's fiancée, defense attorney Morgan Dane, could also provide useful insight on Olivia's dilemma. Morgan's legal advice might be particularly helpful. "I'd like Morgan's and Lance's thoughts as well. Could you see if they're available?"

"Hold on. Let me check their digital calendars." The line went quiet for a few breaths. "Lance should be here in the afternoon. Morgan has a client meeting at nine a.m. Her calendar is clear the rest of the day. How about I put you in the one p.m. spot?"

"Perfect." Olivia lowered the phone and made a note in the calendar app. "I'll see you tomorrow then."

"You know, when you texted"—Sharp's voice deepened—"I had hoped this was a booty call."

A little thrill rushed through her, followed by another burp. Olivia rubbed the fire behind her breastbone. "Tonight isn't a good night. I ate way too much of my mother's food."

He snorted. "That happens. She's an incredible cook."

"Plus, I have to get up early to take her to the doctor." Her mother had offered her the couch for the night, but Olivia preferred her own bed.

"Is everything all right?" he asked.

"She's worried about my sister's separation, and her blood pressure has been up. She likes me with her as an extra set of ears."

"Makes sense. I'll see you tomorrow then. Get some rest and feel better."

"Good night." Olivia lowered the phone.

Satisfied he would help her make her decision, she slid into bed and picked up a book. At midnight, she still wasn't sleepy. She set down the book and redirected her mind. Lincoln was teaching her to meditate. Closing her eyes, she concentrated on her breaths. She conjured a mental image of the beach in her mind and synced her breathing to the ebb and flow of the imaginary waves. At first she had trouble concentrating, but eventually her body felt heavy.

Olivia jolted, her heartbeat quickening, sweat dampening her T-shirt.

What was that?

A glance at the clock on her nightstand told her hours had passed. It felt as if she'd just closed her eyes, but she must have fallen asleep. She scanned the darkness of her bedroom. Her gaze passed over her dresser and chair. Had she heard something real, or had it been a dream?

She concentrated, listening hard to the sounds of her house, but she heard nothing unusual. A thunk and hum signaled the heater switching on. Hot air blew out of the floor vent and moved the sheers that hung over her windows.

The alarm hadn't sounded. She reached for her cell phone. It was far too early to rise for the day. She double-checked the security system app on her phone. The house was secure. She needed to go back to sleep.

She shifted her legs under the covers, closed her eyes, and tried to get comfortable.

Something whooshed. Her eyes snapped open. A large shape rushed toward her. A heavy body landed on top of her, pinning her to the mattress. The weight and size of her attacker felt male. She flailed and tried to push him off, but her arms and legs were trapped as he straddled her. She was cocooned in her comforter like a swaddled baby. Her throat constricted. She couldn't scream.

Panic sprinted through her bloodstream as she stared up at the dark assailant looming over her. His face seemed distorted, his features brighter and flatter than normal. He was wearing a mask.

With a bolt of gut-twisting horror, she recognized the character as Michael Myers from the movie *Halloween*.

A flash of terror shot up her spine. She inhaled, preparing to force a scream out of her tight throat.

He slapped her across the face. Pain, bright and sharp, sang through her cheekbone but faded in seconds as her adrenaline surged. The scream died in her chest.

He waved a knife in front of her face and then pressed a gloved finger to the rubber lips of the mask. *"Shhh."*

Olivia stilled. Given their positions, she couldn't move anyway, and it was unlikely a neighbor would be able to hear her scream, not with her insulated windows closed.

Pretend to cooperate. Wait for an opportunity.

Her instinct was to flail, but he'd disabled both her flight and her fight responses. Her pulse echoed in her ears, each beat of her heart ramming against her breastbone. Her breaths came faster, until she was nearly hyperventilating.

What was he going to do?

After shrugging off his small backpack, he tossed it onto the bed next to her and unzipped it. Putting the knife in his pocket, he shifted his weight from knee to knee and jerked her hands one at a time out from under the covers. He held both her wrists in one of his hands. She tried to pull away, but her wrists were thin and his grip secure. He pulled something from his bag, and fresh fear raced through her. She swallowed the metallic taste as he wrapped duct tape securely around both of her wrists. Once her hands were bound, he slapped a piece of tape across her mouth as well.

Tears ran from her eyes. Her nose clogged. She couldn't draw in enough air through only her nose. She grew light-headed. Could she suffocate with her mouth covered? Her vision dimmed. Spots appeared in front of her eyes.

She needed to control her breathing. Lincoln's voice echoed in her mind. *Inhale, two, three, four. Hold, two, three, four. Exhale, two, three, four.* After three breath cycles, her vision cleared.

The intruder climbed off the bed and yanked the blankets off her body. Under her flannel pajama bottoms and sweatshirt, Olivia shivered, fighting the panic that threatened to debilitate her. Whatever he was going to do, she needed to be ready to react. If he was going to rape her, he'd need to take his hands off her to unfasten his pants. But he made no movement in that direction. Instead, he bound her ankles with duct tape.

Olivia's muscles went rigid. If he was going to kill her, he would have done it already, right?

While she was battling panic, he appeared calm. His movements were efficient and smooth, calculated, as if he was simply performing a chore. He didn't hurry, and he didn't appear to be excited.

Maybe he just wanted to rob the house. He acted almost professional. Hope blossomed inside her. She didn't care what he took as long as he left.

Please.

He showed her the knife again and whispered, "Don't move."

She froze. Standing next to the bed, he picked up her cell phone and the fob to the security system that she had set on her nightstand. He slid both items into his pockets, then zipped his backpack and put it on.

Take what you want and go.

Olivia held completely still and tried not to make any noise—an effort to make him forget she was even there. She would give him no reason to harm her.

But he turned to face her again. His eyes were hidden behind the dark holes in the mask. She felt rather than saw his scrutiny. A whimper sounded deep in her throat.

No.

Please.

He leaned over, grabbed her by the arms, and hauled her to a sitting position on the side of the bed. The truth rushed over Olivia like ice water. He wasn't there for her things.

He was there for her.

Suddenly, his calm was terrifying rather than reassuring. He was going to take her somewhere else.

She'd recently finished writing a book about killers and kidnapping. One thought dominated her brain: she could not let herself be taken to a place where he had the time and privacy to do anything he wanted to her.

Most victims taken to a secondary location didn't survive.

She had nothing to lose at this point. She had to fight.

Olivia shoved both hands at his face, but the mask protected his skin. He grabbed for her wrists. She jerked them out of his grasp and went for his eyes. He swatted, an automatic response. Olivia kicked out with both legs, but she was wearing only socks. When her toes slammed into his heavier shinbone, pain shot through her feet. With barely a grunt, he stepped sideways, trapping her feet between his legs.

She attacked his face again, this time tearing at the edge of the mask, trying to rip it from his face. Her nail caught in the mask. A piece of rubber broke free, and she went after the soft skin of his neck. Her nails raked his skin, and he flinched. His body tensed, anger radiating in his posture for the first time.

He drew his arm back and hit her with a jab. His fist connected with her face. Even as pain bloomed through her cheek and her vision darkened, she realized he'd held back. He could have hit her much harder.

He ducked and hauled her over his shoulder. Her hands and upper body dangled down his back. His small nylon backpack rubbed against her face. Olivia flailed, but he held her in place with a firm hand on her back. His shoulder dug into her belly, further inhibiting her breathing.

Hopelessness swamped her. There was nothing she could do.

She was helpless.

She bobbed against his back as he walked down the hall. He knew her house. Too well. How long had he been inside with her?

Frantic thoughts sped through her mind. They were going toward the garage. He was going to kidnap her with her own vehicle.

When she didn't show up at her mother's house and Sharp Investigations tomorrow—no, today—Lincoln would call. If she didn't respond, eventually he'd come looking for her. Her purse and car would be gone. Other than the bedclothes being mussed, there would be no indication she'd been kidnapped. She needed to leave a sign that she'd been taken.

She sawed her hands back and forth, trying to free herself. It didn't work. The tape dug deeper into the thin skin of her wrists. Frustration and desperation bubbled up in her throat and nearly choked her.

Lincoln had told her she needed to upgrade her security system. He'd even offered to do it for her. She hadn't thought it was a priority and had blown him off. She hadn't wanted to be inconvenienced, even just for a day or two.

Now she was going to die.

Maybe she'd be lucky and he'd kill her quickly.

In the kitchen, he grabbed her purse and keys from the island. Using the fob, he turned off her alarm. Then he walked into the laundry room and paused to open the door that led to the garage. Olivia reached toward the wall and grabbed the molding around the door with both hands. She held on as tightly as she could. With an angry jerk, he yanked her fingers off the wood trim. Pain shot from Olivia's fingertip as her nail tore. Was she bleeding? Just in case, she thrust her hands forward once more and wiped her fingers across the bright-white trim paint. In the dark, she couldn't see if she'd left a mark.

He carried her into the garage, then closed and locked the interior door.

In one last desperate move, she pulled out her right earring and dropped it on the floor. Then she did the same with the left one.

But that was the best she could do. He put her in the cargo area of her car. The Prius didn't have a trunk, just a hatch. She'd be able to sit up, possibly draw attention to herself as he drove. Before her hopes rose, he pulled a rope from his backpack and tied it around her neck. He drew it tightly enough to dig into her throat. Then he forced her body into a tight curl and snugged the rope around both her ankles and wrists.

She flinched as the sharp prick of a needle pinched her thigh. Fear burst fresh in her mind. He'd injected her with a drug. Soon, she would be truly vulnerable.

Something soft fell over her body and head. She touched it with her fingers. The lightweight throw she kept over the back of the sofa?

The vehicle shifted as he closed the cargo hatch.

Olivia wiggled, testing the restraints. The slightest movement of her body tightened the noose around her neck. If she tried to escape, she'd strangle herself. She would have to lie still and wait to see where he took her. Maybe she'd be able to escape later. But considering how easily he'd nabbed her, the odds didn't feel good. He'd planned tonight down to the smallest detail. He'd been prepared.

She clung to the thought that he hadn't killed her yet. He'd gone to great trouble to take her alive. But why?

Fear cramped her stomach as drowsiness overtook her.

Maybe she didn't want to know what else he had planned. Not that she would have a choice. Whatever was going to happen to her, she was helpless to prevent it.

But no plan was perfect. She couldn't give up.

For now, all she could do was hope Lincoln came looking for her.

And that until he found her, she could survive.

Chapter Three

Defense attorney Morgan Dane ushered Lena Olander into her office.

The woman's watery-blue eyes were red rimmed and swollen. She'd been ugly crying.

Guilt weighed on Morgan. "Would you like some coffee or tea, Mrs. Olander?"

"No. Thank you." Mrs. Olander clutched a small brown purse in both hands. She wore dark jeans and a light-blue sweater. Limp straight hair brushed her shoulders, and there was a clear line three inches from her roots that indicated she'd suddenly stopped coloring her gray hair blonde. "I have to get back to the farm before lunch. Kennett doesn't know I'm here. He wouldn't approve."

"Kennett is your husband?" Morgan asked.

Mrs. Olander's head bobbed in a tense nod. "He likes his meals on time."

"You own a dairy farm, correct?" Morgan had Googled the family. Olander Dairy was a midsize family-owned commercial dairy farm.

"Yes." Mrs. Olander's gaze roamed around the office without focus.

Morgan closed the door and gestured to the two guest chairs that faced her desk. "Please, sit down."

Mrs. Olander eased into the chair as if every bone and muscle in her body ached. Though tall, broad shouldered, and physically fit looking for a woman in her midfifties, she acted frail. Her upper body curled forward, as if protecting her vital organs from a possible attack.

Morgan rounded her desk and sat. "What brings you to my office?"

"I want to hire you." Mrs. Olander set her purse on her knees, her fingers digging into the brown leather like a raptor's talons. She opened her purse, removed a tissue, and blotted her eyes, wincing slightly as if they were sore. "I'm sorry."

"There's nothing to be sorry about." Morgan's job was guiding people through some of the most traumatic times of their lives.

Mrs. Olander sniffed. "Are you familiar with Erik's case?"

"I know the major details." Morgan had skimmed through a number of articles.

A few weeks before, Erik Olander had been convicted of murdering his wife, Natalie. The trial had held the media's attention for a solid week.

"My son is innocent. Erik would never have killed Natalie. He loved her."

"He was convicted of strangling her with a lamp cord."

"He didn't do it. A man broke into their home and killed Natalie. It was like that movie with Harrison Ford." Mrs. Olander circled a hand in the air. "The one where he played a doctor who was falsely accused of killing his wife."

"*The Fugitive*?"

"That's it." Mrs. Olander nodded.

"Natalie had been researching domestic violence shelters at the library the day before her death."

The fact that Natalie had utilized the library's computer suggested her husband had monitored her internet activity.

"She was mentally ill." Mrs. Olander's response sounded rehearsed.

"Natalie had never been diagnosed with a mental illness," Morgan said.

"No, but she was always as jumpy as a deer. She must have had anxiety."

"The prosecutor painted Erik and Natalie's relationship as abusive, and several witnesses testified that she was afraid of your son."

"I never saw any bruises." Mrs. Olander looked at the floor and shook her head hard. Was she trying to convince herself? "She was paranoid."

Morgan had prosecuted domestic abuse cases. Some men were very skilled at not leaving visible marks, but she didn't argue with the woman.

"He deserved a fair trial." Red splotches colored Mrs. Olander's sharp cheekbones. "His lawyer barely tried. He wanted Erik to plead guilty. Now he *says* he has someone reviewing Erik's trial, but he seems to have lost interest. He doesn't return my calls."

Morgan had seen nothing in the articles she'd read to indicate the case had been controversial in any way. The jury had deliberated for only a few hours before returning a guilty verdict.

"Why do you think Erik's trial was unfair?" Morgan asked.

She probably would have advised Erik to take a plea deal too. The case against him had been solid. He could have received twenty-five years rather than life in prison. He was only thirty-two. He would have had some years left after his sentence had been served. Convicted, he'd been sentenced to life without parole.

Mrs. Olander's lips puckered. "Because the jury foreman didn't disclose the fact that she'd been a victim of domestic violence."

"How do you know this?" Morgan made a note on her legal pad.

"She was interviewed last week." Mrs. Olander's chin came up. "The TV show host did a better job of researching her background than the court."

The court did not research every juror's background. Prospective jurors filled out a brief questionnaire and were questioned during jury selection in a process known as voir dire.

"Being a domestic violence victim would not automatically disqualify her from serving on the jury," Morgan explained.

A deep, despondent frown dragged at Mrs. Olander's mouth. "Well, it should." Her eyes misted. "How could she possibly have been fair to my Erik?"

While a juror with a personal history of domestic violence *might* identify with Natalie, it was hardly a given. The situation wasn't as cut and dried as Mrs. Olander thought. She'd probably watched too many episodes of *Law and Order*. In real life, courtrooms were far less dramatic.

"The juror would have been asked if there was anything in her background that would make her incapable of being impartial," Morgan said.

"Clearly she lied." Mrs. Olander blotted her eyes with the tissue again. "My son's conviction should be overturned."

"It's not that simple. Even if the juror's background *did* prove to be grounds for appeal, the best possible outcome for Erik would be a new trial. The court would not just set him free."

Mrs. Olander's shoulders caved in. "Well, it should. The woman concealed her background. If that isn't enough to overturn his conviction, what is?"

"There are no perfect juries," Morgan said. "This is understood by the court. Every person who serves on a jury brings a lifetime of experience with them. The court asks only that jurors enter each case with open minds and base their decisions solely on the evidence presented at trial."

"That's not right!" Mrs. Olander spat out the words. "How can a prejudiced juror not be grounds for appeal?"

"I didn't say it *wasn't* grounds for appeal, only that it wasn't a certainty. How long ago did the juror's domestic abuse allegedly occur?"

"I don't remember exactly." Mrs. Olander rubbed the brass clasp of her purse with her thumb. "Maybe twenty years or so. What does it matter?"

"That's a long time ago. The juror may have truly believed she could be impartial."

"That's impossible."

Is Mrs. Olander speaking from personal experience?

Morgan let it go and changed the subject. "What is your financial situation? Erik's defense must have been costly."

"Yes. It was." Mrs. Olander's frown nearly met her jawline, and her swollen eyes were bleak. "And business hasn't been good for years. Small farms like ours are being squeezed out of the market. Only the big operations can survive."

"You sold the farm."

Mrs. Olander nodded. "We took out a mortgage to pay for Erik's initial defense, but it wasn't enough. We couldn't keep up with the new attorney bills and make the mortgage payments. We're behind on everything. We've lived in that house for twenty-five years, but the truth is the cows barely earned enough to feed themselves. We have to move out soon. I thought I'd care, but I don't."

"Appeals involve large amounts of legal research and the writing of long, intricate briefs, which translates to many billable hours. An appeal would be expensive."

Mrs. Olander's eyes were desperate. "My son is sitting in a prison cell, and he will remain there for the rest of his life unless we do something."

As much as Morgan sympathized, mother to mother, the case wasn't right for her. She opened her desk drawer and withdrew a small notepad. On it, she wrote the name of a larger legal firm in the area. They occasionally referred clients back and forth, depending on the circumstances. Some clients were better served by a one-lawyer shop, like Morgan's. Others—like Erik Olander's appeal—required a full staff of clerks.

Also, Mrs. Olander's seeming lack of grief for her daughter-in-law seemed off to Morgan. Everything about the woman felt wrong. Morgan's instincts said Erik Olander had killed his wife in a fit of rage, exactly as the prosecutor—and the evidence—had described.

She tore the paper from the pad and offered it to Mrs. Olander. "Appeals aren't the sort of cases I usually handle. I'm a trial lawyer. You need an appellate lawyer. It's a different process that requires a different skill set. You will get the most for your money if you hire an attorney who specializes in appeals."

"You're turning me down?" Mrs. Olander stared at the slip of paper as if it would bite her.

"Yes. You really need a bigger firm."

Mrs. Olander took the paper, held it at arm's length, and squinted. Her face fell. "They already said no."

No doubt they hadn't seen legs on the appeal either.

"I'm sorry." Morgan empathized, but she couldn't change reality for Mrs. Olander.

Mrs. Olander set the paper on Morgan's desk. "You were my last hope. I've seen you on TV. You always seem so . . . righteous." Her gaze rose, meeting Morgan's. Mrs. Olander's eyes were filled with disappointment, sorrow, and pain deep enough to scar the soul.

Yet she had spoken of her dead daughter-in-law almost with disdain. Had her maternal instincts blocked out her feelings for Natalie? Or had her son's case drained Mrs. Olander to a point where she had no remaining emotional reserves?

Mrs. Olander studied Morgan for a few heartbeats; then her mouth pressed into a bloodless line. "What do I owe you for your time today?"

"Today's meeting was a free consultation." Morgan wanted nothing from the poor woman.

"Thank you." Mrs. Olander rose and tucked her purse under one arm. "You could have taken the case and run up a huge bill, but you were honest with me. I do appreciate that."

She turned and walked out of Morgan's office with the stiff, painful gait of a beaten woman. Needing air, Morgan escorted her into the hall.

The door to the next office was open. Lance sat behind his desk. He took in Morgan's face and the client's in one glance, no doubt also reading the hopelessness in Mrs. Olander's body language.

Morgan saw the woman out. When she closed the door and turned around, Lance was leaning in his doorway. Six two, blond, and buff, he wore tactical cargos, a snug black T-shirt, and a Glock. He looked more like a SWAT team member than a PI. Despite his badass appearance, his blue eyes were soft and concerned as they met hers.

"Is everything all right?" he asked.

Morgan nodded. She rented office space from Sharp Investigations. Since her cases often required the services of an investigator, the arrangement was convenient. The PI firm occupied the bottom half of the duplex. The firm's founder, Lincoln Sharp, lived upstairs.

Morgan headed for the kitchen at the rear of the building. She poured a glass of filtered water from the pitcher in the fridge. She turned and leaned against the counter. The window that overlooked the backyard was open, and cool air wafted into the room, bringing with it the scents of falling leaves and woodsmoke.

"You look like you need something stronger than water." Lance turned and leaned next to her. Their arms touched, his contact grounding her as always.

Morgan's husband had been killed in Iraq a few years before. She'd spent two years burrowed under depression and grief. Last year, she'd reconnected with Lance, whom she'd dated briefly in high school. Their reconnection had blossomed into a relationship filled with love and respect. He'd asked her to marry him last spring. She was grateful every single day that she'd been given a second chance at love.

Morgan sighed. "That was a rough one."

"What did she want?"

Morgan summed up the meeting in a few sentences. "I *could* have taken the case. It would have required a marathon of overtime, but I'm capable of filing an appeal. I would have charged her a fraction of what an appellate lawyer at a big firm would cost." Doubt crept into Morgan's chest.

As a former prosecutor, she was still adjusting to being on the defense side of the courtroom. When she'd first opened her practice, she'd been skeptical. Her years as a prosecutor had convinced her that almost all suspects were guilty. But her attitude had shifted. She'd proven a number of people innocent who had been charged with serious crimes. She could think of few things worse than going to prison for life for a murder one didn't commit.

"We both know it's unlikely that prejudice from one juror could cause an innocent man to be found guilty," Lance said. "It takes all twelve jurors to convict. They have to reach a unanimous decision."

"This is true," Morgan agreed. "I felt terrible for Mrs. Olander, but I didn't see an appeal going anywhere."

"You were honest with her. You *are* a trial lawyer—and a damned good one at that. You don't need to take every case you're offered. You have other clients."

"None of those are very challenging at the moment."

"Every case doesn't have to make headlines. That high school senior facing a month in jail for vandalism needs your help too. You need to listen to your instincts. If the case doesn't feel right, there's probably a reason."

"You're right." Morgan finished her water and set the cup on the counter. "I have total control over which clients I accept, and routine cases are wonderful. I have no desire to work a hundred hours a week."

"Damn right." Lance turned to face her, putting his hands on her shoulders. "That's the best part of being self-employed. I like being home for dinner with the kids."

"So do I. Family dinners are important."

Lance's house had burned down six months before. He'd moved in with Morgan's family and had bonded with her three young daughters. The girls had embraced him as their soon-to-be stepfather. Lance had even become the preferred bedtime story reader. He put serious effort into voice-acting every character, sometimes sending the girls into giggling fits that didn't exactly encourage sleep.

The children didn't miss their biological father the way Morgan did. Only her oldest, at age seven, had even the faintest memory of him. Morgan was glad her kids were happy. The thought of them not remembering their father made her sad, but she kept it to herself.

Lance let his fingertips slide down her arms until he was holding her hands. "We're getting married in just over two weeks. We don't have time for a long and complicated case."

"No, we don't." Morgan put aside her morning meeting. She deserved to enjoy every moment of pre-wedding excitement. "Now tell me where we're going for our honeymoon. I need to pack."

"It will be warm." Lance laughed. "And that's all I'm telling you. The rest is a surprise."

"That's not fair."

"Your sister will make sure you are adequately prepared." Lance's smile turned smug.

Before Morgan could protest about their secret honeymoon destination, the sharp, unmistakable sound of a gunshot came through the open window.

Chapter Four

The gunshot sent Lance's hand to his sidearm. Pulling the weapon was a reflex. Tucking Morgan behind him was just as automatic. His brain knew she didn't require his protection, but his heart didn't care.

Morgan dropped to one knee and ducked her head below the level of the countertop, her own gun in her hand. She whispered, "Could you tell where the shot came from?"

Lance shook his head, duckwalked to the window, and peered over the ledge. The small rear yard appeared empty and quiet. Reaching up, he closed and locked the window. Then he turned and jogged in a crouch out of the kitchen and into the hallway. Morgan was right behind him.

"Sharp!" Lance called.

"In here." Sharp's voice came from his office. Lance and Morgan slipped into the room. The original living room of the duplex, Sharp's office had a large window that overlooked the street. Lance's boss, PI Sharp, was peering around the window frame, gun in hand, his lean face grim. As a result of a strict exercise regimen, a green and crunchy lifestyle, and pure stubbornness, the fifty-three-year-old retired police officer was in better shape than most college kids.

"Could you tell where it came from?" Lance asked.

"Out there." Sharp nodded toward the street. "See anyone out back?"

"No." Lance angled his body on the opposite side of the window. The tree-lined street was empty. "Have you seen anyone?"

"All I see is that van parked across the street in front of the accounting firm."

Lance focused on the white minivan parked at the curb. Sunlight reflected off the windows. "I can't see if anyone is inside the vehicle."

"Should I call 911?" Morgan asked. "Are we sure it wasn't a car backfiring?"

Sharp's lean face creased. "Sounded like a gunshot to me, but it's possible." He headed for the door. "Let's check it out."

Lance followed Sharp. Looking over his shoulder at Morgan, he said, "Stay here and keep watch. Someone needs to be able to call the police."

She nodded and took a position at the edge of the window.

In the hall, Sharp turned toward the back of the house. "We'll go out the back door and circle around."

In case there was a shooter outside, they wouldn't want to walk out the front door.

They went into the kitchen. Lance checked the rear yard. Still empty. He moved into position behind his boss. Lance's pulse throbbed in his throat as Sharp slipped out the door. They crept across the back porch and jumped over the railing into the side yard. Moving quickly, they jogged in the shadow of the house to the front corner.

Shoulder to shoulder, they pressed their backs against the siding.

Sharp peered around the corner. "Looks clear."

"I'll cross to the tree at the curb."

Sharp nodded, stepping into position to provide cover.

Lance darted around a low trimmed shrub and then ran in a crouch across the front yard. He stopped at the oak tree, pressing his back into the bark and scanning the street in both directions. He listened intently, but adrenaline—and the echo of his own heartbeat—drowned out most external noise.

His gaze fell on the minivan parked on the opposite side of the street. The sun's reflection turned the windows into mirrors. Lance looked back at Sharp, then motioned toward the minivan. Sharp tapped his own chest and pointed toward the tree. Lance waited for Sharp to cross the lawn and join him at the tree before jogging across the blacktop. He circled the van, angling off onto the lawn of the accountant's office.

From his position, the sun no longer bounced off the vehicle windows, and Lance had a clear view inside. A figure was slumped over the steering wheel.

He moved closer, peering into the front and back seats. Rounding the rear of the van, he cupped one hand over his eyes and looked through the tinted glass. The cargo area was empty.

Lance headed for the front of the minivan. His initial inspection had concentrated on looking for threats. Now that he knew the rest of the vehicle was clear, he turned his attention back to the driver.

Even after hearing the gunshot, the sight still shocked him.

The inside of the driver's window and front corner of the windshield were splattered with blood and gore. Lance moved around to the passenger-side window for an unobstructed view.

It was the woman who had just left Morgan's office. There was a hole in her temple, just above her right ear. Her right arm lay on the seat next to her thigh. Her open fingers extended just beyond the seat of the van. On the floor was a Glock 43.

"GSW. Call 911." Using the hem of his T-shirt, Lance tried the vehicle door. Locked. He ran around to the driver's side. Also locked. The windows were all closed.

Sharp jogged across the street, his phone pressed to his ear. He gave the dispatcher the address, then held the phone away from his face. "Could she still be alive?"

"Doubt it." But the possibility, even if it was a long shot, trumped preservation of evidence. Lance turned his gun in his hand and used the butt end to break the driver's side window. Reaching inside the vehicle, he pressed two fingers to the woman's neck. "She's dead."

Sharp relayed the information on the phone, then turned and walked a few feet away.

Lance holstered his gun, took his phone out of his pocket, and began taking pictures. If questions arose regarding the death, he wanted his own records. The police didn't always want to share, and once law enforcement arrived, the vehicle would be off-limits.

Crouching, he squinted at the spatter of gore on the inside of the windows. Along with blood, bits of bone and brain matter were stuck to the glass. Lance bent lower to get a better view of her face and head. Her eyes were open and empty. He checked the passenger-side windows but saw no sign that a bullet had been fired into the vehicle.

On the passenger seat, a brown purse sat open. The Glock 43 on the floor was a lightweight, compact 9mm—a solid choice for concealed carry. Had the woman taken her handgun from her purse?

Lance went cold from the inside out. Mrs. Olander had likely been carrying that gun during her meeting with Morgan. A shoe scraped on the pavement behind him. He turned to see Morgan standing a few feet away. She rubbed her arms. Her slim gray skirt and silk blouse offered little protection against the morning chill. Her long black hair was coiled at the nape of her neck.

"Who is it?"

He stood and blocked her view of the body. "The woman who just left your office."

"Is she all right?" She tried to look around him.

He shifted, putting a hand on her arm. "No. There's nothing anyone can do. She's dead."

Morgan's face froze in horror for a few seconds. Then she shook her head. "I don't know why that's a surprise. We heard the gunshot."

She'd been a prosecutor for years, and they had worked several murder cases together after she'd opened her own criminal defense firm. She had seen dead bodies before. She didn't need to be sheltered, but doing so was a reflex for him.

He dropped his hand, and she walked around him. He watched her steel herself as she examined the body and vehicle. Sadness creased her face. Morgan never lost her empathy. Her refusal to be hardened to violence and its impact on the innocent made her job tougher, but it also gave her the passion to fight for her clients.

Her mouth flattened. "Suicide?"

"Probably."

She shot him a glance.

"This is not your fault," he said.

"I know." But responsibility was all over her face. The heart didn't always believe what the brain told it.

"I mean it."

"She killed herself within minutes of leaving my office." Morgan hugged her waist. "She said I was her last hope, and I refused to take the case."

"This is not your fault," Lance repeated in a stronger voice.

A siren sounded in the distance, and he put his phone in his pocket.

Sharp lowered his phone too. All three of them stepped a few feet farther from the vehicle. A Scarlet Falls PD patrol vehicle parked a few yards from the minivan.

Officer Carl Ripton climbed out. Lance and Sharp had worked with Ripton on the SFPD. Carl verified the victim was dead, then approached Sharp, Lance, and Morgan. "What happened?"

"We heard a shot." Sharp gave Carl a quick summary of the discovery of the body.

Carl returned to his patrol vehicle to make calls. A few minutes later, he returned with a small notepad and pen. He separated Morgan,

Lance, and Sharp, took a statement from each of them, and asked them to wait on the sidewalk.

"The ME is on his way." Carl retrieved a camera from his vehicle and began taking pictures and notes.

A half hour passed before the medical examiner and Morgan's sister, Detective Stella Dane, arrived. Stella and the ME examined the body and conferred with Carl. The ME's team unloaded a gurney from the back of the van. It was already outfitted with an open black body bag. Neighborhood looky-loos were gathering on the sidewalk. People craned their necks, trying to see the body.

Stella glanced at the gawkers, then turned to Morgan, Sharp, and Lance. "Can we go inside to talk?"

"Certainly." Sharp led the way through the front door. "I'll also pull the surveillance camera feeds for you." He turned into his office.

"Perfect." Stella followed Morgan and Lance back to the kitchen.

Stella sat down at the table next to her sister and produced a small notebook from her pocket. "Tell me about your client."

"Mrs. Olander wasn't my client," Morgan corrected. She detailed her meeting with Mrs. Olander. Lance corroborated Mrs. Olander's arrival and departure times.

"So no one saw her after she walked out the door," Stella clarified.

"That's correct." Morgan nodded.

Sharp returned with his laptop and set it on the table. "It's all here."

He tapped on the keyboard to wake the computer. The screen came to life, and Sharp clicked "Play."

On the screen, Mrs. Olander walked out of the office, crossed the street, and got into her minivan. Once she closed the vehicle door, her figure became a blur behind the glass. She seemed to sit still for a while. Lance imagined her staring through the windshield, full of hopelessness. Then her shadow moved.

The silent splatter on the inside of the window made them all flinch. Lance's stomach turned over. No one spoke for a few heartbeats.

Sharp cleared his throat, then pointed to the screen. "Both cameras in front of the house actually cover the minivan, but the other one is at a bad angle. All you can see is the reflection of the sun. I'll give you both videos, though."

"Did you watch any more of the video?" Stella asked. "Does anyone approach or leave the van?"

Sharp clicked on "Fast-Forward." "As you can see, there's no one on the video until we find her. In the download I included the entire time period until Carl arrives."

"OK." Stella sighed and nodded. "That makes my job much easier."

It didn't get much clearer than having the suicide caught on video.

"I'll make tea." Sharp filled the kettle and then lit the burner under it. He dropped a mesh tea ball into his ceramic pot. When the kettle whistled, he filled the pot and brought it to the table, along with four mugs.

Morgan didn't argue, even though Lance knew she'd rather have coffee. But then, maybe she was as queasy as he was. Besides, they all knew when Sharp went into mother-hen mode, there was no stopping him. Sharp was not satisfied with living his own neo-hippie lifestyle. He wanted to pawn it off on everyone around him.

Sharp poured.

"Thank you." Stella added a teaspoon of sugar to her cup.

Sharp's phone rang, and he excused himself, leaving the room to answer the call. His voice faded.

Stella wrote a few notes, then pocketed her notepad. "Considering the video and other evidence, Mrs. Olander's death appears to be a suicide. I don't see any sign of foul play."

"The woman was clearly despondent about her son's conviction," Morgan added, her voice riddled with guilt. Lance covered her hand with his, and she gave him a small smile of appreciation.

"I'll let you know when the ME finishes the autopsy and issues an official cause of death." Stella's cell buzzed, and she glanced down at it. "I have to go. So much crime. So little time."

"Where's Brody?" Lance asked.

Stella was one of two detectives in Scarlet Falls.

"He's on vacation," she said. "He and Hannah are drinking rum on a beach in Aruba."

"Good for them." Lance rose to walk Stella to the front door. He could see Sharp in his office, talking on his phone. An unusual stiffness to his posture caught Lance's attention.

Sharp turned, his eyes grim.

Something's wrong.

Chapter Five

"Take a deep breath." Sharp tried to calm Mrs. Cruz, but the fear in her voice gripped his gut like a fist.

"Olivia gave me your number in case of an emergency," Mrs. Cruz said. "I hope it is all right to call. I don't know who else to contact."

Emergency?

The pit of Sharp's belly chilled. "What's wrong?"

"Olivia was supposed to be here hours ago to take me to the doctor, but she never came." Mrs. Cruz spoke faster, urgency speeding up her words. "I thought maybe she had car trouble. My husband drove me to my appointment. But I'm back home now, and Olivia isn't answering her cell phone or her house phone." Mrs. Cruz wheezed. "She would never forget me."

"No, ma'am. She wouldn't." Sharp ran a hand over his fresh buzz cut. Possibilities spun in his mind. After twenty-five years on the SFPD, he immediately thought of worst-case scenarios. But scaring Mrs. Cruz would be pointless and cruel.

"What time was your appointment this morning?" Sharp asked.

"Nine thirty," Mrs. Cruz said, the pitch of her voice rising.

Sharp checked the time. Eleven thirty. "Maybe she had a flat or her car broke down."

"She would have called." Mrs. Cruz blew away his suggestion.

"There are spots with poor cell reception between here and Albany. I'll go looking for her right now."

"You'll call me if you find her?" She sniffed.

"Of course. Try not to panic. I'll call you soon." Sharp disconnected. He dialed Olivia's cell. The call went to voice mail. He left a message. Then he sent her a text just in case she *was* in an area with poor reception. Sometimes a text would go through when a call would not. Even though she rarely answered her home phone—only her mother and telemarketers used that line—he tried that number too. After three rings, her digital answering machine picked up. He left her a message there as well.

He shoved the phone back into his pocket and returned to the kitchen. Stella was gone. "That was Olivia's mother." He explained her news to Morgan and Lance. "I'm going to her house. Olivia told me about that appointment last night on the phone. She'd intended to be there."

"I'll come with you." Lance fell into step beside him. They walked to the door.

The medical examiner's van blocked the driveway to Sharp Investigations. Two morgue assistants were wheeling a gurney to the back of their vehicle. The body had been zipped into the black bag.

"You two go." Morgan's brows lowered. "I'll stay here in case Carl needs anything. Let me know if you find Olivia."

"Will do. Thanks." Sharp took his keys from his pocket.

"I'll drive." Lance headed for his Jeep, parked at the curb. "Your car is blocked in."

Reluctantly, Sharp followed him, putting his keys away.

"Morgan is inside if you need anything, Carl," Lance said on their way past.

"Thanks," Carl called. "I'm waiting on the tow truck."

With a wave at the cop, they climbed into Lance's Jeep. Lance steered around the ME's van and drove the short distance to Olivia's house.

Lance parked in front of her bungalow, and Sharp looked for signs that something was amiss. But her house looked normal. They got out of the Jeep. Sharp went to the garage door, shielded his eyes with both hands, and peered in the window. The spot in the garage where she normally parked her car was empty. Had she gone out and forgotten about her mother?

That wasn't like Olivia. She'd remembered the appointment the previous night. As the only unmarried sibling, Olivia was the first person her mother called on for help. She doted on her parents.

Lance appeared beside him.

"She's not here." Worry tugged at Sharp.

Lance nodded. "Let's drive the route between here and her parents' house."

Alarm rose in Sharp's chest.

"You talked to her last night?" Lance asked.

Sharp hurried back to the Jeep. "Yes. She was going to bed. She wasn't feeling well." A warning itched Sharp's spine.

"She was sick?" Lance asked.

"Just some indigestion." She would have called him if she felt worse, right? Was their relationship at that point? They hadn't talked about any sort of commitment. They were both independent and wary of being too clingy. Both had been burned in the past and without romantic entanglements for some time. She seemed as content as he was to take things slowly.

But suddenly Sharp felt very alone.

"Let's not get ahead of ourselves," Lance said, steering the Jeep toward the main road that led out of town. "Don't you always say, if it looks like a horse and smells like a horse, don't go looking for a zebra?"

"Yes." Sharp scanned the shoulder of the road. He suppressed the disaster scenarios popping into his mind. "Her car doesn't have a spare. If she got a flat and the tire repair kit couldn't fix it, she'd have to call for roadside assistance. If she couldn't get a cell signal, she'd have to walk."

But wouldn't she have found a phone in three hours?

"Why don't you call Morgan?" Lance turned right at the stop sign and accelerated. "Get her to make the usual calls to police departments and hospitals between here and Albany. It's premature, but you'll feel better."

It didn't feel premature to Sharp. "Good idea."

"Do you want me to call my mother and see if she can locate Olivia's cell?" Lance's mother suffered from depression and anxiety and rarely left her home. She was also a computer genius who often assisted with their investigations. Finding Olivia's cell without a warrant would require some illegal hacking, but Sharp doubted Olivia would complain.

"Yes," he said.

Lance talked to his mother, then Morgan, on speakerphone as he drove. By the time the calls were made, he was merging onto the interstate. Sharp sat up straighter and focused on scanning the sides of the road. Olivia could have driven off the shoulder. There were ditches, ravines, and lakes. Her car could be buried in underbrush—

Or submerged underwater.

The empty chill in the pit of Sharp's gut deepened as the miles passed with no sign of Olivia.

Just short of her parents' house in Albany, Lance slowed the Jeep. "Do you want to stop at her parents' house?"

"Not yet." Sharp didn't want to waste time.

Lance turned the Jeep around. Sharp closely watched the opposite side of the interstate all the way back to Scarlet Falls.

Sharp saw no cars abandoned on the side of the road and no breaks in the foliage to indicate a car had gone off the road. The ditches were empty.

Where is she? He rubbed the center of his chest. In his mind's eye, he saw Olivia, her dark eyes shining with mischief, wearing the feminine trench coat and the pointy-heeled shoes she loved.

Lance exited the interstate onto the ramp that led to Scarlet Falls. "Where do you want to go now?"

"Back to Olivia's house." Sharp dreaded calling her mother and telling her he hadn't found any sign of her.

Lance's phone buzzed on the console. "It's my mom." He put the call on speaker. "Hi, Mom. You're on speaker in the car. Sharp is here too."

"Hello, Sharp." Jenny Kruger's voice came through the car's speaker. "I tried to track the GPS on Olivia's phone, but there's no signal."

"Nothing?" Sharp's apprehension grew.

"No," Jenny said. "No signal at all. I'm sorry. The last activity recorded on her number was a phone call to you at eleven p.m. last night. That call was made from her home."

No signal meant Olivia's phone battery had been removed or destroyed or the phone was out of cell range.

Lance parked in front of Olivia's house. Sharp jumped out of the vehicle and rushed up the walk.

Lance hurried to catch up with him. Almost at the front door, he caught Sharp's arm. "Take it slow."

"Something is wrong." Sharp paused and inhaled. The hollow pressure in his chest intensified.

"Then take precautions." Lance dug into the pocket of his cargos and offered Sharp a pair of gloves. "We don't want to destroy evidence."

Reluctantly, Sharp took them and tugged them onto his hands. He didn't want to think about a crime having been committed in Olivia's house.

Lance was more than his partner; he was the closest thing Sharp had to a son. When Lance was ten, his father had vanished. Sharp had been the Scarlet Falls detective assigned to the case. He hadn't found Lance's dad back then, and when he'd discovered Lance's mother suffered from crippling anxiety and was incapable of handling her husband's disappearance or raising her son, Sharp had stepped in to help.

He had also hit rock bottom at the time, with a divorce and the death of his partner in the line of duty. In the end, Lance and his mom had become Sharp's family. He'd dated over the next two decades, but he hadn't let anyone else get close—until Olivia.

Who would have thought a reporter would sneak into his heart? But she had.

He swallowed his fear and unlocked Olivia's front door using the key she'd given him a few weeks before. He opened the door and stepped inside. Lance followed Sharp down the hall to the kitchen. The alarm system beeped. Sharp punched the deactivation code into the panel.

"Can you see the system history?" Lance looked over Sharp's shoulder.

Sharp pushed buttons and read the screen. "At two thirteen this morning, the alarm was deactivated and rearmed as Away." He moved to the center of the kitchen, his critical gaze scanning the room. "Where could she have gone in the middle of the night?" His ignorance of her current work felt acute.

"Has she ever slipped out that late at night before?"

"Not that I know of." But then, Sharp wasn't with her every night. They spent a couple of nights a week together. Then each retreated to their own private spaces.

"Would she call you if she was going to meet someone that late?"

"Apparently not." Sharp brushed off his irritation. Olivia didn't owe him a call before she went out. He wouldn't have notified her if he had to work in the middle of the night.

Sharp walked around the kitchen. "She was researching new topics for another book. That's all I know."

He had to face facts. He'd been sleeping with Olivia for months, and yet he knew very little about her.

Last night's phone call was the first sign she was willing to share her research with him. They slept together but kept their work to themselves.

"Where does she keep her phone, keys, and purse when she's home?" Lance circled the kitchen, scanning surfaces.

"On the island." Sharp pointed. The square of recycled glass was empty. "She carries her phone from room to room with her most of the time. In the middle of the night, it would be on her nightstand."

He headed for the hallway. Lance stayed close. They walked into Olivia's bedroom. The covers were on the floor.

"Olivia always makes the bed as soon as she gets up." Sharp felt his voice crack, and he took care not to touch any of the surfaces. In case Olivia's house was a crime scene, he needed to preserve evidence.

The words *crime scene* pooled fear in his gut.

"Maybe she was in a hurry," Lance said. Morgan and Lance lived with three children, two dogs, a nanny, Morgan's grandfather, and a seemingly endless string of renovation projects. For them, chaos was more normal than order. But Olivia thrived on organization.

"Olivia likes to keep things neat and organized." Sharp walked out of the bedroom. On the surface, the house looked as expected. He went into the second bedroom, which she'd converted into an office. Her laptop sat in the center of the desk. He lifted the lid. It was password protected. "I have a key to her house and the code to her security system, but she hasn't shared her laptop password."

Their professions required them to maintain a level of confidentiality. Sharp certainly hadn't shared any client information with Olivia. She had essentially morphed from a journalist into a true crime writer over the past five years. But in the back of his mind, she was still a reporter—a label that made him wary.

Lance went back through the kitchen to the doorway that led into the laundry room. "Sharp! Over here."

Sharp hurried to join him in the narrow hallway. Lance pointed to a door. "Is that the garage?"

Sharp nodded. His gaze followed Lance's pointer finger to a dark-red smear on the white molding around the door.

"Could be blood," Lance said.

"There's only one way to find out. Do you have an RSID kit in your car?" Sharp asked, his face drawing tight.

A Rapid Stain Identification Kit would detect the presence of human blood.

"No," Lance said. "Because we are not cops anymore. We don't swab and possibly contaminate evidence. I'll call Stella. She'll handle it. I'll call Morgan too. She might notice things we haven't."

Lance stepped back to make the calls.

Sharp crouched and took a long look at the molding around the door. Small scratches marred the wood. His gaze traveled down the length of the door. Something was stuck in the soft caulk around the frame. It was bright pink. A broken fingernail was embedded in the bright-white sealant.

Sharp's heart squeezed as he remembered the color of Olivia's nails when she had stroked his bare chest two nights before.

Bright pink.

His chest tightened, and he pressed a hand to it.

"Sharp!" Lance grabbed him by the arm.

"I'm OK." He gestured to the fingernail.

Lance examined the caulk, then straightened, his face grim. "Morgan will be here soon. Stella didn't answer her phone. I left a message. Do you want to call the SFPD?"

"And tell them what?" Sharp asked. "That Olivia missed one appointment, didn't make her bed, and broke a nail on her way out of the house? We both know that's not enough to launch a missing persons case."

He ran out to Lance's Jeep for a flashlight. He would touch as little as possible, but no one could stop him from searching for clues.

When he returned to the laundry room, Lance had marked the locations of the blood and the broken fingernail with yellow sticky notes.

He tested the garage door. "The dead bolt is locked, which means it was either locked from the inside or the key was used." He turned the dead bolt and went into the garage. It was as tidy as the rest of Olivia's house. Her bicycle stood in a rack near the wall. Opposite the empty space where she parked her car, some basic tools were organized on a pegboard over a small worktable. The concrete was swept clean. Sharp shone the flashlight on the floor. No footprints.

"I thought she liked to garden." Lance scanned the space. "There isn't even any dirt in here."

"There's a potting shed out back where she keeps the messy stuff." Something shiny caught Sharp's attention. He bent down.

"What is it?" Lance asked.

Sharp recognized the small diamond stud as one of Olivia's staple pieces of jewelry. "An earring."

Lance stuck a note to the concrete near the earring.

Checking the floor before setting each foot down, Sharp searched in a spiral pattern. He spotted a glint of metal near the base of the overhead door, where the hatchback of Olivia's Prius would have been located. "Here's the second earring."

"Maybe she was getting something big out of the back of her car and knocked her earrings loose," Lance suggested.

"I don't know." Sharp didn't like it. "I could buy her losing one earring, but two? *And* breaking a nail on the doorjamb?"

They went back into the house. Sharp rubbed his solar plexus. Behind it, fear coiled itself into a tight ball.

Where is she?

Chapter Six

Morgan watched the tow truck drive away with Mrs. Olander's vehicle secured on the flatbed. The Scarlet Falls patrol car pulled away from the curb and followed.

She stared at the empty space where the minivan had been parked. The wind blew, and a few dead leaves tumbled along the gutter. The street showed no sign that a woman had taken her life there just a few hours before.

I am not responsible.

She knew it wouldn't be easy to shelve Mrs. Olander's desperation and despondency. But finding Olivia took priority, and Morgan was relieved to lock up the office and leave. She arrived at Olivia's bungalow a few minutes later. When Sharp opened the front door, she followed him back to Olivia's kitchen.

Lance crossed the room to give her a quick kiss. "Any luck with the hospitals?" He didn't ask about morgues, even though he knew she'd have called those as well.

"None," she said. "I checked with all the hospitals within a hundred miles of here. No sign of Olivia or any Jane Does that fit her description."

"I'm going to check the outside of the house." Lance went out the front door.

Sharp paced the kitchen like a trapped animal. Morgan's heart bled for him. Sharp kept his world small, but he'd fallen hard for Olivia, even if he hadn't wanted to admit it.

Stella arrived. Morgan let her sister in and led her to the kitchen.

"You have a key?" Stella asked Sharp.

"Yes," Sharp answered. "And the codes for her alarm system. Thanks for coming. I know a detective wouldn't normally be the first responder."

A uniform on patrol would have taken the initial report. A detective would have been summoned only if the uniform found evidence of foul play.

He walked Stella back to the laundry room, pointed out the broken fingernail, and explained the call from Olivia's mother. He showed Stella the earrings in the garage. Normally athletic, his movements were jerky and agitated as he identified the small bits of seemingly random evidence.

Stella wrote on her notepad. "Was the alarm set and the house locked when you let yourself in?"

"Yes," Sharp answered. "The alarm had been turned off and reactivated at 2:13 a.m. this morning."

"Olivia was supposed to meet with us at the office this afternoon as well," Morgan said.

Stella walked through the house. She checked doors and windows and then returned to the kitchen. "I don't see any signs of a break-in or struggle. The most obvious explanation is Olivia left the house to meet someone. Maybe a contact for a story she was working on."

"Jenny Kruger already pinged her cell phone. Nothing, and Olivia's last call on her cell was with me at eleven. I didn't check the house phone." Sharp reached for the handset and checked the call log on the caller ID screen. "Two missed calls from a market research company today. No calls came in last night."

Stella propped one hand on her hip, her brow furrowed with thought. "I'll fill out a report." Contrary to public belief, a person did not have to be missing for any specific length of time in order to be reported missing. Trails ran cold quickly, and police appreciated being brought in as early as possible. But the extent of their investigation would depend on the particular circumstances.

Stella continued, "I'll also put out a BOLO alert. The SFPD, county sheriff's deputies, and state police will be looking for her car. Hang on while I grab a blood evidence collection kit." She retrieved the kit from her car, then photographed and swabbed the smear and bagged the fingernail as evidence. She pulled fingerprints from the doorknobs, molding, and light switches.

"It would be most efficient if we coordinate our efforts," Stella said when she had finished.

"Right," Sharp agreed. "We'll talk to family, friends, and neighbors. Morgan has already called local hospitals."

"Copy me on everything." Stella packed up her kit.

With her partner on vacation, Stella would have to juggle cases. She also had to respect privacy laws. In contrast, Sharp, Lance, and Morgan could drop everything and focus on the search for Olivia. And Sharp could—and would—ignore the law and hack away as he pleased.

Stella wrote down a physical description of Olivia. "Does she have any identifying tattoos or birthmarks?"

"No." Sharp shook his head.

"Chronic medical conditions?" Stella asked.

"None that she's mentioned to me," Sharp said. "But I'll ask her mother."

Stella's phone buzzed. She looked at the screen without removing it from her belt. Frowning, she silenced it with her thumb.

Sharp rubbed his forehead, his movements unsteady. His relationship with Olivia had been progressing in a slow-but-steady fashion.

Though both Sharp and Olivia were stubbornly set in their ways, there was something special about their relationship.

"Do you know what she was wearing last night?" Stella asked. "Did you video chat?"

"It was a phone call," he said. "I don't know what she was wearing, but she's usually in her pajamas at that hour."

"Is her suitcase or cosmetic bag missing?" Stella asked.

"I haven't looked yet." Sharp swept one hand over his scalp. "And I wouldn't know what they look like anyway."

The three of them walked back to Olivia's bedroom. Sharp opened the walk-in closet.

"Are any clothes missing?" Morgan joined him in the closet. The racks and shelves were jam-packed with clothes and shoes. "I guess it's impossible to say."

"There's a suitcase." Sharp pointed toward an upper shelf, where a hard-shell carry-on was stowed. Then he led the way out of the closet.

"What about a toiletry kit? What would she use for a trip?" Morgan had reservations about invading Olivia's privacy, but she pushed them aside and went into the bathroom. Olivia would understand.

Sharp looked over Morgan's shoulder. "I don't know. We haven't traveled together. When she stays over at my place, she goes home to get ready if she has an early appointment."

The medicine chest was full of high-end, mostly organic, and fair-trade cosmetics. Olivia shared Sharp's green streak. In a narrow linen closet behind the bathroom door, Morgan found a travel toiletry kit and a waterproof TSA-approved bag full of travel-size liquids.

"It doesn't look as if she planned to be gone overnight." Morgan spotted an inhaler behind the toiletry bag. The box was unopened, and the prescription label was dated the previous winter. "Does Olivia have a lung condition?"

"Not that I know of." Sharp peered around the bathroom door to examine the box. "I've never seen her use an inhaler."

"Maybe it was from an illness." Morgan set the box back on the shelf and followed Sharp out of the bathroom.

Stella crouched next to the bed, examining something on the bamboo floor. "It looks like a piece of rubber."

She donned gloves, then picked up the object by its edge. It was a beige-colored square of rubber about an inch wide.

"What is that?" Sharp asked.

"I have no idea." Stella patted her pockets and produced a paper evidence envelope. She slid the piece of rubber inside. "I'll have the lab take a look at it." She stood.

They went into Olivia's office. Bookshelves lined the walls.

Stella went to the desk and lifted the top of Olivia's laptop. "It's too early to take her computer and have the nerds hack into it." She glanced over the surface of the desk and opened its drawers. "I don't see anything out of order."

Her phone buzzed again, and she silenced it. "Let me get out of here. The BOLO will go out as soon as I get to my car, and I'll drop the evidence at the lab. If you learn anything, please let me know. I'll do the same." She gave Sharp a hug. "She'll probably turn up tonight. Hang tight."

He nodded, sat in Olivia's office chair, and stared at her laptop.

Morgan walked her sister outside. Dead leaves were piled up against the picket fence that surrounded Olivia's garden. Lance appeared from around the side of the house.

Stella showed him the piece of rubber in the evidence envelope. "Did you find anything?"

"Nothing. No marks outside the windows or doors. No footprints. Nothing amiss in her gardening shed." Frustration tightened his face. "Where's Sharp?"

"Inside," Morgan said.

"I'm not sure what else we can do at this point." Lance turned back to the house.

After he'd walked away, Morgan said goodbye to her sister, then followed Lance inside. She found him and Sharp in Olivia's office. Olivia's work space was as pristine as a museum. There wasn't even a single coffee stain on the white blotter.

Looking lost, Sharp still sat behind the desk. He tapped the closed cover of Olivia's laptop. "We'll talk to her friends, family, and neighbors. If nothing pans out, we dig into her work files."

"Sounds reasonable. Let's make an action plan for this evening." Morgan perched on the corner of the desk. "We'll update it in the morning depending on what happens tonight."

If Olivia didn't come home.

"I want to drive the route to her parents' house again. Maybe I missed some sign on our earlier trip." Sharp scrubbed both hands down his face. "And I'll talk to her parents." He checked the time on his phone. "It's almost five o'clock. I should be going. Her family must be panicking at this point."

"Either Lance or I should go with you," Morgan said.

Sharp shook his head. "That's not necessary."

"You can't look for Olivia's car and drive at the same time," Morgan argued.

"Morgan should go." Lance pushed off the wall. "Olivia's sister and mother might open up more to her."

Sharp had mad skills getting people to talk to him, but Morgan went along with it. She didn't want him to be alone or driving in his current state of distraction.

"Maybe you're right," Sharp said.

"While you two are gone, I'll talk to her neighbors," Lance offered. "And check her usual stops around town. Can you make a list of places she frequents? Does she have a favorite coffee shop or restaurant?"

"I'll make a list." Sharp opened the top desk drawer and took out a notepad.

"I'm going to call Grandpa and let the family know we won't be home for dinner or bedtime." Morgan left the office.

Lance followed her into the kitchen. He glanced at his phone. "I can still make bedtime. Questioning neighbors shouldn't take more than an hour or so."

Nodding, Morgan dialed her grandfather's number. When he picked up the phone, she explained about Olivia being missing.

"Of course, we understand," Grandpa said. "Don't worry about the kids. Gianna and I have everything under control."

Morgan was grateful for the thousandth time for her grandfather and her live-in nanny.

She heard a small voice in the background. "Is that Mommy?"

"Ava wants to talk to you. Hold on." Grandpa handed the phone to Morgan's seven-year-old daughter.

"Mommy, you promised to take us shopping for Halloween costumes tonight," Ava said in a strident voice that carried into the room.

Morgan opened her mouth to apologize, but Lance tapped her arm and whispered, "I can do it."

"Hold on, honey." Morgan lowered her cell and covered the microphone. "Halloween isn't for six more weeks. We have plenty of time."

"But we did promise to take them tonight." Lance looked at his watch. "I'll be home by six thirty. Shopping for costumes won't take more than an hour. I'll have them in bed by eight."

"Are you sure?" Morgan didn't doubt his ability to care for the girls, but Halloween generated a level of excitement surpassed only by Christmas. The girls would be revved up.

"Positive," Lance said. "It's not a big deal."

Morgan raised the phone to her ear. "Lance said he'll take you tonight."

"Yay!" Ava squealed. In the background, her sisters echoed her enthusiasm.

Morgan moved the phone a few inches from her ear. When the high-pitched sounds stopped, she and Ava exchanged *I love you*s, and Morgan disconnected.

Sharp emerged from Olivia's office. "Let's roll."

Morgan kissed Lance goodbye. "One costume each. No negotiating. And don't let them talk you into buying the candy at the register. I love you."

"Love you too. See you at home. Good luck."

Hopefully, one of Olivia's friends or family members would have information about her whereabouts. But as Morgan followed Sharp out the door, she couldn't shake the apprehension roiling like storm clouds in her belly. Whatever had happened to Olivia hadn't been good.

Chapter Seven

Lance approached the house diagonal to Olivia's, a blue Cape Cod with red shutters. At five thirty, people were returning home from work. He'd already driven to the organic grocery store and Perk Up, a local café.

No one had seen Olivia that day.

He'd had no luck at the first few houses he'd visited either. None of the residents had seen Olivia for several days. Most people had jobs and didn't spend much time outside unless it was the weekend.

He walked up two steps, stood on the front stoop, and rang the doorbell. Inside the house, a small dog exploded into a frenzy of high-pitched barking.

"Hush!" a voice yelled. An elderly man in gray chinos, a red plaid shirt, and bright-orange track shoes opened the door. A four-pound Yorkshire terrier yapped and growled at his feet, trying to slip past his legs, as if it wanted to tear Lance's ankles apart with its tiny teeth. The man backed out onto the stoop, pushing the furious dog back inside. Chuckling, he closed the door. "Sorry about that. Grizz is fifteen years old and still has no manners. I don't suppose he's ever going to."

Lance handed the old man a business card and introduced himself.

"I'm Bob Johnson." Bob squinted at the card, then pulled a pair of black-framed reading glasses from the chest pocket of his shirt. "A private investigator? I've never talked to one of those before." He sounded excited. "What can I do for you?"

"I'm looking for your neighbor, Olivia Cruz. Do you know her?"

"Yes. I know Olivia. She inherited her aunt's house. Knew her aunt too. I've lived in this house for sixty years. My wife and I bought it after our third child was born."

"Is your wife home?"

Bob shook his head, his eyes misting. "No, she passed away last year, right after our sixtieth wedding anniversary."

"I'm sorry." Lance felt the old man's sadness. He couldn't imagine losing Morgan. Ever.

Bob's smile was bittersweet. "I'm grateful for all the years we had together. She kept me in line." He winked, brushing off his nostalgia. "Someone had to." Bob was probably in his early eighties, but he seemed pretty spry for his age.

"When did you last talk to Olivia?" Lance asked.

Bob rubbed his chin. "A couple of days ago, early in the morning. She was working in her garden. I asked her advice on ground cover for my flower beds. I can't get down to pull weeds like I used to."

"Do you remember what day that was?"

"What's today?"

"Friday."

"I'm retired, and the days all blur together now," Bob explained. "I'd say it was Wednesday."

"But you haven't seen her since then?"

Bob's brows drew together. "She drove by the house last night. I was walking the dog. Neither one of us sleeps through the night anymore. Grizz was sniffing his way around the side yard when we saw her drive by."

"Do you know what time that was?" Lance asked.

Bob rested a fist on his lower back. His head tilted as he concentrated. "I guess it was actually early this morning, probably between two and three. I don't know the exact time. Grizz and I went back to bed."

"Was Olivia behind the wheel? Was anyone else in the car?"

"I didn't see her face." Bob pointed down the street. "She was driving that way, so the passenger side of her car was facing me. But I didn't see anyone in the passenger seat. I assume she was alone."

Lance assumed nothing. "You're sure it was her car?"

"I didn't check the license plate." Bob lifted one shoulder. "But she's the only one on the street with a white Prius."

"Have you seen anyone else around Olivia's house recently?"

Bob rubbed his chin. "There was a guy knocking at her door last night about seven o'clock. He knocked. She didn't answer. He left. That was it."

Lance snapped to attention. A lead. "Can you tell me what he looked like?"

Bob frowned. "He was tall, blond hair. I couldn't see his face in the dark."

"Thin, fat, average?" Lance prompted.

"He was wearing a jacket, but I'd say average."

"Did you see what kind of car he was driving?"

"Yes!" Bob's voice rose, and he pointed to his own chest with his thumb. "I'm a car guy. It was a 1971 Chevy Nova. I'm pretty sure it was black, but it could have been dark blue."

"Is that an expensive car?" Lance was not a car guy.

"Not particularly, but if you like muscle cars—and I do—it was in very good condition."

And distinctive. How many dark-blue or black 1971 Chevy Novas could be in the area?

Lance took a small notepad out of his pocket. "Could I have your phone number, Bob?"

"Sure."

Lance wrote down Bob's contact information. "Have you seen anyone unusual around the neighborhood lately? Salespeople, meter readers, construction crews . . ."

Bob gestured toward the brick house a few doors down the street. "The Browns have been renovating their house for a year. There's always a work vehicle of some kind out front."

"You saw workers there this past week?"

Bob tucked his hands into his front pockets and hunched as if he were cold. "There was a white van parked there on and off for the past two weeks."

"Can you describe the van?"

"White, no windows in the back. A little dinged up." Bob closed his eyes. "Sorry. I don't remember what kind of tradesman it was. I'm afraid I've gotten so used to seeing vehicles there, I don't pay much attention anymore."

Lance thanked him and left the porch. He walked to the brick house and knocked. A blonde woman in her late thirties opened the door. Tall and slim, she wore a long blue sweater over yoga pants.

"Mrs. Brown?"

At her nod, Lance offered her a card and introduced himself.

She frowned down at the card, and suspicion lifted her chin.

"I'm a friend of Olivia Cruz. She lives in the white house over there." Lance motioned toward Olivia's bungalow, catercorner to the Browns' house.

"I don't talk to strange men." She moved to close the door.

Lance wished Morgan were with him. She would be less threatening to a woman. But Sharp needed her more.

"Please wait!" He took one step back, away from the door, and tried not to look intimidating. It wasn't something he did very often.

She hesitated.

Lance smiled. "You can call the Scarlet Falls Police Department. Almost anyone who answers the phone can vouch for me. I was a police officer for ten years."

With a humph, she closed the door. Lance heard the dead bolt slide into place.

Was she going to call? Or was he out of luck?

He turned away from the door and leaned on the porch railing. He'd give her a few minutes. If she wouldn't talk to him, he'd go back to Bob and beg for an introduction from him. He studied Olivia's quiet street. Mature oak trees lined both sides. Sprawling branches shaded the sidewalk. There were lots of shadows to hide in.

He was so engrossed in his thoughts that the click of the door at his back startled him.

Mrs. Brown shook a lock of hair out of her eyes. "The sergeant says hello."

She had actually called. Lance respected her for her caution.

"Do you know Ms. Cruz?" he asked.

From inside the house, Lance could hear children's voices and the thuds of running feet.

Mrs. Brown stepped onto the porch and closed the door behind her. "I know her enough to wave. That's all. I didn't even know her name until you told me." She flushed. "We've lived here for a year, but we don't know many of the neighbors."

"Have you seen her around the neighborhood in the past few days?"

Her face lit with alarm. "Why? Has something happened to her?"

"Olivia missed an appointment today. We hope it's just a misunderstanding, but her mother is worried and asked us to look into it."

Mrs. Brown clutched the edges of her sweater together. Shoeless, she propped one pink-socked foot against the opposite leg like a stork. "I think we saw her over the weekend." She pursed her lips. "Yes. On Sunday. My husband and I were raking leaves. She was doing the same. I work part-time, and I have three boys who play travel soccer. During soccer season it feels like we are never home." She checked her watch. "In fact, I have a pickup in about ten minutes. I'm sorry I wasn't more helpful." She started to turn away.

"A white van was seen in front of your house over the past couple of weeks. Did it belong to one of your contractors?"

"No." She frowned. "Our renovations were finished a month ago. No one has been working here. I really do have to go. I hope you find Ms. Cruz."

Mrs. Brown went back inside, and Lance walked away from the house. He talked to the remaining neighbors on the street. None had seen Olivia for several days. Two had noticed the white van, but like Bob, they had ignored it. No one on the street had hired a contractor recently.

So why had a white van been parked across the street from Olivia's house?

Lance walked back toward his Jeep. He pulled up short as a JBT News van turned the corner and stopped in front of Olivia's house. A camera crew climbed out and began to set up on the sidewalk. A man in a suit applied powder to his face.

A reporter. *Already?*

Irritated, Lance made a beeline for his vehicle. He was in no mood. "You're Lance Kruger," the suit said.

Lance took a deep breath and let it out. He stopped. "And you are?"

The man handed his face powder to one of his crew. His tanned skin and dark hair were too . . . perfect. A crewmember handed him a microphone that he, in turn, extended toward Lance. "Are you working the Olivia Cruz case?"

Lance crossed his arms. As far as he knew, Olivia's disappearance wasn't public knowledge yet, but the Scarlet Falls PD had a long-standing problem with information being leaked to the press. Morgan had called Stella on her cell phone. They hadn't used the police dispatch. Had the call somehow gone out over the police scanner? "How do you know Ms. Cruz?"

The reporter met Lance's gaze. He blinked, then lowered the mic and switched it off. "Look, I have a contact who says Olivia was reported missing. Is that true?"

Lance couldn't decide if it would be beneficial to use the media this early in the investigation. He needed to discuss the situation with Morgan and Sharp.

"No comment." Lance brushed past the reporter and strode to his Jeep.

"I'll find out," the reporter called after him. "I have other sources."

Lance had no doubt that he did.

Chapter Eight

Olivia opened her eyes to blurry dimness. She squeezed them shut again. Confusion flooded her.

What happened? Where am I?

She lay curled on her side. The kidnapping rushed back to her in a kaleidoscope of images and sensations. Her eyes flew open. Blinking, she cleared her vision, but all she could see was a dark surface about a foot from her face. She reached out and touched it. Her fingertips brushed cold, rough stone.

She rolled to her back. A single dim light cast just enough brightness that she could see her surroundings. She lay on a floor of packed earth. Stone walls formed a ten-by-ten space. The low ceiling was constructed of heavy wooden beams. There were no windows. Empty wooden shelves covered the far wall. On the other side of the space, near the source of the tiny light, a set of narrow, steep stairs led upward.

A root cellar?

She was underground.

Horror raced through her. Adrenaline sharpened her senses and tasted coppery in her mouth. Her heartbeat surged, thudding like a drumbeat in her head.

On the bright side, her hands and feet were no longer bound, and the rope had been removed from around her neck. Her lungs tightened, as if a boa constrictor had wrapped itself around her torso. Her breathing became rapid and shallow.

Not enough air.

Lack of oxygen—and fear—made her almost giddy.

Breathe.

She had to think straight.

Panicking will not help.

Air stirred over her face. There must be some sort of ventilation. She should not run out of oxygen.

Her shortness of breath must be a product of her anxiety. But knowing this and controlling her fear were two completely different things. She counted, again hearing Lincoln's words in her mind as she fought to regulate her breathing and the claustrophobia that threatened to lead her straight into a major anxiety attack. Even in her imagination, his deep, soothing voice calmed her. Her tongue stuck to the cotton-dry roof of her mouth, a likely side effect of whatever drug she'd been administered.

Several minutes passed as she focused on breath control. Once her light-headedness had passed, and her heart rate slowed, she became aware of pain throbbing in her face and her foot.

She assessed her overall physical condition. The air was chilly and damp. She was still dressed in her flannel pajama bottoms, sweatshirt, and thick socks. Her cotton throw was draped over her and tucked around her feet, but it wasn't enough to ward off the dampness. A chill radiated from the stone wall, as if she were lying next to a block of ice.

She probed her cheek with one hand. A goose egg had formed over the bone, but she doubted it was broken. Her foot was a different matter. She tried to wiggle it, and pain surged. The entire front half of her foot was swollen and hot to the touch. In hindsight, kicking him while only wearing socks hadn't been a good idea.

Even if she escaped, she wouldn't be running away anytime soon. Maybe there was a vehicle she could steal. She rolled to her hands and knees, then stood and hobbled to the steps. Ignoring the pain, she crawled up the stairs. The wooden doors above were set on an angle in a frame of heavy timber, like bulkhead doors. Pressing her hands to the thick wood, she pushed. But there was no give, no looseness.

She felt the edges for hinges but found none. They must be on the outside. She pressed her shoulder to the doors, but nothing budged. She was not getting out that way. Turning around, she sat on the steps. Next to her face, the tiny light was a round disk attached to the wall about two inches in diameter and made of plastic. There were no wires, and it appeared to be battery operated. Not a good option for a weapon. She pressed the switch on the light, and it went out, leaving her in complete darkness.

No!

Panic surged inside her. She quickly pressed the light again. It brightened. Relief flooded her, leaving her light-headed once more.

Don't do that again.

The air smelled organic, like earth and wet leaves. Straining her ears, she listened for any sounds that might give her a clue to her location. She heard a faint splash. She was near water.

Should she call out?

She wanted to, but fear dried up her throat. Swallowing, she mustered her courage, turned to the doors, and shouted, "Hello, is anyone out there?"

No one answered.

She faced her dungeon again. Two items she hadn't noticed before caught her attention. In the far corner stood a chemical toilet, and a brown grocery bag sat in the shadows next to her blanket. She limped over to the bag and opened it. Two six-packs of water sat beneath two protein bars—enough to keep her alive for a few days if she rationed.

Her lungs tightened again. She sat still and waited for the shortness of breath to pass.

There was no way out. She would have to wait until whoever kidnapped her opened the door. As much as she wanted to escape, what happened when her prison room was opened might be worse. The walls seemed to lean closer to her.

No. She must remain calm—or as calm as she could be under the circumstances. A man had gone to a lot of trouble to kidnap her. He'd left her provisions. That meant he wanted her to stay alive.

Right?

Who was he, and why had he kidnapped her? Had she made herself a target by asking questions about the two murder cases she'd been researching? She'd raised issues with each one. Maybe one of her theories had been too accurate. Maybe one of those convicted killers *was* innocent. Perhaps whoever had committed the crime didn't want her to reveal the truth. But then, why hadn't he simply killed her?

She glanced around the space. Had other women been kept prisoner here?

A slight burst of adrenaline bumped her pulse. Lincoln's voice floated in her imagination, telling her to breathe.

Would she ever see him again?

For the past couple of months, they'd been dancing around making any sort of real commitment. They had recently exchanged keys and alarm codes, but that had been born of convenience, not real progress in their relationship. The sex was great. Neither one of them had any issues with physical intimacy. Emotional dependency seemed to be a bigger hurdle.

Both had been single and set in their ways for a very long time. Olivia had become comfortable living alone. The thought of having to make daily compromises, to alter her space, to change her structured life had seemed too disruptive.

Their arrangement over the past few months had stalled. They'd both been stubbornly careful not to leave personal possessions in each other's spaces other than a toothbrush and deodorant, certainly nothing that would require a drawer and the level of commitment *that* would imply.

But now that she was shivering and alone in the dark, all their desperate maneuvers to maintain their independence felt stupid, and all the ways she'd actively avoided compromise seemed shallow.

There was a very good possibility her life would end soon. People were not taken from their homes in the middle of the night for innocuous reasons. Her kidnapper had some sort of dark plan in mind.

Her claustrophobia picked at her determination to remain calm. Her throat constricted, and her breathing accelerated.

She needed to keep busy or she'd go crazy. She hobbled around the perimeter. She would check every inch of her prison for a way out or a potential weapon.

How long would she be locked underground?

Chapter Nine

Lance drove toward home and dialed Sharp on speakerphone.

"Did you learn anything from the neighbors?" Sharp asked.

"Maybe." Lance turned right. "The retired man who lives diagonal to Olivia saw a white utility van parked across the street multiple times over the past two weeks. He assumed it was a contractor working for the family down the street. I've spoken to all the neighbors. No one was having work done over the past couple of weeks. I plan to check with the township and utility and cable companies in the morning. There could very well be a legitimate source for the white van."

Sharp paused, as if mulling over the information. "How reliable is this guy?"

"He's probably in his eighties, but he seemed articulate and coherent. The same neighbor says he saw a tall blond man knock on Olivia's door last evening around seven p.m. She didn't answer, and he left. He was driving a 1971 Chevy Nova in black or dark blue."

"A white van is too vague of a description to search vehicle registrations, although it could be good supporting evidence after we've located a suspect. But a black or dark-blue '71 Nova is a very specific vehicle. We should be able to find out if any are registered in Randolph County."

"I called my mom. She's on it," Lance said. "I'll let you know if she gets a hit."

"Thanks." Sharp ended the call.

Just after six thirty, Lance opened the front door to be greeted by an avalanche of kids and dogs. When he'd first moved in with Morgan's family, he'd been wary of the noise and activity level. Six months later, he embraced chaos.

Morgan's youngest, Sophie, catapulted herself into his arms. Expecting the leap, he caught her and set her on his hip. She hugged him with all four of her spindly limbs. Ava, at seven, was normally more reserved, but tonight she flung her arms around his waist. Six-year-old Mia gave him a quick hug and hopped away like a rabbit.

"Let Lance get in the door." Gianna stood at the rear of the pack, drying her hands on a dish towel. With a shiny brown ponytail and slender body, she looked younger than nineteen. The young woman was in much better health than when she'd first come to live with Morgan. Kidney disease and required dialysis treatments kept her thinner than she should be, but her smile was wide and her patience unending as she attempted to quiet the girls. "Did everyone use the bathroom and wash their hands?"

The girls turned and raced for the half bath down the hall.

"That should give you a minute." Gianna laughed. "I made chicken parm. Do you want to eat now or when you get back from the store?"

He heard the toilet flushing and water running. They'd be back in seconds.

"I can wait," Lance said.

Springs creaked, and Lance glanced into the family room, where Morgan's grandfather, Art Dane, was levering his body out of his recliner.

Art used his cane to walk into the foyer. "The kids are a little excited."

"I can see that." Lance greeted the dogs at his feet. French bulldog Snoozer snuffled his shoes, while rescue dog Rocket leaned on his leg. He gave each dog an ear rub.

"Halloween," Gianna explained with one word. She tossed the towel over one shoulder. "Do you want me to go with you?"

"No. We'll be fine." Lance shook his head. Today was Friday. Gianna had had dialysis that morning. She'd be tired.

The girls returned at a run. Ava and Mia put on their sneakers. Mia's tongue stuck out from between her teeth as she concentrated on tying her laces. Sophie shoved her feet into a pair of knee-high rubber rain boots. They were bright yellow and covered with red ladybugs, and she'd worn them everywhere for the last two weeks.

"Hurry up!" Sophie bounced on her toes as she waited for Mia to finish.

Mia looked up, fumbled the shoelace, and had to start over.

Sophie exhaled an exasperated breath through her nose. If she were a dragon, she would be breathing fire. "Let Lance do it. The store is gonna close."

Mia frowned at her little sister. "I want to tie my shoes myself."

"There's no rush," Lance said. "The store won't close for hours."

Sophie bounced to the front door, hopping on both feet like Tigger on his tail.

Mia tightened her final knot and grinned. "I did it."

Lance stooped and high-fived her. Then he straightened and ushered the girls to the door. He said over his shoulder to Gianna, "We'll be back in about an hour."

"Good luck," Gianna called.

As the kids bolted through the front door, a little voice in the back of his head warned him he might need it. He strapped the children into their car seats in Morgan's minivan, and they chattered nonstop for the next fifteen minutes. In the parking lot of the Halloween store, he helped them out of the van. He took firm hold of Sophie's hand. She was the runner of the bunch.

"Mia." Lance held his free hand out, and she grabbed it. "Ava, hold Mia's hand."

Getting three small children across a parking lot safely took more precision and planning than executing an arrest warrant on a violent offender. A bell jingled as Lance opened the glass door and herded the girls inside.

"I know exactly what I'm going to be." Ava took off down the princess aisle.

"Hold on!" Lance picked up Sophie, grabbed Mia's hand, and hurried after the oldest. Normally, Ava made a point of acting more mature than her younger sisters, especially in public. But Halloween costumes were too exciting.

Ava turned, her eyes huge as she scanned the high walls covered with colorful ruffles and tiaras. "I have to be Elsa. Where is she?"

"Elsa from *Frozen*?" Lance asked. Over the past six months, he'd seen every animated princess movie in existence.

"Yes." Ava spun in a circle, her eyes widening and her voice rising in desperation. "I don't see her!"

Proud that he could identify all the princesses on the wall, Lance pointed to a blue dress. "What about Cinderella?"

"Kaitlin is being Cinderella," Ava said. "And Jessie is gonna be Belle. Kinsey picked Ariel." She rattled off several more names. Her second-grade class was going to be a sea of princesses.

Lance spotted the shiny blue-green dress hanging high on the wall. "I see Elsa. Hold on. I'll get it for you." Lance set Sophie down and released Mia's hand with a firm, "Don't move."

He reached up and tugged an Elsa costume from the hook. Turning, he handed it to Ava. "Here you go."

"Yay!" Ava's squeal could have ruptured an eardrum. She hugged the costume to her face.

Lance spun around. *Shit!*

Mia and Sophie weren't in the aisle.

"Where are your sisters?" Panic sparked in Lance's chest like a struck match. *How far could they go?*

Ava lowered the costume. "What?"

"Your sisters?" Lance took her by the hand and hurried to the end of the row. They went around the corner and looked up the next aisle. Relief stole his next breath when he spotted the two little girls about twenty feet away. He caught up with them and let go of Ava's hand.

"Look what I got!" Ava thrust her shiny costume at her sisters.

"That's the one I want!" Mia was jumping up and down and pointing to a white unicorn costume. It was a wearable stuffed animal with four dangling legs, a pink mane and tail, and a shiny silver horn. On her next jump, she caught a leg and yanked. A dozen costumes cascaded to the floor. Lance picked them up to replace them on their hangers, but all the legs were tangled. He gave up with a prickle of guilt.

Job security for the clerk, right?

"Girls, you cannot walk away from me," he said.

Ava hugged her costume. Mia danced in a circle with the unicorn. Both nodded and looked appropriately apologetic—for about two seconds.

The girls were usually well behaved. What had gotten into them?

Gianna's voice echoed in his head. *Halloween.*

"Where is Sophie?"

Ava pointed. "Right there."

She was only about six feet away, but her little body was half-hidden by an adult-size cardboard cutout of a zombie. She extended a hand toward a display of rubber zombie masks. They were gory and bloody and completely inappropriate for a four-year-old. If she wore one of those to school, every kid in her class would have nightmares for a week.

Lance felt a tug on his pants. Mia had wrapped one arm around his thigh. She looked up at him with tear-filled eyes.

He crouched down to her level. "What is it, Mia?"

She pointed at the zombie mask and whispered in his ear, "That's scary."

"It's all right." He wrapped an arm around her shoulders. "It's just a mask."

Mia leaned into him, sniffed, and wiped her nose on the unicorn. He was definitely buying that costume now.

He turned to Ava. "You two stand right here. We found your costumes. Now it's Sophie's turn."

"OK." They nodded. Mia moved to stand next to her sister.

Lance turned back to Sophie. The way her eyes glowed with excitement reminded Lance of Drew Barrymore in *Firestarter*.

Or that kid from *The Omen*.

Lance walked forward to stand next to her. "That costume isn't for a kid, Soph."

She didn't say a word, but her expression was all *So what?*

What is she going to be like as a teenager? Lance shuddered.

Wisely, Sophie chose bargaining over confrontation. "Ava and Mia got to pick the costumes they wanted."

"Yes, but they picked from the kids' section. These are adult costumes." Lance stared at the mask. There was something about it that nagged at him. He tore his gaze away. "How about we look at the rest of the kids' costumes, OK?"

Sophie tilted her head, as if she was contemplating how far she could push him on the issue. She was a cagey little thing, and he admitted, he was usually a pushover. She glanced back at Mia, who was wiping her eyes. "OK." Sophie turned away from the zombies, slumped her shoulders, and dragged her rain boots on the floor.

Lance took her by the hand. They turned back to the kids' section and strolled up the aisle. Mia and Ava fell into step beside them.

He spotted a display of puppy and kitten costumes. "How about this kitten? You like kittens. Isn't this Marie from *The Aristocats*?"

"I don't want to be a kitten." Sophie shook her head hard enough to sway her pigtails.

"You spent most of last year dressed as a kitten," Lance reasoned.

"I'm *four* now," Sophie said. "I want a scary costume."

Mia's lip quivered.

"Let's keep looking." Lance scanned the walls. He spotted a zombie princess across the aisle. Ragged purple dress, greenish-white makeup, no splashes of blood. He pulled it down from the hook. "How about a zombie princess?"

Sophie deflated with exaggerated disappointment. "There's no blood."

Exactly.

"It's still scary," Lance said. There was no way he was buying Sophie a Halloween costume that made Mia cry and would terrify half the kids in her preschool class. Morgan would kill him.

"I could get two costumes," Sophie offered. "One for school and one for trick-or-treating."

He steeled his gaze. "One costume."

Sophie scuffed a yellow boot on the waxed floor.

Lance spotted a vampire makeup kit. "But we could buy some red makeup and draw a little blood on your face. But not for school, all right? Just for trick-or-treating. We don't want to scare your classmates."

She gave him a deadpan look that suggested that's exactly what she'd wanted to do.

Lance met her gaze head-on.

"OK." Her sigh was long-suffering.

"So we're done." Lance plucked the makeup kit from its peg, hung the costume over his arm, and steered the girls toward the front of the store. The wall of adult masks caught his attention again as they walked past. They were made of rubber and were meant to be worn over someone's whole head. There were witches, skeletons, and horror-movie characters. His gaze lingered on the zombie mask Sophie had wanted. It was flesh colored, with open wounds and sunken eyes.

It reminded him of something.

The girls were at the head of the aisle.

With no time to study the mask, he grabbed one and hid it under Sophie's costume. He hurried to catch up with the children. At the checkout counter, he distracted them with lollipops, pretending not to hear Ava whisper to Mia, "Mommy never lets us get the candy."

He purchased the adult mask without them noticing and quietly asked the clerk to put it in a separate bag that he tucked under his arm as they navigated the parking lot.

Back in the van, Lance hid the bag under the passenger seat. Then he buckled the girls into their car seats and drove home. Once inside the house, the girls stampeded to their rooms to put on their costumes. Lance returned to the van for the mask. He took it to the bedroom and shut the door. Sitting on the edge of the bed, he pulled the mask from the bag and stretched the material between his fingers. It had plenty of give, but it could be ripped.

More important, the mask was the same texture, color, and thickness as the piece of rubber they'd found in Olivia's bedroom.

Chapter Ten

Morgan drove Sharp's Prius south on the interstate slowly enough to elicit three horn honks and two middle fingers from passing vehicles.

Sharp responded to the gestures in kind. "Those drivers are assholes. They can get around you."

Morgan ignored them.

Sharp stared out the window, his gaze searching the roadside. Morgan slowed even more as they approached a bridge, and Sharp craned his neck to get a view of the sloping riverbank. But his tight-lipped expression told Morgan there were no breaks in the guardrail or tire tracks in the soft earth to indicate a car had driven off the road. Morgan glanced at the dark water as they crossed the river. Could her car have gone off a different road?

Leaving the bridge behind, Morgan brought the Prius back up to the minimum speed. "Does Olivia always take the same route to her parents' house?"

"Unless there's an accident or other major traffic delay," Sharp answered without taking his eyes off the roadside. "I checked. There were no traffic issues this morning."

"Is there anywhere else she would have stopped along the way? A reason she might have left the interstate?"

"I don't know." The sigh that eased from Sharp's chest made her heart hurt. "But I also don't know why she would have left her house at two in the morning. I don't know why I'm even looking for her car. I doubt she was headed to her parents' house at that hour. What was she doing?"

"It does seem strange. Maybe surveillance?"

"Maybe. But of whom?" Sharp's voice was heavy with frustration. He motioned toward the windshield. "Take this exit."

They drove the rest of the way in silence. The sun dipped below the horizon, casting the road in darkness. Morgan wished she had words of comfort, but Sharp's head was no doubt full of every violent crime he'd investigated over the past thirty years. As was hers. In their professions, they had both seen the worst humanity had to offer. Neither one of them could be fooled into a blissfully ignorant but false sense of security.

Morgan turned Sharp's car into a development. Olivia's parents lived in a senior community of one-story cookie-cutter homes.

"That's the house." Sharp pointed to a tiny white house with red shutters. Light glowed from the windows. A blue minivan was parked at the curb.

Morgan parked the Prius behind the van, and they got out of the car.

Sharp stood on the sidewalk for a minute. "I don't know what to say to them."

A curtain moved in the window. Someone had been watching for them.

Morgan took his arm and steered him up the cracked concrete walk. "It'll come to you."

"I've talked to families before, but this is different," Sharp said. "I know these people."

The door opened before they reached the stoop. A short woman with a head of dyed-brown curls stood in the opening. Morgan assumed she was Olivia's mother. Her eyes were dark and worried. Morgan and Sharp continued up the steps.

"You have not found Olivia," Mrs. Cruz said in a flat voice.

Sharp shook his head. "No, ma'am. I'm s—" He began to apologize, but his words were cut off by the woman's embrace.

She held him tightly, as if she knew he needed as much comfort as she did. She released him and patted his arm. "You will find her. I know you will."

When Sharp stepped back, his eyes were wet. "This is my partner's fiancée, Morgan Dane. She and Lance have offered to help."

Morgan and Sharp followed Mrs. Cruz into the foyer. Then it was Morgan's turn to be hugged. For a small woman, Olivia's mother had strong arms.

Releasing Morgan, Mrs. Cruz held her at arm's length. "Thank you. Olivia has spoken of you often. She thinks you're a brilliant lawyer."

"We'll do everything we can to find her," Morgan said.

"I know." Mrs. Cruz led them down a short hallway. The kitchen was small but modern. Two people sat at the table. Mrs. Cruz introduced her husband and Olivia's sister, Valerie. The family's anxiety was as palpable as the scent of coffee.

"Let me get you some coffee." Without waiting for their responses, Valerie bustled around her mother's kitchen, using the movement to expel some of her anxiety.

"A reporter called a few minutes ago. How did he find out about Olivia?" Valerie asked.

"I don't know." But Morgan should have expected the news to get out. Stella might keep her end of the investigation under wraps, but every department had leaks. "What did you tell him?"

"My mother answered the phone." Valerie's eyes softened as she looked at her mother.

"He was rude, and I hung up," Mrs. Cruz added.

Morgan preferred she be the spokesperson for the family. The press could be a useful tool, but they had to be managed, especially this early in a case. Stories generated false leads that used up valuable investigation time.

"You will probably get more calls from reporters," Morgan said. "Next time, if you don't want to talk to the press, you can refer them to me. I can handle them for you. Or we can set up a formal press conference to make a public request for help."

Mrs. Cruz looked from Morgan to Valerie and back. "What do you think we should do?"

"Let me think about it," Morgan said. "Have you received any phone calls or messages about Olivia?"

"No." Valerie shook her head. "I also checked my parents' email as well as their physical mailbox."

So no ransom demand.

Morgan glanced at Sharp, who stood silently, his eyes bleak, as if he had no words.

She continued, "What time did Olivia leave here last night?"

"About nine." Valerie took cups out of a cabinet.

"She texted me around ten o'clock, when she arrived at home." Mrs. Cruz sat next to her husband. "I know it's silly. Olivia is a grown woman, but when she leaves my house, I can't sleep until I know she's home safe." Her husband took her hand, and their fingers intertwined.

"It's not silly at all." Morgan couldn't imagine one of her daughters vanishing, no matter how old they were. The mere thought was enough to generate a rush of anxiety. She sat across from Mr. and Mrs. Cruz. "Mothers are allowed to worry."

Sharp eased into the seat next to Morgan.

"Olivia indulges me." Mrs. Cruz pushed a notepad toward Sharp. "We made a list of Olivia's friends."

Sharp seemed frozen, so Morgan read the short list. She picked up a pen from the center of the table. "Can you tell me how Olivia knows each of these people?"

"Olivia doesn't have many real friends. She works too much. But these are the people she talks about." Mrs. Cruz tapped on each name. "This is her best friend from college. They haven't seen each other for a while, but they talk on the phone now and then. Olivia has known this woman since high school, but I don't know when they spoke last." She continued down the brief list of names.

"How about professional contacts?" Morgan asked.

Valerie brought two cups of coffee to the table. "I don't know. Years ago, when she worked for a newspaper, she had reporter friends. But the industry changed. Before she wrote the book, she'd been freelancing for years. I haven't heard her talk about seeing other journalists in a long time. Jake Riley is her editor, and Kim Holgersen is her literary agent. I don't know their phone numbers."

"That information will be easy enough to get," Morgan assured her and wrote both names in her notepad. "How about boyfriends? Does she have any jealous or violent exes?"

"No. Before she met Lincoln, she hadn't dated in some time." Valerie stood next to her father and smiled sadly at Sharp. "She talks about you a great deal. You're the first man she's brought home in a decade."

Morgan's eyes grew moist. A muscle near Sharp's eye twitched.

He wrapped his hands around the mug without drinking. "Does she have any medical conditions?"

Mrs. Cruz nodded. "She had asthma as a child, but now it rarely bothers her except for an occasional flare-up in the winter, when the air is cold and dry."

Which explained why Sharp didn't know about it. He'd met Olivia last spring.

He cleared his throat. "Has Olivia talked to any of you about being followed or mentioned anyone she was concerned about in her neighborhood?"

Heads shook all around.

"What about her work?" Morgan asked. "Was she excited about anything in particular?"

Her sister frowned. "Last night, she said she had an important decision to make. She seemed conflicted, but she didn't elaborate."

Was this decision the reason Olivia had wanted to talk to Sharp, Lance, and Morgan? Was it also the reason she was missing?

Valerie twisted her wedding ring. "We talked about me most of the time. My husband and I recently separated. The kids are having issues. I'm afraid I monopolized the dinner conversation." Her eyes welled with tears.

Mrs. Cruz passed the tissues and patted her daughter's hand. "It's not your fault. Olivia was happy to listen. That's what sisters are for."

Valerie wiped her eyes. "She always does more listening than talking. That's what makes her a great journalist."

"She didn't say anything about meeting someone last night?" Sharp asked.

"No," Valerie said.

Mr. and Mrs. Cruz shook their heads.

"She doesn't talk to us about her work." Mrs. Cruz pressed a knuckle to her mouth. "We worry too much." A small sob shook her. "But she's always dealing with the wrong sorts of people. She even went to a *prison* to do interviews." She bowed her head and crossed herself.

Olivia interviewed criminals, which was inherently dangerous, as Morgan knew well.

"If you want to know more about her research, you should talk to her agent," Valerie said quietly. "Olivia talks to her a lot."

Morgan and Sharp continued to question Olivia's sister and parents about her interests and any upcoming activities she might have mentioned, but Valerie's impending divorce seemed to have dominated family discussions for the past month.

Morgan checked her notes. "Do you know who has a key to Olivia's house?"

"We both have keys." Mrs. Cruz gestured between herself and Valerie.

"No one else?" Sharp asked.

Mrs. Cruz turned up both hands. "I don't know."

"Has Olivia ever spoken of being threatened by a subject of one of her investigations?" Morgan asked.

Shaking her head, Mrs. Cruz burst into tears. Her husband wrapped an arm around her shoulders. They bowed their heads toward each other, their foreheads touching. Morgan felt as if she was intruding on a private moment. Their shared fear was both painful and beautiful to witness.

Sharp looked away, his expression shuttered, and then he stood. "We should be going," he said in a hoarse voice.

"We'll touch base in the morning." Morgan put a hand on Mrs. Cruz's shoulder.

Mrs. Cruz put her own hand on top of Morgan's and squeezed. Her eyes shifted to Sharp, then back to Morgan. "Thank you both. We would not know what to do without your help."

Valerie walked them to the front door and followed them onto the stoop, closing the door behind her. "My parents are strong, but they're not young. I don't know how they'll cope if—" A sob cut off her words. She covered her face with a hand. Her next breath hitched. Then she sniffed and took a deep breath, exhaling hard as she collected herself. Her hand dropped in a balled fist to her chest. "If you have bad news, promise me you'll call me first, so I can be here with them when you tell them?"

Sharp nodded, his mouth a grim, flat line. "We will."

Valerie gave them her home and cell phone numbers.

Morgan sent her a text. "Now you have my number. Call if you remember anything that might help us locate Olivia."

Sharp and Morgan headed for the sidewalk. The air had cooled since night had fallen. Morgan tugged her suit jacket around her.

"I'll drive." Sharp headed for the driver's side. "It's too dark to see the roadside, and the focus will help me think."

Morgan unlocked the doors with the fob. They climbed into his car, and she handed him the keys.

"Olivia used to cover the crime beat." He started the engine. "I wonder if any of her former subjects have gotten out of prison lately."

"Finding out sounds like a job for Lance's mother," Morgan said. "We should make a list of people for background checks too. You never know what or who you might find in someone's past."

"We'll get her phone records and find out how many of these people she actually communicated with recently." Sharp pulled away from the curb.

During the hour-long drive back to Scarlet Falls, Morgan texted Lance, but he didn't respond. She also called Olivia's brothers and the friends on Mrs. Cruz's list but learned nothing. Olivia hadn't spoken to any of them in weeks.

Sharp headed to Morgan's house. It was after ten o'clock when he finally pulled into her driveway. The skeleton of the new master-suite addition loomed on the side of the house.

"Where are you going now?" Morgan asked.

"Back to Olivia's place." Sharp stared out the windshield. "I'm going to walk the house again, then start going through her desk."

"Why don't I come with you?" Morgan hated to see him alone with only his worry to keep him company.

He shook his head. "It's late. Get some sleep. I'll see you in the morning. Maybe I'll have found a lead by then."

"Call us if you discover anything important." Morgan reached for the door handle and waited for his reply.

"I will."

Morgan climbed out of the car. Sharp didn't drive away until she was inside the house. She removed her heels in the foyer and left them by the door, then went looking for the family. She found her grandfather in his recliner in the family room, watching the news.

She leaned down and kissed him on the cheek. "Is everyone in bed?"

"Gianna went to sleep early. She wasn't feeling great. Lance put the kids to bed at eight, but Mia had a bad dream. I haven't seen him since he went in to talk to her."

She set a hand on his shoulder. "Thanks."

He put his hand on hers and gave it a squeeze. "Good night."

Morgan walked down the hallway to the girls' bedroom. Once the new master suite was finished, Gianna would move into the old master, and her room would become Sophie's. Morgan's youngest daughter still occasionally suffered from night terrors—aptly named because her screaming was terrifying to everyone *except* Sophie, who slept right through them.

Morgan opened their bedroom door. Light slanted from the hallway into the room. Three twin beds were crammed into the space. Lance lay next to Mia's bed. His eyes were closed. After such a disturbing day, Morgan indulged herself in a few minutes watching him sleep. He was on his back on the hardwood floor, using a stuffed seal as a pillow, one hand clasped behind his head. The other held Mia's hand. Morgan's heart swelled with love and gratitude, and tears filled her eyes.

How did I get this lucky?

She'd found love a second time, with a man who was willing to take on the intimidating job of being a father to three young children. Morgan wiped her eyes and checked the girls. They were sound asleep. She nudged Lance's shoulder. He opened his eyes and rolled his head as if his neck ached. He wore navy-blue sweatpants and a gray T-shirt. Silently, he stood and stretched, then followed Morgan from the room.

In the hallway, he whispered, "Did you eat dinner?"

"No." Her stomach grumbled at the suggestion of food.

He took her hand and pulled her into their brand-new enlarged kitchen. The white cabinets gleamed, and undercabinet lights shone on the gray granite counters.

"Gianna made you a plate." Lance opened the fridge and transferred a plate to the microwave. He pushed a button, and the machine hummed. "I'll be right back." He rushed out of the room and returned in a minute. "I bought this at the Halloween store." He held out the rubber zombie mask. "Does it look like the piece of material Stella found next to Olivia's bed?"

Morgan rubbed it between her fingers. "Yes. We should give it to Stella so the lab can compare the pieces. The color seems a little lighter to me."

"There must have been fifty different masks in the store. Thousands must be available online." Lance got up to pace. "Why would there be a piece of a Halloween mask in Olivia's bedroom?"

Morgan's brain whirled with possibilities. "I can think of no good reason."

The microwave dinged, and Lance set her plate in front of her. She ate without tasting the food, her mind on the case.

Gianna walked into the kitchen, her face pale.

"Do you feel all right?" Morgan didn't like her pallor, but Gianna was often fatigued after dialysis. Ironically, the process that kept her alive also drained her of energy.

"I think I'm getting a cold." Gianna washed two Tylenol tablets down with water. "A bunch of kids in Ava's class are sick."

"The back-to-school virus. Maybe you should go to the doctor tomorrow," Morgan suggested.

"It's just a cold." Gianna went back to bed.

Morgan and Lance walked back to their bedroom together. Lance doubled his pillows and lay down, his hands clasped behind his head.

Exhausted but also restless, Morgan changed into pajamas, washed her face, and brushed her teeth.

She climbed into bed beside him and told him about her evening visit with the Cruz family. "It's heartbreaking. They're so scared."

"So is Sharp." He pulled her closer, wrapping an arm around her shoulders and kissing the top of her head. She rested her head on his chest. He turned off the light.

Morgan listened to his heartbeat and closed her eyes, but sleep did not come. Twenty minutes later, she shifted position, restless.

"Can't sleep?" Lance whispered.

"No." She sat up.

"Me either." He turned on the light. "Did Sharp say where he was going after he dropped you off?"

"To Olivia's." Morgan checked the time on her phone. Eleven thirty. "He's probably still there."

Lance reached for a pair of pants on the bedside chair. "Let's go."

Chapter Eleven

Sharp stood in the middle of Olivia's kitchen. He pictured her standing at the island, chopping homegrown herbs and drinking a glass of red wine. For a quiet evening at home, she'd wear worn jeans or yoga pants. Her hair would be up in a ponytail. She'd look up at him as he came into the room. Her face would brighten. She'd smile, and his step would lighten.

He could see her in front of him as if she were there. But the image faded too quickly. Bowled over by a rush of emotions that bombarded him faster than he could identify them, his chest tightened and he lost his breath. When the onslaught of emotions ended, he was left with only two: love and fear, intertwined like a Celtic knot.

Bowing his head, he hooked a hand around the back of his neck.

She couldn't be gone. Their relationship was just getting off the ground. Missing her was a force, a pressure within his body that he wouldn't have suspected existed yesterday.

Why did it take losing someone to make one appreciate them?

He had to find her. She'd only recently entered his life, but in a few short months, she'd become the first person he called when he received important news, good or bad. He enjoyed her quick wit, her clever banter, and the way she took absolutely zero shit from anyone, including—maybe especially—him. She was brilliant, often several steps ahead of him in any conversation. If *he* had vanished, *she* would have figured it out immediately.

He couldn't imagine life without her.

Did she leave in the middle of the night to pursue a story for her next book?

She *was* a reporter. But no one had called her, either on her home phone or her cell, so the outing would have been planned. Olivia had plenty of street smarts. He couldn't believe she would go somewhere dangerous without taking minimal safety precautions. She would have told someone where she was going, or she would have left a note. She'd been in the crime reporting business for twenty-five years. She took calculated risks for her job, not stupid ones.

Olivia's call the night before played in his mind. She had wanted to talk to the three of them about a conflict she was having over her research. Was the issue with her research related to her disappearance?

A car engine sounded from outside. Sharp whirled and strode down the hall to the front door. Through the narrow panes of glass next to the door, he saw headlights approaching. His heart broke into a gallop.

Olivia?

The vehicle came closer and drove under the streetlight. Lance's Jeep pulled to the curb. Disappointment washed over Sharp. The space behind his ribs felt hollow, and his heart hurt. He rubbed his sternum.

Lance and Morgan climbed out of the SUV and walked to the door. Sharp let them inside. Lance was carrying a plastic shopping bag. He reached inside and pulled out a rubber mask. Without a word, he held it out.

Sharp took it, turning it over in his hands. "This looks like the scrap of rubber we found next to Olivia's bed."

"That's what we thought," Lance said.

"Was Olivia planning to attend a costume party for Halloween?" Morgan asked.

"She didn't mention one to me. We usually compare calendars, but Halloween is still six weeks away."

"We'll double-check her calendar," Morgan said. "But I didn't see any other parts of a costume when we searched the house earlier."

"How hard is this to rip?" Sharp tested the mask, digging his fingers into the rubber and pulling. The material tore. He twisted and a square of rubber broke free. "That answers that question." He stared at the rubber, dread gathering in his gut. "It seems to me we can eliminate the possibility that she left on her own."

"Someone took her," Morgan said quietly.

"But how?" Sharp turned to the house again, trying to reconstruct Olivia's evening in light of this new disturbing clue. "Her security panel showed her disarming the system when she arrived home at about ten o'clock. Two minutes later, the system was reset using the At Home setting. Then at 2:13 a.m., the system was disarmed again and reactivated in Away mode."

Lance walked to the panel. "Her alarm is outdated."

"And she doesn't have motion detectors or cameras." Sharp could kick himself. He should have insisted on updating her system. "I didn't see any sign that the alarm system was hacked, but I can't rule it out. Everything that operates on Wi-Fi is vulnerable to hacking."

Lance turned away from the alarm panel. "Let's walk through the house assuming her security system was compromised and her house breached. Then she was kidnapped."

Sharp went down a short hallway to the bedroom. Lance and Morgan followed him.

Sharp stood in the doorway and stared at the covers spilling onto the floor. He imagined what could have happened. "He surprised her while she was sleeping."

"Wearing a Halloween mask." Morgan shivered, rubbing her arms.

Sharp remembered a night three months back when he and Olivia had gotten themselves into a jam with two goons. She'd fought hard, scratching and clawing for her freedom. She was tough.

"Olivia would not have gone quietly. She would have put up a fight." Sharp pictured the events unfolding in front of him. "She would have gone for his face with her nails."

"But he was wearing a mask," Lance added. "Which she tore."

"He overpowered her, restrained her, or pulled a weapon." Sharp imagined a masked man dragging Olivia from her bed, the covers being pulled off the mattress along with her body. "And forced or carried her to the garage."

They retraced their steps to the kitchen.

"Her purse would have been on the island." Sharp pointed. "So the intruder would have her phone, the security system fob, and her car keys. He could have turned her alarm system on and off easily using either the fob or the app on her phone."

They walked to the short hallway that led to the laundry room.

"He exited through the garage." Sharp stared at the wood trim. Stella had taken the broken fingernail and sampled the blood, but the smear was still visible. "She grabbed the doorjamb on the way out."

"If she had broken away right here"—Morgan opened the door and stood in the doorway—"then she could have closed and locked the door with him on the garage side." To demonstrate, she motioned for Lance to walk down the two wooden steps to the concrete floor while she stayed in the laundry room.

"But that didn't happen"—Lance walked farther into the garage—"because he put her in the back of her car."

"Her car is a hatchback. It doesn't have a trunk." Sharp walked to where Olivia's Prius was usually parked. "He would have had to incapacitate her in some way."

"He clearly planned this down to the smallest detail," Morgan said. "He would have brought something to restrain her. Rope. Zip ties."

Or used drugs, a Taser, or a blunt instrument to render her defenseless.

Sharp's mind jumped in with other possibilities. He stared at the two yellow sticky notes that marked the locations of Olivia's fallen earrings, and he knew.

How did he not see it the first time he'd walked the scene?

She was clever, clearly smarter than Sharp, and she would never give up.

"She left us a trail." His gaze locked on the empty concrete. Trying to absorb the scene playing out in his mind, Sharp rubbed his scalp with both hands. "I should have known. I should have assumed she'd been kidnapped."

He'd let her down already.

"Sharp." Morgan's voice was clipped. "You had no way of knowing. Now let's start looking in her office for a motive."

"Right." Sharp nodded. *Back to work.*

"She keeps her calendar and contact information on her phone, which is missing, but it syncs with her computer. She keeps her laptop on her desk." Sharp turned and led the way back through the house to Olivia's office. He flipped the wall switch, and light brightened the room. A built-in desk and bookshelves lined the walls.

"I should be able to break into her laptop," Lance offered. "I'll have to hack around her screen passcode, but it's not hard."

Sharp gestured toward the desk, and Lance took the chair behind it. He opened the laptop and went to work. In less than two minutes, he bypassed the opening-screen password.

"I'm in." Lance looked up.

Morgan walked toward the shelves and began scanning them. Olivia had research books on every aspect of the criminal justice system, from police procedure to criminal defense. "We need to know which cases she was researching." She stopped at a row of binders. "Is all Olivia's research on her laptop, or does she keep written notes as well?"

"Both." Sharp leaned over Lance's shoulder. "She transcribes her interviews and notes onto the computer, but she keeps the originals. She organizes everything in those binders in some sort of elaborate system." Sharp remembered seeing a black and a red binder on Olivia's desk earlier in the week. He spotted the two binders lying on their sides on the shelf over the desk. He picked up the first one and opened it, scanning the page. "Olivia was researching the case of Cliff Franklin, who was convicted of murder in 2016."

Lance looked up. "I see two recently accessed folders on her computer. One is entitled 'Franklin Case.' You're never going to guess the name of the second case."

Morgan turned away from the shelves. "What is it?"

Lance looked up and met her gaze. "Olander."

Morgan froze. "Olivia was interested in Erik Olander's case?"

Sharp retrieved and then opened the second binder. "Yes. This book is labeled 'Olander.' Isn't that the name of the woman who shot herself outside the office?"

"Yes." Morgan looked troubled.

"That's a hell of a coincidence." Sharp moved behind the chair and read the computer screen over Lance's shoulder. If Olivia was interested in the case, Morgan would be second-guessing her decision to turn down Mrs. Olander.

Morgan reached for the binders.

Sharp let her have them. He didn't like the coincidence, and he knew Morgan wouldn't either.

"I wonder if she found something to suggest Erik Olander was innocent." Shaking her head, Morgan closed the binder and splayed her hand on its cover. "It's too much material to read quickly. I'd like to take all of this back to our office and put it on the whiteboard."

"I agree." Lance closed the laptop and tucked it under his arm. "We need to get organized."

The three of them could divide and conquer all this information. Plus, Lance and Morgan saw different patterns. Over the past year, they had learned to work as a team. Their different skill sets complemented each other, and Sharp needed their help.

The clock was already ticking.

Olivia had been gone for twenty-two hours. Sharp had already misinterpreted several clues. Now he had to hope Olivia didn't die because of his mistakes.

Chapter Twelve

Back at Sharp Investigations, Lance tossed his jacket on his chair and then hustled into Morgan's office. Sharp was right behind him.

"I'm going to try to hack into Olivia's online accounts," Lance affirmed.

Morgan gestured to the whiteboard that hung on her wall. When they worked complicated cases, her office became their war room. "Why don't you stay here and use the board? I'll take the binders into the kitchen and start reading." She grabbed her laptop and withdrew.

Sharp sat in Morgan's chair. Facing him across the desk, Lance opened his laptop. They spent the next few hours hacking into Olivia's online cell service and credit card statements. Luckily, Olivia used the same password for most of her accounts.

"I'll tackle these phone and financial records." Sharp flexed his fingers over the keyboard of Olivia's computer.

"And I'll move on to social media." Lance found several social media accounts in Olivia's name. All were professional. Olivia did not post personal information. She scheduled her posts in advance. They automatically went live three times per week. He scrolled through her posts for the last several months and noted the topics: bail reform, local crimes, her upcoming book publication. A few of the articles she'd shared had long lists of comments. Lance expanded the comments and began making a list of hostile responses. He moved from post to post, looking for repeat commenters, aggressive trolling, and threats.

The printer hummed. Sharp got up and retrieved a piece of paper. He took it to the whiteboard and used a magnet to place it in the center. It was a picture of Olivia. He stared at it for a few seconds, then picked up a marker and wrote a time line of her disappearance on one side of the board. When he turned to face Lance, his eyes were bloodshot.

Lance rolled a kink out of his neck.

"We need to review and organize our evidence on the board." After setting the marker on the ledge, Sharp went back to the desk. He took off his wire-rimmed reading glasses, tossed them on the blotter, and squeezed the bridge of his nose.

"I'll get Morgan." Lance stood and stretched.

"OK." Sharp picked up his glasses, cleaned them with the hem of his shirt, and put them back on.

Lance headed for the kitchen. Morgan sat at the table, a cup of coffee and a box of powdered donuts at her elbow. Her own laptop and Olivia's binders were open in front of her. White sugar dotted the table.

"How many of those have you eaten?" he asked.

"I don't know." Morgan lifted the lid of the box to peer inside. "Almost all of them. There's one left. Do you want it?"

"No." Lance's stomach turned at the thought. "A massive overload of sugar isn't going to cut it."

Morgan lifted one shoulder. "To each his own."

"Sharp wants to review."

"All right." She closed her computer.

Lance whipped up two protein shakes and carried them back to the war room. Morgan followed, finishing her last donut as she walked through the doorway. She stood in front of the board and studied Sharp's notes for a few seconds.

Still sitting behind Morgan's desk, Sharp looked up from his computer screen as Lance set one of the drinks in front of him. "Thanks."

Morgan picked up a marker. "What do we know?"

"I've found a few hostile social media trolls, but none felt particularly personal." Lance perched on the corner of the desk.

Morgan wrote SOCIAL MEDIA TROLLS? at the bottom of the whiteboard. More promising leads would take up the center of the space.

Sharp drank his shake. "Olivia had several long calls with her literary agent over the past two weeks. She received messages from her editor but apparently didn't return his calls."

"I'll call them both in the morning," Morgan said.

Sharp set down his glass. "I'm still cross-checking her calls and contacts with her calendar. She calls and texts her mother almost every day. There were multiple marathon conversations with her sister. She had a lengthy call with Erik Olander's attorney on Tuesday and one with Cliff Franklin's lawyer the week before that." Sharp shifted forward and propped on elbow on the desk. "She prefers email for professional correspondence and has multiple accounts, including an anonymous one."

"Let's look at her calendar." Lance opened it on his computer. The lethargy that nagged at him almost made him wish he'd taken Morgan up on her donut offer. "I'll send a list of names to my mother so she can start on background checks. We'll start with the major players in the Franklin and Olander cases and anyone who had an appointment or phone call with her in the last two weeks."

"Did you email a copy of her calendar to Stella?" Morgan asked.

"Yes." Sharp leaned back in his chair.

Lance scanned the entries. "There is no costume party on her calendar."

"No." Sharp ran a hand over his short salt-and-pepper hair. "There isn't."

They were quiet for a few seconds. If Olivia was kidnapped the way they'd envisioned, she must have been terrified. Lance was trying not to think about her waking up and seeing a man in a rubber mask in her bedroom. And he was trying even harder not to imagine the same thing happening to Morgan. The mere thought made his heartbeat stutter.

Sharp seemed to have aged overnight. Usually he looked—and acted—like a man half his age. But today, exhaustion and stress lined his face, and his eyes were clouded with worry.

Lance locked his own feelings away. Sharp was already emotionally compromised. Lance needed a clear head. As much as he liked Olivia, he'd serve her better if he could compartmentalize his feelings and be objective.

"Olivia used initials extensively in her calendar." Sharp read from a notepad in front of him. "I've sorted out some of the abbreviations. Most are boring. *TOY* stands for the Toyota dealership. She took her Prius in for regularly scheduled maintenance two weeks ago. *AHA* stands for A-1 Heating and Air. They serviced her heater on Wednesday. She calls her parents *M&D*."

"Let's focus on the current week." Lance studied the most recent calendar entries. "She talked to her literary agent on Monday morning, and she met with Lena and Kennett Olander at their farm on Monday evening."

"Her mother's doctor appointment and the meeting at our office are on Friday's agenda. She has nothing at all scheduled for Saturday or Sunday. Next week, she has lunch with her literary agent on Monday and a dental cleaning on Tuesday."

"Plus, the usual Thursday night dinner with her parents," Morgan said.

"Yes." Sharp scratched his chin. "Morgan, what can you tell us about the cases she was researching for her book, other than both Olander and Franklin were convicted of murder?"

She started a new column labeled FRANKLIN CASE. "Three years ago, Cliff Franklin was convicted of the murder of twenty-six-year-old Brandi Holmes. Do you remember the case, Sharp? I wasn't paying much attention to the news back then."

She'd been mired in grief over her husband's death.

"The boys talked about it quite a bit." Sharp rubbed his temples in a circular motion as if he was trying to stimulate his brain.

The boys were Sharp's retired cop buddies. Sharp was the youngest. They met at least once a week at a local bar. Despite being retired, the boys knew almost everything that went on in local law enforcement.

Sharp lowered his hands. "The sheriff's department linked Franklin to Brandi and five other missing women. Only Brandi's body was found. As far as I know, the other women are still officially missing. Brandi's murder was the only one he was charged with. The boys were all convinced Franklin was a serial killer, but they couldn't prove it. Everyone was relieved he was convicted and sentenced to life, but they really wanted justice for those other five women and closure for their families."

Under Franklin's name, Morgan wrote 5 MISSING WOMEN and VICTIM—BRANDI HOLMES.

"There must be a special reason Olivia was interested in the case," Lance said. "Was she trying to find the five missing women?"

"It seems that was part of her angle." Morgan capped her marker. "But there are repeated notations that Olivia wanted to interview Cliff's brother, Joe. I don't see any notes indicating that meeting ever took place."

Sharp nodded, his face grim. "I found multiple calls to Joseph Franklin lasting approximately thirty seconds."

"She was leaving messages for him," Lance suggested.

"Maybe he wasn't answering." Morgan stood back to scan the whole board. "In his initial interviews, Cliff claimed his brother, Joe, could give him an alibi. He'd been living at Joe's house at the time of the murder. However, the alibi was weak, and the physical evidence was solid. Cliff had worked on Brandi's car. Hairs found inside Cliff's trunk were identified through DNA as belonging to Brandi."

Sharp rubbed his chin. "What was weak about the alibi?"

Standing in front of her desk, Morgan set down the binder and opened it. "Joe is hard of hearing and removes his hearing aids at night. If Cliff had left the house during the night, Joe would have slept right through it."

"Not a good enough alibi to counter DNA evidence." Sharp got up to pace the floor behind the chair.

Lance searched his memories. "Bryce prosecuted the Franklin case, right?"

Morgan flipped a few pages. "Yes. I'll make an appointment to talk to him. I'm sure he remembers a win on a case this prominent."

District Attorney Bryce Walters was an experienced trial lawyer. DAs were elected. For a politician, Bryce was usually a straight shooter, but he would have made good use of this case in his campaign.

"What about Olivia's meeting with the Olanders?" Sharp asked. "What did she discuss with them?"

"Hold on." Morgan headed for the door. "Let me get the other binder. I haven't gotten to that case yet."

Lance took over recording facts on the board. He started a new column for the Olander case, beginning with the potential bias of the jury foreman.

Morgan returned with the binder open and in the crook of her arm. "They discussed the general details." Her finger moved over the page as she skimmed. "Oh. Wait. Here's a surprise. Olivia was the one who brought the juror issue to Mrs. Olander's attention."

Lance doubled-checked the calendar. "That was Monday."

"Yes." Morgan underlined her note. "The same day that Mrs. Olander made the appointment with me. Mrs. Olander had said the information came from a television interview."

"Maybe I can find it on YouTube." Lance went to his computer, opened YouTube, and typed in the search bar. Even knowing the subject of the interview, it took him several tries to locate the video. "Here it is. It's part of a series on injustice in the justice system."

He pressed "Play" and they watched the six-minute clip. Two women sat in chairs angled toward each other. The host, a sharp-looking man in his forties, wore a gray suit. He summarized the charges against Erik Olander. Four minutes in, they got to the meat of the discussion.

The host leaned forward. "Tell us about the domestic abuse you suffered."

The jury foreman, a middle-aged woman in navy-blue slacks and a pale-blue blouse, shook her head. "A jerk I used to date slapped me once during an argument. He was arrested, and I broke up with him. That was the end of it. It was a onetime assault, not a case of prolonged domestic abuse."

The interviewer pressed his lips flat. "When the judge asked you if there was anything in your past that could prevent you from being impartial, you didn't bring it up."

"It happened more than twenty years ago," the juror said. "It didn't even occur to me."

The interview went on for another minute, but there were no more revelations.

"It sounds like we need to talk to Mr. Olander." Lance closed his computer. "Olivia met with both Erik's parents, right?"

Morgan checked the binder. "Yes. He was there, but I might not be the right person to approach Mr. Olander. His wife committed suicide minutes after I refused to take her case. I doubt he'll want to see me."

"I'll do it," Sharp said. "First thing in the morning."

"I'll go with you," Lance volunteered.

"All right." Sharp shrugged.

"I'll contact both Olander's and Franklin's attorneys in the morning." Morgan set the marker on the whiteboard ledge. "I'm going back to the files. I've only skimmed the surface of these cases."

Sharp said, "If someone involved with one of them took Olivia, she must have rattled him."

"I can't see why anyone would be nervous about a closed case." Lance crossed his arms. "Unless the wrong person was convicted of the crime."

"And the real killer doesn't want that made public because he likes walking around scot-free." Sharp shifted forward and pressed the button on the side of his cell phone. "It's two a.m. She's been gone for twenty-four hours, and we have no idea where to look for her."

Chapter Thirteen

Morgan lifted her head from the table. Early-morning light brightened the office kitchen to a hazy gray. She massaged an ache in her neck, rolling her head to stretch the cramped muscles. Her face itched, and she reached up to peel a sticky note from her cheek. She must have fallen asleep while reviewing files.

She glanced down at Olivia's thick Olander binder. Her own laptop was open beside it. Lance had copied Olivia's digital files and emailed them, so Morgan had all of the information in one place. Olivia's research was extensive and often repetitive. Each source was verified multiple times, each fact triple-checked.

Olivia had also requested the official courtroom transcripts for both cases. Except for special cases and juvenile records, trial information was public record and was available online for a fee. Olivia had received Cliff Franklin's trial transcript electronically. As Erik Olander's conviction was recent, his trial transcript had been ordered but not yet received. Olivia had accessed and downloaded the digital audio recording of the trial, but Morgan could not listen to all ninety hours of it. She didn't need a law clerk. She needed seven.

It would take her the rest of the week to get through all the pages of the Olander file alone, and the Franklin case was just as complicated. Morgan did not have time to review all of Olivia's documents.

Morgan's eyes burned, and she'd only read a portion of the material. Since she didn't have a law clerk, she would utilize the next best thing—her grandfather, a retired NYPD detective.

She stood and stretched her arms toward the ceiling.

"You're awake." Lance walked through the doorway. One side of his short hair was mussed, suggesting he'd also dozed off. He leaned over and kissed her. "Good morning."

"Morning." She kissed him back.

Morgan headed for her office—and her coffee maker. "Coffee?"

Sharp wasn't at her desk, but he'd been busy writing notes on the whiteboard during the night. Morgan needed caffeine before she could review his additions.

"Yes, please." Lance followed her into the room. He ran a hand over his head, setting his hair back into place. "How do you feel?"

"Better. The nap helped." Morgan checked the time. Seven o'clock. She turned on the machine. "Where's Sharp?"

"He went back to his office." Lance wrapped his arms around her.

Morgan indulged herself and leaned into him for a moment. As always, the solid contact with him grounded her. "I don't suppose he fell asleep at any point."

"No." Releasing her, Lance shook his head grimly. "I'm worried about him."

"Me too." Morgan started the machine brewing.

She handed him the first cup of coffee and brewed a second. She lowered her voice. "I don't think we should leave him alone right now."

"I agree." Lance drank.

"But will *he*?" Morgan waited, impatiently, for her morning caffeine.

"All we can do is try. Why don't you go home and have breakfast with the kids? You can shower and change. I saw the girls last night. I can shower here and go to the Olander farm with Sharp."

"Good idea. I'll call my sister and let her know what's going on." Morgan missed her children. She hadn't handled a big case for months and had become accustomed to seeing them in the morning and evening every day. The thought of hugs, a hot shower, and fresh clothes perked her up. "But isn't it early to knock on Mr. Olander's door?"

"He's a farmer. He should be up. Plus, I doubt I can get Sharp to wait any longer." Lance turned to leave her office. "Kiss the kids for me," he said over his shoulder on the way out.

"Will do. Be safe," she called after him.

A few minutes later, she heard the front door close as Lance and Sharp left. She set her coffee on her desk and gathered information on Cliff Franklin for her grandfather to review. While she sorted files, she called Stella and gave her a quick recap of their investigation so far.

"I have less news," Stella said. "There were no matches to the fingerprints from Olivia's house. As for the blood sample, the rapid stain ID kit shows the blood on Olivia's doorjamb is human. The lab will enter the DNA sample into CODIS, but it'll take weeks to get a hit, if we get one at all. Considering the torn fingernail was pink, I suspect the blood is Olivia's, but I want to cover all the bases."

CODIS, the Combined DNA Index System, was FBI software that compared DNA samples to DNA criminal justice databases. Matches could be offender hits and generate an actual suspect, or forensic hits, where the sample would match DNA found at another crime scene.

"Thanks." Morgan said goodbye and ended the call. While she had the phone in hand, she called both Olivia's editor and agent. Neither answered, so she left them voice messages. Both numbers were identified as cellular, but that didn't guarantee that either the agent or editor would answer calls on the weekend.

After her bag was packed and she had enough caffeine in her system to safely get behind the wheel, she put on her coat. With her tote slung over her shoulder, she left her office.

She opened the front door and was startled to see a man standing on the stoop. The man looked down at her with piercing blue eyes. His face was gaunt and haggard, his clothing wrinkled. She wrinkled her nose at the smell of body odor. He hadn't showered recently. Was he homeless? She glanced over his shoulder and saw a battered green pickup across the street.

"Can I help you?" she asked.

"I'm Kennett Olander."

Morgan didn't know what to say. She'd dealt with victims' families in her prosecutor years, but this was an entirely unique situation.

"My wife came to see you yesterday." He stepped closer, wobbling on shaky legs. The bags under his eyes were deep and dark. His eyes were bloodshot, and his pallor suggested long-term sleep deprivation, inadequate nutrition, and killer stress.

Morgan found her voice. "Yes. I'm so sorry for your loss."

He nodded, his eyes growing moist. In his midfifties, Olander struck an imposing figure. Tall, with thick white hair and a beard that needed trimming, he could have passed for an aging Viking.

"I wanted to talk to you about my wife." Mr. Olander stepped forward and held out a hand.

Morgan hesitated for a second, then shook it.

Heavy calluses on his big hands indicated many years of manual labor. He wore dark jeans and a wrinkled blue button-down shirt with the sleeves rolled up to his elbows. The morning was too cold to be out without a jacket. Chilly air was blowing inside the open front of Morgan's peacoat.

"Come inside." Morgan moved back, allowing him into the foyer.

She led the way to her office. Inside, she removed her coat and set her tote on her credenza. "Can I make you a cup of coffee?"

"All right." Mr. Olander looked lost.

Morgan gestured to a chair facing her desk. "Please, sit down."

He lowered his frame into the seat, resting trembling hands on the arms of the chair. Morgan opened her credenza drawer and found a package of cookies. She put a few on a plate and brewed a cup of coffee. When it was finished, she handed the mug to Mr. Olander and set the plate of cookies on the desk in front of him. "Cream or sugar?"

"No, thank you." He picked up a cookie.

Morgan settled behind her desk, content to wait until he was ready to talk. Understandably, he seemed to need to collect himself. While he did, she held her phone in her lap under the desk and sent Lance a quick text, letting him know Mr. Olander was here and not at his farm. After Mr. Olander had eaten two cookies and sipped his coffee, his color improved.

He settled back in the chair and stared into the coffee. "I'd like to say I can't believe my wife killed herself, but that would be a lie. It didn't surprise me one bit." He wrapped all his fingers around the mug.

"I'm sorry for all that has happened to you."

His life had been destroyed.

He nodded once. "She was at a breaking point. I honestly thought she was going to do it when Erik was convicted. I'm almost surprised she held out this long."

"Did she get counseling?"

He huffed. "No. She refused. It was almost like she didn't want to feel better. Plus, our health insurance deductible is so big, we can't afford to use it. We mortgaged the farm to hire the best lawyer. We even sold off some of our furniture. We eventually put the farm up for sale, although it took a while to find a buyer. No one wants a dairy farm these days."

He'd lost his son, his wife, and his home. What did he have left?

Hope that his son might win an appeal.

"Where will you go?" she asked.

"We're moving to a small house in town. I can't imagine living so close to other people, but it's all I can afford. But I guess it doesn't matter. The farm is just an empty shell now. I sold the equipment. The livestock is gone." He sighed. "Everything is gone."

"What can I do for you, Mr. Olander?" Morgan asked in a soft voice.

"My wife wanted to hire you right before she . . ." He inhaled and steadied himself.

"Yes. That's correct."

"Erik's conviction broke her, until that writer lady came to see us. She got Lena all fired up." He dug into his pocket and produced a wrinkled business card. "Olivia Cruz." He shoved it back into his pocket. "Ms. Cruz told us she was researching Erik's case. When she said the jury foreman had lied about her background, Lena went ballistic."

"Did Ms. Cruz actually say the juror lied?" Morgan asked. Olivia's previous book had been based on one of Morgan's former clients. Olivia knew legal procedure. She would have understood the technicalities of the jury selection process.

"I don't remember if she used the word *lie*." His forehead wrinkled. "She might have said something like *neglected to disclose*, but that's the same thing."

Not exactly.

So often, people heard what they wanted to hear.

"Ms. Cruz said she was going to continue researching and she'd let us know if she found anything else. Erik's lawyer already filed a notice of appeal, but he doesn't think we'll get any traction with what Ms. Cruz discovered. He's working other angles."

Morgan agreed with the attorney, but Mrs. Olander hadn't.

"For all I paid him, he should be able to get some results!" Mr. Olander's voice rose. He looked away, his jaw sawing back and forth, as he composed himself.

Morgan gave him a minute to cool down. Then she changed the topic. "How did your wife find me?"

"She saw you on TV a while back, about the same time Erik was first arrested. She wanted to hire you to represent him then." He shifted his weight. "But our funds were limited. I wanted someone with more experience in criminal defense. Your practice had just opened."

Morgan had additional experience as a prosecutor, but now was not the time to mention it. She wasn't selling her services. She'd already refused the case.

Mr. Olander set his mug on the desk. "Here's the thing. The damned prosecutor was such an arrogant prick in the courtroom. It wouldn't surprise me if he knew all about the juror and picked her on purpose."

ADA Anthony Esposito had prosecuted Erik's case. Morgan had a sometimes adversarial, sometimes cordial relationship with Esposito. His moral code seemed as gray as the charcoal suits he favored. He could be arrogant, and he liked to win. But Morgan couldn't see him committing an ethical violation and jeopardizing his career by withholding critical information from the defense, especially not in a case where he already had a clear advantage.

Morgan said, "In most cases, neither the prosecutor nor the defense counsel would know about an event from a juror's distant past."

"Well, he treated Erik like dirt."

Of course he had. Esposito had wanted the jury to feel his certainty that Erik was guilty. He had wanted them to feel—and share—his disgust. Much of what happened in the courtroom was theatrics. The truth was irrelevant if an attorney could not convince the jury.

Olander's fist suddenly slammed down on her desk, rattling it— and surprising Morgan with the rapid shift in his demeanor.

"Erik's trial was a farce." Olander's face twisted until he barely resembled the man she'd let into her office. "I paid a lot of money for a good lawyer, and the first thing he did was suggest Erik plead guilty."

The firm the Olanders had hired was based in Albany. Morgan was familiar with their attorney's reputation. He was experienced and seemed competent.

The skin of Mr. Olander's already-lean face had tightened with anger. Maybe Erik had inherited his father's volatile temper. She considered Olander's behavior on the doorstep. He'd lost his entire life. Some emotional instability should be expected, but Morgan had interviewed hundreds of suspects, victims, and witnesses. Mr. Olander set off her well-honed bullshit detector.

Was he truly volatile, or had his depression been an act? Had he been trying to manipulate Morgan's sympathy and cooperation? Which one was the real Mr. Olander?

Morgan remembered Mrs. Olander's statement when she'd first entered Morgan's office: *Kennett doesn't know I'm here. He wouldn't approve.* At the time, Morgan hadn't thought much of the comment, but now she wondered if Mrs. Olander had been afraid of her husband.

Erik's wife had been researching domestic violence shelters on the sly. Maybe wife beating and being a control freak ran in the family.

"Our fucking lawyer should have found out about the juror's partiality," Mr. Olander said. "We shouldn't have learned about it from a reporter."

"As I explained to your wife, being a domestic violence victim more than twenty years ago would not automatically disqualify her from serving on the jury."

"That's bullshit!" Mr. Olander spat out the words. "I hate lawyers." His voice rose, and he banged a fist on his thigh. "Can't I get a fucking straight answer from you either?"

"Mr. Olander, it isn't that simple."

"No shit. I'm not stupid," he snapped. "I'm pissed off. I sold my farm, and I've nothing to show for it."

Had he thought with enough money he could buy his son's freedom?

"The past few years have been tough. I have nothing left. The fucking lawyers took what was left, and then Lena comes to me saying we need to hire another one. I told her"—his voice dropped off abruptly and his gaze shifted, as if he had barely stopped himself from saying something he knew he shouldn't—"I told her, *'No. We already have a lawyer. I'm not throwing more money at a different one.'* I need you to give me whatever money my wife gave you as a retainer."

"She didn't give me any money. I turned her down. As I told your wife, you need an appellate lawyer—"

"Fuck you!" He leaped to his feet. "I know she gave you money. She took a check, and it wasn't in her purse."

Morgan had a brief but vivid flashback to the last time she'd dealt with an impulsive, violent client. He'd punched her in the face in the middle of the courthouse corridor. She'd suffered a concussion. Her face had healed, but the incident had left a mark on her confidence. Her heart sprinted, its beats echoing in her ears, and sweat broke out under her arms.

Was Mr. Olander just a bully? Or was he out of control and dangerous?

Chapter Fourteen

Lance stared through the windshield of Sharp's Prius at the Olander farm. "Does anyone even live here?"

"The place looks abandoned." Sharp turned off the engine.

They stepped out of the car in front of a sprawling single-story house. A second house of the same style stood on the other side of a meadow the size of a football field.

"This is Kennett Olander's address." Lance pointed to the home in front of them. With few trees to protect it from the elements, the primary house was old and had been weather-beaten to a dull gray. The second house appeared newer, the sheen of its blue shutters and white clapboards suggested vinyl siding. "He built the second house for Erik and Natalie."

Sharp crossed his arms and studied the two structures. "Looks almost like a compound."

Behind the houses, a long, low barn stretched out, surrounded by empty pastures and smaller outbuildings.

Lance headed up the walk to the single step that led to the front porch of the first house. "Someone will probably turn the whole property into a housing development of McMansions."

Sharp rapped on the front door.

Wind blew across the open space. Other than the rustle of dead leaves across the porch, the entire place was eerily silent.

Sharp knocked a second time. They waited several minutes, but no one answered.

"Let's look around." Sharp walked to the nearest window, cupped his hand over his eyes, and peered inside.

Lance followed his boss around the side of the house, looking in each window as they passed. Normally, Sharp was nosey but tried to color mostly within the lines of the law.

"I wonder how long they've lived on the farm." Sharp pivoted on his heel and strode across the grass. "Let's check out the barn."

They followed a dirt footpath from the house to the barn.

"From the smell of this place, I wouldn't want to buy their milk." Sharp skirted the carcass of a large rat. A scurrying sound inside the barn wall suggested there were live ones as well.

"Agreed," Lance said. "Let's hope the place was better maintained when they were in business."

"I doubt it. This looks like long-term neglect."

They walked into the large indoor enclosure that had housed the animals. Even with the cows gone, the pungent scents of manure and urine bit into Lance's nostrils. Cobwebs clung to the few pieces of rusted equipment that remained.

The center space was two stories high. On either side, the building had two floors of offices and storage. Windows overlooked what appeared to be the area where the cows had been milked. Across the back of the building, a catwalk connected the two sides and presumably gave management a bird's-eye view of the operation.

The barn was empty except for a few feral-looking cats. Lance poked his head into an office. Dust coated the file cabinets and battered desk. A gray tabby arched its back and hissed before darting through an open doorway into an adjoining office.

"I guess Mr. Olander isn't here." Sharp walked outside and headed back toward the house.

"We'll have to try again." Lance fell into step beside him. "Maybe we should call first."

"When you warn suspects, you give them the opportunity to hide the incriminating shit." Sharp liked to drop in on people.

"True. But consideration can produce cooperation. We aren't police anymore. We can't compel anyone to talk to us." Lance stopped. "Wait. Do you have some reason to suspect Olander took Olivia?"

"No, but it would be easy to hide a woman in a big empty place like this." Sharp turned in a circle.

"What would be his motivation?" Lance asked.

Sharp propped one hand on his hip. "Mrs. Olander came to Morgan's office alone. Why didn't her husband go with her? Maybe Mr. Olander didn't want to appeal his son's case."

"Why wouldn't he?"

"Maybe he killed his daughter-in-law."

"Do we have a reason why he might have done that?"

"No." Sharp was reaching. "What if he knows his son is guilty, and he helped him try to cover it up?"

"That sounds more plausible."

Sharp resumed walking. "Let's go look at the other house."

Lance followed Sharp to the footpath to Erik's house. They peered through each window and moved on. The rooms seemed empty, not just of people but of personal possessions as well. The furniture had been pared down to the bare essentials, and cardboard moving boxes were stacked in what Lance assumed was the family room at the back of the house.

"This window is unlocked. Give me a boost." Sharp tugged on a pair of gloves and pushed up a window sash. "We have the place to ourselves. We might not get this opportunity again."

Lance boosted him over the sill. Then he returned to the rear corner of the building to watch the long driveway in case Mr. Olander came home. Sharp returned in fifteen minutes. "I checked the closets, attic, and basement. She's not here. Let's look next door."

They jogged across the meadow and repeated the process at the main house, except Sharp had to jimmy a window to gain access.

"There's no interior basement door," Sharp said as he climbed out of the window and dropped onto the grass. He reached up to close the window.

"It's an old house. It was common to only have an exterior entrance to the basement."

They moved to a set of bulkhead doors around back. A chain and padlock secured the handles.

"We've already searched ninety percent of the property. We can rule out this last space pretty quick." Sharp took lockpick tools from his wallet and began to work on the lock.

Lance didn't bother to argue. This was not a normal investigation. If there was any chance—no matter how remote—that Olivia was in the Olanders' basement, then they would look.

Sharp had the padlock off in two minutes.

"Wait." Lance pulled gloves from his pocket and put them on.

They each grabbed a handle. The doors were rusted around the edges but opened easily. Wooden stairs descended into darkness. Sharp took a flashlight from his jacket pocket and shone it into the opening. All they could see was a few square feet of hard-packed earth and footprints.

"Someone's been down there recently." Sharp descended the steps with no hesitation. He shone the flashlight straight down and examined the footprints in the dust. "Looks like the same pair of boots made all these tracks."

Lance followed him, switching on his own flashlight. Partitions divided the basement into what appeared to be storage areas. Shelves covered with dusty boxes lined the first area. Block print labeled the boxes as CHRISTMAS DECORATIONS and ERIK'S LITTLE LEAGUE TROPHIES.

Lance lifted a few lids. The labels seemed to be accurate.

They moved to the next section, a huge shelved closet where labels on the shelves indicated the family had stored a large quantity of non-perishable food. A box of MREs and a few mason jars of home-canned tomatoes and peaches remained.

The last area held four old steamer trunks.

"What do you think is in here?" Sharp stood in front of a trunk and examined a keyed padlock that secured the lid.

Dirt and cobwebs coated the trunks, and the concrete around the trunks was covered in a thin layer of dirt that was clear of footprints.

"It doesn't look as if anyone has accessed them lately, but there's only one way to find out. We've already committed a B and E. We might as well finish the job." Lance went to the second trunk. He kept his own set of lockpicking tools in his wallet.

"Good point."

The trunk was old and the lock simple. Lance had it open in less than thirty seconds.

Sharp raised the lid of his trunk and whistled softly. "Holy shit."

Lance looked over. Sharp's trunk was full of rifles.

Sharp whistled. "These are AR-15s."

Lance raised the lid of his trunk. It was full of boxes of bullets. "There's enough ammunition in here to supply a small militia."

The third trunk held more weapons, while the fourth was full of body armor and gas masks.

Sharp waved a hand over the trunks. "What the hell is Olander doing with all this?"

"I don't know." Lance closed the lid and relocked it. "But Olivia isn't down here."

With a short nod, Sharp returned his crate to its original locked state. "The pistol grips on those rifles are not legal."

In New York State, a permit was not required to own a long gun, but certain features on semiautomatic rifles were illegal.

"Neither are these high-capacity magazines," Lance said. The sheer volume of weaponry was also highly suspect. "We should tell Stella."

"How do we explain finding them?"

"Good point," Lance said. "We'll have to find a way around that. She'll need to coordinate with the ATF."

The Bureau of Alcohol, Tobacco, Firearms, and Explosives would be interested in the possible illegal trafficking of firearms.

"You're right," Sharp admitted with a sigh.

Lance led the way out of the basement, blinking at the daylight. The overcast day felt bright compared to the darkness underground. They locked the bulkhead doors and returned to the Prius.

"Maybe my mom will turn up some dirt on Mr. Olander." Lance slid into the passenger seat. He took his phone out of his pocket and checked his messages. He'd missed a text from Morgan. He'd been so focused on the search, he hadn't felt his phone vibrate.

"He's neck-deep in something." Sharp started the engine.

Lance read Morgan's message. His belly tightened. "Mr. Olander is at the office."

"Shit." Sharp turned the vehicle around. "I don't like her being alone with him."

Neither did Lance. He called Stella and put the call on speakerphone. "Hey, I need to tell you something as a confidential informant."

Her sigh was audible over the connection.

"Would you rather me call from a pay phone?" he asked. Could he even find one that worked?

"Just tell me." Weariness edged her voice.

"There are trunks full of guns and ammunition in the Olanders' basement," Lance said.

"And how do you know this?" she asked.

"An anonymous source told us," Lance suggested.

Stella snorted. "Never mind. I don't want to know the details. I assume you found no evidence of Olivia there?"

"None," Lance answered.

"OK," Stella said. "I'll call the ATF office in Albany."

"I have a contact there," Sharp said. He had contacts everywhere in local law enforcement. "Do you want me to call him?"

"Who's your contact?" Stella asked.

"Ryan Abrams," Sharp answered.

"I've heard of him," Stella said. "But we've never met."

Ryan was a fifteen-year ATF veteran. He and Sharp had worked two cases together involving illegal gun sales while Sharp was with the SFPD.

"OK," Stella agreed. "You call. Try to stay out of trouble." Her tone suggested she didn't have much faith that they would.

"We'll try." Lance glanced at Sharp, who was gripping the wheel with white knuckles. If Olivia wasn't found soon, keeping Sharp out of danger was going to get harder.

The connection broke off, and Lance lowered his phone. "Maybe the ATF will send an agent."

"They'll need more than an anonymous claim that some guns were seen at a private residence to establish enough probable cause to obtain a search warrant," Sharp said. "Other than the guns, we haven't turned up any dirt on the Olanders."

"I can't think of any legitimate reason for a dairy farmer to have trunks full of guns and ammo."

"Could he be an illegal arms dealer?" Sharp suggested as he drove away from the house.

"I don't know. The guns seem to have been there awhile. I wouldn't think a dealer would want to hang on to them for long periods of time."

Sharp turned onto the main road. "Maybe he's a collector."

Lance jerked a thumb over his shoulder at the rear window. "That is not a collection. That is an arsenal."

Chapter Fifteen

Morgan reminded herself that she was armed, and even if she wasn't, she came from a family of cops. She'd been taught to defend herself at a young age. She didn't believe in taking careless risks, but she certainly didn't need to take this man's abuse.

She summoned her cross-examination face and assessed Mr. Olander.

His face was flushed, and a vein on his temple throbbed. But there was no sign of wildness in his eyes. Instead, they were focused and sharp.

Calculated.

He was a bully, plain and simple.

Morgan no longer saw any sign of the devastated father and husband who had talked his way into her office. Mr. Olander was a skilled manipulator. He'd used her empathy for him against her. She would not allow that to happen again.

"Mr. Olander, I think it's time for you to go." Morgan stood. In her heels, she was nearly six feet tall, and she leveled him with a firm gaze.

But he didn't leave. Instead, he leaned forward, slapping both palms on her desk. He was obviously accustomed to using his bluster to browbeat people. But in her prosecutor years, Morgan had been threatened by hardened killers, and she'd dealt with men much more intimidating than Mr. Olander—which was why she wore a Glock on her hip.

Her previous client attack in the courthouse had been a bizarre and isolated event. The man had had mental issues. He'd been unable to control himself, even knowing surveillance cameras would capture the entire scene. Mr. Olander was smarter.

Their gazes locked for four heartbeats as Olander sized her up. Morgan didn't blink.

One giant hand swept toward her.

Morgan moved backward as Mr. Olander struck out. Her hand went automatically to the weapon on her hip under her blazer. But the blow hadn't been aimed at her. Instead, he swept the contents of her desk toward the wall. Morgan's notepad and blotter skidded across the floor. The ceramic mug hit the whiteboard and shattered. Coffee dripped down the dry-erase board.

The childishness of the act sent a burst of anger through her.

Keeping her gaze on his, she chilled her voice and put on her best interview-an-alleged-killer face. When she had faced accused murderers as a prosecutor, the suspects had been handcuffed to a table and law enforcement officers had been watching her back. As a defense attorney, she had no protection. "This meeting is over."

His gaze fell to her hand, still hovering over the butt of her weapon. He backed off, his weight shifting backward, but his scowl said his temper had not defused.

Mr. Olander studied her for a few heartbeats; then his mouth pressed into a disdainful line. "Fine. Bitch."

With a curt nod, he spun on the heel of his work boot and stomped out of her office. Morgan wiped her palms on the sides of her legs. Relief loosened the muscles of her thighs. Needing air—and wanting to be sure he left the building—she followed him into the hall.

Lance was in the hallway, leaning on the wall just outside her office door. His posture was deceptively relaxed. His eyes practically bored holes into Olander as he passed. Olander quickened his steps and skirted around Lance. As a former cop, Lance was trained in defense and arrest tactics, and every inch of him was poised to attack. Lance was the alpha male, and Olander recognized his own inferior status in an instant.

But when the older man went out the front door, he slammed it hard.

"You're back." Morgan took a deep breath. "I didn't hear you come in."

"Mr. Olander?" Lance asked.

"Yes." She turned to Lance, warmth filling her. "How long were you out here?"

"Long enough." He assessed her, then leaned over and kissed her on the mouth. "We got back about five minutes ago."

"You were listening at the door." Morgan went back into her office, crouched, and began picking up broken pieces of ceramic. Lance brought the trash can closer and fetched napkins from her credenza. They cleaned up the mess together.

They stood, and Lance slung an arm around her shoulders. "Normally, I wouldn't eavesdrop, but I was concerned. He was a belligerent ass."

"I know." Morgan tossed the shards into the trash can. She appreciated that he respected her ability to do her job.

"But the sound of shit literally hitting the wall was too much. I was this close to barging in and throwing him out of the building." Lance demonstrated his patience by pinching his forefinger and thumb nearly together.

"I appreciate your self-control, and the fact that you stood outside the door."

"I had my ear pressed to it," he admitted. "But you handled him just fine."

Sharp peered into the office. He looked bleary-eyed. "Is everything OK?"

"Mr. Olander came to see me," Morgan said.

"Get anything interesting out of him?" Sharp squeezed his eyelids shut a few times, as if to clear his vision.

Morgan summed up her meeting in a few sentences. "The most interesting part of the conversation was that while Erik's mother professed her son's innocence, Mr. Olander never made the claim. Not once."

"I don't know if innocence is all that important to Mr. Olander." Lance filled Morgan in on what they'd found at the farm.

Goose bumps lifted on Morgan's arms. She was so disturbed, she didn't even admonish them for breaking and entering. "If the weapons were illegal, maybe Erik's wife knew about them. Maybe that's why she was killed."

"That would make sense," Lance said. "Sharp left a message for his contact at the ATF."

Morgan picked up her coat and bag. "Now I'm going home, but I won't be long."

"Thank you." Sharp exited her office.

Lance's gaze followed him. "He looks dead on his feet."

"He needs sleep." Morgan's phone buzzed. She read the screen. She needed to schedule Lance's wedding present for delivery. The wedding—and all the last-minute details that needed to be addressed—hadn't entered her mind since Olivia had disappeared.

"Everything all right?"

She turned the phone away from him. "Yes."

His brows lifted.

"Maybe you're not the only one keeping a secret. Are you going to tell me where we're going on our honeymoon?"

"Nope."

Morgan shoved the phone into her pocket. "Then I'll see you soon. Take care of Sharp. Text me if you need anything from home."

Morgan needed energy. On the way home, she detoured to the bakery for fresh donuts. Fifteen minutes later, she was in her foyer, being happily bombarded by three kids and two dogs. Kisses and hugs with all five of them improved her mood. Since it was Saturday, Ava and Mia were still dressed in their pajamas. Ava took the box of donuts and ran. Sophie, clad in her Halloween costume, leaped into Morgan's arms.

Settling her youngest on her hip, Morgan walked into the kitchen. "No donuts until after breakfast."

"Yay. The pancakes are done." Sophie pushed away from her mother, and Morgan set her on the floor.

Grandpa stood at the stove, using a spatula to remove pancakes from the new griddle. Bacon sizzled in another pan. The girls scrambled onto stools at the island, and Grandpa set plates of pancakes in front of them. "Easy on the syrup, girls."

Hoping the kids would be sloppy, Snoozer and Rocket took up strategic positions beneath the kids' stools.

Grandpa met Morgan's gaze, his eyes asking the question he wouldn't voice with the children in the room. Morgan shook her head, and he frowned.

Gianna sat at the island. Her face was pale.

"How do you feel?" Morgan poured a mug of coffee.

"OK. I can cook." She shot Grandpa a look.

"Just sit there and take it easy." Grandpa ate a piece of bacon and passed the platter to Morgan. "I enjoy cooking now and then." Grandpa sat down to his own breakfast.

Having given up nagging him about his diet, Morgan took a slice of bacon. Her phone chimed with an email. It was from the caterer. Morgan had forgotten to call her the day before. She couldn't even think about the wedding today.

"What's wrong?" Gianna asked.

Morgan set down her phone. "Nothing. Just a few calls I was supposed to make about the final wedding details."

"I can make the calls for you." Gianna buttered a slice of toast. "It'll give me something to do, since Art won't let me cook."

"Are you sure?" Morgan asked.

"Positive." Gianna bit into her toast.

"Well, you did plan half of the reception anyway. You have a real flair for party planning."

"I loved every minute of it." Gianna sighed wistfully.

"All right, then," Morgan said. "The caterer needs a final head count. I'll make a list of everything else."

Morgan was relieved to delegate the reception details to Gianna. And Gianna seemed equally as happy to accept the responsibility.

Would they even want to go through with the wedding if they didn't find Olivia in the next two weeks?

Morgan ate, spending a precious thirty minutes with her family—and downing two more cups of coffee—before heading for the shower. The meal and a fresh suit revived her. When she returned to the kitchen, Grandpa was scanning the leftover donuts.

"The kids and Gianna are watching cartoons." He selected a chocolate cruller and dunked it in his coffee.

"Great, because I could really use your help today." Morgan summarized their investigation. "Would you read the trial transcript and case files for an old murder?"

Morgan would concentrate on Erik Olander and let her grandfather pick through Cliff Franklin's case.

"I'd be happy to. Email me everything you have."

Morgan removed her laptop from her tote and opened her email.

What would she do without Grandpa?

Morgan's father had been killed in the line of duty as an NYPD detective. Morgan's older brother had been in college at the time, but her mother had moved her three daughters out of the city. She'd claimed the move was to get away from the violence, but everyone knew she'd been running away from memories. Grandpa had moved to Scarlet Falls with them. Mom had died shortly after, and Grandpa had stepped in to finish raising them.

Years later, when Morgan's husband had died in Iraq, she had quit her job as a DA and moved back in with Grandpa. He'd been her rock.

His hand trembled as he opened his iPad and confirmed receipt of her email. His hair was pure white, and he needed a cane to walk. The thought of him aging twisted her insides into knots.

"Thank you. I don't know what I'd do without you." Morgan stood, rested a hand on his shoulder, and kissed him on the cheek.

"You would be just fine. You're stronger than you know."

Tears filled her eyes.

"Aw, don't cry. I'm not dead yet." He patted her hand. "I have no intention of going anywhere anytime soon. But someday in the distant future—very distant—you *will* have to manage without me. I have no doubt you'll make me proud."

"I know." She swiped a fingertip under her eye. "I'm just wired."

"Let me know if there's anything else I can do," he said. "My body might be giving out, but my brain still works."

Grandpa had decades of experience as a detective. He'd helped with several cases over the past year.

"I will." Morgan packed up her laptop. "I have to go back to the office."

Stepping into her pumps, she gathered her coat and bag. After a quick stop in the family room to kiss the girls goodbye, Morgan went outside and hopped into the Jeep.

She checked her messages. Neither Olivia's agent nor her editor had responded yet. Frustrated, Morgan headed for the office. How would they find Olivia if no one would talk to them?

Sharp had dealt with a lot of tragedy and trauma in his life. It had taken him decades to let a woman into his life. If the worst happened, Morgan sensed he would not recover from losing Olivia.

Chapter Sixteen

Screech.

Startled, Olivia woke to a sprinting pulse. She had a moment of déjà vu, wondering if she'd been awoken by a noise or if it had been her imagination. She had no idea how long she had been underground or why he had taken her. Had he sent her parents a ransom demand? They didn't have much money.

When she heard nothing for several breaths, she slowly stood. Her legs were wobbly. Pain blasted through her foot, but she limped across the room and back. She needed to move.

She stood on one foot and leaned on the wall, breathing hard. The effort of walking had stolen her wind. She tried to draw in a deep breath and failed. The effort triggered a wheeze.

No. Not just the effort.

Her asthma had been triggered by the cold air. The temperature had fallen last night, and the cellar was damp.

This was not good. Not good at all. She had no medicine. She needed to find a way out.

She caught her breath, leaned on the wall, and drank some water. Tremors burst through her and she coughed, choking on the water. Liquid dribbled down her chin. She wiped it on the sleeve of her sweatshirt. The cold drink set off another bout of shivers. She'd already consumed two full bottles of water and one protein bar. Not knowing how long she'd have to survive on her meager supplies, she was rationing.

How long had she been in the ground?

She'd examined every inch of the cellar. There was no way out other than the double doors. The cellar had been designed to store food over the winter. Carrots and potatoes didn't need an emergency exit.

Above her, something squeaked.

Her skin prickled with alarm, and she listened intently. The high-pitched squeal of rusty hinges sliced through the quiet. She flinched at the harsh *fingernails on blackboard* tone. Fear catapulted her heart into her throat. Footsteps on gravel approached. Her heart rate spiked. Her lungs tightened, making her breathing rapid and shallow. Her grip on the water bottle tightened.

A little voice—one that sounded a lot like Lincoln's—said, *Don't show him your fear.*

She focused on deep breathing and let her imagination conjure up a picture of his steady gray eyes. But it wasn't enough. Fear still dried her throat and drove her to the back of the cellar. Her hand touched her swollen cheek, remembering her captor's blow.

The crunch of shoes on dry dirt came closer. On the other side of the doors, it sounded as if something heavy was being moved. With another squeak, the doors opened, revealing a dark silhouette against a pale-gray sky.

Twilight. But was it morning or evening?

He shone a light into the cellar. The brightness blinded her, and she put a hand up to shield her eyes. Heavy steps fell on the wooden stairs. The light moved off her face, and she lowered her hand to watch him descend. He carried a white bag down the steps.

She flinched as the scant light in the stairwell fell upon the oddly proportioned features, creating shadows that made his face even more terrifying. The Michael Myers mask sent an unreasonable spark of horror through her. She should be glad he wasn't showing her his identity. As long as she couldn't identify him, she had a chance. Hopefully, he wanted her for some reason that didn't require her to die.

But her response to the mask was instinctual. The character represented murder and pain and terror.

He lifted a hand, the palm facing her in a stop gesture. Behind him, she saw that he'd left the doors open. Could she rush around him and escape?

She shifted her weight. Pain throbbed through her foot. Even if she got to the steps, she wouldn't be able to outrun him. He'd catch her before she reached the top.

She couldn't see his face, but she noted as many things about him as she could. He was over six feet tall and muscular. He wore khaki pants, boots, and a black jacket. A knife was sheathed on his belt. The mask covered his whole head, so she couldn't see hair color. His eyes were far enough behind the holes in the mask that she couldn't determine their color either.

"Why—" She tried to ask why he'd taken her, but her throat was too dry to speak, and the word came out as an unintelligible croak.

He stood still for a moment, facing her, his posture stiff. A cold pang gripped her empty belly. Her sore cheek throbbed. He knew how to hurt people.

"What do you want from me?" she wheezed, her teeth chattering as she spoke.

He took three steps forward and slapped her. The blow stunned her, both the speed of his hand and the sting of her already-bruised face.

"Shut up." He spoke in a throaty whisper, odd and raspy, as if he was purposefully disguising his voice. He lifted the white bag. "Come here."

She limped forward, feeling like a hungry dog that was regularly beaten but still relied on an abusive human for food. Like a feral animal, she drew closer to the smell of hot food in spite of the risk.

"Stand up straight," he commanded.

She shifted her weight and winced.

He held the bag over her head, just out of reach. "Ask nicely."

Olivia sensed that refusing would be the wrong move. "May I please have the bag?"

He lowered the bag into her hand. Tucking her water bottle under her arm, she opened the bag. It was a sandwich, wrapped in foil. When she removed it from the bag, it was warm in her hands. She unwrapped the foil. Hot ham and melted cheese on a long roll. Despite her nerves, the smell made her stomach rumble.

She took a tentative bite. Her shortness of breath made eating difficult, but she took a second bite. She had one protein bar left. Who knew when she would get food again?

After three bites, a coughing spell interrupted her meal. She sipped some water, needing to catch her breath before she continued eating.

"What's wrong with you?" he asked in a disgusted tone.

"Asthma." She lowered the sandwich. She could feel her airways narrowing. Without access to her medicine or a way out of this cold, damp basement, she would grow worse. "The air is too cold in here. I need my—" A cough cut off the word *medicine*.

He propped his hands on his hips, his posture tensing. "You have a blanket."

The thin cotton throw was insufficient for the temperature in the cellar, but that wasn't the real problem.

Still short of breath, she shook her head. "It's the cold air in my lungs."

"Don't try to bullshit me. I'm not stupid." He stepped closer, leaning forward. His body vibrated with rage.

Olivia's next breath whistled. Her pulse scrambled, and her stomach cramped around the sandwich.

The backhand came faster than she could react. It hit her bruised cheek with an explosion of light and pain. She stumbled backward. Her sandwich and water bottle went flying. Her injured foot gave out, and she fell backward. Pain rang up her tailbone. The impact expelled what little air she had managed to suck into her lungs. She sat still, gaping like a fish, struggling to draw a tiny bit of air into her chest when her rib cage felt like it was made of steel. Her lungs refused to expand.

"I bring you a hot meal, and you repay me by lying." His whisper had turned hostile. "That's not how it works here."

Olivia couldn't respond. She couldn't do anything except try to breathe.

He picked up the sandwich and stuffed it back in the white bag. "Next time, you'll be respectful. Not that I should feed you. Only the strong survive, and you don't seem very strong."

What did that mean? Was there going to be a test of some sort?

Taking the sandwich with him, he stomped back up the steps. On the way out, he slapped the light in the stairwell, extinguishing it. The doors slammed shut with a bang that seemed to rattle the ground, leaving Olivia shivering, gasping for air, and alone in the dark.

She crawled toward the steps, feeling ahead with her shaking hands and using her memory to guide her, desperate for the tiny source of light. Sweat soaked her pajamas, and fear nearly choked her.

Her hand hit the wood of the bottom tread. She crawled upward. How many steps until the light? She turned, sweeping her hands across the wall of the stairwell. Her fingers touched the plastic disc.

Please work.

She pressed it. The light came on, and tears of relief flowed down her cheeks. She barely felt the fresh pain throbbing through her cheek.

What was he going to do to her?

She didn't want to find out. But how could she get past him? He was armed, and she had nothing but the clothes on her back.

Chapter Seventeen

Lance's pulse pumped as he sprinted down Second Street and turned left. His running shoes hit the blacktop in an even rhythm. He checked his watch. Sharp had promised to close his eyes for thirty minutes. Lance had been staring at his computer screen for hours and had wanted some air.

Checking his watch, he made a U-turn and jogged back. Morgan was climbing out of his Jeep. She rose onto her toes and kissed him.

He held his body away from hers. "I'm sweaty."

"I don't care." She kissed him again. "Where's Sharp?"

"I talked him into a power nap."

"Good. He was looking ragged." Morgan raised an eyebrow at his sweat-soaked T-shirt. "You went in a whole different direction."

"I slept a little last night, and I needed to clear my head."

She shook her head. "I had a huge breakfast, lots of coffee, and donuts."

"We all do what works for us." He opened the door, and they went into the building.

Morgan put a finger to her lips and pointed. The door to Sharp's office was open. He was still asleep. Lance figured he'd be awake in another ten minutes.

He followed Morgan into her office. "How were the kids?"

"Fine. You were right. I feel recharged." She set her tote on her desk. "Grandpa is reviewing the Franklin files. I'm still plugging away at the Olander material, and I'm meeting with Esposito at noon."

It didn't surprise Lance the ADA would be in his office on a Saturday. For the prosecutor, weekends were often used to prepare and review for trials.

"Good luck with that." Lance held on to his opinion that the ADA was an asshole.

Morgan was a softie. A few months back, Esposito had showed a few signs that he could be a decent human being, and she was ready to believe in him. But then, believing in people is what made her a great defense attorney. Lance knew she'd been a successful prosecutor but suspected she was even better on the defense side of the courtroom.

Lance collected clothes from his office and took a two-minute shower, not bothering to shave. Dressed in clean cargos and a long-sleeve T-shirt, he went back into his office. His phone beeped, and he read a text message from his mother. She wanted to video chat.

He dropped into the chair behind his desk, opened the app on his laptop, and called her. She accepted the call, and her face appeared on the phone screen. "Hi, Mom."

"Hello, dear." She was in her office, as usual. Lance's mother still lived in the same house in which he'd grown up. Her mental illness had likely always been present, but after his father had vanished when Lance was ten, Jenny Kruger had withdrawn from the world.

On the screen, she smiled sadly. "I'm so sorry to hear about Olivia."

"Thanks, Mom." Lance angled the screen to see her better.

Stress and time had not been kind to his mom. She looked older than sixty-one. But since she'd started virtually dating a man from her group therapy session, her eyes—and outlook—seemed brighter. Today, her gray hair was combed, clean, and almost shiny, and she was wearing lipstick. She must have been video chatting with her manfriend, Kevin. Before

Kevin, Lance had never seen his mother wear makeup. Kevin worked in computers and had many of the same anxiety issues as Jenny. Their relationship made her happy, and that was all that mattered to Lance.

"I haven't finished with the background reports yet," she said. His mom taught online computer classes and designed, maintained, and secured websites. She also helped with the online legwork in some of their more complex cases. "But I wanted to give you an update." She opened a file. "I've been working on Olivia's investigative pieces. I found several articles exposing people of criminal wrongdoings. In the past ten years, Olivia's stories directly resulted in three people going to prison. According to the New York State Department of Corrections online inmate lookup, two are still in prison. The third was released six years ago."

"Who is he?"

"A contractor convicted of grand larceny. He defrauded homeowners, mostly senior citizens, out of more than ninety thousand dollars. He served eighteen months in prison. He promised he would get even with Olivia."

"Sounds like a possible suspect."

"Except that he was released six years ago and moved to Oregon. He posted photos of himself in Oregon yesterday."

"Then he's probably a dead end."

"I'll email you the details. Expect the rest of the reports later today," his mom said. "Also, I have not found a black or dark-blue 1971 Chevy Nova in Scarlet Falls or the surrounding towns. I'm expanding the search. Is it possible he had the year or color wrong?"

"He seemed sure." But it had been dark, and Bob's eyes were not young. "Maybe expand your search to other dark colors."

"OK. I checked out both Olivia's agent and editor and found no criminal records for either of them in the tristate area."

Private investigators did not have access to the same national criminal databases that law enforcement used. They had to piece together background checks from county and state records.

"What about Cliff Franklin?" Lance asked.

"You know he was an auto mechanic before he went to prison," his mom said. "But in addition to working at a local auto shop, he also had his own business, specializing in antique car restoration."

"Could that be related to the sighting of the '71 Nova?" Lance thought aloud.

"I can't find a link. Neither Cliff nor his brother, Joe, has a Nova registered to him."

"The vehicle could be unregistered."

"True," his mom agreed.

"No wives or exes?" Lance asked.

"None," Jenny answered. "He operated his side business at his brother's place."

"Joe Franklin?"

"Yes. Joe is a game developer. He owns a company called JF, Inc. No criminal record. No civil suits. No marriages or divorces. No current social media activity. Almost every hit in my search results is from before his brother was accused of murder. Joe seems to have gone off the radar after his brother's arrest. He did not give a single interview after the trial."

"The media attention must have been brutal."

"Yes. The press hounded him," Jenny agreed. "Joe Franklin owns a chunk of wilderness about twenty miles from here. He and his brother inherited the land from their parents, who died in a car accident when the brothers were in their late teens. Cliff is the oldest, and for two years following their parents' deaths, Cliff was Joe's guardian. They shared the same address until Cliff was arrested."

"We need more info on Joe Franklin." Lance rubbed the back of his neck. Too many hours hunched over his laptop had knotted his muscles. "Did you find anything on the Olanders?"

"Now that's where things get interesting." His mom clicked her tongue. "Kennett bought the farm in Randolph County and moved here twenty-five years ago. This is the weird part. No mortgage."

"A cash buy?" Lance was surprised.

"Yes," his mom answered. "They bought everything: several hundred acres of land with a house, barns, cows, equipment, customer lists, the works. It was just under a million dollars."

"Where did the money come from?" Lance asked. "Family?"

"I didn't find anything in his family's history that suggests they had that kind of money, but it's possible."

But Lance suspected the source of the money was related to the arsenal he'd found in the Olanders' basement.

Chapter Eighteen

The peal of Sharp's phone alarm jolted him back to consciousness. It took all of three seconds before he remembered Olivia's disappearance. He scanned his empty office, then checked his phone for messages and emails.

Nothing.

Disappointment crushed him as if a car were parked on his chest. Sitting up on the couch in his office, he rubbed his stubbled jaw. He hadn't wanted to close his eyes, but Lance had insisted. Lance had been right. Even through the fog of waking, Sharp could feel his neurons beginning to fire.

He was still groggy as hell, but the small amount of sleep would enable him to function.

Rising, he went across the hall and ducked into Lance's office. "Anything?"

"I called the cable company, utilities, and township," Lance said. "None of them sent a white van to Olivia's street in the past couple of weeks. Stella is on the way. She says she has news. Why don't you get a cup of tea? You look like hell."

But Sharp's brain felt like mush. "I don't think tea is going to cut it."

He went into Morgan's office and called out, "How do you work this coffee machine?"

Lance appeared in the doorway, looking shocked. "When was the last time you drank coffee?"

"I don't know." Sharp took a clean mug from Morgan's shelf. "Sometime in the nineties, I think. But I'm desperate. I can hardly think straight, and I really need to be on my game."

"Lift the handle, insert a pod, and press the flashing blue button."

"These plastic pods are terrible for the environment." But Sharp followed his instructions. In less than a minute, he had a cup of coffee. He took a tentative sip. It didn't taste as good as he remembered, but he'd drink it anyway.

"What you really need is more sleep," Lance said.

"That's not going to happen. Not until we find her." Sharp turned, panic scrambling for a toehold in his chest. "What if we don't?"

With every minute that passed, the chances of Olivia returning alive and well decreased.

"You can't think that way. Not yet. It's only been a day and a half." Despite his words, Lance's mouth was set in a grim line. "Let's see what Stella has to say."

"You're right." Sharp carried the coffee back to his office. The caffeine wasn't helping. He opened his laptop and tried to remember what he'd been reading when he'd almost fallen asleep on the keyboard. His office door was open, giving him a view of the foyer.

Morgan walked in. "Stella's here."

Following her sister, Stella entered Sharp's office and unbuttoned her jacket. Physically, the sisters looked similar. Both were tall, with long black hair and blue eyes. But Stella dressed like a cop. Plain black pants, flat black boots, and a black jacket over her gun and handcuffs. She'd contained her hair in a utilitarian bun. Morgan dressed like the successful trial attorney she was. She wore a feminine, fitted gray suit;

white blouse; and heels. She'd left her hair down, and it waved just past her shoulders.

"Jenny Kruger called this morning," Morgan said. "She hasn't found a '71 Nova, but Joe Franklin lives on a secluded property where Cliff used to restore antique cars."

"We need to pay Joe a visit." Stella tossed her jacket on a chair. "Let me give you a quick update on my end. As I told Morgan, the fingerprints taken from Olivia's house didn't have any matches in AFIS." The Automated Fingerprint Identification System was a national database of fingerprints maintained by the FBI. "Also, the heating and air company that was on Olivia's calendar for Wednesday checks out. They do background checks on all of their employees. None have criminal records, and the technician who serviced Olivia's heater has an alibi. He was at a bachelor party at a strip club until three a.m."

"Then it's unlikely he's involved." Sharp leaned back in his chair.

"Right. The chief has called a press conference." Stella checked her watch. "He'll put out a tip line and ask for the community's help."

"He didn't want *you* to talk to the press?" Sharp knew the current asshat of a police chief liked to trot out Scarlet Falls' only female detective for the press. The chief was all about politics.

Stella sighed. "I told him I had to run down a lead. Thankfully, the chief likes to be in front of the camera."

Sharp rubbed the top of his scalp. "It'll generate a hundred calls about everyone's suspicious neighbor and at least one false confession."

"There's nothing we can do about it now," Stella said. "It's going to happen. The story was all over the news last night."

"And the chief wants a piece of the press coverage." Sharp's phone went off, and he glanced at the screen. "It's Olivia's sister. I should have called her already." How could he feel any shittier? He answered the call. "Valerie. I'm sorry. I should have called you with an update."

"That's not why I'm calling." She sounded upset. "We trust you to update us when you know something."

"Then what's wrong?" he asked.

"There is a crowd of reporters outside," Valerie said. "The street is full of them. They're broadcasting from the sidewalk in front of the house."

"Can you see any particular news stations?"

"Yes. JBT News."

Sharp covered the phone mic and turned to Morgan. "See if there's some live coverage on the website for JBT News."

Morgan turned her laptop around and typed on the keyboard. "There is. I can see vans from other stations as well. They're all in front of the Cruz house."

Sharp lowered his hand and spoke into the phone. "Do you want us to come down there and talk to the press?"

Valerie paused, as if thinking it over. "Not unless you think it will help find Olivia."

"The police chief is holding a press conference later," Sharp said. "He's going to give the public a tip line to call. I don't see how stressing your mom and dad out with a horde of reporters is going to accomplish anything."

"Then we'll sit tight and ignore them," Valerie said.

"If you change your mind, Morgan can set up your own press conference. For now, we have a few leads to follow up on this morning." Sharp didn't want to get their hopes up with specifics. Nor did he want to give them information in case a reporter got to them. "I'll call you if I have any news."

He ended the call and turned to Morgan. "Are the reporters giving any real information?"

"Not really." Morgan shook her head. "Feels more like entertainment than news, but they are showing her picture and encouraging anyone with information to call the SFPD."

Stella sat in a chair facing his desk. "I want to interview the former manager of Olander Dairy. His name is Ronald Alexander. He was fired a few months ago when the farm went belly-up."

Sharp shifted forward, his fingers curled around the arms of his chair. "Why do we want to talk to Ronald?"

"Because I have questions about the Olander dairy farm, and I want to ask someone besides Kennett Olander." Stella pulled her chair forward and rested her forearms on his desk. "Kennett and Lena Olander married in Iowa in 1982. Lena was sixteen. Kennett was twenty-three. Erik was born in Iowa. Kennett Olander has no criminal record in the state of New York or in the National Crime Information Center, which is normal. But get this. He also has no employment record with Social Security prior to 1994. He didn't file a tax return before moving to Scarlet Falls."

The National Crime Information Center, or NCIC, was an FBI database that tracked crime at the national level.

"What about Lena?" Morgan asked.

Stella shook her head. "There are barely any records for Lena at all, even here and now. She isn't listed on the deed of the farm. Kennett's name is the only one on the property tax records or recent mortgage. Lena Olander had a driver's license, but no vehicles are registered in her name. She had no credit cards. The couple had one joint bank account. The rest of the accounts are in his name only. The gun she used to commit suicide is registered to Kennett. His license on the weapon was for on-premises only. He didn't apply for concealed carry."

"So Lena, who married very young, had no assets, no credit, and no income separate from her husband." Morgan leaned on the corner of the desk. "When she came here to speak with me, she acted anxious."

Abusive men often maintained control of their wives by making sure they did not have access to money. Financial dependence could be a heavy chain.

"Hopefully, Ronald is a disgruntled former employee and will tell us all about his former boss." Stella rose.

Sharp stood. "Do you have a current address for this Ronald Alexander?"

"I do." Stella nodded.

Sharp grabbed his keys. "Let's go talk to him. Maybe he can tell us what official reports won't. We can drive out to Joe Franklin's place too."

"OK." Stella held up a hand in a stop gesture. "I'll let you come with me on one condition."

"I'm not sure I can make promises. I'm going to do whatever it takes to find Olivia." Sharp was prepared to work around, over, or through any obstacles. "If you don't want me along on the interview, I can always catch up with Alexander when you're done with him."

He was being a dick, but he couldn't help it.

Stella gave him a look. "Or you could play nice. I have enormous respect for you as a detective. You helped train me when I was a rookie. With Brody on vacation, I could use a second set of ears and eyes. Your experience is invaluable."

"What do you want me to do?" Sharp grumbled.

"Not break any more laws," Stella said. "At least not when you're with me."

"All right." If necessary, Sharp could ditch her and circumvent the law afterward. "Let's go."

"Morgan and I are headed for the DA's office," Lance said. "Let us know what happens in the interview."

Sharp grabbed his jacket and led the way into the hall.

Stella zipped her jacket and followed him. "Unlike the Olanders, Ronald has a colorful history. He worked for Olander Dairy for ten years. But before that, he served a year in jail for criminal possession of a firearm and did a six-month stint for assault. He beat up a neighbor who let his dog poop on his lawn."

They walked to her unmarked police car. Sharp went around to the passenger side.

Stella drove away from the office. "In an interesting twist, his assault victim refused to sign a complaint. Alexander was convicted on the eyewitness testimony of another neighbor."

"The victim was afraid of him." Sharp had seen it before.

Unlike on TV, no citizen can press charges against another. Only the DA can charge someone with a crime. It wasn't unusual for a victim to refuse to sign a complaint or to withdraw their complaint for fear of retribution. The DA does not need the cooperation of the victim. Although getting a conviction can be more difficult without a victim's support, the DA can charge a suspect as long as there is sufficient evidence.

"Does he have a wife?" Sharp stared out the passenger window as the houses rolled by. They passed Olivia's street, and the air left his lungs, the hollowness aching.

Is she still alive?

"Yes. He's been married to the same woman for twenty years." Stella looked both ways at a stop sign, then turned onto the main road that bisected the small business district. "Once he started working for Olander Dairy, he stopped getting into trouble."

But Alexander was definitely capable of violence.

Chapter Nineteen

In the conference room of the DA's office, Morgan opened her file. "Thank you for agreeing to meet with us. We won't keep you long. You're already working overtime. Big case?"

"No." Across the table, ADA Anthony Esposito tugged at his french cuffs, then leaned on his forearms. Dark and precisely groomed, Esposito was slick from his whitened teeth to his black Ferragamo shoes. Even on a weekend, he was dressed in a custom-tailored gray suit. "I work every Saturday. It's the only time the office is quiet."

Morgan had almost worked for the Randolph County Prosecutor's Office the previous year. After she'd agreed to defend her neighbor's son, who'd been accused of a horrible murder, her offer of employment had been withdrawn. Eventually, Anthony Esposito had been hired to fill the vacancy.

She did not regret her decision one bit. Morgan was able to keep her caseload to a more manageable size. She only worked weekends when she accepted a high-profile case, which wasn't often. Most weekdays she was home by five thirty, and she did her best to reserve Saturdays and Sundays for family time.

When she accepted a high-stakes case, like Olivia's disappearance, she could work overtime without guilt.

As if that were possible for any working mom.

But at least she could keep her guilt to a minimum by working reasonable hours most of the time.

"I assume you've heard that Olivia Cruz is missing." Morgan clicked her pen open and held it poised over her notepad.

"Yes," Esposito said. "I'm sorry to hear about Ms. Cruz, but I'm not sure how I can help."

"We're not sure either," Lance commented from the seat next to Morgan. "But one angle we've been working is her current book research. Olivia was digging into the Erik Olander case."

"Why would that case interest her?" Esposito leaned back and crossed his arms. He kept his eyes on Morgan and ignored Lance. "It was a relatively easy case to prosecute. Erik tried to stage the scene to look like an intruder had killed his wife. But forensic evidence was able to cut through that little piece of bullshit like a chain saw through butter."

"How?" Morgan was still waiting for the full transcript of Erik's trial.

Esposito shifted forward and rested his elbows on the table. "His wife was beaten and strangled. Despite all his efforts to make it appear as if someone had broken into the house, the latent fingerprint examiner was able to lift two of Erik's thumbprints from his wife's throat."

"Nice break," Lance said. "It isn't easy to lift prints from human skin."

"The tech used black magnetic powder and lifted them with white silicone, and we got lucky. They were beautiful." Esposito's eyes gleamed. "And, if that wasn't enough, the lab was able to extract touch DNA from the prints."

Touch DNA was exactly what it sounded like, the skin cells left behind when a person touched an object.

"With Erik's thumbprint taken from his wife's neck, the DNA presence was overkill, but juries love forensics." Esposito understood his job wasn't to *prove* the defendant guilty. It was to *convince* a jury the defendant was guilty.

"Did he explain his DNA on his wife's neck?" Morgan would have argued a husband's DNA would naturally be on his wife's body.

"He said he touched her neck after she was dead to see if she had a pulse, but the positioning of the prints was perfect for strangulation, not medical assistance." Esposito opened his fingers and mimicked wrapping them around a person's neck. He wiggled his thumbs. "The thumbs were on each side of her neck, as if he had been straddling her."

"Hard to check someone's pulse that way," Lance said.

"There was bruising as well, so it wasn't the gentle, loving touch he claimed." Esposito flicked a brief, irritated glance at Lance. "Also, Natalie's friends testified she was terrified of her husband and that he tried to keep her isolated. They'd seen bruises on her body in the past. We also got a big break with Natalie's use of the library internet to research domestic violence shelters."

"You never had any doubts Erik killed his wife?" Morgan asked.

Esposito shook his head. "Never."

Lance leaned forward. "Did you have any suspicions that someone helped Erik?"

"Are you thinking the father?" Esposito asked.

Lance nodded. "That's exactly what we were thinking."

"It's possible." Esposito shrugged. "But there was no evidence of it. The old man doesn't even have a speeding ticket on his record, let alone anything criminal. He was so clean, he squeaked. But there was one thing that bugged me during the trial preparation."

"What was that?" Morgan asked.

"Erik's mother." Esposito's brow furrowed. "Mrs. Olander claimed Erik was innocent. She repeated a few lines about an intruder killing her daughter-in-law. Every time I asked her, she said the exact same words, verbatim."

"Her statement was rehearsed." Morgan took notes.

"Yes." Esposito's chair squeaked as he suddenly leaned back. "And every time she spoke, she'd glance at her husband. I swear she didn't breathe until he approved."

"Did you try questioning her alone?" Morgan would have separated the couple immediately.

"Of course we did." Esposito all but rolled his eyes. "As did the original officer who responded to the farm about the intruder call. All of her statements were identical. She was even more nervous alone, and she repeated the exact same sentences. No matter how the questions were phrased. If we deviated from questions about the night or crime, she stopped talking. I think she would have exploded if I asked her what her favorite color was."

Morgan set down her pen. "You think she was afraid of her husband."

Who Lance and Sharp suspected was trafficking illegal guns.

"I do." Esposito frowned. "Erik's mother shot herself in her car right after she met with you."

Remembering, Morgan swallowed. "Yes."

Lance tapped a knuckle on the table. "Erik killed Natalie, and Mrs. Olander was afraid of her husband. Possibly both wives were victims of domestic abuse. But neither of those things feels like a reason to kidnap Olivia."

Lance was right. They needed to focus on Olivia, not Mrs. Olander.

Morgan checked her notes. "What about the issue with the jury foreman?"

Esposito scoffed. "Olander's attorney filed a notice of appeal, but we all know it won't go anywhere. The jury didn't deliberate long. Their decision was unanimous. No holdouts. No hint of a hung jury. Nothing."

Maybe the Olander case, as strange as the family was, had nothing to do with Olivia's disappearance.

"You said Ms. Cruz was working on two cases," Esposito prompted. "What was the second?"

Lance volunteered, "Cliff Franklin."

The smallest glimmer of surprise showed in the ADA's eyes.

"That wasn't my case." Esposito stood, smoothing his already-perfect hair. "You'll have to ask Bryce about it. I have to get back to work." He reached for Morgan's hand and shook it for a few seconds too long. "Ms. Dane. Always a pleasure." He shot an arrogant glance at Lance. "Kruger." The tone was dismissive and smug. Esposito took two strides to the doorway.

Morgan had to control rolling her eyes. Esposito liked to tweak Lance whenever possible. The ADA was a skilled trial attorney. Unfortunately, arrogance often accompanied that ability, and Esposito was full of it.

"Is Bryce in today?" Morgan called after him.

"No." He paused to shake his head but offered no additional information before he left the room.

"What now?" Lance got to his feet and stretched. He pulled out his phone and glanced at it. "No word from Sharp."

She followed Lance from the room and out of the DA's offices. Once the elevator doors closed, she asked, "Why did you insist we invite Esposito to the wedding again? He works hard to aggravate you."

"Because I want him to see us get married." Lance grinned.

Morgan shook her head. "You two are ridiculous."

Lance shrugged. "He started it."

They left the building and crossed the parking lot to Lance's Jeep. Morgan's phone vibrated in her pocket as they climbed into the vehicle. She pulled it out and opened a text. "Grandpa says he found something."

She fastened her seat belt, then called her grandfather's cell phone. He answered on the first ring.

She raised the phone in front of her face. "You're on speaker, Grandpa."

"Let me go into my room." He huffed and puffed.

Morgan worried about his heart and blood pressure and the butter and bacon he loved. She could hear the television and the kids in the background and guessed he was hauling himself out of his recliner. A door closed.

"OK, I'm here." His voice was breathless. "So I started with Olivia's notes on the Franklin murder trial. She made following her research easy, cross-referencing her comments with the trial transcript." Grandpa cleared his throat. "Olivia flagged two evidentiary errors. First of all, there was a minor error in the original search warrant. The house number in the address was incorrect by one digit. Cliff Franklin's attorney called this out during the trial and motioned to have all evidence obtained via that search suppressed. However, the judge overruled his objection. There were enough additional details describing the house to establish it was the correct location."

Contrary to public belief, minor errors on search warrants do not automatically disallow all evidence found during that search. As a failsafe, the police add descriptive elements to search warrants. Sometimes they include directions on how to arrive at the house; a description of the residence, including details such as house color and trim; and the official tax lot description on file for the location. If a reasonable person would still know which house to search, even with the street address error, then the warrant can generally be upheld.

"The second error Olivia found was not called out during the trial, and it's a big deal." Grandpa paused for a breath. "One of the key pieces of evidence was the victim's hairs that were found in Cliff Franklin's trunk. But more hairs were submitted to the lab than were logged in by the exhibits officer. So it appears that not all the hairs went through the proper chain of custody."

There should have been no doubt as to where every single piece of evidence was located at any time during collection, testing, or storage. Failure to maintain the chain of custody allows the defense to suggest that evidence could have been contaminated, tampered with, or even planted.

"Let me guess." Morgan rubbed the bridge of her nose. "The hairs that matched the victim were the ones missing from the evidence log."

"Bingo," Grandpa said. "There was other evidence, but the majority of it was circumstantial. One of Brandi's friends stated that Brandi thought Cliff was creepy. He'd been seen near her apartment building, and she'd texted that friend that she thought he was following her to the grocery store."

"What about additional physical evidence?" Morgan asked.

"Her body had been washed, and the dish soap residue matched the brand found under the kitchen sink in the Franklin house. But it's a common brand."

"Tell me more about her death," Morgan said.

"Her car was found on the side of Gravelly Road," Grandpa said. "Brandi was on her way to the community college, where she was taking night classes. Her engine had seized. Someone had put sugar in the gas tank. Cliff Franklin was an auto mechanic, so he'd know how to do that, but there's no evidence he was the person who did. The security cameras in her apartment complex's parking lot were not working. A silver Honda Accord was caught on the surveillance camera feed of the convenience store across the street from the apartment complex. It pulled out behind Brandi as she left for class. Cliff Franklin drives a silver Honda Accord. However, the license plate was covered in mud and the vehicle had no distinguishing features. The video from the night camera was grainy."

"He followed her." Morgan could picture it.

"Unfortunately, there are three hundred thousand Honda Accords registered in the state of New York, and silver is one of the most popular colors." Grandpa sighed. "So again, good supporting evidence, but not enough to get him convicted."

"What about the rest of his house?" Morgan asked. "Where do they think he killed her and washed her body?"

"They don't know. Cliff lived with his brother, Joe, on a small farm. The house and outbuildings were clean. No evidence was found that Brandi was killed there. However, Joe slaughters his own animals. He stocks coveralls, gloves, and tarps and rinses his floors with oxygen bleach. The drains were full of blood and animal matter and oxygen bleach. The sheer amount of biological evidence would have been overwhelming."

Morgan took out her notepad and wrote notes. "How was she killed?"

"She was strangled with her own belt," Grandpa said. "A neat, bloodless kill."

"Was she raped?" Morgan lifted her pen.

"The weather had been unusually warm that autumn. The body was too badly decomposed for the ME to tell." Papers rustled over the connection; then Grandpa said, "The state sent cadaver dogs to Joe's property and to the area where Brandi was found. The dogs didn't find any additional bodies."

"Without bodies, there's no physical evidence to connect Cliff with the other five missing women." Lance frowned at the phone.

"That's correct," Grandpa said. "Appeals have to be legal not factual, correct? Can Franklin file an appeal based on the incomplete chain of custody?"

"That's a little murky, but the answer is maybe." Morgan clicked her pen. "It's true that appeals are normally made for legal errors, not evidentiary ones. Counsel objects to the inclusion of a piece of evidence, and the judge then rules if said evidence is admissible. The objection puts the legal issue on record. The judge's ruling becomes the legal grounds for appeal. If the defense counsel fails to object, then the error is implicitly waived."

"Franklin's attorney didn't object. So technically, there's no basis for appeal," Grandpa clarified.

"Correct, but appeals can be granted for ineffective assistance of counsel. Franklin's attorney missed a chain of custody error on the biggest piece of evidence in the prosecutor's case. If I were going to file an appeal for him, that is the route I would take."

"Well, shit." Lance smacked the steering wheel. "I can't believe the sheriff's department screwed up that badly collecting the evidence from Cliff's trunk."

"Similar errors occurred in the OJ trial." Morgan's thoughts whirled. "If the appeal were granted, the DA would have an opportunity to bring a new trial. Is there enough evidence?"

Grandpa huffed. "I don't know. The exhibits aren't included with the trial transcript. I'd need to see the murder book."

The trial transcript only included the words spoken at the trial. Copies of evidence had to be obtained separately.

But Morgan had to wonder if Cliff Franklin was innocent.

And who might not want the truth revealed.

Chapter Twenty

Lance hated to think an innocent man was sitting in prison for a murder he didn't commit. But it was equally hard to believe that Franklin had been set up.

Morgan pulled her notebook out of her tote.

"The sheriff investigated this murder, correct?" Lance tapped his finger on the steering wheel.

"Yes." Morgan made more notes in her file.

Lance said, "We already know he was corrupt."

"Yes, he fudged evidence in one investigation. There's no reason to believe he wouldn't have done it in others." Morgan lifted her pen. "But why would he have wanted to convict the wrong man and presumably let the real killer escape justice? It doesn't make sense."

"Too bad the sheriff is dead and we can't ask him."

Morgan lifted the phone to talk into the speaker. "Grandpa, did you find an interview with Bryce Walters in Olivia's documents?"

"No," Grandpa answered. "But I found several notes about her leaving messages for him."

Had the DA been avoiding Olivia?

Someone called for Grandpa in the background.

"I have to go," he said. "The kids are looking for me. That's all I have for now anyway. I'll let you know if I find anything else. There's still plenty of material to read."

"Thanks. You're the best." Morgan lowered the phone.

"I know." Grandpa ended the call.

Lance started the Jeep's engine. "Where do you want to go now?"

Morgan bounced her pen on her fingers. "Let's drop in on Cliff Franklin's attorney, Mark Hansen. The firm is located in Redhaven." She read the address into her phone and asked it for directions. Then she called her sister and gave her the information on the evidentiary error in Cliff Franklin's case.

Redhaven was a neighboring town to Scarlet Falls. The law offices of Hansen, Adams, and Green occupied a small suite in an office complex. Lance parked directly in front of the glass door. Morgan got out and tried the door. It was locked. She cupped her hand over her eyes and tried to see inside.

Morgan returned to the car. "It doesn't look like anyone is in today, but I don't want to leave a message. Any ideas?"

"Let's stop by his house." Lance backed out of the space.

Morgan called Jenny and asked her to get the attorney's home address. Jenny called back in a few minutes with the information, and Morgan plugged the address into her phone's GPS. Mark Hansen lived close to his office. In less than ten minutes, Lance turned onto a country road.

He slowed in front of a black mailbox. "It looks like Hansen does all right as an attorney."

Lance steered the Jeep onto the long driveway. Mark Hansen lived in a converted barn that sat well off the road. The front lawn was the size of a soccer field and just as well kept. Large windows had been inserted across the front of the boxy stone structure. Ornamental cabbages lined the flower beds, and a collection of straw bales and pumpkins was artfully arranged on either side of the front door. He parked at the end of the driveway, and they got out of the Jeep.

"I don't see any cars," Morgan said as she walked around the front of the vehicle.

Lance joined her. He pointed to a four-car detached garage behind the main house. "I wouldn't expect to."

They went up the front walk. A gust of wind hit Morgan in the back and blew her hair into her face. She held it back with one hand. Lance reached for the doorbell. Inside the house, chimes echoed. A few seconds later, the sound of footsteps approached.

A petite redhead of about thirty opened the door. "Can I help you?" She wore black slacks and a black blazer over a white blouse.

"We're looking for Mr. Hansen." Morgan handed her a business card. "Are you his wife?"

"No. I'm the housekeeper. You should leave a message at Mr. Hansen's office." The redhead moved as if to close the door.

Lance placed one boot in the opening. "This is an emergency."

Morgan put a hand on Lance's arm. "We apologize for disturbing Mr. Hansen at home. But as my associate just said, this *is* an emergency. A woman is missing, and she might be tied to one of Mr. Hansen's old cases."

"You'll have to wait here." The redhead frowned down at Lance's boot, which prevented the door from closing.

Lance withdrew his foot. "Sorry."

The door closed. Another gust of cool wind blew across the open field. Morgan drew the edges of her jacket together as they waited. Several minutes passed before the door opened again, and a man of about forty stepped outside.

He zipped a puffy down vest over a blue crewneck sweater that looked like cashmere. "I'm Mark Hansen. My housekeeper said it was an emergency."

"Thank you for speaking with us," Morgan said before Lance could jump in. "A woman is missing."

"Let's walk." Hansen started walking across the manicured lawn. "I don't allow my profession anywhere near my family."

"I understand. I feel the same way." Morgan took a position between the two men.

Lance fell into step beside her. "This is about the Cliff Franklin case."

Mark hesitated midstride. "That case is several years old. I don't know how it could be related to a current missing persons case."

"The woman who is missing is Olivia Cruz," Morgan said. "Do you remember speaking with her about the Franklin case?"

"Yes. Now that you mention it, I remember speaking with her on the phone." Hansen shoved his hands into the pockets of his down vest. "She wanted some background on the case. I don't recall everything that was said."

In Lance's opinion, *I don't recall* was lawyer code for *I don't want to tell you.*

"You were assigned the Franklin case?" Morgan asked.

"That's correct." Hansen kept his gaze on the horizon. "Judge Miller felt the public defender's office was too overwhelmed to give the case the amount of time and energy it required. He asked me to handle it."

"How did you feel about the assignment?" Morgan asked.

Hansen lifted a shoulder. "You know how it is. The case required a large number of man-hours, but the extra publicity was good for the firm."

"You lost," Lance pointed out. "How is that good publicity?"

Hansen shot him a look. "The prosecutor's case was strong. I advised Mr. Franklin to plea bargain. There was a question on one of the search warrants. Not enough to get the evidence thrown out, but enough to give me a little leverage. I could have gotten Franklin a twenty-five-year sentence. He could have been paroled in seventeen years."

"But he refused." Morgan brushed the hair out of her face.

"Yes. He insisted he was innocent, so we went to trial." He shrugged. "I discredited witnesses and argued that everything discovered in the property search should have been disallowed, but the judge did not agree."

Morgan's mouth pursed, as if she was considering how to phrase her next question. "What about the chain of evidence issues with the hair samples?"

His eyes widened, but he recovered his poker face in a heartbeat. "I don't know what you're talking about."

But did he?

Morgan kept her tone neutral. "The hair samples taken from Franklin's trunk were not properly logged when they were taken into evidence. Chain of custody was not maintained. These were the very samples that matched the victim's DNA."

She let the implication hang.

This was the evidence that convicted Cliff Franklin.

Mark said nothing for a full minute. Lance was impressed with his smooth expression, but behind his flat eyes, he could see Mark's thoughts churning.

Finally, he stopped walking and met her gaze directly. "I would have to review the case before I could comment on your assertion."

Annnnd now he sounded like a lawyer on the defensive.

"This never came up in your conversation with Olivia Cruz?" Lance didn't bother trying to sound neutral. His voice dripped with disbelief.

"I don't recall my entire conversation with Ms. Cruz." Hansen's words were clipped and precise.

"Are you sure?" Morgan asked. "It seems a piece of information *that stunning* would stand out."

"I've already commented on that." Hansen turned back toward the house. "Is there any way I can help you locate Ms. Cruz?"

"You tell us," Lance challenged. Instead of leaving Morgan between him and Hansen, Lance smoothly moved into position on his opposite side, so that they were flanking him. He wanted Hansen to feel pressured. "Where were you at two o'clock in the morning on Friday?"

Hansen pulled out his phone. "I was in Rochester overnight on business. I didn't get home until noon on Friday."

"Can you prove that?" Lance asked.

"Yes, but I don't have to." Hansen quickened his pace and walked them directly to the Jeep. "If you want to talk to me again, please call my office. I wish you luck finding Ms. Cruz." And with that, he left them at their vehicle and went into the house.

They didn't speak as they slid into the Jeep. Halfway down the driveway, Lance glanced in the rearview mirror. "I can't tell if he was lying, but I hate that *I don't recall* bullshit. It was a big case. He wouldn't have forgotten so many details."

"But I can't decide if he blew the case on purpose or through neglect. Either way, this discovery could open a path to appeal through incompetent counsel."

"Then our options are incompetent or corrupt?"

"Seems like it," Morgan agreed. "But the real question is, did he kidnap Olivia to keep her from exposing his failure?"

"Or did the real killer take her to keep his guilt a secret?"

"Ugh." Morgan gathered her hair at her nape and bound it into a quick ponytail. "*Someone* took her."

"Hansen is a creep. We should stake out his house for a while." After leaving the lawyer's driveway, Lance uncurled his fingers from their too-tight grip on his steering wheel. Hansen's evasion had left him with a bad taste in his mouth. The attorney knew more than he was saying, and not even the possibility that Olivia's life could be at stake got him talking.

Morgan glanced up and down the road. "This is a very rural road. There's no way we can sit here and not have him notice us."

She was right. The terrain around the house was wide open.

"He does not want his screwup revealed." Lance was sure of it. "Even if it means his client stays in prison for a crime he didn't commit. I'll bet he resented having to work for less than his usual hourly fee. He didn't put the time in on the case, and he missed the chain of evidence error."

"So why did Olivia sit on this revelation?" A line formed between Morgan's brows.

"Maybe she was saving it for her book."

Morgan frowned. "Do you think she would do that?"

"She *is* a reporter." But Lance didn't like his answer. "But she also *seems* to have a strong sense of ethics. And she did make an appointment to talk to the three of us, maybe about this. The sheriff's department tied Franklin to five additional missing women, but the bodies were never found. Maybe Olivia wanted more information on the other possible victims before she committed herself to this particular story."

"What if Olivia wasn't sure if she wanted to reveal this evidence issue? What if she didn't want a potential serial killer to be set free?"

"We need to talk to Todd Harvey." Lance scrolled through the contacts on his phone. The current Randolph County chief deputy was acting as sheriff. "He was working for the sheriff when this investigation was underway."

"The sheriff liked to keep his evidence to himself," Morgan reminded him.

"There must be a file somewhere." Lance dialed the chief deputy's cell phone number and asked him about the file.

"I honestly don't know," Todd said. "You are welcome to come and look through the old files I boxed up from the sheriff's office."

"Thanks," Lance said. "We're on our way."

They drove to the sheriff's station. The chief deputy met them in the lobby and escorted them behind the counter.

"I put the murder book and other files in the conference room." The chief deputy led the way into a small office. A row of cardboard boxes sat on a round table.

"There's everything I could find relating to the case. Help yourself to coffee if you need it," the deputy said on his way out of the room.

Lance and Morgan took seats and opened the first box, hoping they would find something that might generate a lead. They divided up the remaining boxes and dug in.

Two hours later, Morgan brewed a second cup of coffee. "Brandi Holmes went missing in September 2014. While he was investigating her disappearance, the sheriff discovered Tawny Miller, who disappeared in October 2012."

"He looked further back and discovered four more women who had gone missing in the fall, approximately two years apart." Lance leaned back and drank some water. One more cup of coffee would set his gut on fire. "Cassandra Martin, November 2010; Samantha Knowles, September 2008; Jessie Mendella, October 2006; and Brenda Chase, September 2004."

Morgan carried her Styrofoam cup back to the conference table. "None of those other women have been found."

"No, but each of those women had had their cars serviced at the auto shop where Cliff had worked for fifteen years. He didn't personally work on every one of their cars, but he could have seen them in the shop. And he would have been able to access their names and addresses through the shop's customer records."

"But there were other employees who could have done the same," Morgan pointed out.

Lance rose and stretched his aching back. "Yes, but Franklin was the only one working at the shop throughout that entire period. The owner was cleared as he was in Italy the week Brandi went missing."

"None of the other women have been found."

"But Brandi's body turned up in November 2014. Her grave was shallow, and animals had been at the corpse. She was badly decomposed. But the sheriff's department had already made the link between Franklin and the six missing women, and they had enough supporting evidence to establish probable cause and obtain a search warrant. They found the hairs in his trunk and that was the critical piece of evidence that convicted him." Anger surged in Lance's chest. The biggest piece of evidence in the case had been mishandled.

Morgan turned a page in the file. "The county would have the DNA profiles of those other five women on file."

Lance added, "But none of their hairs were found in Franklin's trunk. If Brandi's hair was disallowed, is there enough additional evidence to bring a new trial?"

"I doubt it." Morgan closed the file and rested her hand on it. "Probable cause isn't even close to the standard applied by the court to establish beyond a reasonable doubt. If an appeal is granted, Franklin could walk."

"And possibly kill again."

Chapter Twenty-One

Jittery from the vat of coffee she'd consumed at the sheriff's station, Morgan climbed out of the Jeep in front of Sharp Investigations. She stood on the sidewalk, hoisted her tote higher on her shoulder, and glanced at the front door. A package sat on the porch.

Lance locked the Jeep and caught up with her. "Sharp hasn't called. I guess he's still tied up with Stella."

They turned up the walk. Their shadows fell over the box. Next to it, a tiny red light blinked. Morgan hesitated. Had that dot been a trick of the sunlight? It blinked again.

The hairs on the back of her neck prickled, and she reached for Lance's forearm. "What's that red light next to the package?"

Lance stopped. Under her hand, his muscles tensed. "It looks like an infrared light."

And it was blinking faster.

The package emitted a faint beep and then a second.

"Get down!"

She barely heard the third beep. Before she could process what was happening, Lance hooked an arm around Morgan's waist and tackled her to the lawn. She went down hard in a full sprawl. Her chin bounced off the grass. The impact jarred her head and knocked the wind from her lungs. Lance crawled on top of her and wrapped his arms around his head.

A boom sounded. Bits of debris showered them. A chunk of something hard nicked her calf. The slice of pain brought her brain back into focus.

A bomb.

Morgan gasped. Her heart slammed against her ribs. Her face was pressed into the grass, and Lance's weight on her back prevented her from inflating her lungs. Lance had covered her body with his own and used his arms to protect their heads.

The air went quiet, and she tapped his arm. "Are you OK?"

"I think so." His weight shifted slightly. "You?"

"I can't breathe."

He slid off until he was lying on the grass next to her, one arm still protectively over her back. "Are you all right?"

Rolling over, she drew in a deep breath. All of her limbs moved. No major pain. "Yes." Morgan spotted blood dripping down his arm. "You're bleeding."

But he ignored it. He was scanning the front yard and the street. "I think that infrared beam was the detonator, but let's find cover just in case there's a second package."

He rose into a crouch, tugged her to her feet, and pushed her back toward the Jeep. Without breaking stride, she grabbed her tote bag from the grass where it had fallen. One of her shoes had come off. She left it and ran awkwardly with Lance in one heel and one bare foot.

Once inside the vehicle, Lance started the engine and moved the Jeep down the street, his head swiveling as he looked for threats.

While he drove, Morgan called 911, then looked back at the duplex. A hole gaped in the front porch and scorch marks colored the siding next to the door. Most of the debris that littered the front walk and lawn appeared to have come from the porch railing and the bomb packaging. The front window that looked into Sharp's office was broken.

She'd expected more damage, but the explosion seemed to have been limited to a six-foot radius centered around where the bomb had been placed.

She turned back to Lance and his bleeding arm. "Let me see."

"It doesn't hurt."

"Yet." She found the source of the bleeding immediately: an inch-long gash in his biceps. "This might need stitches."

Lance didn't seem concerned.

Sirens signaled the approach of the first responders. The Scarlet Falls Police Station was only a few blocks away. Two police cars roared around the corner.

"Wait here." Lance stepped out of the Jeep and waved them down. They parked in the middle of the street, their lights swirling. Two officers emerged from the squad cars. She recognized Officer Carl Ripton. Lance conferred with his former coworker. Morgan changed into the flats she kept in her tote bag. Then she joined Lance in the street as the officers moved away.

Lance steered her back toward their vehicle. "They want us to wait here. The SFPD is going to evacuate the block and sit tight until the county bomb squad gets here to clear the scene."

Carl blocked one end of the street with his vehicle. The second officer drove to the other end of the street and did the same. Then the two cops left their vehicles and ran toward the buildings on either side of the office.

The thought that there could be additional bombs around the property made Morgan feel ill. The blood dripping from Lance's fingers onto the sidewalk wasn't helping. She wasn't normally squeamish. The explosion had left her shaky. Plus, little aches were blooming where her chin, knees, and hands had hit the ground. She opened the hatch and rummaged in the back of the Jeep for two bottles of water and the first aid kit. Lance stocked his vehicle the way she stocked her tote bag.

She opened three gauze pads and held them against Lance's cut. The blood soaked through them in seconds. She'd need twenty stacked together. She needed something more absorbent. The ACE bandage in the kit wasn't sterile. Unzipping her tote, she found a Maxi Pad, opened the package, and pressed it against his wound.

Lance looked down and lifted one brow.

Morgan shrugged. "It's clean and absorbent." She wrapped the ACE bandage around his arm to hold the pad in place. "Would you rather go to the ER?"

"Nope. This is fine." Lance took his phone from his pocket. "I need to call Sharp."

With Lance's wound addressed, Morgan cleaned the scratch on her calf and covered it with a Band-Aid. Sirens wailed as more officers arrived. In ten minutes, they were joined by two fire trucks, an ambulance, and a paramedic unit. Morgan flagged down a paramedic, who opened his kit on the hood of the Jeep.

He unwrapped the makeshift bandage and paused for just a second before nodding at Morgan. "Resourceful."

He cleaned the wound. "This could probably use a couple of stitches. I'll close it with butterfly bandages, but if it doesn't stop bleeding, you should go to the emergency room. Have you had a tetanus booster recently?"

"I'm sure I have," Lance said.

The paramedic bandaged the wound, then turned to Morgan. "How about you?"

"I'm fine." Because Lance had played human shield.

The paramedic cleaned up his supplies and took his kit back to his vehicle.

Morgan turned and leaned against the Jeep next to Lance's good arm. "Thank you for throwing yourself on top of me."

"Anytime."

"Is Sharp still with Stella?" With the excitement fading, the chill wrapped around her, and she shivered.

"I assume so. He didn't answer his phone. I left him a message." Lance scrolled through apps on his screen. "I can access the security camera feed on my phone. The cameras should have caught our bomber."

"Let's hope." But that seemed too easy for Morgan. They weren't usually that lucky.

"Here he is." Lance angled the phone so she could see the screen.

A man in jeans and a hoodie ran up to the front porch, set down the package, and retreated.

"Damn. He kept his face turned away from the camera," Lance said.

"He knows it's there." Morgan pointed at the screen. "Show the feed from camera two. It covers the street."

Lance switched camera feeds. "He parked outside the camera's view."

"Go back to number one and run it again." Morgan watched the man leave the box. She touched the screen to freeze the video. "We can approximate his height and body type."

"He looks fairly average."

"Average can rule people out."

"True."

She squinted at the image. "Do you see any logos on his clothes?"

Lance zoomed in and moved the image around on the screen. "He's wearing Timberland boots."

"He's also wearing leather gloves." Morgan zeroed in on a small strip of skin between the hoodie sleeve and the glove. "Zoom in here. He's Caucasian."

"We were bombed by an average-size white guy in Timberland boots."

"Not much of a description." *But better than none at all,* she thought.

"Uh-oh. Here comes the press." Lance sighed.

Morgan lifted her head. Two news vans turned the corner and stopped just shy of the command center established by the SFPD and fire department. Before the crews could exit those two vans, another pulled up.

"On the bright side, our bomb has drawn the press away from Mr. and Mrs. Cruz's house." Lance's eyes narrowed until he looked almost wolfish.

"There is that." Morgan watched the crews unload from the vans. "But how did they get here so quickly? Albany is an hour away."

"Maybe they got a tip, like that reporter who randomly showed up at Olivia's house yesterday while I was canvassing the neighborhood."

A reporter spotted them. But Morgan and Lance were behind the command center barrier. Morgan was grateful the press couldn't get to them. Reporters lined up to give sound bites with the police activity as a dramatic backdrop.

"Are you going to talk to them?" Lance asked.

"No. I'm going to ignore them." With a normal case, Morgan gave interviews to manipulate public opinion in favor of her clients, but there was no need for her to indulge the media today.

"Good. I hate to see them sensationalizing Olivia's disappearance and hounding her family for ratings."

Hours passed as the bomb squad set up and then cleared the office and surrounding buildings. As soon as the area was proclaimed safe, the ambulance, fire engines, and half the police vehicles drove away. Neighbors were permitted into their homes and businesses.

The fire chief approached Lance and Morgan. He was holding a small silver object in his gloved hand. "The building is clear. There was only the one device."

"What's that?" Morgan pointed to his hand.

"An infrared motion sensor. It seems your package contained a small pipe bomb with a mechanical switch triggered by the IR sensor.

In theory, it's smart. There's no obvious trip wire, and the assailant can be far away from the scene when the bomb goes off. But you got lucky. The sensor picked up your movement while you were still a good distance from the bomb. If you two had been closer when it went off, you would have gotten faces full of shrapnel."

Considering a bomb had detonated and they had suffered only minor injuries, Morgan felt very lucky indeed. "I would have expected a larger explosion from a pipe bomb."

"We'll know more when we've fully investigated, but I suspect the bomber didn't use enough explosive." The fire chief shrugged. "Whether that was intentional or not is the question."

"We have the security camera feed showing the bomber in action." Lance lifted his phone. "Unfortunately, you can't see his face or vehicle, but I'll email it to you."

"The arson investigator and bomb squad are still working the scene. I'll let you know when we have answers."

"Can we go inside?" Morgan asked.

The fire chief looked back at the duplex. "The explosion was limited in scope. There's no structural damage, except to the porch. We've roped off the front porch and lawn. Forensics needs to comb the grass. Stay off the lawn and use a different door."

Lance and Morgan left the Jeep at the end of the street and walked back to the office. They stood on the sidewalk and stared at the gaping hole in the front porch.

"And how is this tied to Olivia's disappearance?" The afternoon waned, and the shadow of the building fell over Morgan. She shivered. "Is this a warning?"

"I think it's a good bet that our investigation provoked this attack." Lance pointed to the blackened porch. "But who did we trigger?"

Chapter Twenty-Two

"Slow down." In the passenger seat of the unmarked sedan, Sharp scanned the side of the road. "We should see Joe Franklin's driveway any second. There it is."

A break in the forest marked the entrance to the property. Stella turned the vehicle, but a heavy gate barred the way. Two signs hung on the gate: BEWARE OF DOG and NO TRESPASSING. A split rail fence surrounded the property. On the other side of the gate, the driveway curved sharply to the right. The house was not visible.

"Franklin must be a very private man." Stella lowered the window and pressed the intercom button on a kiosk alongside the driveway. No one answered. She pressed the button again but received no response.

Sharp climbed out of the car.

Stella joined him a moment later. "We can't go around that gate without a warrant."

Sharp wished he'd come alone. He'd be over that gate in a heartbeat. "I don't see how we're going to get one."

"We need evidence. We don't have anything even remotely close to probable cause."

Sharp walked to both sides of the gate and tried to peer through the woods, but the trees were too thick. With most houses, a cop could walk up to the front door and knock. But the fence and locked gate created an expectation of privacy. They were stuck.

"We'll have to come back." Stella turned around.

Sharp hesitated. "We *need* to talk to Joe Franklin."

Stella headed for her car door. "I'm sorry, Sharp, but we have to obey the law. This is private property. We cannot enter without a warrant."

Is Olivia somewhere on the other side of that gate?

Sharp did not miss the intricacies of police procedure. Stella's hands were tied. As soon as possible, he was coming back without her.

They climbed into the car, and Stella drove to Ronald Alexander's house. The Olanders' former foreman lived in a small ranch-style home not far from the dairy farm. The house was basic, no frills but well maintained.

She pulled to the curb alongside the mailbox. They got out of the vehicle and stood on the sidewalk.

The curtain shifted in the window as they approached the front door. Stella knocked, and a haggard-looking woman answered the door. Her gray-streaked hair was scraped away from her face and bound in a tight knot. She wore old jeans and dirty sneakers. Deep frown lines bracketed her mouth, and Sharp doubted the crow's-feet around her eyes had been caused by too much smiling.

Standing in the doorway, she narrowed suspicious eyes at them. When her gaze settled on Sharp, she clutched the edges of her cardigan sweater together. When she spoke, she directed her question to Stella. "What do you want?"

"Are you Mrs. Ronald Alexander?" Stella asked.

The woman hesitated, then gave them a single small nod.

Stella flashed her badge and introduced herself and Sharp. "We'd like to ask you a few questions about your husband."

The woman immediately stepped backward and tried to close the door. "No. You'll have to talk to Ronald." Her voice and hands trembled. "He ain't home right now."

Sharp put a hand on the door to prevent her from closing it. "Can you tell us where he is?"

"No." Mrs. Alexander shook her head almost violently. The whites of her eyes shone. She bowed her head and studied the tiles under her feet. "I can't."

Her fear was palpable.

"Thank you anyway." Sharp lowered his hand and inclined his head in understanding. She flushed, almost looking ashamed, but fear overrode any sense of pride she might have. She closed the door, and the dead bolt slid home with a loud click.

Stella and Sharp turned away from the house. As he reached the passenger side of the vehicle, Sharp spotted a middle-aged neighbor rolling her trash can to the curb. The neighbor gave Stella's sedan a curious look. She didn't hurry into her house but watched them.

"She looks talkative. Let's get the neighborhood gossip." Sharp led the way across the street. "Excuse me, ma'am. I'm looking for Ronald Alexander."

"Better you than me." She lined her garbage can up with the curb. "Ronald is one miserable SOB."

"Is that so?" Sharp asked.

The neighbor frowned at the Alexander house.

Sharp offered her a business card and introduced Stella as his associate.

"I'm Iris." The neighbor inclined her head toward the house. "I don't suppose *she* told you anything. I'm surprised she even answered the door." She lowered her voice to a conspiratorial tone. "I don't think he lets her out of the house by herself."

Sharp frowned in disapproval but didn't comment. Iris was on a roll, and he didn't want to interrupt.

"It wouldn't surprise me if he beats her." She shook her head. "He's the type."

"Type?" Sharp prompted.

"He thinks all women should be subservient to men. Every time he sees my husband—which is rare because Fred can't stand him—he tells him that a woman belongs in the home, and that he should teach me to stay in my place." She barked out a laugh. "That is so not Fred. Ronald would be funny if he wasn't so scary."

"Scary how?" Stella asked.

"He beat the hell out of a neighbor, Larry Brown, for not picking up his dog poop. Just ran out of the house, tackled him, and started punching him in the face." Iris shuddered. "Larry put his house up for sale as soon as he got out of the hospital. We were all hoping Ronald would move when he got out of jail, but he didn't."

"That's terrible," Stella said. "Does he frighten you?"

"Yes and no." Iris tilted her head. "It isn't anything he *does*. It's how he looks at me. I can't explain it, but I know he's angry. I can feel his rage from across the street, like heat radiating off a sidewalk in August, and I haven't done anything to him. I avoid him. If he comes out of his house, I go inside mine." She gave a high-pitched, nervous laugh. "Thank goodness Fred was a linebacker for his college football team. Ronald won't mess with him."

"Did you see him beat your neighbor?" Sharp wondered if this woman was the witness.

Iris shivered and rubbed her arms. "No. I came home from work just as the ambulance picked up Larry. His face . . ." She closed her eyes for a few seconds. A tremor passed through her. "It happened a long time ago, but everyone who lived here back then remembers."

"Do you know where he might be now?" Sharp asked.

"Sure." Iris looked at her watch. "Ronald just got a new job at Frederick's Garden Center. It's on Highway 12. I used to buy my perennials there. This year I went to Home Depot."

"Good call." Sharp pointed at the business card still in her hand. "If you remember anything else, you can give me a call."

"I will." Iris pocketed the card. "The entire neighborhood would love it if Ronald went back to prison and stayed there."

Stella and Sharp returned to her vehicle.

Stella fastened her seat belt. "Let's try the garden center."

When he and Stella were engrossed in the investigation, he could almost pretend he was working a normal case. But the moment his brain was unoccupied, Olivia appeared front and center. He rubbed the aching emptiness above his heart as Stella drove away from the Alexander house.

Frederick's Garden Center was only a few miles away. The rural roads had little traffic, and the drive took just a few minutes.

After she parked next to a pallet of pumpkins, Stella used her dashboard computer to pull up Ronald's driver's license photo. "This is who we're looking for."

Ronald Alexander was about fifty years old, with a mean squint and the veiny red nose of a longtime alcoholic.

They stepped out of the car and walked down several aisles of plants. They found Ronald in front of a greenhouse, loading trays of purple cabbages onto a display table. He was an average-size man, but his body and face looked hard, as if he had spent most of his life doing physical labor and being pissed off about it. His hairline had receded past his ears, leaving him with a crown of greasy brown-and-gray hair. Over his jeans and sweatshirt, he wore a green apron displaying the Frederick's logo.

"Excuse me, Mr. Alexander?" Stella moved her jacket aside to show the badge on her belt.

Ronald's eyes widened, and for a split second, he looked scared. "What do you want? I haven't done anything."

"Is there somewhere we can go and talk?" Stella glanced around. "Can you take a quick break? We only have a few questions."

"No. I'm working." Ronald turned to the plants and gave the two investigators his back.

"I'd be happy to run it by your manager." Stella smiled. "I'm sure he wouldn't mind you cooperating."

"Cooperating with what?" He shifted a tray of plants.

"My investigation," Stella said. "Your former boss's wife, Lena Olander, is dead."

"I know. I saw it on the news." Ronald spun to grab another tray of cabbages. "I am under no legal obligation to answer your questions."

No one understood his rights better than an ex-con.

But Stella was no pushover. "We'd like to ask you a few questions about Lena and Kennett Olander. You worked for Olander Dairy, is that correct?"

Shiny sweat broke out on Ronald's head. "Get this straight. I will not talk to you. Lena killed herself. That has nothing to do with me."

Sharp had no time for his bullshit. "Does your new boss know you're an ex-con?"

"It doesn't matter." Ronald licked his lips. "This is harassment."

"Why don't you want to talk about the Olanders?"

"You had no right to come here." His eyes darted up and down the aisle, as if he expected someone to be watching. He lowered his voice. "You don't understand."

"Then explain it to me," Stella said.

Ronald opened his mouth but quickly closed it. He set his jaw, but underneath his determination was fear. "There's nothing to tell. I worked for Mr. Olander, but he had to sell the farm. Obviously, there was no job for me once the cows were sold. He had to let me go."

"Were you on the farm when Erik killed his wife?" Stella asked.

"I don't know anything about that."

"Did you ever see Erik and his wife fight?" Stella pressed.

"I rarely saw Erik's wife," Ronald evaded.

Sharp jumped in. "You didn't answer the question."

"I don't have to." Ronald crossed his arms and took a step backward.

"OK, Ronald." Stella backed off. Unfortunately, Ronald was right. He was under no obligation to speak with them, and they had no leverage.

Sharp wasn't ready to give up. He stepped closer, eating up the space Ronald had put between them, getting in his face. "Why don't you tell us what you're afraid of?"

"I'm not afraid of anything." But a muscle on the side of Ronald's face twitched.

He was lying. Sharp could feel it. Anger rose into his throat, as bitter as Morgan's coffee. If Stella weren't here, Sharp would make Ronald talk any way he could.

He didn't normally condone threats or physical violence, but with Olivia missing, nothing was off-limits.

Stella put her hand on his arm. "Let's go, Sharp."

Reluctantly, he followed her back to her car. "Are you sure we just can't beat it out of him?" He was only half kidding.

"The interview wasn't a total loss. We learned that he's terrified."

"But what is he afraid of? Olander? Or something else?"

"Whatever it is, it's scarier than the police. Now I want to talk to Mr. Olander." Neither of them spoke as Stella drove out to the dairy farm. The twin houses looked even more depressing than they had when Sharp had been there with Lance.

They went up to the front door of the main residence and knocked, but no one answered.

"Let's try the barn." Sharp turned away from the door.

"All right, but we cannot search the premises," she warned. "We can only call out for Mr. Olander. Your hunches are not enough to get a search warrant."

"Uh-huh," Sharp said vaguely. He wasn't making promises.

"This place is creepy." Stella followed him around the side of the house. The sun broke through the clouds. "There should be animals. It feels like a ghost farm."

165

"It looks like they sold everything that had value." Sharp used his hand as a visor to block the sunshine. He stopped at the entrance to the barn. The brightness outside made the barn's interior appear black.

"Mr. Olander!" Stella called through the wide doorway.

One of the barn cats slunk across the opening, giving Sharp and Stella the stink eye as it raced away.

"The barn smells worse than I remember." Sharp waved a hand in front of his nose. "All I can smell is shit."

Stella cupped a hand around her mouth. "Mr. Olander, are you here?"

Somewhere in the darkness, wood creaked. Sharp stepped across the threshold, the unreachable spot between his shoulder blades itching in warning.

"We can't go in without a warrant," Stella reminded him.

As if he'd forgotten. He hadn't. He didn't care. He was never going to find Olivia following the rules.

"What if we think something is wrong?" he asked.

"What could be wrong?"

"I don't know, but it's something." Sharp couldn't shake the feeling, and he didn't want to. His survival instincts had saved his ass more than once over the past thirty years.

Yet, the need to know—and to find Olivia—drew him forward. He took one more step. Once out of the direct sunlight, his vision began to adjust to the dimness within. The inside of the barn took shape.

"Sharp," Stella warned, "I don't have a warrant."

"I'm not a cop. I'm a concerned citizen, worried about Mr. Olander." Sharp ignored Stella's irritated huff. It was all well and good for him to make excuses. It would be her ass on the line if the situation went sideways. But Sharp didn't much care.

The barn looked mostly the same as it had that morning. Sharp looked down and saw footprints in the dirt. He thought back to his earlier visit but couldn't remember if he'd noticed them before. The hairs on the back of his neck lifted, and a primitive alarm clenched his gut. His hand automatically sought his weapon.

Something was definitely wrong. But what?

Another cat shot past, the low streak of its body startling him. A bird flew in the open door and soared up to the rafters. Sharp followed the sound of its wings in the empty space. He scanned the catwalks that spanned the middle of the barn.

And then he saw it. The sight repelled him, a visceral human reaction to death.

From just outside the doorway, Stella called out for Olander again.

"He won't be responding." Sharp drew his gun and scanned the big lofty space. Nerves prickled along his skin, raising goose bumps on his arms.

"How do you know?"

Reaching behind him, Sharp pulled Stella into the barn and pointed to the catwalk on the far side of the barn. From it, Mr. Olander was hanging by the neck. The rope had been tossed over the railing and tied off to a support beam. The farmer's dirty boots dangled several feet above the ground. Had Olander been so depressed he had jumped?

Sharp looked at the fresh footprints in the dirt.

Or had the farmer been pushed?

He approached the body.

"Shit." Stella pulled her gun. "Any chance he's alive?"

If there were, they would cut him down and attempt to revive him. If not, they would preserve the scene.

The body faced away from them. Sharp walked in a wide circle, skirting Mr. Olander so he could see the victim's face. Sharp took in the purple skin and swollen, protruding tongue. "Nope. He's dead."

"Suicide?" Stella took out her phone and called for backup.

Sharp zeroed in on Olander's hands, dangling at his sides. He moved a little closer and took out his phone. Using his flashlight app, he shone light on the corpse. Several of the fingertips were bloody and raw, a few nails torn below the quick. Pulling a pen from his pocket, he used it to lift the cuffs of the farmer's jacket sleeves. Angry red lines ringed the corpse's wrists. "His fingernails are torn, and I see ligature marks around his wrists."

Sharp scanned the ground but didn't see anything that could have been used to bind the farmer's hands.

"So a probable no on suicide." Stella leaned in for a better view. Then she put her back to Sharp's and scanned their surroundings.

"Let's clear the building." Sharp moved toward the first doorway.

Stella called him back. "No. We'll wait outside for backup. There's a unit on the way. ETA is eight minutes. This place is too big for us to clear on our own."

Sharp hesitated.

"Sharp," Stella warned in a firm voice, "we don't know if whoever did this is still here or not. You can't find Olivia if you're dead."

"All right." Sharp didn't like waiting, but Stella was right.

They backed out of the building and waited next to the car.

Sharp knew she was right, but the time seemed to tick by in slow motion. He paced. There were no sounds coming from the barn or either house.

The house!

"Hold on." Sharp spun and ran up toward the main house.

"Sharp!" Stella yelled. "Get back here."

He heard her boots hitting the dry ground behind him.

Sharp reached the back of the house. The bulkhead doors stood open, and the chain that had secured them lay on the ground. Several links were severed. Sharp opened the flashlight app on his phone again.

Stella caught up, breathing hard. "We can't go down there."

"You're right," he said.

Stella had procedure to follow.

Sharp shone his light on the steps and started down. "*We* can't, but *I* can."

He descended, leading with his gun. He swept his light around the space. Footprints covered the concrete, lots of them, and scrape marks showed where something heavy had been dragged. He followed the same path he and Lance had used earlier that morning.

Even before he got to the area where the trunks had been stored, he knew. The room was empty. Four clean rectangles on the concrete marked the spaces where the trunks had sat.

Disappointment crushed Sharp.

"The guns are gone," Sharp said to Stella as he returned to the stairwell from the back of the basement.

On the way up the stairs, Sharp checked the time on his phone. Five o'clock. He opened a text from Lance and read the message. "Holy shit."

"What's wrong?" Stella asked.

"Someone left a bomb at the office."

Stella stared at him.

"Everyone is OK," he said quickly. "It detonated but only did minor damage to the porch."

Stella's eyes turned back toward the barn. "None of this makes sense."

Sharp agreed.

"But is this connected to Olivia's disappearance?" Stella asked. "Did she discover something about the guns in the basement?"

Every lead they followed generated far more questions than answers. Mr. Olander had been murdered. The Olanders had been into something dangerous. They were no closer to finding Olivia, and now someone had tried to blow up his office.

"Did Olivia stumble onto an illegal arms deal?" Sharp asked.

The thought of Olivia in the hands of an arms dealer gave Sharp a pain behind his sternum. He bet Mr. Olander had been executed. If Olivia had been abducted by the same person or people and they considered her a threat, would they have any reason to keep her alive?

Chapter Twenty-Three

Lance stood in Morgan's office, staring at the whiteboard, when he heard the back door open and close. He glanced at the doorway. A moment later, Sharp appeared. His face looked leaner, and the bags under his eyes were more pronounced than they'd been that morning. Of course, none of them had slept much the night before, and it was nearly four o'clock in the morning.

"Where's Morgan?" Sharp walked into the room and stood next to Lance, his tired eyes on the board.

"Asleep on the couch in your office." Lance had taken a nap earlier, but he was sure he didn't look fresh either.

"You're back." Morgan entered her office and beelined for the coffee maker on the credenza behind her desk. She was barefoot. Her skirt was rumpled and her blouse untucked. On the way past the men, she stopped and rested a hand on Sharp's shoulder. "Are you all right?"

"Honestly, no." Sharp shook his head. "And I'm not going to be until we find Olivia. But I don't know what else to do except keep looking for her."

Morgan gave his shoulder a squeeze. "And that's exactly what we're going to do."

Realistically, they couldn't maintain the pace at which they were working for much longer. Mental function declined drastically with sleep deprivation. Naps would hold them for only a couple of days. But when would Sharp agree to back off? It was Sunday. Olivia had been missing for two days.

Morgan checked her phone as she brewed a cup of coffee. "Olivia's agent left me a return message while I was asleep. She's available this morning."

Sharp perched on the corner of Morgan's desk. The exhaustion in his eyes went beyond lack of sleep. Worry for Olivia was wearing him down. "Would you make me a cup of that poison?"

Morgan's eyebrows shot up. "Again? Are you serious?"

"Yes. Very." Sharp rolled his neck. Something cracked.

Morgan pulled a clean mug from her shelf and inserted a pod into the machine. A minute later, she handed him the mug. She pulled a bag of cookies from her drawer and ate one.

Sharp took a cookie.

"Did you eat dinner last night?" Morgan asked.

Sharp shook his head.

"You need some real food." She rounded her desk and left her office.

Lance felt helpless. What if they didn't find Olivia? "You're sure Mr. Olander was murdered?"

Sharp nodded. "The medical examiner confirmed the red rings around his wrists were ligature marks."

Looking for energy in any form, Lance helped himself to a cookie.

"Since the guns were at the farm yesterday, and now they're gone, I assume his murder was related to them." Sharp bit into his cookie.

"Seems likely someone stole them." Lance could hear the soft beeping of the microwave in the kitchen.

"It does." Sharp washed the rest of his cookie down with coffee.

A few minutes later, Morgan returned with a bowl of soup, a spoon, and a steaming mug of tea. "Sit." She gestured toward her desk.

After Sharp sat in her desk chair, she put the soup and tea in front of him. He picked up the spoon and dipped it into the bowl. "Thank you. This is just what I needed."

Morgan smiled. "It's your soup from the freezer, but you're welcome."

"Who put the pipe bomb on our doorstep?" Sharp blew on a spoonful of soup.

"Are we agreed it was related to Olivia's disappearance?" Morgan asked.

Lance nodded. "Yes."

"Did they want to kill us or scare us?" Morgan stood next to Lance and studied the whiteboard.

"Good question." Lance's eyes were dry and his vision blurry. Not that it mattered. He had been staring at the board most of the night, trying to make connections or generate ideas about where Olivia might be or who might have taken her. Unfortunately, the investigation wasn't narrowing. Instead, the leads were spiderwebbing.

They didn't speak again until Sharp had finished his soup.

"I set up some additional motion detectors and cameras outside," Lance said. "Turn on notifications in the app, and you'll get an immediate message whenever anyone approaches the house, and you can see their approach in real time."

"That's great. At least no one will sneak up on us." Sharp pushed away the bowl. "Stella let me walk Olander's murder scene with her."

She was smart enough to make use of Sharp's experience.

"The way Olander was killed suggests more than theft of the guns. A pair of cut zip ties was found on the catwalk above him. His hands were bound; then he was forced onto the catwalk in the barn. They put a noose around his neck, cut the zip ties, and shoved him off. The drop was only about six feet. His neck didn't break, and the way his fingertips and nails were torn and bloody, we know it took him a few minutes to die. He hung there, tearing at the rope around his neck, until it strangled him."

Lance's belly cramped at the visual running through his head. Next to him, Morgan shuddered. He put an arm around her shoulders.

"Sounds like an execution," Morgan said.

"Yes," Sharp agreed. "I got the sense of punishment or revenge."

"Or they were making an example of him," Lance pointed out.

"Maybe all of those things." Morgan crossed her arms. "But why? Who are they? Did he betray them in some way?"

Lance wrote the possible motives under a new column headed with OLANDER'S MURDER. "Maybe *he* stole the guns from *them*?"

"It's possible." Sharp massaged his scalp with both hands as if his head hurt. "But how are the guns or Olander's death related to Olivia's disappearance?"

"We don't know that they are," Morgan said quietly. "There's no mention of guns in Olivia's notes."

"Shit." Sharp lowered his hands, shot to his feet, and paced the narrow space between the desk and credenza. "Are we any closer to finding her?"

Lance didn't insult Sharp with meaningless encouragement. The chances of finding Olivia alive decreased with every moment that passed. They all knew it. There was no pretending.

"Let's table the Olander case for now," Lance said in a firm voice. "Let the forensics team and medical examiner do their jobs."

"You're right. Whoever killed Olander literally didn't bother to cover their tracks. There'll be evidence, but it will take time to process. Same with the materials from the bomb left on our porch. An arson investigation is not a fast process either." Sharp walked two steps, pivoted, and took two more strides in the opposite direction. "Did we find any sign that a former subject of one of Olivia's investigative journalism pieces could be behind her abduction?"

"Nothing that makes sense." Lance tapped the note on the board. "The only real possibility is in Oregon."

"Where are we?" Sharp's voice echoed his frustration.

"My mother sent the rest of the background reports," Lance said. "I've started skimming them. So far, nothing has jumped out at me."

Sharp swept a hand through his hair, leaving it standing up in tufts. "Have you made any headway with the Franklin case? What did you learn at the sheriff's station?"

"Morgan and I read the murder book. The sheriff was convinced Franklin was tied to the disappearances of five other women who went missing over the past ten years. But his theory is mostly conjecture with a small amount of circumstantial evidence." Morgan picked up her file on the Franklin case. "What if he's innocent?"

A shadow passed over Sharp's eyes. "Then the real killer certainly wouldn't want Franklin freed and the Brandi Holmes murder case reopened."

Lance picked up the marker and wrote REAL KILLER? in the FRANKLIN CASE column. "The attorney, Mark Hansen, also has motive. He royally screwed up Franklin's case."

"Maybe he didn't miss the error," Morgan said. "Maybe he purposefully let it go."

"Why would he do that?" Lance asked.

"Blackmail and bribery come to mind." Sharp scrubbed both hands down his face.

Lance circled his name. "He claims he was in Rochester overnight Thursday, but he refused to prove it."

"We can't make him provide receipts, but we can keep his name on the short list." Morgan sighed. "What other leads do we have?"

"I'm going to talk to the brother, Joe," Sharp said. "Today. Without Stella, if that's the way it has to be."

"I'm going to track down Olivia's editor after I talk with her agent," Morgan said. "I know it's the weekend. He could be away, but I'm not waiting any longer."

"I'll go with you," Lance offered.

Morgan was more than competent, but so was Olivia, and she had been kidnapped. Morgan's New York State concealed carry permit was not valid in the city. She'd be going unarmed. Lance did not like that. As a former cop with more than ten years of experience, he could carry a gun anywhere as long as he maintained his certification. He would go with her and play bodyguard.

"We'll have to leave soon," she said. "It's a three-hour drive without traffic."

Lance turned to Sharp. "When are you checking in with Stella today?"

"We're touching base later in the morning. We were tied up at the Olander farm most of the night. I came back here, and she was going to catch a nap if she could manage it." Sharp studied the board. "I feel like we're missing something."

Morgan's eyes were heavily shadowed, and she looked like she'd slept in her clothes—which she had. "I need to shower and change."

Lance hesitated, looking back at Sharp. "Do you want me to stay here?"

"No. Go with Morgan." Sharp waved away his offer. "Stella will call in a few hours. I'll be fine." He rose and picked up his soup bowl and mug. "As much as I don't want to rest, I'll be more useful if I sleep for a couple of hours. Maybe my brain will reboot and things will start to make sense." He carried his dishes to the door. "Please go. I can't be everywhere at once. I need you two to chase down leads in the city."

Lance and Morgan collected their jackets and followed Sharp toward the kitchen, and all three left through the back door. The air outside was cold, damp, and cutting. Sharp armed the security system, locked up, and walked around the side of the duplex. Morgan buttoned

175

her wool jacket and followed Lance to the Jeep. The police and arson investigators had finished with the porch, but it was still roped off for safety's sake.

Lance slid behind the wheel and watched Sharp climb the wooden staircase on the outside of the house. A minute later, lights brightened the windows of his second-story apartment.

"Think he'll be all right?" Lance drove away from the curb.

Morgan rubbed her hands together. "No. I don't think so."

Chapter Twenty-Four

Olivia wheezed. Drawing air in and out of her lungs felt like she was trying to breathe through a cocktail straw. Her inhalation caught in her throat. The coughing fit left her breathless. Again. Her chest and back ached.

On her hands and knees, she breathed shallowly, trying not to trigger another coughing spell. All of her concentration focused on inhaling and exhaling as slowly and steadily as possible. She had no time to worry about her claustrophobia or the pain in her foot and face.

For the next few minutes, sucking oxygen into her lungs was a full-time job. Her chest felt tight and her ribs hurt.

What was she going to do?

What *could* she do?

Nothing.

Suffocate.

Die, maybe.

She fought the panic that shook her. Fear would only make breathing harder. But the tightness of her lungs amplified her claustrophobia. She thought of Lincoln and imagined his voice in her head, calming her.

She shivered and continued searching through the dirt, crawling on all fours. The temperature was falling. It would be best to continue moving, keep her blood flowing. Lying down usually made her asthma worse. She was an asthmatic locked in a damp cellar. If she didn't get medical help soon, her situation wasn't going to end well. It couldn't. He didn't have to do anything to her for her to die. She could do that all on her own.

Her fingertip encountered a small rock. She wrapped her fist around it for a second. The cellar was old. A century of feet had packed the earthen floor. But underneath, there were rocks. Crawling back to her blanket, she added the rock to the few she'd accumulated, but none were large enough to use as a potential bludgeon.

She'd considered trying to remove the lid to the chemical toilet, but it was made of light plastic and wasn't heavy enough to be used as a weapon. She could not think of a way to use empty plastic water bottles as weapons either. She had one more option, but it was a long shot. She'd reserve it as a last resort.

Footsteps sounded outside, startling her. Then she heard the rusty squeal of the door hinges. The door opened, and the beam of a flashlight shone down the steps. A minute later, he descended. Even though she expected to see the Halloween mask, the unnatural rubber face sent fear spiking through her.

Carrying a small white bag, he tromped down the steps. How long had it been since he was here last? A day? The sky through the door was gray, but again, she didn't know if it was morning or evening twilight or just overcast.

He stared at her through the mask. "Are you going to be respectful today?"

Did that mean one day had passed?

Olivia nodded. Best to act submissive. It was what he seemed to want.

He held a white bag toward her. "Say please."

She cleared her throat. "May I please have the food?"

"That's better." He put the bag in her hands.

Inside was a white take-out container. The unmistakable smell of chicken soup wafted to her. Instantly starving, she dug the plastic spoon out of the bottom and ate some. It was lukewarm, but the liquid soothed her throat.

She swallowed and paused for a breath. "Thank you." Her voice was barely audible.

He nodded, and the arrogant incline of his head made it seem as if he was pleased with her obedience.

There was no way to escape. The only way she was getting out of this alive was if someone found her or if her captor decided to let her go. She should talk to him. Engage him. Try to make him see her as a person. If she could connect with him, she might foster some empathy.

If only she could talk and eat and breathe at the same time. Eating took priority. She'd eaten the second protein bar and gone through half the water originally stocked in the cellar. She needed the food for fuel in case she had an opportunity for escape.

Halfway through the soup, she gagged. The coughing started up again, and she feared she would vomit what she'd eaten. She set the spoon in the soup and waited for the spell to pass. She needed to pause every few mouthfuls, and it took her a long time to finish. Even though she couldn't see his face, his posture became impatient. He shifted his weight and checked the time on his watch.

"I got you medicine." He pulled a plastic bag bearing a drugstore logo from his jacket pocket. He opened the bag and pulled out a bottle of cough syrup and a bag of cough drops.

Olivia shook her head. "They won't"—*cough*—"help." She wanted to say *I don't have a cold,* but all she could do was hack.

"Fuck you." He threw the bottle of syrup and the cough drops to the ground. "You ungrateful bitch. Haven't you learned anything? I'm gonna be so happy to be done with you."

But Olivia was focused on getting enough oxygen into her lungs. She was using up all of her energy on the fear of suffocation. Her lungs were betraying her. She was strangling from the inside out.

"I'm sorry," she wheezed.

He shook his head and crossed his arms, disappointment emanating from his stiff body. "Doesn't matter. You only have to survive two more days. Then it'll all be over for you."

A chill swept over Olivia. He was going to kill her in two days? Her brain scrambled, her panicky thoughts scattering like rats. Her hand went to her pocket. It felt like last-resort time.

He turned and headed for the steps. Olivia pulled the drawstring from her pajama bottoms out of her pocket, wrapped an end around each hand, and lunged forward. She looped it around his neck, pulling tight with all her strength.

The string was a half-inch-wide woven cotton cord. She had tied a knot at each end to give her a better hold.

He made a choking sound. His hands flew to his neck, and he tried to get his fingers under the cord. Unsuccessful, he reached over his shoulder to grab her. Olivia leaned back, put her weight into the effort, and stayed out of his reach. He staggered, but the mask over his head protected his neck. She pulled harder, her feet digging into the dirt for leverage.

Was it working?

But before hope could bloom, he grabbed hold of the string at the back of his neck. He spun. The cord caught on the mask and pulled it off his head.

Their eyes met for one tight breath.

He leaped forward. His fist struck her temple before she could register what had happened. Pain burst behind her eyes. Her vision blurred, and she crumpled to the ground. She watched his leg draw back, and she braced herself. The first kick caught her in the ribs. She curled into a ball, protecting her head with her hands as the next two swings of his boot struck her thighs.

He left the cellar without saying a word. The doors slammed shut with a resounding, angry bang. Footsteps in gravel faded away.

Her head pounded from the blow. She wheezed, lungs aching. She tested her limbs. The places where she had been kicked ached. She would be bruised, but her legs worked. Nothing was broken.

Sweating, shivering, and dizzy, she dragged herself to her hands and knees and resumed her hunt for rocks. She had to find another way to escape.

If she didn't, she would die in two days. What was driving the time line? It didn't make sense. Had he asked for ransom and not gotten it? Had he asked for ransom but was planning on killing her anyway after he received it?

He couldn't let her live.

Not now that she had seen his face.

Chapter Twenty-Five

At eight o'clock, Morgan read from her file in the passenger seat of the Jeep while Lance drove into a parking garage in Manhattan. "Kim Holgersen was born in Redhaven, but she's lived in New York City for the last twenty years. She worked for two literary agencies before opening her own firm in 2015. She married Brandon Sykes in 2007. He's a real estate investor."

Lance stopped the vehicle next to the attendant booth, handing over his keys and collecting his ticket. Morgan shoved her file into her tote and climbed out of the Jeep. She led the way out of the garage. They walked two blocks and stopped at a crosswalk on the opposite side of the street from Kim Holgersen's Upper East Side condominium building.

"Nice building." Lance gazed upward. "Looks expensive."

"Everything in this neighborhood is expensive." Morgan watched the traffic signal. "Kim and her husband bought this condo for nine hundred thousand dollars in 2007. Since then, the value has more than doubled."

The walk signal flashed, and they crossed the street.

"Is Holgersen successful?" Lance asked.

"According to your mother's background report, Kim brokered some large book deals this year, and her client roster is impressive." Morgan recalled a few of the agent's well-known clients she'd seen on the website. "Your mom also noted that a typical literary agent receives a fifteen percent commission from their authors."

"Then they need to close frequent deals to make money." Lance opened the glass door and held it for Morgan. She stepped into the sleek modern lobby decorated in shades of gray. Two huge sprays of fresh red chrysanthemums brightened either end of a reception desk finished in a rich mahogany stain.

Morgan gave their names to the doorman. He called up to the agent's apartment, then waved them toward the elevator. They rode it to the fifteenth floor and found unit 1511.

A tall woman of about forty opened the door. She wore slim black pants and a tunic-length sweater. Her face was pale, even for a redhead. Her eyes were shadowed with dark circles as if she hadn't slept. "I'm Kim Holgersen. Please, come in." She backed up to allow them inside.

By Manhattan standards, the place was huge. Lance and Morgan followed Kim past a kitchen with a long gray granite island to a shockingly spacious living room. The apartment was decorated in the clean, clutter-free style of professionals with a regular cleaning service and no kids. A few photos in matching silver frames were artfully clustered on a side table.

Morgan leaned closer to look at the pictures. In one, Kim stood in front of a lake with two elderly people who looked like older versions of her. The man held a large fish by the gills.

"Your parents?" Morgan pointed to the photo.

Kim smiled. "Yes. That was a few years ago, when my dad could still fish. He had a stroke."

"I'm sorry." Morgan scanned the other pictures. In most of them, the person with Kim was holding a plaque. She squinted to read the print. "Your clients have won quite a few publishing awards."

Kim nodded. "I've been very lucky. The industry has been good to me."

"You're being modest," Morgan said. "You must have an eye for spotting talent."

"I love good books," Kim said simply. "I knew Olivia was special when I read the first page of her manuscript."

"Thank you for seeing us, Ms. Holgersen." Morgan perched in one of the chairs.

"Please, call me Kim." She chose the love seat opposite Morgan. "I apologize for not getting back to you right away. I was under the weather and mostly asleep for the past couple of days."

Lance eased onto the chair next to Morgan, as if unsure whether the delicate structure would hold his weight. "We have three kids. I couldn't imagine living in an apartment, although this one is bigger than I expected."

Kim clasped her hands together. Her nails had been chewed ragged. "I grew up in the country, but I fell in love with the city." Leaning forward, she rested her forearms on her knees. "I had no idea Olivia was missing, or I would have returned your call immediately. Since you're here, I assume there's been no sign of her?"

"None," Morgan said. "We're very concerned."

The crow's-feet around Kim's eyes creased. "Her parents must be frantic."

"You spoke to Olivia earlier in the week?" Morgan prompted.

"Yes." Kim nodded. "I called her."

"Can you tell us what you discussed?" Lance leaned forward and rested his forearms on his thighs.

"I don't know." Kim hesitated. "I shouldn't discuss Olivia's business without her permission."

"We would love to have Olivia's permission too," Morgan agreed. "But she's been missing for more than two days now. She didn't show up to take her mother to the doctor on Friday."

Kim's eyes widened, and she sat back. "That's not like Olivia."

"Her family is worried," Morgan pressed.

Kim nodded. "I'll tell you in general terms, which is all I know anyway. We talked about her next book—more specifically, her next book proposal. Her editor wanted it weeks ago."

"But you don't know what she's going to write about?" Lance's clasped hands fell between his knees.

"No." The agent hesitated again. "Other than she was focusing on several crimes committed in upstate New York, she wouldn't give me any specifics about which cases she was considering. And believe me, I pressed. Her editor has been calling me daily."

"Her editor was pressuring her?" Morgan asked.

"Yes. The publisher bought her first manuscript at auction. They paid a lot for it. They want to get her next title into their lineup for the following year, but in order to do that, they need a proposal from Olivia. Ideally, they'd have her second book available for preorder when her first is released." The agent exhaled hard. "I'm afraid I've been applying pressure too. A film studio has expressed interest in her first book. They talked about a movie or a true crime miniseries, something along the lines of *Making a Murderer*. I want to get Olivia a film deal and a nice fat advance on a second book while the market is still hot for her. It's possible her first book won't even be a bestseller. It won't release for another eighteen months. A lot can happen between now and then. The market changes every day."

"You think she was stressed?" Lance asked.

"I do," Kim said. "She even told me she'd stopped responding to her editor's emails. She couldn't deal with him anymore. I told him to give her some space, but he refused. I know she's thorough with her work. Olivia doesn't half ass anything. It can be frustrating because I'm trying to do right by her career, but at the same time, I have to respect her professionalism, which is exactly what I told Jake Riley."

"Do you know why she wouldn't share her research with you or her editor?"

"No, but she promised I'd have a proposal next week."

"Her calendar says you're meeting tomorrow at a restaurant in Redhaven," Morgan said. "That's a long drive for you just to have lunch."

Kim smiled. "My parents still live in Redhaven. I usually stop and see them before I meet with Olivia."

"Do you see them often?" Morgan asked.

Kim frowned. "I drive up at least every other week. I tried to move them closer to me after Dad's stroke. I got them into a senior community, but my father will not leave Redhaven. Olivia has the same issues with her parents. She stressed about her mother's blood pressure. Her mom was very upset over Olivia's sister's separation. I understood because my mother freaked out about mine. We've been separated for two months, and when I talk to her, that's all I hear." She paused, picking at her cuticle. "Olivia would never have missed that appointment."

"We're lucky," Morgan said. "My grandfather lives with us. It makes it easier. Plus, one of my sisters is nearby. Do you have any siblings to help you?"

Kim shook her head. "My brother helps as much as he can."

"Support is important." Morgan thought about support. "Is Olivia close to any other authors? Anyone she might have discussed her book research with?"

"Not that I know of." Kim frowned. "I get the impression she's a loner. I offered to take her to publishing parties, but she always declined. She told me she'd rather go home, put on pajamas, and have a cup of tea."

Which was Morgan's idea of a perfect evening.

"Do you know where her editor would be today?" Lance asked. "We'd like to speak with him."

"I usually reach him by cell phone. He's been working from home a few days a week. He mentioned some sort of family emergency last time I talked with him." She picked up her cell phone from the black coffee table. "Do you have his number?"

"I think so." Morgan checked her own phone and read the last few digits of the number they'd taken from Olivia's contact list.

"That's it." Kim lowered her phone and stood. "Please let me know if you find her, or if there's anything else I can do to help."

"We will." Morgan gathered her tote and got to her feet.

She and Lance thanked Kim and left her apartment.

Outside, they walked back to the garage where they'd left the Jeep. Lance handed the parking attendant their ticket, and the man disappeared inside.

"So Olivia's editor and agent were both hounding her for her book proposal," Lance said as they waited.

"Yes." Inside the garage was colder than the street. Morgan shivered. "Kim looked upset."

"She said she'd been sick."

"That would explain her dark circles," Morgan agreed. "But her nails were bitten to the quick, and she was picking at them when she admitted pressuring Olivia."

"Maybe she regrets giving Olivia a hard time."

Once they were in the vehicle, Lance turned the heater on full and aimed the vents at her.

Morgan pulled out her notepad. She wrote a few notes on the interview with Holgersen, then moved on to scan the editor's background report. "Olivia's editor, Jake Riley, is thirty-four. He was born in New York, went to college in New York, and currently lives in Brooklyn." She plugged the address into the GPS for directions.

It took thirty-five minutes to drive the nine miles through Lower Manhattan and over the Brooklyn Bridge. On the other side, Lance cut off a taxi with a feral smile, then continued onto Middagh Street into Brooklyn Heights.

Morgan pointed to an upcoming intersection. "There's the street on the left."

Lance turned left and slowed down in front of an old brownstone. "Keep your eyes open for a parking spot."

They drove around three blocks, like a shark circling for prey, before Morgan spotted a space. Lance parallel parked the Jeep, practically kissing the bumper of a MINI Cooper.

They walked back to the brownstone, and Lance led the way up the stone steps to the front stoop. He pulled on the handle of the double doors, but they were locked. Morgan shaded her eyes and peered through the glass panes. The building had a tiny foyer with a staircase running up one side. The paint was peeling, and the dark stain of the wooden steps and banister was worn through.

"It's a walk-up." She saw a resident carrying what looked like a racing bike down the steps. He wore an aerodynamic helmet and skintight cycling clothes. She backed up to scan the call buttons next to the door. There were eight apartments listed, two per floor. Morgan pressed the button for 4-B.

The cyclist opened the door.

Lance grabbed the handle and held it open while the man tipped the bike onto its rear tire and maneuvered it outside. It sounded like he was wearing tap shoes. "Thanks. Who are you looking for?"

"Jake Riley in 4-B," Morgan said with a smile.

The man shook his head. "He's not home. Haven't seen him much lately. Try Riley's Place." He gave them directions. "It's only about a half mile. You can walk from here." His shoes clicked on the concrete as he lifted the bike down the steps, set it on the road, and pedaled off.

Morgan and Lance followed his vague directions and walked up Hicks Street to Atlantic Avenue. The sun came out from behind the clouds, and unlike in Manhattan, its warm rays actually reached the street in Brooklyn.

Ten minutes later, they approached Riley's Place, which appeared to be a dive bar. They passed the narrow alley that ran next to the building.

"Morgan." Lance stared down the alley.

In the back, the front end of an old black muscle car stuck out from behind a dumpster.

"Hold on." Lance jogged down the alley and back. His eyes were bright. "It's a Chevy Nova."

"It was Olivia's editor who knocked on her door Thursday evening." Excitement flushed warmth through Morgan. Could this be the lead they'd been looking for?

Lance nodded. "It's only a three-hour drive."

They walked to the door of the bar.

Morgan glanced at her watch. "It's ten thirty. I don't see the hours posted. Do you think they're open?"

Lance looked through the glass. "I see people at the bar."

"Kind of early."

"Hard-core," he agreed.

Inside was dark, and the floor felt vaguely sticky underfoot. The wooden bar formed a letter *J*. A dozen tables were lined up along the wall. An upright piano was squeezed into the space between the bar and the doorway that led to the restrooms and back office.

Despite the early hour, several people sat on wooden stools, lifting tumblers of amber-colored liquid. The bartender dried glasses with a towel at the back. Morgan headed for him. Some of the attention that turned on her felt inexplicably hostile. As if he sensed it too, Lance deftly slid around her to place himself between Morgan and the patrons, as usual.

The bartender set the glass on the bar. "What do you want?"

"We're looking for Jake Riley." Morgan smiled.

The bartender didn't return the pleasantry. "You look like a lawyer."

He said the word *lawyer* as if it were synonymous with Satan.

Morgan glanced down. Her suit and heels were not the sort of attire she'd normally wear to a dive bar. But then, she'd expected to interview a literary agent and a book editor. Professional attire had seemed best.

"I *am* a lawyer." She slid a business card across the bar. "I just want to talk to Mr. Riley."

The bartender's gaze dropped to her card for two seconds. "I ain't seen him."

A footstep scuffed on the hardwood to Morgan's right. Next to her, Lance stiffened, and she turned her head. An old man stood in the doorway between the back rooms and the bar. Artificial light from the room behind him fell on the shotgun he pointed at Morgan and Lance.

Chapter Twenty-Six

Sweat trickled down Lance's back. The old man with the shotgun was swaying like a maple tree in a nor'easter. The old guy was bald and pale, with sunken eyes that suggested a terrible sickness. Jeans and a sweatshirt bagged on his skeletal frame.

"What do you want?" He stepped closer. The fingers that clutched the gun were as thin as talons. "To serve me with another subpoena?"

"No. We just came here to talk." Lance raised his hands, simultaneously sliding his shoulder in front of Morgan. But he didn't dare step in front of her for fear of setting off the old man. He debated pulling his own weapon. But he couldn't clear the holster faster than the old man could pull the trigger. The guy looked desperate and shaky, not a stable combination. Lance couldn't take the chance. A handgun wasn't accurate outside of eight or ten feet, but a shotgun at that range was deadly.

Morgan held her hands in front of her chest, palms out, in the classic *hands up* position.

A younger man hurried through the doorway behind him. "Dad! Put that down."

"No." The old man gestured toward Lance and Morgan with the gun barrel. "I won't have one more fucking lawyer trying to get a piece of us. I'm dying, for crying out loud. I don't have anything to lose."

Lance shifted an inch sideways, putting more of his body in front of Morgan.

"Dad, come on." The younger man put his hands over his father's and tipped the barrel of the shotgun to the floor. Then he gently eased it away. He ducked into the back room and reappeared a few seconds later without the shotgun.

Lance glanced at Morgan. She lowered her hands. Behind her, the patrons shot them disapproving frowns.

"Can't you people just leave them alone?" the bartender snapped. "Can't you wait until he's in the ground to take his bar?"

"We're not here to take the bar," Morgan said softly.

"Are you from the bank?" the younger man asked.

Morgan shook her head. "We don't know what you're talking about."

The younger guy seemed more exhausted and frustrated than hostile, but Lance kept his body between him and Morgan just in case.

But Morgan stepped in front, offering the younger guy her business card. "I'm Morgan Dane, and this is my associate Lance Kruger. We're looking for Jake Riley."

The young man took the card and read it. "Which Jake Riley, junior or senior?"

"The book editor," Morgan clarified.

"That's me." The tension in Jake's shoulders eased. "I'm a junior." The young man reached for his father's arm. "Come on, Dad. Let's get you back to bed."

"No." His father jerked his arm away. Then he sagged and collapsed onto the piano bench. "Buddy! Pour me a whiskey."

The younger man frowned. "Dad, you can't—"

"Don't tell me what I can and can't do. I'm gonna die no matter what." The old man plinked at a few keys, then spread his hands over the keyboard. His hands trembled too hard to play. "I just want five fucking minutes of normal."

The bartender poured two fingers of amber liquid into a tumbler and set it on the bar. The old man pushed himself off the piano bench and shuffled to a stool. He eased onto it and pulled the glass closer, his shoulders slumping over his whiskey. His eyes closed as he sipped. He swallowed, coughed, and set down the tumbler. "Son of a bitch. Can't play my piano. Can't drink my whiskey. Might as well kill me now." He took another sip, this time barely wetting his lips. "That's better." He eyed Morgan and Lance. "You're not here from the bank?"

"No, sir." Lance walked over to the piano and sat down.

"May I use the restroom?" Morgan asked.

Jake gestured to the doorway at the back of the bar, and Morgan walked through it.

Lance stretched his fingers over the keyboard. "I'm a little rusty, but . . ." He started into the opening notes of "Piano Man." He hadn't touched a piano in six months, not since his house and the piano in it had burned to the ground. But he'd played most of his life. Music calmed him. It helped him think. And during all the stressful years after his father's disappearance, it had been his escape. Maybe someday he'd figure out a way to squeeze one into Morgan's house. Sophie had showed interest—and talent.

Twenty seconds into the song, muscle memory took over, and his fingers sorted themselves out. He started singing without thinking, and for the next few minutes, he lost himself in the song.

Morgan returned as the final notes faded. The old man finished his whiskey and set the glass down on the bar with a solid thunk. "You wouldn't want to come and do that Friday and Saturday nights, would you?"

Lance shook his head. "Sorry. Just a hobby for me."

"Ah, it was worth a shot." The old man shrugged.

His son scanned the line of patrons watching them and listening to their conversation. "Let me grab my jacket. We can talk outside."

He took a jacket from behind the bar and led them to the door. They walked out into the sunlight. Lance, still sweating from the shotgun incident, removed his jacket.

"Thanks for that. I haven't seen him that relaxed in a long time." Jake leaned on the brick exterior wall and lit a cigarette. "You'd think watching my father die of lung cancer would encourage me to quit. Maybe when he's gone, I'll be able to."

"I'm sorry your father is sick." Morgan shoved her hands into the pockets of her wool jacket.

"He has two months, at best." Jake sighed. "This place isn't much, but it's all he has left. It's what got him through my mother's death. It's what's getting him through his own. After he's gone, the lenders can have the fucking bar. I don't want it." He took an angry drag of his cigarette, then sighed again.

"I saw the Nova out back. Sweet car. Is it yours?" Lance asked.

Jake shook his head. "Belongs to our bartender."

Convenient, thought Lance. "We're here to ask you about Olivia Cruz."

Jake sucked in another lungful of smoke. "What now?"

"She's missing." Lance watched him for a reaction.

Jake flicked ashes off the end of his smoke. "How do you know?"

"She hasn't been seen since Thursday evening," Morgan explained. "She isn't answering her cell phone or returning messages. We're concerned."

"I wouldn't be too alarmed." Jake sounded irritated. "Olivia isn't exactly prompt with returning messages. Maybe she's just avoiding you."

"Has she been avoiding *you*?" Lance asked.

Jake didn't answer the question, but Lance saw the flash of truth in his eyes.

Jake exhaled a plume of smoke. "I'm not going to give out personal information on her just because you say you're looking for her."

"I understand your hesitation." Morgan moved her head to avoid the trail of smoke. "In fact, I applaud your commitment to client confidentiality, but her family and friends are worried about her."

"I still can't tell you anything." Jake lifted a palm. "And Thursday evening was only a few days ago. Maybe she just went somewhere. She's a grown woman. She doesn't have to report her every move to her family."

"But this isn't typical behavior for Olivia." Morgan's voice grew firm. "She missed her mother's doctor's appointment."

"Look, I have family too." Jake's gaze shot to his father. Through the glass door, they could see him laughing with his buddies at the other end of the bar. "But I don't share my daily calendar. Have you thought that Olivia could have forgotten the appointment? No one's perfect. It's also possible she simply left town to get away from her stress and all those people asking for things she isn't delivering."

Lance waved smoke out of his face. "Why would you say that?"

Jake dragged on his cigarette. The embers burned almost to the filter. "I can't tell you."

"We talked to her agent," Lance said. "She told us Olivia was late with her proposal."

Jake's lip curled. "Her agent isn't any help. Holgersen has always hustled for her clients. She's pushy and demanding when *she* wants something for her authors but has no consideration for anyone else. Since her husband left her, she's gone full bitch. She told me to leave Olivia alone, and then she had the nerve to ride me about contracts for two other authors she reps. The gossip mill says her divorce is getting nasty and she needs money. Whatever the reason, she couldn't care less about me."

Because her job is to further her clients' interests, not yours.

"Did Olivia ever mention that she was concerned about her safety?" Morgan asked. "Or anything that had worried her about her current research?"

"Has she been reported as missing? Are the police involved?" Jake challenged.

"Yes." Morgan nodded. "You can speak with Detective Stella Dane with the Scarlet Falls Police Department. Would you like the phone number?"

"Um. No." He paused, as if he was searching for words. "That won't be necessary." He dropped his cigarette and ground the butt beneath his heel. "If the police want to talk to me, they can pay me a visit." He shot them both dirty looks. "Not a lawyer and a PI."

"You were seen knocking on Olivia's door Thursday evening," Morgan bluffed. Technically, the Nova had been seen. They couldn't prove the blond man driving it had been Jake. Olivia's neighbor hadn't seen his face.

Jake froze. "I'm not admitting anything. But bonus time is coming up and having another big deal to take to the acquisitions committee would help." He studied his shoes. "Money is tight. I'm running the bar and doing my own job. I don't have time to discover the next great author."

"So you went to her house?" Lance leaned closer. He wanted a damn confession.

"If she called me back, I wouldn't have had to," Jake snapped. He closed his mouth abruptly, as if realizing he had just admitted being at Olivia's house. "Look, she didn't answer her door, and I realized how stupid and inappropriate it was for me to be there. I turned around and drove home."

"What time did you get back?" Morgan asked.

"Around midnight," Jake said. "The bartender will vouch for me. I borrowed his car."

Or he'll lie for you.

"If you find her, tell her to return my calls. I have to go." Jake turned and disappeared into the bar.

Morgan frowned at the closed door. "Do you think he'll call Stella?"

"I doubt it." Lance turned away from the bar. "He sounded surprised that the police were involved, but he didn't think Olivia being out of touch for a couple of days was a big deal. He clearly thinks she skipped town to avoid her responsibilities."

"And he's angry at her for avoiding him. Now that we know about the Nova, maybe Stella will come and see him or get a local cop to talk to him." Morgan slid her hand through Lance's arm. "While you were playing the piano, I might have checked the back room and the apartment upstairs. There was no sign of Olivia anywhere."

Lance looked down at her. "You broke the law?"

"Not really." Her lips twisted. "The apartment was open, and he gave me permission to use the restroom. He didn't specify *which* restroom."

"That's a load of bullshit." He laughed. "You entered a personal residence without permission." Lance wrapped an arm around her shoulders and squeezed her biceps. "That's kind of hot."

Morgan rolled her eyes. "You think everything is hot."

He leaned close to her ear. "Only everything *you* do."

Morgan shook her head. Then she paused midstep and inhaled. "I smell food."

"It's only eleven."

She shoved her hands into her pockets. "I'm hungry. I need extra food to compensate for the lack of sleep."

"If we get sandwiches to eat on the way home, we won't have to stop."

They walked to a bagel place down the block and ordered sandwiches to go. Morgan added cookies, coffee, and a dozen bagels to the order.

"Bagels?"

"For Grandpa." Morgan collected the bag of bagels and her coffee from the counter. "He says bagels from anywhere other than New York City aren't real bagels."

Lance paid and accepted the sandwich bag from the clerk. They carried the white take-out bags back to the Jeep. By eleven thirty, Morgan and Lance buckled into the vehicle.

Lance unwrapped his sandwich on his lap. "What do you think of what we learned today?"

Morgan sipped her coffee. "Olivia kept her work close. No one knew what she was working on. Both her agent and her editor were pressuring her for her new book information."

"Olivia's lack of response is creating problems for her editor at the publishing company. And he's already under an enormous strain with his father's illness and financial situation."

"Definitely." Morgan wiped her mouth with a napkin. "Jake Riley needs money, he was at Olivia's house the evening before she disappeared, and his stress level is through the roof."

"But what would kidnapping Olivia accomplish?"

"I don't know."

"Maybe he pressured her for the proposal and lost control," Lance said. "He's angry and desperate."

Maybe he accidentally killed her.

"Maybe," Morgan agreed. "According to Jake, Kim needs money, but again, it seems like she would need Olivia alive and well to bring in more income."

"There could be something we're not seeing." Lance took a bite of his sandwich.

Morgan stuffed her used napkin inside the empty paper bag. "While you drive home, I'll search tax records and see if I can find any other properties owned by either Jake or his father."

Lance backed up the Jeep as far as he could without hitting the vehicle behind him. Then he pulled away from the curb and headed for the Brooklyn Bridge. Jake's or Kim's possible motivation might be unclear, but a desperate need for money had driven people to do some very bad things.

Chapter Twenty-Seven

Light streamed through the window and fell across his bed. Sharp reached for Olivia. He could almost feel the silkiness of her shining dark hair. But his hand fell on an empty pillow. The past couple of days came flooding back. He wanted to go back to his dream state and pretend she was with him. To drag her out of bed for a morning run. Or even better, to tuck her against him and spend the next hour making love to her.

But he could do none of those things.

She was gone.

He rolled over and pressed his face into her pillow. She only slept at his apartment once a week, but his pillow smelled like her. The faint citrus scent of her shampoo filled his nose, clogged his throat, and opened up the hollow ache around his heart.

I have to find her.

He simply could not consider a future in which Olivia was not part of his life. Before this week, he'd been more concerned with easing into any commitment. Now he realized all that posturing had been a huge waste of time.

Time he could have spent getting to know her better.

Time he might not get back.

What would he do if he never found her? Or if he did and she was—

With his years as a detective, he understood the odds of bringing her home alive and well were slipping through his fingers like drops of water. Missing persons reports and autopsy photos played a slideshow in his head.

Too many.

When he'd been a patrol officer, he'd performed death notifications after vehicle accidents. He'd thought that was the worst duty. Then Lance's father had gone missing, and Sharp had learned that *not knowing*—that never being able to give a family closure—could be just as devastating. Lance and his mother had lived with not knowing what had happened to Vic Kruger for twenty-three years. Sorrow had gnawed at their hope over those decades, until nothing had been left but grief. Lance had moved on, mostly, but Jenny had burrowed into her pain.

Until today, Sharp had not appreciated the depth of the emotional damage *not knowing* could inflict. But he also couldn't imagine learning Olivia *was* dead. Or seeing her naked and bruised body on an autopsy table in the morgue. His imagination superimposed Olivia's face on victims he had watched being autopsied during his police career. He could smell formalin in his nose, taste decaying flesh in the back of his throat, see organs being lifted from the open abdominal cavity, hear the sound of the bone saw cutting the skull.

He blinked the image away. He needed to get back to the investigation. Letting his brain wander was dangerous. He'd seen too much—knew too much—to deny the possible outcomes. His mind needed to be busy.

At the moment, he'd rather have hope, even if it was dimming by the hour.

The pity party won't bring her home. Get a grip and get crackin'.

Sharp turned away from Olivia's pillow, sat up, and swung his feet over the side of the bed. A glance at his phone told him Lance and Stella had left messages for him—and that it was just nearly two o'clock in the afternoon. He'd slept for six hours.

After turning the case over in his mind for several hours, he'd stretched out for a short nap, and he'd slept right through his phone alerts.

He checked the messages. Neither were urgent. Lance and Morgan were on their way back. Stella was attending Olander's autopsy. She promised to touch base with Sharp afterward.

Grogginess and depression weighted his head as he rose. He needed to get his shit together. He took a cold shower to clear his head. While he was shaving, his phone beeped with a text from Stella. She would pick him up in ten minutes. He wiped the remaining shaving cream from his face and brushed his teeth. After he'd dressed, he almost felt human.

He grabbed two protein bars from his kitchen and went downstairs to the office, leaving the back door unlocked for Stella.

She walked into his office a few minutes later, carrying two take-out cups of coffee. She offered one to him. "I know you don't normally drink coffee, but I thought you might need the energy."

"Thank you." Sharp took the cup. "Rough morning?" Sharp opened a protein bar and sat in his chair. Opening his laptop, he waited for it to boot up.

Stella eased into one of the chairs that faced his desk. "I hate autopsies."

The image of Olivia's naked and gray body on a stainless-steel table punched through Sharp's mental barrier again. He set the bar on his desk and forced down a mouthful of coffee. Bitterness coated his throat and unsettled his stomach. He set down the cup and stood. "I'm getting some water. Do you want anything?"

Stella shook her head.

When he returned with the water, he sat back down and braced himself. "How did Olander's autopsy go?"

"The ME officially declared his death a murder. In addition to the ligature marks and torn nails, blood and tissue were found embedded in the noose. Olander had defensive bruises on his arms. He'd also suffered from repeated blows to the abdomen and several broken ribs."

"They beat him."

"Yes." Stella rose and paced, coffee in hand. "But why? Was it punishment? Or did they want information from him?"

"I don't know."

Sharp's phone buzzed. He read the screen. "It's Ryan Abrams at the ATF." He answered the call. "Thanks for the call back, Ryan. Detective Stella Dane from the SFPD is with me. She's working a murder case related to the guns. Can I put you on speaker?"

"Yes," Ryan said.

Sharp switched the call. "Did you find anything for us?"

"Yes, I did." Ryan exhaled. "I didn't find anything on Kennett Olander in New York State, but I found old records from Iowa that associate Kennett's father with the LMS, a national anti-government militia group."

"What does LMS stand for?" Sharp asked.

"Last Men Standing," Ryan said.

Sharp took out a pen and paper for notes. "Where do they operate?"

"They're a large group, with several thousand members," Ryan answered. "They prefer rural areas, specifically farms and big patches of wilderness." Papers rustled on Ryan's end of the connection. "We've uncovered members in fifteen states. It's a quiet organization. For the most part, they go about their business."

"Which is?" Stella asked.

"Mostly, they stockpile food, fuel, guns, and medicine to get them through an end-of-days scenario. They run survival retreats and military-style training camps. Members blog and use social media accounts to compare survival tips and techniques. They pop onto the scene every few years when a member gets caught buying or carrying guns illegally.

We've arrested a handful of members for possession of illegal weapons. The LMS doesn't believe in registering guns with the government, so their offenses vary according to local laws."

Every state had different gun laws. In most of New York State, long guns did not need to be registered, and no permit was required to purchase one. But handguns were highly regulated.

Sharp said, "Olander had a stash of illegally equipped AR-15s, ammunition, and some body armor."

"Sounds like his farm is being used as a storage facility," Ryan said. "Did you take pictures of the guns?"

"No." Sharp gave himself a mental kick in the ass.

"Are the LMS involved in money laundering?" Sharp wondered if the Olanders' association with the militia group explained the cash purchase of the dairy farm.

"We think so," Ryan said. "They keep their operations small and spread them out, so they don't draw attention to their activities."

"Kennett Olander was found hanging from his barn rafters yesterday," Stella said.

Ryan whistled. "Suicide?"

"No," Stella answered. "Murder. And the guns have disappeared."

"He pissed off somebody," Ryan said.

Sharp tapped his fingers on his desk. "You said the LMS works hard to stay off your radar? What did you mean by that?"

"Rather than living in large easy-to-find compounds, they spread their resources and people out," Ryan explained. "Even if we uncover one site, we only find a small portion of their armaments, and they utilize the Dark web for activities they want to keep secret."

There were three levels of the internet: the Surface web, the Deep web, and the Dark web. The Surface web was the normal searchable internet most people accessed every day. The Deep web was a layer of the internet that couldn't be accessed through search engines. Most of these sites were legitimate, such as online bank accounts that required registrations, logins, and passwords to protect customer information. But users of the Dark web purposely hid their identities and spoofed their locations with encryption tools. The anonymous nature of the Dark web made it the ideal tool for criminal activity.

Sharp had encountered a local militia group in a previous case. "How many militias can operate in one area?" he asked.

"The number of anti-government militia groups has doubled over the past decade. A few individuals in the LMS have been convicted of weapons offenses, and several members have gone missing or turned up dead. But we haven't been able to prove the organization orchestrated any of these crimes. LMS discourages members from drawing too much attention to themselves or to the group. On the surface, they're all about education and survival training."

"Can't you follow the money?" asked Sharp.

"They used to run their money through the Caymans and Swiss banks, but international banking laws have changed. It's harder to hide funds these days. We now believe they buy and use legitimate businesses to cover their activities. As I said before, they make a serious effort to stay off the radar of law enforcement."

"Would having your son convicted of murdering his wife annoy the group leadership?" Sharp asked.

"That's exactly the kind of attention they *don't* want," Ryan agreed.

Sharp gave Ryan the basic details of Erik's murder conviction. "Is that enough to earn a death sentence from the group leadership?"

Ryan paused. "I don't think so. I feel like there should be more. Guns, money, serious betrayal."

"We don't know how all of this might be connected to our missing reporter," Stella said. "I'd like to send you a list of the people involved in this case and see if you recognize any of their names."

"Sure," Ryan said.

"Thank you." Stella's phone rang. She excused herself and left Sharp's office to answer the call.

Ryan continued, "As I said, we've had suspected members turn up dead, but we've never been able to trace the killings back to anyone in the group."

"What if a member wants out of the organization?" Sharp asked.

Ryan sighed. "With some of these organizations, there's only one way out."

"And Olander found it," Sharp said. "Thanks for your help, Ry."

"Anytime. I'm going to do some more digging and see what I can come up with," Ryan said. "I'd love a solid lead on this group if they're dealing in illegal weapons."

"You'll call me or Stella if you find anything?" Sharp asked.

"I will," Ryan promised.

Sharp disconnected. He looked up to see that Stella had walked back into his office. She was staring at him, grim-faced.

His heart stuttered, and his stomach curled up in a defensive ball. "What?"

"Olivia's car was spotted about twenty minutes from here."

Sharp jumped to his feet. "Where? Is she in the car?"

Stella held up one hand. "They don't know yet. It's in a ravine."

He felt the blood drain from his face, leaving him light-headed. A moment later, Stella was holding his arm, but he hadn't noticed her walk closer.

Had Olivia been in a ravine, dead, for the past two and a half days? Could she be alive? People had survived longer. So many thoughts, hopeful and dire, ricocheted through his head. Sharp could barely form questions.

He sputtered, "What condition is the car in?"

"I don't know." Stella shook her head. "I spoke to the state trooper on scene. They can only see the rear bumper. It looks like the car went off the road just before the bridge. The trooper was driving by, noticed snapped saplings, and pulled over. The incline is steep and covered with trees and brush. They're going to need rappelling gear to get down to the car."

Sharp headed for the door on shaky legs.

Stella lifted his jacket from his coat hook and handed it to him. "Why don't you call Lance and let him know?"

He nodded. His throat felt rusty, and he couldn't form words. In silence, he put on his jacket. Adrenaline pumped through his system, and his pulse felt thin and too quick. Nausea churned in his empty belly as he led the way out of the building and locked the back door. In the passenger seat of Stella's cop car, he used his phone app to engage the office security system. He performed these functions on automatic pilot. His brain was consumed with only one train of thought.

In what condition would they find Olivia?

His thumb sat poised over the buttons to call Lance. It felt stupid, but he hoped Lance could get to the crash site. He was the closest thing Sharp had to family.

In thirty minutes, would he know whether she was alive or dead? And would he then wish he didn't know?

What if not knowing *was* better?

Stella had her radio turned low. He stared out the windshield and listened to the soft chatter. She drove out of town and picked up speed on the interstate. He wanted her to drive faster, but at the same time, he didn't.

Because most of all, he was dreading arriving on scene in time to identify Olivia's dead body.

Chapter Twenty-Eight

Lance pulled over behind two state trooper vehicles and Stella's dark-blue cop car. "I don't even know what to hope for."

"Neither do I." In the passenger seat of the Jeep, Morgan exchanged her heels for the flats from her giant bag. "What could this mean?"

"I don't know. Let's wait and see what we find in the car." He glanced at her. She was shivering. "There's a warmer jacket in the back."

They'd been close to Scarlet Falls when Sharp had called. Lance had changed course to head west toward the crash site. Then he'd pushed the Jeep to ninety.

They climbed out of the Jeep. Morgan opened the hatch and exchanged her wool jacket for his heavier coat. It was wind- and water-proof. She pulled gloves from one pocket and a hat from the other.

Lance spotted Sharp and Stella behind the ambulance and hurried over. Sharp's face was as white as the line running down the shoulder of the road. Stella introduced the two troopers. Lance didn't catch their names. He was focused on Sharp—his pallor and the darkness swirling behind his gray eyes. Then Lance moved to the side of the road and looked over the edge.

He tracked a line of broken underbrush and small trees. At least forty feet down, a white car was ass end up. The vehicle appeared to have been stopped by a stand of large trees. The first half of the descent was steep, but then the slope dropped straight down for the last twenty-five feet. They definitely needed rappelling equipment.

Could anyone have survived that crash?

"We just got here a few minutes ago," Stella said. "A fire crew is en route with rescue gear."

Trooper One said, "ETA is ten minutes."

Sharp pointed toward the ravine. "That's my girlfriend's vehicle. I'm not waiting. I'm going down." He moved away from the group. He turned to Lance. "You have rope in your Jeep?"

"I do." Lance pivoted. There was no changing Sharp's mind. If it had been Morgan's car in that ravine, nothing could have stopped Lance from climbing down. Nothing. But he wasn't going to let any harm come to Sharp either. "I'm going down with you."

"Thanks."

Lance opened the cargo area of his Jeep. He kept his vehicle stocked with emergency supplies, and this was not the first time he'd needed to use them. He handed a coil of nylon rope and a carabiner to Sharp and set the same aside for himself.

Starting with the midpoint on his left side, Sharp fed the rope around his waist, between his legs, and around both thighs, forming a half hitch on each hip. He tied the rope off with a few more knots on his left side, away from his dominant or brake hand, giving him an emergency rappel harness, also known as a Swiss Seat. He attached a carabiner to the front of the makeshift harness.

Lance followed suit. He slung two more sections of rope over one shoulder. Sharp returned to the group, and Lance backed the Jeep closer to the ravine. With no tall trees on the side of the road, they tied their ropes to the tow bar on the back of the Jeep.

They picked their way around rocks, brush, and tree trunks, then paused at the top of the drop-off. From this angle, Lance had a better view of the vehicle. "The car isn't at the bottom. Those trees are keeping it from sliding any farther."

Sharp looked over his shoulder. "The clearest path is on the driver's side."

"Right," Lance said. "We don't want to land on the vehicle in case our weight makes it fall the rest of the way to the bottom."

Another twenty-foot drop could kill anyone who might still be alive inside.

"Watch the broken trees." Lance went over the edge backward, letting out his rope slowly, making his way down the ravine. Sharp descended next to him. They stopped parallel to the car. The roof was partially caved in, and the exterior badly dented and damaged. Spider cracks and holes covered the windshield. The driver's door hung open. Lance stopped, bracing his foot on a tree root, to lean out and peer into the vehicle. The driver's seat was empty.

"She's not in the front," Lance said.

Broken glass and debris filled the inside of the car. The airbag had deployed and deflated. Despite the damage, the interior of the vehicle remained intact.

Sharp stared down at the ravine floor. "The occupants could have been ejected in the crash or fell or climbed down afterward."

"It's possible." Lance looked for blood on the seat, steering wheel, and dashboard. "I don't see any blood in the car. I would expect to see some blood if a person rode this car all the way down that slope."

Sharp nodded. "Maybe whoever was driving got lucky."

"Maybe." But Lance doubted it. Even restrained by a seat belt, a person would have been banged up in that crash.

"The driver would have been hanging by the seat belt. The belt wasn't cut. It wouldn't have been easy to get out of it and the vehicle."

"No." Sharp paused. "We've already decided Olivia was kidnapped from her house."

"We could have been wrong about her being put in the cargo area. Maybe he sat in the back and forced her to drive at gunpoint." Lance scanned the car. "Or she somehow caused the driver to crash the car."

Sharp scanned the inside of the vehicle. "I really think there should be blood."

"Maybe no one was inside the vehicle." As Lance considered the interior, this seemed the most likely scenario. "The car could have been pushed off the road to dispose of it."

Sharp dropped a few feet. "I'm going to the bottom."

Lance followed him to the ground and unclipped his carabiner, letting the rope dangle. At his feet was a side mirror ripped from the Prius. Pieces of broken red plastic, possibly from the brake light cover, were scattered on the ground. He looked up at the car precariously perched in the trees above them. The wall of the ravine was nearly vertical at the bottom, but there were some thin trees and brush protruding from the earth. But would they hold an adult's weight?

Lance took out his cell phone and sent Morgan a text: No Olivia. Checking ravine.

"I'll go this way." Sharp headed south.

Lance went in the opposite direction. He kept his eyes on the ground, looking for broken underbrush, footprints, drops of blood, scraps of fabric, anything that would suggest a wounded person walked that way. But he saw nothing. He traveled about a hundred feet and turned back.

Lance returned to the vehicle. He cupped his hands around his mouth and called out, "Sharp!"

"I'm coming," Sharp called and appeared two minutes later.

"The sooner we climb back up, the sooner the troopers can organize a search. I didn't see any tracks, but it's still possible."

Sharp nodded. "I didn't see anything either. I don't know whether to be relieved or not."

"I know." Lance started climbing. The trip to the top took longer than the descent had. By the time they reached the road, an ambulance, fire truck, and tow truck had arrived.

They relayed their findings to the responders and stepped aside while the firemen and tow truck driver discussed extracting the Prius from the ravine. Lance stepped out of his Swiss Seat. Sharp did the same. They stood on the side of the road.

Sharp gestured to the ribbon of blacktop. "There aren't any skid marks. If I were driving toward the edge of the road, I'd lay on the brakes."

"Me too," Lance agreed.

"I think you're right. No one was in the car, and whoever took Olivia pushed it off the road."

Morgan brought Lance and Sharp bottles of water from the Jeep. Sweat coated Lance's chest after the climb. The exertion had put some color into Sharp's cheeks, but his eyes were lost.

Morgan's phone rang. She stepped away to answer the call.

"What did you find out in the city?" Sharp asked.

Lance summed up their interviews with Olivia's agent and editor. "The editor was the man who visited Olivia Thursday night. But even if we could weaken his alibi, Morgan couldn't locate a property owned by him or his father. Olivia wasn't at the bar, and it seems unlikely he could hold a woman captive in a fourth-floor walk-up."

"What is our most likely lead?" Sharp asked. "Joe Franklin is the only person we haven't been able to question."

Morgan hurried across the pavement, her mouth set in a grim line. "Gianna is really sick. Grandpa was worried enough to call Mac and have him take her to the ER."

Stella approached, took one look at her sister's face, and asked, "What's wrong?"

Morgan explained.

Stella had known Gianna before Morgan. More than two years before, Gianna had overdosed. Stella had saved her with a dose of

Narcan. But the young woman's kidneys had suffered irreversible damage.

"I'm going to the hospital now." Morgan turned to Lance, her brows raised in question. "You can stay with Sharp."

"Go, take care of Gianna." Stella waved them away. "I'll take Sharp back to the office later. I'm sure he wants to stay here until we pull the car out of the ravine."

"I do." Sharp's eyes were dark. Was he thinking of Lance's father, whose car had spent twenty-three years on the bottom of a lake? When it was finally discovered and pulled out, they'd found a skeleton in the trunk. Sharp would want to examine the vehicle more closely. Sharp turned to Lance and said, "You go with Morgan. Gianna is part of your new family. They need you."

Morgan was already striding toward the Jeep.

"I'll drive Morgan to the hospital and come back for you." Lance fished his keys from his pocket and pointed at Sharp. "Promise me you won't go to Joe Franklin's place without calling me."

"OK." Sharp held up both hands in surrender. "I promise. Recovering the Prius isn't going to be quick or easy. We'll be tied up here for hours anyway."

Lance turned and jogged away.

"Call me when you have news about Gianna!" Stella called after him.

Lance waved over one shoulder. He ran to the Jeep and climbed behind the wheel.

Morgan fastened her seat belt and white-knuckled the armrests. "I should have insisted she go to the doctor yesterday."

"People get sick. It's not always serious. I'm sure your grandfather was just being cautious. She could have a simple virus. As soon as school starts, one of the kids always seems to have a runny nose." Lance pressed the gas pedal and hoped he was right.

Chapter Twenty-Nine

Morgan jumped out of the Jeep in the ER parking lot. Not waiting for Lance, she hurried across the pavement. Lance caught up before she reached the entrance.

"Hold up." He grabbed her arm.

Distressed, she whirled and shook off his hand. "What?"

"Take a deep breath. You will scare Gianna if she sees you like this."

"Grandpa doesn't panic. If he sent Gianna to the ER, it's serious." Morgan brushed her hair out of her eyes. Her stomach was clenched into a tight fist. Emotions swirled inside her, fear and guilt tumbling over and over until she couldn't tell them apart.

She should have been paying better attention. Dialysis put Gianna at risk for complications from illnesses that were mild for most people. But Gianna's overall health had improved so much since she'd come to live with Morgan that they'd all become complacent.

Lance put his hands on her biceps. "Just take three deep breaths, and then we'll go inside."

She inhaled. The chilly air cooled her.

"Better." He squeezed her arms, then dropped his hands.

Morgan faced the doors. She reached for Lance's hand and held it. The automatic doors swished open, and they walked into the waiting room side by side. She scanned the room. No Mac or Gianna. They walked up to the registration desk and gave the nurse Gianna's name.

The nurse checked her computer. "She's in bed number seven. You can go on through."

She pointed to a set of double doors. When Morgan and Lance approached, the doors swung open. Gurneys were lined up in curtained-off bays like cars in an auto shop.

Morgan spotted number seven and hurried over. Mac sat on a folding chair, but the bay was empty. Morgan's stomach turned over. "Where is she?"

Mac stood. "They took her for some tests. She'll be back soon."

"How bad is she?" Morgan gave him a quick hug.

Mac frowned. "She spiked a fever this afternoon, and your grandfather didn't like the way she looked."

"He has good judgment." Morgan checked the hallway. No Gianna yet.

"The doctor thinks her dialysis graft could be infected." Mac swept a hand through his shaggy surfer hair. A biology professor at the local university, he spent a good deal of time outdoors and volunteered with search and rescue. He was perpetually tan.

Lance shook Mac's hand. "Thanks for bringing her."

"I'm glad to help." Mac gestured toward the chair. "Why don't you sit down, Morgan? You look tired."

She shook her head and paced. "I assumed she'd caught a cold. I should never assume anything with Gianna. She's been so normal, sometimes I forget how sick she is."

"They didn't rush her into ICU or anything," Mac said. "The doctor isn't panicking, so relax."

But Morgan worried. Before Gianna had come to live with her, no one had cared about the girl. Her mother had been a prostitute who had started her daughter hooking at age thirteen. Gianna's mother was currently in jail for cooking meth. The girl had never had a father in her life. Coming to live with Morgan was the first break Gianna had ever received.

The squeak of wheels caught Morgan's attention. An orderly was pushing a gurney down the hall. On it, Gianna huddled under a white thermal blanket. Morgan moved aside as the orderly turned the gurney into the bay.

Gianna was pale, with a feverish splotch of ruddy color on each cheek. Morgan used the hand sanitizer mounted on the wall, went to the bedside, and touched her forehead. Her skin was warm.

"I'm all right," Gianna said in a weak voice.

"Do you need anything right now?" the orderly asked.

Gianna shook her head.

"OK then. The doctor will be in soon." The orderly closed the curtain and left.

Morgan squeezed Gianna's fingers. "I'm sorry I wasn't home."

"You can't be everywhere." Gianna pulled herself a few inches up on the gurney.

"We should have gone to the doctor yesterday," Morgan said.

Gianna lifted her arm and frowned at it. The dialysis access site was normally a hard lump under the skin, but today it was swollen and red. "My arm didn't look like this yesterday, and I didn't have a fever. There was no reason to think it was anything serious."

"Hello?" The curtain swished aside, and a doctor in blue scrubs walked in. He introduced himself. "As I suspected when she first came in, her dialysis access is infected. We're going to schedule her for surgery to remove the infected graft. We're also putting her on IV antibiotics."

"How will she get dialysis without a graft?" Morgan asked.

He shone a penlight into Gianna's eyes. "We'll use a central venous catheter until the infection is cleared, and then the surgeon can decide where to place a new graft."

She'd need at least three surgeries just to get back to where she'd been before this weekend, and she'd have to live with a temporary catheter poking out of her chest for the next month or two. Gianna would never complain, but this had to be disappointing.

The doctor checked Gianna's vital signs. "Unfortunately, this is not uncommon." He patted Gianna's foot. "Are you OK?"

Gianna nodded.

"Do you have any questions?" he asked.

"No." She shook her head.

He checked her chart. "Your fever is down a few degrees. Did the acetaminophen also help the pain or do you need something stronger?"

She'd been in pain? She hadn't said a word.

Gianna shook her head vigorously. "I don't want anything stronger."

The doctor's brows rose.

"I was a heroin addict," Gianna said without blinking. "I've been clean for over two years. I won't take any risks. I'm on the transplant list. I won't do anything to hurt my chances of getting a new kidney."

"Good to know." The doctor opened a laptop on a wall-mounted shelf and typed. "I'll make a note. But if you are in pain, there are other options. You don't have to suffer."

Gianna nodded. "I'm OK for now."

He closed the laptop. "Then you hang tight until they find you a bed. No food or water. The surgeon wants to get that graft out tonight."

The doctor left. A few minutes later, a nurse came in and shooed everyone out of the room. "Give us ten minutes."

Morgan, Lance, and Mac withdrew to the waiting room.

"Where is she on the transplant list?" Mac asked.

"It's hard to say." Over the past year, Morgan had helped Gianna with her transplant application process and had become a minor expert in all things related to kidney failure. "Gianna has been on dialysis for a little over two years. The average wait for a kidney from a deceased donor is three to five years, at minimum."

"Shit," Mac said.

"Exactly." Morgan turned to Lance. "Are you going back to get Sharp?"

"I should. After the car is recovered, there's only so long he'll wait for Stella before he goes off on his own," Lance said. "I don't trust him to be careful. But the kids are a handful for your grandfather."

"I'll take care of the kids," Mac offered. "Stella won't be home anyway. She'll be working all night. The kids will be great company."

"Thank you, Mac." Morgan kissed him on the cheek.

"Hey, family is family," he said. "Tell Gianna I'll see her tomorrow. I'll grab a pizza for the kids."

Morgan thanked Mac again, and he walked away.

"Are you staying here?" Lance wrapped his arms around Morgan.

Morgan nodded, slipped her hands around his waist, and pressed the side of her face against his chest. "I'll stay with Gianna until she's out of surgery."

"Do you want me to get you anything from home?" Lance kissed the top of her head.

"No." She leaned back and patted her tote bag. "I have a toothbrush and change for the vending machine. That's all I need."

Sleeping in her clothes was going to start feeling normal.

His blue eyes were concerned. "I don't like splitting up, but there are only two of us."

"Thank goodness for Mac and Stella." Morgan pulled her hands free, then settled them on his broad chest. "I'll be fine here."

Lance held on, hooking his hands together behind her back. "What about Peyton and Ian? Could either one of them help out?"

Morgan's older brother was NYPD SWAT. Her younger sister was a forensic psychiatrist in California. "I'll give them both a call, but they have careers. They can't just drop everything to watch my kids. Besides, they both requested their vacation days to come for the wedding." Morgan paused. "Speaking of the wedding, maybe we should think about postponing it."

Disappointment flashed in Lance's eyes for just a second.

It had taken her a long time to put the grief over losing her first husband behind her and make room for Lance in her heart. He'd waited patiently for her to be ready. She'd been excited about the upcoming wedding. Everything had been going so well for them.

"It's not that I want to," she said. "I just . . ." She couldn't verbalize her emotions. "I don't want to go forward with our wedding if Gianna is in the hospital and Olivia is still missing or . . . worse."

"I know." He looked away. "And you're right."

"I don't want our anniversary to carry the weight of . . ." Morgan trailed off. She didn't want to say *Olivia's death.*

Lance nodded. "I know there's more at stake here than our wedding. Finding Olivia and getting Gianna healthy are more important. But I really want to marry you. Living together is great, but it's not enough for me."

She rose onto her toes and kissed him. "Maybe you'll find Olivia today, and Gianna will be fine. Then we won't have to cancel."

The look in his eyes was not a hopeful one. But he kissed her. "I love you. Wedding or no wedding."

"I love you too." She pressed her lips hard against his and hugged him, grateful to have him in her life. "It feels really selfish in light of everything else that's happening, but I'm disappointed. I was really looking forward to our wedding."

"Me too." He smiled sadly and cupped her jaw with one hand. "Call me if you need anything."

"I will." What Morgan needed was three clones of herself.

Lance's phone buzzed, and he read the screen. "Sharp wants to go talk to Joe Franklin. Stella just got called back to the station for a press conference."

"Be safe. Take care of Sharp—and yourself."

Chapter Thirty

"I'm not so sure this is a good idea," Lance said.

Sharp ignored him and got out of the Prius.

Lance followed, tugging his jacket over the butt of the Glock on his hip. The sun had set, and trees bowed over the narrow dirt lane, blocking the moon and casting them deeper in shadow. Cold wind shifted through the branches and rustled leaves overhead.

"He doesn't answer the gate intercom or his phone, and we need to talk to him." Sharp walked around the front of the Jeep and stared at the metal-and-wood gate that barred access to Joseph Franklin's property.

"This guy is serious about his privacy." Lance surveyed the dark woods. Joseph Franklin owned fifty heavily wooded acres.

"Yep." Sharp squeezed through a gap between the gate and fence post.

With a sigh, Lance followed him.

"We're just going to knock on the door." Sharp started up the driveway without hesitation. He was getting more desperate—and more reckless.

"It doesn't feel like a *knock on the door* type of place."

The driveway narrowed beyond the gate. Branches met over their heads and formed a tunnel of foliage. *It also feels like a trap.*

"Your mom said Joe Franklin is a game developer," Sharp said. "He's a nerd, not a member of any militia."

They rounded the curve and stopped.

"Not what I expected." Sharp stared ahead.

"Me neither."

Landscape lights brightened the property. Instead of a fortified cabin, the house was a three-story stone structure built to mimic an English manor. It looked like a drawing in one of the girls' fairy-tale books. In front of the stone steps, the driveway circled around an empty fountain.

Sharp nodded toward the house. "State-of-the-art satellite dish."

Lance saw brand-new surveillance cameras mounted under the crumbling eaves. "Cameras too."

"He'll know we were here." Sharp plowed forward. He jogged up the steps and pressed the doorbell. Nothing happened. Sharp rapped on the heavy door with a fist.

Nothing.

He knocked again, louder.

No answer.

"Too bad. He doesn't seem to be home." Lance stepped away from the door. "We'll have to try again."

But Sharp had other ideas. He pivoted and walked around the side of the house.

Lance broke into a jog and caught up with him. "Where are you going?"

Sharp didn't break pace. "Joe is hard of hearing. Maybe he's working out back and didn't hear us."

"Sharp!" Lance called out but was ignored. He grabbed for Sharp's arm.

Sharp spun. "I know we're trespassing. I don't care. If there's any chance in hell that Olivia is here, I'm going to find her."

Torn, Lance shook his head. "You're going to get yourself shot, and then who will find her?"

"What would you do if Morgan were missing?"

Lance would break every law in the world without regret. It must have showed on his face.

"I thought so." Sharp whirled around.

Behind the house, a wire enclosure surrounded a chicken coop. From inside, chickens clucked. Standing on the ramp that led into the coop, a big red rooster gave them the stink eye. A few goats grazed on the lawn. As they walked across the grass, the goats trotted a few feet away and settled down to graze again.

Lance felt eyes on him. Either they were being watched or he was imagining it. He moved a few feet away, so they presented separate targets. There was no cover as they crossed the open space between the rear of the house and the outbuildings.

He was torn between calling out for the homeowner and sneaking around. Clearly, Sharp preferred not to issue any warnings. Sharp paused at the entrance to a barn. The door stood open and Lance followed Sharp inside and shone his flashlight around. Inside a large pen, four cows raised their heads. Hay hung from their mouths. A second pen held a few pigs. One squealed, the high-pitched sound raising the hairs on the back of Lance's neck. The barn smelled better than he would have expected. The pens appeared clean, and the doors suggested the animals had access to outdoor areas as well.

"Well, he's not in here." Sharp headed for the door.

Lance followed him outside. The temperature had dropped, and the air was a chilly forty-five degrees for September. There were two more outbuildings. They walked to the second: a metal-roofed structure. The wooden door was closed, but Lance detected a familiar metallic smell.

Blood.

Sharp sniffed and nodded. "I smell it too."

It was the smell of death. But no decomp spoiled the air.

A fresh kill.

Sharp drew his weapon. Lance did the same, then stood beside the door so as not to form a target in the center of the doorway. His heartbeat accelerated, and his stomach soured.

But from the odor, what he expected to find wasn't danger—but death.

Sharp knocked. "Mr. Franklin, are you in there?"

Silence greeted them.

Sharp used his shirtsleeve to open the door. They went through the opening like a well-drilled team, sweeping their weapons across the room from corner to corner. The corners were empty.

It was colder inside. In the center of the space, a shrouded figure dangled from a wooden stand. It was tightly wrapped in white cloth, as if a spider had wrapped its prey in silk.

A workbench lined one wall. Lance took a step closer to the body, onto the plastic sheeting that covered the concrete floor. Blood congealed in spots and small puddles.

Sharp was breathing hard. Lance could hear his lungs heaving from several feet away. The color drained from his face, leaving him the gray-white of the concrete under their feet.

"No. It can't be." His voice was half plea, half groan.

Lance approached the body. Several metal buckets were arranged around it. Two were filled with ice. Cold air wafted from them. The third metal bucket sat to one side. He glanced into it, and his belly flip-flopped.

Blood.

Lance said, "It looks too big to be Olivia."

But it could be Joe Franklin.

Sharp made a noise that could have been agreement, or retching. Then he leaned over, rested his hands on his thighs, and wheezed. "Please."

He needed to know.

Lance moved toward the body. Something about the shape was eerily wrong. He reached out and worked the white cloth from around the top of the body. Then he lifted its edge.

"It's a hoof." Lance quickly moved to the bottom of the body and unwrapped it.

A pig's head stared back at him.

Relief nearly toppled him. Lance staggered backward. "Shit. A dead pig."

"Pig?" Sharp raised his eyes and stared at the pig's head for a full minute, the truth slowly sinking in. The color began to return to his face. He exhaled, the stress leaving his body with his breath.

Lance replaced the cloth around the pig's head. He knew little about slaughtering animals but had seen hunters hang deer.

"You going to be all right?" He was tempted to take Sharp's pulse.

Sharp nodded. "Fine. I just aged a few years in the past minute, that's all."

"Let's get out of here." Lance led the way out of the shed. A light from the back of the house blinded him. The sound of breathing lifted the hairs on his neck. He held up a hand to block the light and saw the shadow of an enormous creature.

Sharp whipped his flashlight around. "Holy shit. Is that a dog or a bear?" Sharp asked in a whisper.

"A dog, I think." All the moisture in Lance's mouth and throat instantly evaporated.

The animal was tan with a black muzzle. It had a thick body and square head and was roughly the size of a Volkswagen.

"Back away slowly," Sharp whispered.

"I think we should cut and run." Lance had been chased by a dog in the past. He'd barely escaped with all his body parts.

"Nope." Sharp eased backward. "You'll trigger his prey instinct."

Yep. That's exactly what Lance felt like. Prey.

Chapter Thirty-One

Lance stared at the dog, sweat dripping down his back.

"Hey!" a voice called out.

Lance looked for the voice. A man walked toward them, an ax balanced on one shoulder. He was a lean six three, and he moved like an athlete. If this was Joe Franklin, he did not look like a nerdy game developer.

He lifted a hand to his mouth. A shrill whistle split the air, and the dog abruptly pivoted and trotted back to its master. The man gave it a command, and the dog planted its ass on the ground next to him.

"That's a good girl," the man said in a high-pitched voice as he scratched the dog behind her ears.

The dog wagged the whole back half of her giant body.

The man let the ax fall into his hands. If the guy rushed him, could Lance draw his gun and shoot before the blade hit him?

"You must be Joe Franklin." Lance lifted both hands in front of his ribs, palms facing out. The seemingly defensive position put his hand closer to the weapon at his hip.

"Don't move!" the man ordered. "Didn't you see the No Trespassing signs?"

"We must have missed them." Lance pointed one finger toward the house. "We knocked on your door, then thought maybe you were in the barn."

"I don't give a fuck if you knocked on the door." The man's face flushed angry red. "How did you get around my gate?"

"We walked." Lance could not see his face. "Are you Joe Franklin?"

"Get the hell off my property. Are you reporters? Because I hate reporters." Joe started toward them. "Still calling me, still showing up at my house, years later. I can't go anywhere without someone snapping my picture. Last month, I caught some news guy parked on the road. He was flying a drone over my house."

Olivia was a reporter. Had she come here? Had she made him angry?

Lance faced Joe. "We're not with the press."

Joe's gaze darted back and forth between Lance and Sharp. He stepped closer, his eyes fixed on Lance's face. "Can you repeat that?"

Lance remembered Joe's hearing impairment and raised his voice, trying to speak more clearly. "We're not with the press."

Joe lowered the ax to the ground. He turned to his dog. "Stay." Then he walked toward Lance. "Then who are you?"

Lance pulled out a business card and held it out. The beam of the flashlight blinded him. "You're Joe?"

"Yes." Joe shined the light on the card, then back at Lance. "What do you want?"

"Just to ask you a few questions," Lance said. "It's about a missing woman."

"I don't know anything about a missing woman." Joe backed up a step. "I hardly leave my farm."

"Please. Her name is Olivia Cruz." Sharp moved forward. "She's a true crime writer, and she's my girlfriend. Can we just have ten minutes of your time? She's been missing for days," he pleaded.

225

"All right." Joe turned and strode away without another word. With a snap of his fingers, he summoned his dog. The big animal trotted obediently at his side.

Sharp fell into step beside Lance, and they followed the man and his dog to the house. Joe led the way inside, down a corridor, and into a large kitchen. Like the outside of the house, the kitchen had an old manor feel. The floor was brick-colored tile. Copper pots hung from a rack over a butcher-block island.

In the close quarters of the kitchen, the dog turned, shoved her huge muzzle in Lance's crotch, and wagged.

"She's friendly?" he asked, not liking her giant teeth so close to his important parts.

"Yes." Joe sighed. "Please don't tell anybody. She's scared the crap out of more than one reporter, but she's actually not much of a guard dog. She likes everybody."

Lance rubbed her head, carefully moving the dog's nose from his groin. Encouraged by the attention, she pressed closer, forcing Lance backward a step.

"Place," Joe commanded, gesturing to a dog bed the size of a twin mattress in the corner. The dog walked to her bed and lay down. Joe walked around the island, opened a drawer, and took out two hearing aids. He put them in his ears and faced them over the island. "Now, what do you want?"

Sharp began, "Did Olivia Cruz contact you?"

"She did. Several times. By phone and by email." Joe crossed his arms. "I emailed her back and told her I don't grant interviews."

"Could you hear us outside?" Lance leaned a hip on the counter.

Joe shook his head. "But I can read lips."

And that explained why Joe hadn't heard them calling for him.

"You never spoke to Olivia?" Sharp hooked a thumb in the front pocket of his jeans.

"No." Joe leaned on the counter, spreading his palms wide. "I prefer email and text. I don't like to talk on the phone. Even with hearing aids, it's hard for me to distinguish words without having lips and facial expressions to read."

Sharp's head tilted. "The night Brandi Holmes was kidnapped, your brother said he was here with you. Was he?"

Joe stared at his dog. "As I said in my testimony, I don't wear my hearing aids at night. In fact, I don't like to wear them at all. They aren't like glasses. Hearing can't be returned to twenty-twenty. I've never been able to get used to the way they amplify sound. There's always distortion and background noise. And it's like wearing plugs in your ears all the time."

"You didn't give your brother an alibi?" Sharp asked.

"How could I?" Joe's voice rose. "Even if I had wanted to, it was impossible."

"But did you want to?" Sharp pressed.

Joe blinked. "I wish I could have given him an alibi."

Lance switched gears. "Olivia found a technical issue with the evidence presented in your brother's trial. Did she mention it to you?"

Beads of sweat broke out on Joe's forehead. A vein on his temple throbbed. "No."

Is he lying?

"What was wrong with the evidence?" Joe asked.

Lance explained about the break in the chain of custody of the hair samples.

"I don't understand all that technical legal crap, but my brother will never get out of prison." Joe shook his head, as if trying to convince himself.

"What if he could get an appeal?" Lance asked.

"It's been years," Joe stammered. "Could that even happen?"

"I don't know," Lance said. "But Olivia was onto something. And now she's missing."

227

"Well, Cliff is in prison. *He* didn't take her." Joe began to pace. He propped one hand on a hip and swept the other through his thick black hair. Distress radiated from him in waves.

"You're sure you didn't meet with her?" Sharp asked.

Joe stopped, his mouth dropping open as his gaze darted back and forth between Sharp and Lance. "You can't think *I* had anything to do with her disappearance."

That was exactly what Lance was thinking.

He leaned forward, placing both palms on the smooth wood. "Why does the thought of revealing an evidentiary error bother you? Do you believe Cliff is innocent? Is he going to be mad you didn't give him a better alibi? Has he been locked up for three years for a crime he didn't commit?"

Joe swallowed. "This conversation is over. Get out." His voice roughened. Sensing her master's emotions, the dog rose to her feet, her attention riveted on Joe.

Sharp didn't break eye contact with Joe until Lance guided him toward the front door. They walked outside into the cold night air. They didn't speak until they reached the car.

Sharp unlocked the vehicle with his fob.

"Let me drive." Lance walked to the driver's door.

Sharp didn't argue and climbed into the passenger seat. "What did you think?"

"I'm not sure." Lance turned the vehicle around. "He wasn't happy about the idea that his brother's conviction could be overturned."

"Does he really think his brother is guilty or did *Joe* kill Brandi? Maybe he doesn't want the case reopened?" Sharp leaned his head on the back of the seat. "We don't have anything to tie him to Brandi or any of the other missing women."

Lance steered the Prius onto the main road.

"Maybe we haven't looked hard enough." Sharp reached for his phone. "When he said he wished he could give his brother an alibi, he was lying his ass off."

"Where to?" Lance asked.

"The office," Sharp said. "I want to review everything we have on Joe Franklin and touch base with your mother and Stella. I also have to call Olivia's sister and give her an update."

Lance planned to call Morgan to let her know he'd be sleeping at the office. Sharp was losing control, which was understandable under the circumstances. But Lance wasn't leaving him alone.

Chapter Thirty-Two

Morgan stirred. Pain in her neck jolted her awake. Sitting up in the hospital recliner, she blinked at the dawn light pouring through the open blinds.

A nurse was checking Gianna's vital signs.

"You're awake." Gianna smiled.

Morgan rubbed at the cramp between her neck and shoulder. "How do you feel?"

"Fine," Gianna said, though pain shadowed her eyes. "You should go home and get some sleep."

"I just had some." Morgan checked her watch. She'd slept at least five hours after Gianna had been brought back to her room after surgery.

The nurse left the room.

"Morgan, I appreciate all you do for me," Gianna said.

"It's my pleasure—"

"Let me talk." Gianna rubbed the edge of the clear tape over the new catheter in her chest as if it itched. "A little more than two years ago, I didn't care if I lived or died. Then Stella saved my life and helped me get clean. I had no faith in myself, but Stella did. I had no money. Kidney failure was a hard thing to accept. Even if I'd wanted to get some job skills and make something of myself, I was way too sick to work."

She dropped her hand to toy with the edge of the blanket. "I was pretty depressed, maybe even more than when I OD'd. *That* was an accident. I was careless with my life because I didn't have much to live for. But after I got out of the hospital, I had to make a choice. Did I want to live or not? Dialysis requires commitment. It sucks, and if I didn't really want to live, why bother? I could just stop going. No one could make me."

Gianna spooned an ice chip into her mouth from a plastic cup on her tray.

Morgan had known Gianna had been depressed but not that she'd considered letting herself die.

"But Stella wouldn't give up on me. She checked on me every day. She made sure I had food. She paid my rent twice. I was surprised how much it meant just to have one person who cared. I'd never really had that before." Gianna paused again to swallow and fish out a second ice chip.

Morgan didn't interrupt. She sensed Gianna had more that she needed to get off her chest. The young woman had lived with Morgan for over a year. Yet they hadn't had this conversation. Morgan had been focused on getting Gianna healthier and guiding her through the transplant application process at several nearby centers. She'd been single-minded. She should have been more attuned to Gianna's emotional wellness. Depression was common in dialysis patients, and Gianna had plenty of life baggage piled on top of her medical condition.

"Anyway. That night in the hospital when you said I was going home with you changed my life forever." Gianna had been kidnapped and had nearly died. "Part of me wanted to say no. To just go home and die. Letting you all care about me was hard. As weird as it sounds, it was scary to want to live. What if I wasn't worth all the effort? What if I failed? What if I did everything right and still died?" She paused, swallowing hard. "What if I went back to using?"

Morgan reached out and touched Gianna's hand. "First of all, I don't think you'd do that. Secondly, I would still support you." But it would change things. Morgan couldn't have a drug user in her home with her children.

"People relapse. It happens." Gianna's eyes hardened. "I was in pain every single day. It would have been easier to find some dope and not give a shit anymore. To want to live meant I was going to have to work every day at getting healthy. Even harder for me, I was going to have to let people get close. That was hard." She looked down at Morgan's hand over hers. "But I was too tired to argue with you, so I let you take charge."

"I'm sorry if I was too bossy," Morgan said. She hadn't meant to steamroll over Gianna's insecurities.

Gianna gave a short laugh. "Not too bossy. Just bossy enough. Anyway, those first few weeks at your house were pretty overwhelming. The girls accepted me with no hesitation. They didn't know what I'd been." Gianna's cheeks flushed with humiliation. "All the things I'd done."

Morgan squeezed her hand.

"Your whole family took me in. They didn't seem to care about my past. I can never repay you all for what you've given me. I don't care if we're not related. I love every one of you more than my biological family." She sniffed and wiped a tear from her cheek. Her own mother had done nothing but use her.

"We feel lucky to have you with us," Morgan said. "And we love you back."

Gianna nodded. "Anyway, my point is now I *want* to live. I won't lie. This setback is discouraging, but I won't let it get to me." She gestured to the tube taped to her chest. "As much as I hate this, it's only temporary. The doctor says it's common, and I'll get back to normal in a couple of months. Maybe if I'm lucky, I'll get a transplant before the next graft goes bad."

"Let's hope," Morgan said.

Gianna looked up, meeting Morgan's eyes with a fierce gaze. "But you need to go home and take care of yourself and your family and find Olivia. I'm not that weak, super-sick girl you practically adopted last year. I can speak up for myself now. I'm going to get through this."

Respect filled Morgan. All Gianna had needed was some love and encouragement. How horrible was it that she never received any in the first eighteen years of her life?

"All right." Morgan stood and collected her tote. "But you have to promise to text if you have any problems. If you can't find me, Grandpa can coordinate whatever you need."

Gianna smiled. "He's good at that."

"Yes, he is." Morgan turned toward the door but glanced back. "And for the record, I wouldn't have made it through my husband's death without him. There's no shame in needing people. I was just lucky enough to be born with a built-in support system."

Morgan left the room. On her way to the elevator, she stopped at the nurse's station and gave them her grandfather's cell phone number in case of an emergency. Gianna might be an adult, but she wasn't alone anymore. She had family now. Someone would always be around to help.

Outside, she opened her rideshare app and requested a car. Her minivan was at the house, and Lance had taken the Jeep. Her ride came within ten minutes. Twenty minutes after she was picked up, Morgan opened the front door of her house and went inside. She toed off her shoes in the foyer. The dogs greeted her with sleepy stretches, yawns, and wags, and she scratched behind their ears. Carrying her shoes, she went into the family room.

Mac rose from the couch, where he'd clearly been sleeping.

"How is Gianna?" He rubbed an eye.

"Out of surgery and resting as comfortably as possible. She might be able to come home in a few days."

"That's great." Mac stretched. "You should catch a few hours of sleep. No offense, but you look like hell."

"I'm sure I do."

"Where is Lance?"

"With Sharp." Morgan set down her tote.

"Have you eaten?" Mac asked.

Morgan shook her head. Her hospital sleep had been fitful. Exhaustion weighed on her like a wet comforter.

"The girls will be up soon. I'll make breakfast after I take a quick shower." She went into the kitchen.

Mac followed her. The dogs whined, and he scooped kibble into their bowls.

"Do you teach classes today?" She filled the coffeepot.

"I have one class and office hours this morning." He set the bowls on the floor. "I can take Sophie to preschool on my way to work, pick her up on my way back, and hang out with the kids this afternoon."

"I'd really appreciate that. I don't even know what I'm doing today." Morgan hadn't talked to Lance, Sharp, or Stella since the night before.

"I'm going to run home and shower. Be back soon. I'll take the dogs out before I go." Mac gave her a quick hug before leaving. He and Stella lived just a few minutes away.

"Thank you," Morgan called after him. She scooped coffee and pressed the "On" button.

Morgan hurried to her room and took a quick shower. When she emerged from the bathroom in her bathrobe, Sophie stood in the doorway. "Mommy!"

She'd slept in her Halloween costume. She raced for Morgan and leaped into her arms.

Morgan caught her, kissed her, and carried her to the kitchen. "What do you want for breakfast?"

"Pancakes, but can you make them like Gianna does?" Sophie asked.

"I think I can manage." Morgan filled a cup with coffee, then found the box of pancake mix in the cabinet. "Before Gianna came to live with us, I used to make *all* your pancakes."

"But Gianna makes them special." Sophie climbed up onto a kitchen stool, knelt, and leaned her chin in both hands on the island. "Will she be home today?"

"No. Maybe in a few days."

"I miss her." Sophie sighed.

Ava, Mia, and Grandpa joined them in the kitchen and gathered around the island. Morgan hugged everyone and poured juice. Then she mixed batter and ladled it onto the buttered griddle. She piled the cooked pancakes on a plate and gave the girls two each before setting the plate on the island and sitting down.

"Gianna made bunny pancakes yesterday." Sophie inspected her pancakes, then covered them in syrup. Tasting her first bite, she grudgingly admitted, "They're almost as good as Gianna's."

"Thank you." Amused, Morgan sipped her coffee. Gianna had only been with them for one year, but for a four-year-old, that was a quarter of her life. For Sophie, it was as if Gianna had always been with them.

The girls finished eating, and Morgan sent them to get dressed.

Grandpa pushed the plate of pancakes toward her. "Eat. Coffee isn't enough."

"I'm worried about Gianna."

"She's tough. She'll be all right."

Morgan lowered her voice so the girls wouldn't hear. "What if she isn't? What if she doesn't get a kidney in time?"

Grandpa frowned. "Let's take one day at a time and not borrow trouble. We have enough of our own."

"You're right." But her head was full of doubts as she ate a pancake. She went back to her bedroom, dressed in jeans and a sweater, and walked Ava and Mia to the bus stop. Mac picked up Sophie to take her to preschool, as promised, and Morgan returned to the kitchen for another cup of coffee.

Lance called as she poured.

She answered, "Hey."

"Hey yourself."

Morgan updated him on Gianna's condition, then asked, "How is Sharp?"

"As you'd expect." Lance sounded depressed. "I don't know how he's going to be if we don't find her."

"I know," Morgan said. "The kids are off to school. I can be at the office in fifteen."

"Don't rush. Sharp and I are going to question the former Olander foreman, Ronald Alexander. Stella tried yesterday, but he wasn't very cooperative. Sharp wants to try a different approach."

"Stella isn't going to like that," Morgan warned.

"Probably not," Lance agreed. "But Sharp is going with or without me. I don't want him running off on his own. I'd rather *none* of us be alone."

"All right. I'll review files here while you're gone. Grandpa can help—"

"Hold on," Lance said. "Turn on the news. A reporter is interviewing Kim Holgersen."

With her phone still pressed to her ear, Morgan left the kitchen and turned on the TV in the family room.

On the screen, Olivia's literary agent was standing in front of a small one-story house. The street was lined with similar homes on tiny lots. It looked like a senior community. A news van was parked on the side of the road.

The reporter shoved a microphone at her. "Are you worried about your client Olivia Cruz?"

Kim pushed her long red hair behind her ear. "Yes, I am."

"Have you heard any updates from the police?" the reporter asked, following her.

"I'm not sure I should be talking to you." Kim turned toward the house.

"You live in New York City. Why are you here?" the reporter persisted, bombarding her with questions faster than Kim could answer them. "Did the police ask you to come? Do you know anything about Olivia Cruz's disappearance?"

Kim was no pushover. She faced the camera. "I'm here to visit my parents, but I'm available to the police at any time. Olivia is my friend as well as my client. I wish I knew something that could help bring her home, but all I can do is pray for her safe return. I can't imagine what her family is going through." Kim's voice broke. She paused to compose herself. "If anyone has information about Olivia's whereabouts, please call the police." She turned and walked away.

The reporter added a few lines about Olivia being missing for over three days and signed off.

"How did he find her at her parents' house?" Morgan turned off the television. "The press has been unusually relentless, and someone is clearly feeding them information."

"Probably the usual leak in the police department," Lance said. "Sharp is ready. I have to go."

"Good luck with the foreman."

"I'll call you when we're finished," Lance said. "I love you."

"Love you too." Morgan ended the call and went back to the kitchen.

Grandpa pushed up the sleeves of his sweater. "Let's get to work. How can I help?"

Morgan brought out her laptop. "I want to focus on Joe Franklin. Lance and Sharp talked to him last night, but they both felt he was evasive. They want to know if there's any way he could be connected to Cliff's victim or any of the other five girls who are still missing."

"Are you thinking *he* killed those girls?" Grandpa asked.

"I don't know. But it would explain why he didn't want to talk about an appeal for his brother. If Joe is guilty, he wouldn't want the case reopened."

Grandpa pointed to the doorway. "Would you get my laptop from my bedroom?"

"Sure." Morgan fetched his computer. "Could you find Joe's testimony in Cliff's trial? I'd like to read it."

They sat side by side at the island. Morgan reviewed Joe's testimony and background information but found nothing new. Then she shifted her focus to the auto shop where Cliff worked. To date, it was the only link between all six women besides their disappearances. Morgan was scanning the ABOUT US page when she noticed the initials at the bottom of the website.

"Site design by JF, Inc.," she read aloud, a chill settling over her.

"Joe Franklin's initials are JF," Grandpa said.

Morgan searched her computer for the background report from Lance's mother. Buried on the second page was the name of Joe's game development company. "There it is. Joe owns JF, Inc."

"He must have some relationship with the owner of the auto shop where his brother worked if he designed the website."

"If he designed the website, would he also have access to all of the customer records, including the names and addresses of Brandi Holmes and the other five women who went missing?"

Could Joe have killed six women? Was Olivia number seven?

Chapter Thirty-Three

Lance stared through his windshield at the garden center. The afternoon sun shone on the hood. They'd been watching the exit for hours, waiting for Ronald Alexander to leave work.

Sharp's hand bounced on his knee. He reached for the take-out cup of coffee in the console and shook it. Lance had half a cup left, but he didn't offer it to his boss. Six months before, Sharp had suffered a serious abdominal injury. He'd fully recovered, but he looked gaunt today, as if he'd lost some of the fifteen pounds he'd gained back since his injury. Lance understood. He felt sick and helpless over Olivia's disappearance. If Morgan were missing, he would be out of his mind.

Sharp twisted the cap off a bottle of water. "There he is."

Lance spotted the former Olander Dairy employee leaving the main building of the garden center. A dozen vehicles sat between the Jeep and Alexander's truck. Lance wasn't worried about being seen.

Alexander crossed the parking lot and climbed into his battered pickup.

"What do you want to do?" Lance started the engine of the Jeep.

"Let's follow him and see where he goes." Sharp straightened, rolled his head, and checked his phone for the fiftieth time.

Lance hung back, waiting for Alexander to pull out of the lot before steering the Jeep toward the exit. He drove onto the country road, keeping two cars between the Jeep and Alexander's truck.

"He's not going home," Sharp said as the pickup made a left at a stop sign.

Lance eased off the gas. They'd lost the two-car buffer. He allowed more distance between the vehicles.

Ten minutes later, Alexander turned into the entrance of a small local bar, Wings & More.

Lance parked three rows away. "What do you want to do?"

Sharp reached for the door handle. "Let's go talk to him."

Lance followed him inside. At two o'clock in the afternoon, the crowd was light. A few men sat at the bar, their attention on football highlights that played on a flat-screen TV. Most of the tables were empty. The bar smelled of hot grease and beer. He spotted Alexander alone at the end of the bar, drinking a beer. Lance and Sharp split up and flanked him. Alexander was focused on his drink.

Sharp tapped on the bar. "Whiskey. Make it a double."

Lance raised a brow at him behind Alexander's back. His boss rarely drank hard liquor.

The bartender looked questioningly at Lance, and he ordered a club soda. She poured Sharp's whiskey and slid it across the bar toward him. He lifted the glass, then downed half the liquid in one smooth gulp. The bartender set a glass of club soda in front of Lance and walked away.

Lance turned and put his elbow on the bar, crowding Alexander between him and Sharp.

On the other side, Sharp's arm bumped Alexander's. Beer sloshed over the rim of his mug.

"Hey." Alexander mopped up the bar with his cocktail napkin. He glared at Sharp. Recognition dawned on his face, and his angry stare turned suspicious. "What do *you* want?"

"Remember me?" Sharp drained his glass and tapped it on the bar. The bartender refilled it.

"Yeah. You work with that bitch cop." Alexander's mouth turned smug. "You can't make me talk. Charge me with something or leave me the fuck alone."

"I'm not a cop." Whiskey in hand, Sharp turned to face him.

Lance added, "Neither am I."

With an assessing glare at each of them, Alexander sipped his beer. "Then why are you here?"

"I have a few follow-up questions." Sharp drank another finger of whiskey. "About the LMS."

Alexander choked and almost dropped his beer. "Shh."

"Let's get a table." Lance pointed at an empty table at the back of the room.

"No." Alexander swiveled on his stool, putting his back to the bar. "I ain't saying anything."

Sharp got in his face. "There's a woman who went missing last Friday morning. She's my girlfriend. This is personal. I'm not fucking around here."

"That reporter I saw on the news?" Alexander frowned.

"Yes." Sharp nodded.

"Not my problem." Alexander shrugged.

Sharp's face reddened. He finished his second drink and set the empty glass on the bar. "The LMS could be involved."

"Then the bitch is probably dead." Alexander set his beer on the bar. "You know what happened to Kennett, right?"

A muscle under Sharp's eye twitched.

"Why would the LMS murder Kennett Olander?" Lance asked.

Alexander paled, clearly realizing his mistake. "How would I know?"

"Hypothetically," Sharp said. "Why would an organization like the LMS kill a man?"

Alexander ignored the question.

Sharp grabbed Alexander by the front of his sweatshirt and dragged him off his stool. "The reporter was at the Olander farm last Monday night. Did you see her there?"

"I wasn't there. I got fired, remember?" Alexander spat in Sharp's face. "Fuck off."

Lance moved around Alexander and tried to catch Sharp's arms. "Time to go, Sharp."

But Sharp shook him off. The older man spun, and before Lance could stop him, he punched Alexander square in the face. Alexander's head snapped back, and he stumbled.

"Hey!" A tall, hefty man charged from the back of the room, a beer bottle in his hand. With no hesitation, he swung it at the back of Sharp's head. Sharp was focused on Alexander. He didn't even see the man coming.

Lunging forward, Lance jumped in front of the assailant and blocked the blow, forearm to forearm. The impact rang through the bones of Lance's arm. The man drilled a punch into Lance's solar plexus. The air whooshed from his lungs, and he doubled over.

The man raised the bottle high, his mouth twisting into a mean smile. He was enjoying the fight.

Lance took a breath and grabbed the man's arm as the bottle came down. With a twist of his hips, he threw the man to the floor. The beer bottle flew from his hand, hit the wall, and shattered. The man rolled to his feet, swiped a hand across his mouth, and lunged at Lance, trying to tackle him around the thighs. Lance shot his legs out behind him and centered his weight onto the man's shoulder blades. The man went down on his face.

Spinning around, Lance grabbed the man's arm and twisted it behind his back. Heart sprinting, lungs heaving, Lance paused for air.

Ten feet away, Sharp was straddling Alexander's chest and punching him in the face. Hauling his hand back, he made another fist. "I asked you a question. Why would the LMS have killed Olander?"

"Money!" Alexander spat blood from his mouth. "They paid for the farm. He mortgaged it and took the money for his dumbass son's defense."

Sharp shook him by the front of his shirt. "How do you know that?"

"I worked there for years. I heard things." Alexander wet his lips.

"Did they kidnap Olivia Cruz?" Sharp asked.

Alexander closed his bloody lips.

Sharp raised a fist over his face, ready to pound him again.

"Sharp!" Releasing his opponent, Lance staggered to his feet. He launched himself at Sharp's back and hooked his arms under Sharp's shoulders. He dragged his boss off Alexander and held him in a full nelson. "Calm down!"

"Let me go!" Sharp struggled against Lance's grip. Hooking a foot behind Lance's ankle, Sharp tripped him. They went down to the floor in a heap, with Sharp still fighting him. Frustration and desperation lent him stamina and strength.

Lance didn't want to hurt him, but he couldn't let him beat the hell out of Ronald Alexander either.

As Lance pinned Sharp to the floor with his weight, he heard the sirens approach.

Chapter Thirty-Four

The Scarlet Falls Police Station occupied the entire first floor of the township administration building. Morgan crossed the gray-tiled lobby and walked through an open space filled with cubicles. She saw her sister in her cubicle, staring at her computer.

She stopped in front of Stella's desk. "Where are they?"

Stella hit a key, and her screen went blank. She rose, her body sluggish. Her blouse and slacks were wrinkled. She was putting in as many hours as they were. "I put Lance and Sharp in the conference room. The other two guys are in interview rooms. I didn't have the heart to put Sharp in a holding cell, although I should have. He assaulted Ronald Alexander."

"What exactly happened?" Morgan asked. Stella had been short on details when she'd called.

Stella walked toward a short hallway. "On the Wings & More surveillance video, Sharp was questioning Alexander. Then Sharp lost control and punched him."

"He's not himself." Morgan didn't know how Sharp had held it together this long.

"I know that, and that's why he's cooling off in the conference room instead of a cell." Stella turned down a hallway. A patrol officer stood by a closed door. "Lance tried to stop him but got sucked in when one of Alexander's friends jumped into the fight."

"Do I need to post bail?" Morgan asked.

"No. They're lucky. Alexander has a record. He isn't interested in filing a complaint as long as Lance and Sharp reciprocate. Ronald's buddy also has a record and is willing to call it even. There wasn't any property damage, so the owner of the bar isn't filing a complaint either. Lance and Sharp are banned from the bar for life, and they can't go anywhere near Ronald Alexander."

Morgan rubbed her forehead. "Sharp is not going to like that. We have so few leads, and none of them are panning out."

"I know, but it's the best I could do under the circumstances. Either we cut deals, or he can end up being charged. He could lose his PI license." Stella opened the conference room door.

Lance nursed a cup of coffee at the conference table. In the chair next to him, Sharp held an ice pack on his hand. He looked up as Morgan and Stella walked into the room. Stella closed the door behind her. Bruises surrounded one of Sharp's eyes. Alexander must have gotten a punch in at some point. But it was the bleak look in his eyes that hurt Morgan's heart.

How could she help him?

She greeted Lance with a quick kiss, then turned a chair to face Sharp and sat down. "Are you all right?"

He shook his head. "I don't know."

Morgan outlined Stella's deal. "I think you should agree."

Sharp nodded. "I fucked up. I know it. Alexander said Olivia was probably dead, and he said it like it didn't matter. My brain shorted out. I wanted to kill him with my bare hands." He lifted the ice pack and stared down at his red raw knuckles. They were sore and would hurt even more the next day. "And now we've lost one of our only leads."

"I might have another." Morgan explained how she discovered Joe Franklin had designed the auto shop's website.

Sharp rose. "I need to talk to Joe again. Now."

Stella held up a hand. "No. I'm going to visit Joe as soon as we're done here, and I can't take you with me."

Sharp dropped into the chair, his posture defeated. "I understand."

Stella gave Sharp a pointed look. "But Morgan can come with me if you promise to stay out of trouble."

Sharp nodded. "Deal."

Stella handed Lance a set of keys. "I had your Jeep brought here. One more thing."

Lance closed his fingers around the keys. "What is it?"

"I questioned Alexander after he was brought in. He has an alibi for the night Olivia disappeared. He was drunk in the same bar he was in today. He's a regular. The bartender confirmed that he closed the place last Thursday night. He was so hammered, she took his keys and poured him into an Uber at two a.m. She has the confirmation on her app that he was dropped off, and he was far too drunk to have committed any crime, let alone one that required finesse. If the LMS had Olivia kidnapped, Alexander wasn't the man who did it."

Lance took the keys. "Let's get out of here."

In the hallway, Lance paused. "Sharp and I have to get our personal effects."

Including their weapons.

Morgan touched Lance's arm. "In that case, I'll meet you at the office after Stella and I interview Joe Franklin."

Morgan followed her sister outside. They crossed the parking lot, and she slid into the passenger seat of her sister's unmarked police car. "Thanks for taking me with you."

Stella drove out of the lot. "You know more about the Franklin case than I do. I'm counting on your help. Plus, I don't want to take a uniform. Might put him on the defensive. He's already reluctant to talk about the case."

"Does the chief know you're questioning Joe about a closed case?"

"No." Stella turned left. "There are still five missing women. Their cases are still open. I know the chain of evidence was screwed up and the former sheriff was a corrupt bastard, but planting evidence wouldn't have been easy. The case was big. There were a lot of eyes on it. I have a hard time believing in elaborate conspiracies."

"Do you think it's more likely the chain of evidence error was an oversight, nothing deliberate?" The theory made sense to Morgan. "You don't think it's possible Cliff went to prison for a crime Joe committed?"

"I don't know, but that's what we need to find out. Joe didn't want his brother to get an appeal. Why not? Most brothers would have lied for their sibling. But not Joe. He also designed the website for the auto shop, so he had access to the customer records. If he couldn't alibi his brother for the night Brandi Holmes was killed, then he's in the same boat. Home alone, sleeping, isn't an alibi." As the car cruised along the rural highway, Stella drummed her fingers on the steering wheel. "We can't arrest him for designing a website or for not having an alibi. How would he have met the women? He didn't work at the shop."

"Designing the website is a solid connection with the auto shop, and he could have gone there when Cliff was working."

A short time later, Stella turned into Joe Franklin's driveway, pulled up to the intercom, and pressed the button.

"Yes," said a male voice.

"This is Detective Stella Dane from the Scarlet Falls Police. I'd like to speak with you."

A few heartbeats ticked away before he answered. "All right. Come up to the house."

Morgan got out of the car and opened the gate. After Stella drove through, Morgan closed it and got back into the car. Stella drove around a curve and parked in front of a tall stone house.

Morgan stared at the house. Ivy climbed three stories of gray stone. Three goats trotted across the front lawn. "It looks medieval."

Stella used the radio to report her location. They stepped out of the car and walked up to the house. A tall man answered the door before they knocked. He stepped out onto the porch and closed the door behind him. From inside, the deep bark of a large dog echoed. When Joe turned his head, Morgan could see the top of a small flesh-colored hearing aid. He wore jeans, a flannel shirt, and boots.

"Mr. Franklin." Stella introduced herself and Morgan. "We'd like to ask you a few questions."

"Go ahead." He crossed his arms.

"Do you know about the chain of evidence error in your brother's trial?" Stella began.

Joe met each of their eyes, assessing them, maybe trying to decide if they knew about Sharp and Lance's visit from the previous evening. "I heard about it last night."

"Have you spoken with your brother or his attorney?" Stella asked.

"Not yet." Joe licked his lips.

"You're not excited to help your brother appeal his conviction?" Stella's eyebrows and voice rose.

"I just haven't had a chance, that's all." Joe shifted his weight and looked away.

Liar.

Stella rocked on the balls of her feet. "How do you know the owner of Speedy Auto?"

"Who says I know him?" Joe raised his chin.

"You designed his website," Stella said.

"That was years ago." Joe uncrossed his arms and shoved his hands into the front pockets of his jeans. His voice sounded as if he were calm, but his inability to stand still or maintain eye contact said otherwise. He needed a push.

Morgan went for a major shock. "Did you know Brandi Holmes?"

His gaze snapped to hers.

"No," he said, but his eyes were worried. He understood the implication behind Morgan's question.

Morgan pressed harder. "How about Cassandra Martin, Samantha Knowles, Jessie Mendella, Brenda Chase—"

"No." He cut her off. The color bled from his face. He clearly recognized the names. His voice was harsh as he answered, "Why are you asking me this?"

Morgan pressed. "There's only one reason I can think of you wouldn't want your brother to get his appeal. You killed those women, and you don't want the case reopened."

He shook his head hard. "No."

Stella leaned forward, her voice rising as she jumped in on Morgan's line of questioning. "Did you take your brother's car that night? Did you put sugar in Brandi's gas tank? Did you follow her until her car broke down? Did you kill her?"

"No!" He spun, holding his skull with both hands. "You don't understand."

Stella lowered her voice. "I can't understand unless you talk to me."

"I didn't kill any of them, but their deaths are my fault." He closed his eyes. His hands fell to his sides. "The reason I don't want my brother to get an appeal is because he's a monster."

Morgan exchanged a glance with her sister, and they waited.

"I've known Todd, the owner of Speedy Auto, since college. I talked him into hiring Cliff." Guilt lined Joe's face. "It's my fault those women are dead. If I hadn't gotten him that job, he wouldn't have met them. They'd still be alive."

"Five of them have never been found. How do you know they're dead?" Stella asked in a soft voice.

"Because Cliff told me he killed them." Joe backed up to his door and leaned on it. His eyes darkened and filled with pain. "He told me every detail. I begged him to stop. After each death, he promised me it would be the last one. A year or so would pass, and I'd think it was over.

Then he'd give in to his need again. When Brandi Holmes was found, I hoped he'd go to prison."

"Then why didn't you testify against him?" Stella propped a hand on her hip.

Anger lit Joe's face. "Because he's my brother!" One big hand swept out to point at Morgan. "That's your sister, right? Would you betray her?"

"If she murdered six people? You bet I would." Stella nodded.

"Well, Cliff raised me after our parents died. He took care of me. He is the only reason I didn't end up in foster care. He said, 'Joe, we're family, and family sticks together.'" Joe's eyes glistened. "And now I'm going to have to betray him. I already have the deaths of six women on my soul. He can't get out of prison. He can't control himself. More people would die. I can't live with that."

He looked broken, and Morgan almost wanted to comfort him. But she remembered the five families of the missing women. This man had known their loved ones were dead for years and had let them suffer and hope all that time because he didn't want to betray his monster of a brother.

Coldness swept through her as she realized his guilt went far deeper. He'd known after each woman had been killed.

His silence had allowed his brother to keep murdering.

Yes, those deaths were on his soul.

Almost all of his arguments had begun with *I*. He didn't care about those women and their families. He only cared about himself.

"Will you testify now?" Morgan asked.

Joe blinked the moisture from his eyes. "Maybe. I'd have to make sure I wouldn't be charged with conspiracy, aid and abetting, or accessory."

Anger flared in Morgan's chest. He was using the victims' families as bargaining chips. That was low. And she'd almost felt sorry for him.

"Do you know where those women are?" Stella asked.

He met her gaze. His emotions closed down. His eyes shuttered, and his gaze went cold. "I might. Can you promise me immunity?"

Bastard.

Chapter Thirty-Five

An hour later, Morgan faced the whiteboard. Lance and Sharp stood shoulder to shoulder with her.

"Stella is going to be tied up for the rest of the night," Morgan said. Her sister had taken Joe Franklin back to the station and sent Morgan back to the office in a patrol car.

"She'll be tied up for the rest of the week," Lance added. "Or longer, depending how quickly and where they locate the remains of the five women."

"Which is why we need to concentrate on finding Olivia." Sharp stared at the board and pressed both hands to the top of his head. "Who are the remaining suspects?"

Morgan picked up the marker and wrote ALIBI next to Ronald Alexander's name. Next to Kennett Olander, she wrote DEAD. She drew a question mark next to Joe Franklin's name. "Joe is in Stella's hands now. Assuming his story pans out, we can eliminate him from our list."

Sharp dropped his hands to his sides. "What about Franklin's lawyer?"

Lance shook his head. "Mark Hansen said he was in Rochester, and he could prove it if he had to."

"But he refused to provide evidence," Sharp said. "What about the editor?"

Morgan checked her notes. "He says he was back at his bar in Brooklyn by midnight, and his bartender will back him up."

Sharp waved a hand in the air. "The bartender would lie for him."

Morgan sighed. "We could ask him for his E-ZPass records, but we can't make him give us anything."

"What if it was no one we know?" Sharp's voice cracked. "What if Olivia was taken by some random psycho who saw her on TV and fixated on her? Or what if the LMS orchestrated her kidnapping because she found out about an illegal gun sale? Alexander could be right. Olivia could be dead. She could have been killed the same night she was taken."

They were all quiet for a few seconds.

Lance's phone went off, startling them. "It's my mom."

He answered the call. "Hi, Mom. I'm putting you on speaker. Sharp and Morgan are here."

Jenny greeted them all, and then got down to business. "I've been digging deeper into all the people involved with Olivia, and I found something interesting about Kim Holgersen."

"Interesting how?"

"Holgersen isn't a common name. It wasn't hard to find Kim's parents. Frank and Ethel Holgersen live in Redhaven. I found their current home address and their previous one. A couple of years ago, the former property changed hands from Frank and Ethel to Stephen Holgersen. In the past six months, several creditors have filed against Stephen, and there's a tax lien on the property."

"So he's in financial trouble," Lance said.

"Yes," his mom said. "He owns a company called Primitive Survival School, and the company has filed for Chapter 11 bankruptcy."

Morgan went to her desk, opened her laptop, and pulled up Kim's social media profile. "I don't see a Stephen Holgersen in Kim's social media friend or follow lists."

"They have to be related. Look him up directly." Lance walked behind the desk and read the screen over her shoulder.

"He has his own social media accounts," Jenny said. "As well as separate pages for the survival school. Kim's social media accounts aren't connected to any of Stephen's. But Kim owns half of Stephen's business."

Morgan typed in the search bar. "There he is."

Lance leaned closer. "Oh yeah. He's definitely a relative. He looks like Kim."

In his profile picture, a tall and red-haired Stephen Holgersen was dressed in camouflage from head to toe and held an AR-15. Morgan scrolled down the page, full of blog posts on survivalist tips. "He has a YouTube channel too." She opened a new tab. "More of the same."

"What's the address of the property?" Sharp moved around the desk to watch over Morgan's other shoulder.

Jenny gave them a rural route number in Redhaven. "The survival school uses that address as well. One more thing before I go. Stephen Holgersen drives a white Chevrolet Express Cargo Van."

Was that the white van that had sat in front of Olivia's house?

Jenny said goodbye and signed off.

Morgan plugged Stephen's address into the app. Most of the property was solid green with a blue horseshoe-shaped blotch roughly in the center. "Looks like nothing but woods and a lake." She switched to the survival school's website. "The school offers weeklong classes on wilderness survival. There's a photo gallery."

She clicked through a series of pictures of people fishing with homemade spears and nets, building shelters from natural materials, and setting snares to catch small game.

Sharp stared at the screen. "That would be an excellent place to hide a kidnapping victim."

Morgan tapped a finger on her desk. "But why would Olivia's agent want to kidnap her own client?" Her tired brain whirled. "Could there be a financial motivation?"

"She and her husband were separated. So Kim probably needs money," Sharp said.

"Right," Morgan agreed. "But doesn't she lose money if Olivia doesn't produce more books?"

"It doesn't make sense. She needs Olivia to finish her proposal." Sharp reached for Morgan's computer, still showing the company's website. "We don't know they are working together. There could be a conflict between Kim and Stephen. We have no information about their relationship, and we've all seen enough family disputes to know that being blood relatives doesn't always translate to a close bond. We know Kim is Olivia's agent. We are hypothesizing Stephen took Olivia. The rest is conjecture." He clicked on a tab marked Videos and read the first two titles out loud: "Setting Booby Traps to Keep Your Family Safe; How to Make an Explosive Trip Wire Alarm."

Morgan read several more video headlines: "Know Your Rights on Property Searches and Seizure; How to Stay off the Government's Radar."

"This sounds like the guy who blew up our front porch." Lance stood.

"We should call Stella," Morgan suggested.

Sharp shook his head. "Why? She's tied up with Joe Franklin, and we don't have any evidence that directly links Stephen Holgersen to Olivia—at least nothing that isn't purely circumstantial. The ability to have done something is not probable cause; neither is bankruptcy. Stella wouldn't even be able to get a search warrant."

"She could interview him." Morgan shifted back in her chair.

"This guy is anti-government." Sharp pointed to the computer screen. "He'll know his rights. He'll never agree to an interview. He won't let her onto the property. Requesting an interview will give him advance warning and allow him to get rid of any real evidence on his property. If Olivia is there, he'll move her."

If she's still alive.

Sharp rose to his feet. He glanced at Morgan, and then Lance. "I think I should go alone. I will be breaking a long list of laws tonight—"

Lance stopped him. "You are not going anywhere alone. I'm in."

"In that case, you'll need to have your lawyer on hand," Morgan added.

Sharp could not be allowed to go off on his own. He had already nearly been arrested that night. Who knew what else he might do?

Chapter Thirty-Six

Lying on her side under the blanket, Olivia heard the sound of the doors being unlocked. When had he said she only had two days left?

What day is it?

She lay in the corner, the blanket pulled up over her shoulders. Her breath rattled in her chest. Her body ached from her previous beating. He might not have to kill her. How much longer could she survive down here anyway?

The hinges squeaked as the doors opened, and his boots clomped down the stairs.

"What the fuck?" He walked closer, his footsteps crunching in the dirt until he stopped a foot from her head. His shadow fell over her. A few seconds passed. "Ah, shit."

The flashlight beam looked red behind her closed eyes.

"Get up." He nudged her with his foot.

Olivia groaned and rolled to her hands and knees. She'd tied the blanket around her shoulders like a cape. It hung down around her hands. She paused to cough and suck oxygen into her lungs.

"I said get up." He tapped her thigh with the toe of his boot.

Pain shot up her leg, and she groaned, her head hanging.

"Come on. On your feet. Your time is up. We're taking a walk."

He's going to kill me.

She looked up at him. He hadn't bothered with the mask. Without it, he was just as intimidating. But Olivia had no options. Her time had run out.

She levered one foot under her body and lifted her head, her fist clenching the sock on the ground. Launching herself to her feet, she whipped the sock toward his head. She'd spent the last day filling the toe of her sock with every small rock she could find in the dirt of the cellar. Now those rocks struck her captor in the head with a solid thwack.

He staggered backward, his knees buckling. The flashlight fell to the ground. Olivia advanced, swinging the sock at his head again. It struck him in the temple. His arms windmilled for a second, and he fell backward into the dirt.

She wanted to hit him again, but she'd have to get closer. He might grab her.

Not worth it.

Afraid to take her gaze off him, Olivia snatched the flashlight from the ground and backed toward the stairs. He was half sitting, supporting himself with one hand. The other clutched his head.

Olivia turned and limped up the stairs. Outside, she shut the doors and glanced wildly around. The cellar had been dug into the side of a wooded hill. There was a large metal padlock on the ground next to the bulkhead. It locked with a key, which she assumed was in the cellar with her captor.

She needed to secure the doors. She'd stunned him, but she hadn't knocked him unconscious. He'd be after her soon.

She grabbed a narrow branch and shoved it through the door handles. That was the best she could do. She turned away from the cellar and surveyed her surroundings. In the darkness, all she could see was woods. Were there any other people nearby? Should she risk using the flashlight?

She switched it on and kept the beam pointed toward the ground. A footpath led downhill, into the woods. Which way should she go? Follow the path and hopefully run into a vehicle she could take? Or go in the opposite direction?

Switching off the flashlight, she hobbled toward the path. The ground was sandy in both directions. He would have little difficulty following her trail. Adrenaline flowed in her bloodstream, easing her breathing and quieting the pain in her foot. But she still couldn't move very quickly. She limped down the path.

She'd traveled less than a hundred feet when she heard the first impact of his body against the inside of the doors. He was on his feet. How long would it take him to break out? A few minutes? He wouldn't be far behind her, and she wouldn't be able to outrun him. She needed to find a place to hide.

Fear scrambled her heartbeat. Anxiety tightened her lungs, and she fought for air with each step. Cold, clammy sweat broke out between her shoulder blades. She couldn't let him catch her.

The trail crossed another path. She had no time to think about which direction to go. Turning right, she kept going. There must be a vehicle somewhere nearby. She needed to keep looking. But between her injured foot and her asthma, she was hardly making progress.

How could she throw him off her trail? The trail divided again. She left a few prints in the wrong direction, then turned and backtracked to the intersection. Then she left the trail and walked parallel to it. But the snap of a twig underfoot drove her back to the path.

She couldn't get a break.

The path ended suddenly. She tripped and went down on her knees. Pain shot up her legs. She sat back on her heels, winded and wheezing, her lungs aching. She'd emerged from the trees on a beach. A lake stretched as far as she could see. Moonlight glittered on its rippling blackness, shining like oil. A dock extended over the water, and a shed sat at the edge of the dock. Was there a boat inside? Moonlight turned the rocky beach silver. If she was careful and stayed on the rocks, she could cross the beach without leaving tracks.

But if she hid in the shed and he found her, she'd be trapped.

A loud crack echoed in the night. Olivia froze for a few seconds. She'd thought she was too far from the cellar to hear him burst out, but she'd been wrong. She mustn't have gotten as far as she'd hoped. He was close.

And he was coming for her.

She climbed to her feet and headed across the rocks toward the shed. There were no other hiding places in sight, and she was moving too slowly to stay ahead of him. The shed was her only hope. She opened the door and stepped inside. Disappointment rushed through her, followed by sheer panic. Fishing rods lined the walls. Fishing nets were heaped in the corner. The rest of the space was empty.

Could she hide under the nets? Did she have any other options?

Chapter Thirty-Seven

Lance adjusted the night vision goggles on his head over the black knit cap that hid his bright-blond hair. He flipped up the goggles until he needed them. Next to him, Sharp secured the Velcro on his body armor. Like Lance, he wore black cargos and a black zip-up, with a cap over his short salt-and-pepper hair.

"I don't like waiting behind." Morgan stood next to the Jeep, her black jacket layered over her own Kevlar vest. A dark-gray scarf hid the pale skin of her face.

"If we run into trouble, we'll need someone to call for help." Sharp checked the weapon on his hip.

"You can't bail us out if you're in jail with us." Lance didn't like separating either, but they had no idea what they would run into.

Morgan was wicked smart, and she had many incredible qualities. But athleticism wasn't one of them. She had powered through physical challenges in the past with sheer determination. But Lance and Sharp ran regularly and would be able to move faster on their own.

"There are too many variables that could turn to complete shit tonight." Sharp selected a stick about three feet long from the ground. He took a piece of bright-yellow paracord from his pocket and tied it to the end of the stick. "We need a person on the outside."

"What's that?" Morgan asked.

"A trip wire detector." Sharp held the stick in front of him. The cord fell straight down. He swept it slowly side to side. "The cord is lightweight. It should show us a trip wire without triggering it. An infrared sensor was used on the pipe bomb, but out here in the woods, it might make more sense to go low-tech. Stephen uses fishing line in his YouTube videos."

"I don't like you going into the woods in the dark." Morgan set her jaw. "What if you don't see an infrared sensor?"

Sharp shook his head. "He uses this land as a camp for survivalists. He can't risk blowing up his customers."

Lance wasn't so sure. Holgersen's survival school was in bankruptcy. How long had it been since he'd had students here? He thought of the arsenal he and Sharp had found at the Olander farm. As a survivalist, Holgersen could also have plenty of firepower on hand. Sharp and Lance would be the trespassers. What would Holgersen do if he caught them snooping around his land? Would he come after them with weapons or call the sheriff's department?

But in the end, the worst scenario was if Stephen Holgersen wasn't the man who took Olivia. Then what?

A failing business did not make Stephen Holgersen a criminal. They had no evidence to support their hunch. But Olivia had been missing for three and a half days, and Sharp wasn't going to wait to assess or gather any more information. He'd been twitchy since they learned about Stephen Holgersen's massive debt and watched his YouTube videos on setting booby traps. Lance was lucky he'd talked him into changing his clothes and having a look at satellite images of the area and online pictures of the camp.

The Jeep was concealed behind a clump of trees just past the entrance marked PRIMITIVE SURVIVAL SCHOOL. From this position, Morgan would be able to see the driveway and the road in both directions.

He leaned over and kissed her on the mouth. "Be careful."

She nodded. "You're the ones walking into who knows what."

"We'll be all right." He settled his hands on her arms and squeezed her biceps. "This will be an in-and-out operation. Our goal is to avoid confrontation."

From the online pictures, it seemed as if most of the property had been left in its natural state. People paid to learn to live off the land.

Sharp tapped him on the shoulder. "Let's go."

"Love you." Lance released Morgan's arms.

"Love you too." She stepped back.

Lance and Sharp turned into the woods. Lance lowered his NVGs over his eyes and scanned his surroundings. The newer-generation night vision equipment illuminated the landscape in shades of black and white instead of the traditional eerie green. He took the stick and cord and held it in front of them. Sharp stayed at his right flank, watching for infrared sensors. Thick woods and the potential for booby traps kept their pace slow.

A hundred yards into the forest, they stepped onto a rough trail. A red light shone to his left. Lance grabbed Sharp's arm to stop him and pointed at the light. Sharp took a tiny penlight from his pocket and shone it ahead.

He leaned close to Lance's ear. "Trip wire connected to a sound grenade."

An alarm was better than a bomb.

Lance skirted the device.

They moved back into the woods and traveled north in a line parallel to the trail. The property was on a peninsula that jutted into the lake. Water formed a natural barrier on three sides. Satellite images of the area had not penetrated the thick woods but had showed several structures built at the edge of the water. This likely marked the location of the main buildings. Stephen's residence should also be near the lake.

Most people with lakefront properties built their houses with a view of the water.

A northerly path from where they'd parked at the entrance would take Lance and Sharp through the center of the property. Lance checked his compass and angled slightly to the west to intersect with the shoreline of the lake. A flank approach would be preferable to a direct line.

Pine needles were quiet underfoot. The underbrush thinned, and they increased their speed. An organic, mossy smell hit Lance's nostrils.

The lake must be ahead.

He turned to signal Sharp. A loud snap sounded, and Sharp went down.

Chapter Thirty-Eight

Pain shot up Sharp's leg. He'd hit the ground sideways. His hip landed on a rock.

Lance doubled back and spoke in a low voice. "What's wrong?"

"I don't know. I tripped on something." Sharp jerked his foot, but he couldn't budge it. "My boot is caught."

"Maybe a tree root." Lance knelt down and brushed pine needles aside. "Not a tree root. An animal trap."

Sharp sat up. Moonlight caught the black metal of the spring-loaded leghold trap. His belly churned at the sight.

"You're lucky. You stepped on the edge and the jaws caught the heel of your boot."

If he had hit the center of the device, it could have broken his leg. "Can you open it?"

"If I can't, you'll have to take off your boot." Lance squeezed the levers on both sides of the trap with his hands, but the springs wouldn't give. "Stand up so I can use my body weight." He extended a hand and helped Sharp get vertical.

Sharp balanced on one foot. Lance placed a boot on each side of the trap. He pressed down on both levers simultaneously. The jaws opened, and Sharp pulled his foot free.

Sharp tested his foot on the ground. Other than a slight pang in his ankle from the twist, he seemed uninjured. "I'm good."

"I thought I heard something in that direction." Lance pointed to the northeast.

"Let's go." Sharp left the trap closed, so it couldn't hurt anyone else. Guilty or not, Stephen Holgersen was a nutter.

They moved onto the trail and headed in the direction Lance had pointed. Sharp surged forward. But Lance held him back. "We won't find anything if one of us breaks a leg in a trap."

He went back to using the stick and paracord to check for trip wires. They crept a hundred yards farther down the trail, and Lance stopped. He tapped Sharp on the shoulder and pointed to the ground. The paracord leaned against a fishing line trip wire.

"Damn. This guy is paranoid," Sharp said under his breath. "But we have to move faster."

"I know," Lance whispered. He followed the trip wire to a loop of wire on the ground hidden beneath a layer of sand. "A leg snare."

"I'm sorry I gave you shit about the cost of those NVGs." Sharp circled around the trap and they continued their trek toward the lake. Frustration gripped him. How were they going to find Olivia in a hundred acres of booby-trapped wilderness?

The sound of water lapping caught his attention. They were nearing the lake. Ahead, the trail opened onto the water. Sharp could see the rocky shore and moonlit ripples across the lake's surface.

A squeak stopped them both short. They moved to the side of the trail and crept to the last clump of underbrush before the beach. Ducking behind it, they peered over the top of the foliage. A dock extended out over the water. Next to the beginning of the dock, a man stood in the open doorway of a shed.

His voice floated over the rocks. "Olivia, if you come out now, I promise to kill you quick. It won't hurt."

She's alive?

Hope surged in Sharp, followed by rage. The man had just promised to kill Olivia. Sharp wanted to strangle him with his bare hands. Was she in that shed? There was only one way to find out. Simultaneously energized and furious, Sharp pressed forward.

Lance grabbed his arm and held him back. He made a motion toward the other side of the shed and pointed to his own chest. Sharp breathed through his urge to run headfirst at the man on the beach. To pound on him and make him say where Olivia was. But Lance was right. They should flank the man, otherwise he might escape. He could have weapons.

"Count to fifty," Lance whispered before he raced along the tree line to the right.

Sharp said a quick prayer that neither of them hit another trap. Counting, he turned back to the lake just as the man disappeared into the shed.

Twenty-nine. Thirty.

Sharp counted faster.

Chapter Thirty-Nine

Under the dock, Olivia shivered in the freezing water. The lake bottom was slimy and slick under her bare feet.

Boots clumped on the dock. He was exiting the shed. Thank God she'd changed her mind about hiding in there. He would have found her already.

The footsteps came closer. Her pulse skittered. She wanted to flee, but there was nowhere to go. No boats were tied up at the dock, and she didn't have the wind to swim. Her body remained still, but her heart beat like a wild animal.

Instinctively, she wanted to hold her breath, but that might trigger a coughing spell. She prayed the lapping of the water covered her wheezing. As long as she didn't cough, he wouldn't hear her.

"Where are you?" His angry voice echoed over the water. "I swear, the longer it takes me to find you, the more you're going to suffer."

The sound of his words sent a shiver through her entire body. Still, she tried not to move. Could he hear her teeth chattering? Her arms, wrapped around the dock piling, cramped in the cold water.

Do. Not. Move.

No matter how uncomfortable she was, she had to remain still. The footsteps approached. She breathed shallowly to minimize her wheezing. Olivia looked up. She could see the soles of his boots between the boards of the dock.

So close.

Her heart slammed against her ribs so hard it seemed as if he would be able to hear it knocking. A cough tickled Olivia's throat. She swallowed and concentrated on taking shallow, steady breaths.

Please. *No.*

The cold penetrated her bones. Her teeth rattled, and the cold seemed to burn her skin. The aching in her body slowly went numb. Her hands and feet felt like blocks of ice. How could she hold on to the dock if she couldn't feel her hands?

Don't let go!

Slowly, the footsteps began to walk away. Olivia waited. He would need time to walk back across the rocky beach to the path in the woods.

Her hands slipped on the wet piling. She lost footing in the slippery muck. The cold closed over her head. For a few seconds, she was suspended in the murky water. Then she got her feet under her body again. Her face broke the surface, and she sputtered.

Had he heard?

She listened but heard no more footsteps. Had he left or was he waiting for her to come out? She couldn't wait any longer. Soon, she wouldn't be able to move. Her body would shut down. She'd sink and drown.

She released her grip on the dock. Her arms fell limply into the water. She sank, her head going under again. The cold water burned her eyeballs. But she wasn't ready to die. Her survival instinct kicked in, and her feet followed suit. She came up again. Floundering in the water, she gasped for air as she emerged from under the dock. For a few seconds, she stood in the muck, scanning the beach, the tall weeds that grew at the marshy edge of the lake brushing her face.

The shore was empty, but she could sense a presence. The goose bumps on her skin prickled. Someone was watching.

Where is he?

Maybe she'd gotten lucky. Maybe he'd returned to the woods to search for her. Maybe he hadn't heard her almost drowning in the marshy lake.

Olivia's bare feet were numb as she tried to walk toward the shore. She could barely feel the slime on the bottom of the lake. Tall weeds and cattails tangled around her legs. She tripped over a rock and fell forward. Reaching out, she caught her balance on the side of the dock. Righting herself, she plowed forward. She could do this.

Dry land was ahead. Then what? She was soaking wet, having an asthma attack, and probably hypothermic. She could barely breathe standing still. How could she run away?

A hand reached down from the dock and grabbed her by the arm. "Get up here, bitch!"

Olivia tried to resist as he pulled her from the water, but there was nothing to hold on to. Lack of oxygen had stolen her energy. Not even the panic swirling in her belly could give her the strength to fight back. She flopped like a rag doll. Her leg banged into the wood as he dragged her over the edge. Her legs tangled in her wet pajama bottoms.

He shook her arm. "I've had enough of chasing you through the woods. Did you think you could escape?"

She did not.

As her oxygen levels fell even further, her panic faded to sadness. She'd never see her family or Lincoln again. Her life was over, and she had left too many things undone and unsaid. She had been defeated. She had nothing left. Her lungs were tighter than an industrial vise. She could barely draw in enough air to stay conscious. She couldn't fight, and she couldn't run.

She was at his mercy.

Chapter Forty

Through the black-and-white imaging of his NVGs, Lance watched the man he was assuming was Stephen Holgersen drag a women's body from the water up onto the dock. She fell onto her hands and knees. Was that Olivia?

The woman was the right size and shape. Moonlight brightened the lake, and he could see Olivia.

Relief passed through him.

She's alive.

Lance paused behind a bush to send Morgan a quick text, asking her to call 911 and send help to the lake.

He returned his phone to his pocket and drew his weapon. If Morgan received his message and called for help, emergency response was at least twenty minutes from the entrance to the camp. Then the Redhaven police or Randolph County sheriff's deputies would have to find them. Who knew how long that would take? He and Sharp were on their own. At best, law enforcement would show up to clean up the mess after it was all over.

He had to sneak up on Stephen. Lance removed his NVGs and set them on the ground at the base of a tree. Holgersen was focused on Olivia, who was on her knees in front of him. Lance crept across the beach and hid behind the shed. He peered around the building and saw Sharp approaching from the other side. Slipping out from behind the shed, Lance eased into the lake. He lowered his body until only his head was above the water.

Olivia and Stephen were near the end of the dock, about forty feet away. Lance slid alongside the dock. He moved slowly so he didn't splash. When he'd gone twenty feet, Lance chinned himself up and peered over the top of the dock.

Still on her hands and knees, Olivia coughed and spit water onto the dock. Her long dark hair dripped. Her pajamas were soaked. Her shoulders slumped in defeat. Closer now, Lance could see bruises on her face.

"You thought you were being clever, hiding in the water." Stephen grabbed her by the hair and jerked. "Do you feel smart now?"

She whimpered, and fury stoked inside Lance. Men who hurt women deserved the same treatment tenfold.

Stephen released her hair. Her head fell and hung low. She began to cough, a dry, painful sound. When the spell ended, Lance could hear her wheezing from twenty feet away. Her body moved with the effort to draw in air. Could she even breathe? How long had she been in the water?

Lance moved forward. She needed help. Now. But Olivia was too close to Stephen. He couldn't shoot him without risking hitting her. He needed a better angle.

He eased back into the water and moved through the thick weeds and cattails until he rounded the far end of the dock. A ladder led up. Lance started up the rungs and peered over the top.

A few feet away, Stephen took a big-ass KA-BAR knife from his pocket. He took hold of Olivia by the hair again and pulled her head backward, stretching her neck. Rage rose in Lance's chest. Olivia's eyes were wide. How fast could Lance get over the side of the dock? Not fast enough to keep Stephen from slitting her throat.

Putting the knife to Olivia's neck, he said, "Say goodbye."

From the corner of his eye, Lance saw Sharp leap onto the other end of the dock and draw his gun. "Put down the knife, Stephen."

Stephen's head snapped around. His eyes narrowed as he assessed Sharp. "Who are you?"

"A private investigator," Sharp said.

"A PI?" Stephen snorted. "Don't come any closer, Private *Dick*. One slice is all it'll take." He caressed Olivia's throat with the KA-BAR. A thin line of blood trickled down her neck.

"Then what?" Sharp asked. "I'll be a witness. Are you going to kill me too?"

"Why not, old man? Doesn't look like it'll be that hard."

"Come and try it." Sharp extended his empty hand, palms up, and curled his fingers in a *come here* gesture. "What's the matter? It's easy to best a girl. Are you afraid to take on a grown man? Are you a coward?"

Stephen dragged Olivia to her feet and held her in front of him, using her as a human shield. "Go ahead. Shoot. She's only a woman. No big deal if you hit her."

Sharp didn't move. He kept his gun leveled at Stephen. "Put down the knife."

"I don't think so," Stephen snapped. "One more step, and I will slit her throat. She'll bleed out before you can dial 911."

Sharp eased forward one tiny step. "Why did you kidnap her, Stephen? Why?"

Keep stalling, Sharp.

"Is this the part where I'm supposed to confess and tell you my life's story?" Holgersen mocked. "Fuck that. I'm not telling you anything."

Chest-deep in the lake, Lance went up another rung. Between Stephen's and Olivia's legs, he could see Sharp. Did Sharp see him? Slowly, silently, he pulled his body from the water until he crouched on the dock.

Lance needed a few inches of space between Olivia's throat and the blade. He couldn't risk attacking Stephen with the knife so close. Sharp needed to make him move. Just an inch or two. That's all Lance needed.

Come on.

"You don't have a chance," Sharp yelled. "I didn't come alone. The cops are already on their way."

"It'll take them forever to get way the fuck out here. Put down the gun!" Stephen shouted at Sharp. The knife remained pressed against Olivia's neck.

"OK. OK," Sharp said. "I'll put it down. But you have to move the knife away from her throat."

"Fuck you. I'm making the rules here."

"Know this." Sharp's voice went harsh. "If that knife touches her again, I will shoot you. From this distance, I won't miss. If she gets hurt, you die."

Stephen hesitated. "I guess this is a stalemate."

"Guess so." Sharp's voice was cool. But Lance could hear Olivia wheezing from six feet away.

Stephen glanced sideways. Before Lance could move, Stephen flung himself and Olivia off the dock. They hit the water with a splash. Lance lunged across the dock and looked over the edge, searching for Olivia.

Ripples on the dark surface of the water sparkled in the moonlight. He saw no heads, just bubbles. Sharp rushed down the dock toward him.

Splashing drew his attention to the right. Lance jumped off the dock toward the sound, hoping he had heard Olivia and not Stephen.

Chapter Forty-One

Morgan held the phone to her ear. Her connection with 911 was still open. Lance and Sharp had found Olivia, but they needed help.

"Olivia Cruz has been found. She was kidnapped and held here." Morgan gave the dispatcher the address. "I don't know what condition she's in. Please send an ambulance."

"There's a unit en route. ETA is twelve minutes," the dispatcher said.

"There are two former SFPD officers on-site. Both are armed." Morgan didn't want the Redhaven police to shoot Lance or Sharp.

"Yes, ma'am." The dispatcher asked, "Can you please stay on the line?"

Considering how far out in the country the camp was located, twelve minutes wasn't a bad response time. But Lance had texted that they'd found Olivia and were in trouble. That was all Morgan knew.

What kind of trouble?

Stephen had kidnapped Olivia. He was clearly capable of doing terrible things. What was happening to Lance right now?

She paced the grass. The sound of an engine brought her gaze to the road. She peered out from behind an evergreen. Headlights approached.

She asked the dispatcher, "Do you have another unit closer? Someone is here."

"No, ma'am. The closest unit is en route. ETA is eleven minutes. Please stay on the line. It'll help if you flag down the officer when he arrives."

The approaching vehicle slowed and turned into the camp. The sleek BMW was definitely not a cop car. Morgan stayed hidden.

"Advise the responding officers there could be multiple suspects," Morgan said to the dispatcher.

If it wasn't a law enforcement officer turning into Stephen Holgersen's driveway, then who could it be? Was Stephen Holgersen coming home from somewhere? No. Stephen drove a white van.

A client? A buddy? His sister?

She sent Lance a text letting him know a car had turned into the entrance but the police wouldn't arrive for another ten minutes, at least. She didn't want him to be surprised.

After they arrived, the police would have to drive back to the lake. They might wait for backup before they went in to confront multiple armed people.

Morgan climbed into the Jeep, locked the doors, and kept her eyes on the entrance to the camp.

She hated waiting.

Chapter Forty-Two

Sharp slid to a stop at the end of the dock and shone his flashlight at the water. "Olivia! Lance!"

Something splashed to the right. Sharp turned the beam and spotted Lance and Holgersen fighting in the shallows. Lance punched Holgersen in the face. Holgersen staggered backward. Sharp didn't have a clear shot at Holgersen. He'd have to leave him to Lance.

Where is Olivia?

Sharp saw a trail of bubbles on the surface. He secured his handgun in its holster and jumped into the lake. The cold water closed over his head. He swam for the bottom, feeling in the murky darkness for her body. His hands swept through empty water.

Something long and silky passed through his fingers. Her hair? He grabbed for it, only to come up with a handful of wet weeds. Disappointment flashed through him. At that very moment, she was drowning. If he didn't find her in the next minute or two, she would die. His lungs screamed for oxygen, and he kicked upward.

Sharp surfaced, and he gasped for air. "Olivia!"

Panic stirred inside him. How much longer could she survive underwater? He saw more bubbles a few feet away, took in a breath of air, and dove under again. His hand brushed clothing. *Olivia!* He kicked forward and swam into an arm. Grabbing it, he pulled her to the surface. Was she alive? Once his head was above the water, he flipped Olivia onto her back and towed her to the shore. When the water was midthigh, he scooped her into his arms and carried her through the weeds and mud to the lakeshore. He staggered onto the beach and gently set her down.

"Please." He put a hand on her chest. Was it moving? She hadn't been underwater for more than a minute or two. "You can do it, Liv."

Nothing. She wasn't breathing.

He pinched her nostrils, put his mouth over hers, and gave her two rescue breaths. Then he started chest compressions. He counted to himself, then pinched her nostrils and breathed into her mouth twice more.

She stirred and sputtered, and Sharp's heart jump-started. He turned her on her side so the water could drain from her mouth. She coughed hard, her body heaving with the effort. When the spasm had passed, she inhaled with a whistling sound. He put two fingers to her wrist. Her pulse scrambled under his fingertips.

His belly churned with relief. Light-headed with it, he leaned down and hugged her for a few seconds. Then he pressed a kiss to her forehead. "Welcome back."

She rolled to her back. Her eyes flew open desperately wide. But she wasn't safe yet. Her chest rattled, and she couldn't get enough air to answer him.

Sharp pulled his phone from his pocket to call for an ambulance, but it had been submerged in the lake and wouldn't turn on. Olivia was alive, but she struggled for every breath. She needed a hospital.

He looked for Lance. *Shit!* Where was he?

"Lance!" he shouted.

No one answered.

Chapter Forty-Three

Waist-deep in water, Lance hugged his head to block the punch. Holgersen's hook landed on his biceps. Holgersen shifted his stance and came at him with an uppercut. Lance stepped sideways to avoid the blow. Countering, he fired a jab, catching Stephen in the jaw, and followed up with a cross that snapped his head back. Blood spurted from his nose, and his hands went reflexively to his face.

Shoving Stephen's chest with both hands, Lance knocked him backward and reached for his Glock.

They were fairly well matched in size, and Holgersen had clearly trained in hand-to-hand combat. But Lance had no interest in a fair fight. Fighting honorably was bullshit. The only thing that mattered was not dying.

Before he could draw his weapon, Stephen dove at Lance. The high water slowed Lance's movements. Stephen tackled him around the waist. They went under together, rolling in three feet of water like a crocodile with fresh prey in its mouth.

Water blinded Lance, and he swallowed a mouthful of muddy lake. Choking, he raised his head above the water and sucked in a lungful of air. Stephen twisted, grabbed Lance by the neck, and shoved him underwater again.

Lance held his breath and floundered. His hands went to his throat, and he pulled at Stephen's fingers. Getting hold of just one, he bent it backward until it snapped. The grip on his neck released. Lance pushed out of the water. Stephen staggered backward. His left hand fell awkwardly at his side. One finger bent at an obscene angle, rendering it useless.

Stalking forward, Lance reached for his gun again. But his hand hit an empty holster.

"Looking for this?" Stephen yelled. He pointed Lance's own gun at him. Stephen must have taken it while he was trying to drown him.

Lance didn't waste time talking. He dove sideways and swam for the bottom. He flinched at the muffled sound of a gunshot and waited for the pain, hoping the shot hit him in the vest. A few seconds passed, and he felt nothing.

Stephen had missed.

Lance eased to the surface. Holgersen was turning in circles, the gun aimed out over the water. Another shot rang out. But Stephen was facing away from Lance and shooting in the wrong direction. Lance slipped underwater and swam toward him. He could see nothing but mud and murkiness. Three strokes later, his hand struck fabric.

Lance wrapped his arms around both of Stephen's legs and stood, lifting him out of the water. He twisted and slammed Stephen into the water on his back. The gun went flying and landed with a splash. Stephen thrashed as Lance held him underwater. Lance lost his grip, and Stephen squirmed out from under Lance's hands and started swimming.

Oh, no you don't.

Lance was not letting him get away. He jumped on Stephen's back. Sliding one arm under his chin, Lance locked him in a rear naked choke. He squeezed his elbows together, cutting off the blood supply to Stephen's head.

Seconds later, Holgersen went limp.

Chapter Forty-Four

A gunshot boomed over the lake. Sharp stood slowly, his eyes searching the darkness. Lance had to be all right. He had to be.

Sharp had been so focused on finding Olivia that he had left Lance to fight Holgersen alone. Who knew what kind of weapons a survivalist would have on his person?

A few very long minutes later, a man walked out of the lake, dragging another body by the foot through the shallow water.

Who is it?

Moonlight fell on Lance's face. "Bastard tried to shoot me with my own gun."

Air hissed out of Sharp's lungs.

"Do you have zip ties on you?" Lance asked, patting his pockets. "Mine are missing, and he'll be awake in a minute or two."

"You didn't kill him." Sharp pulled a bunch of plastic ties out of the leg pocket of his wet cargo pants. He handed them to Lance.

"Nope. But I punched him in the face a few times. He might have a concussion. His nose is probably broken too." Lance retreated to the water's edge to bind Stephen's hands behind his back. Then he dragged him farther up the bank, zip-tied his ankles, and attached them to his bound wrists, putting him in a backward C position.

Holgersen's eyes were closed, and his face was a bloody mess. But he was breathing.

Lance dropped to the ground next to Sharp. "How is Olivia?"

"Alive." Sharp turned back to her. Her eyes fluttered open and closed. "Olivia? Can you hear me?"

Shivering hard, she nodded and said one word in a breathy, weak voice. "Asthma."

"We're going to get you help." He touched her shoulder, then turned toward Lance. "I drowned my phone. Do you have yours?"

"No. Mine is waterlogged too. I texted Morgan before this went south." Lance climbed to his feet. "But I don't know if she got the message or responded. I'll see if I can find a phone or run down the road to Morgan."

It had taken Sharp and Lance forty-five minutes to hike through the booby-trapped woods to the lake, but the private driveway would be much faster.

"Look out for booby traps," Sharp warned.

Lance turned toward the shed. "Let me check for a phone."

Sharp rubbed Olivia's shoulder. "Hang on for a while longer."

Focused on her breathing, she barely nodded.

There wasn't much Sharp could do without any first aid supplies. He didn't even have a blanket. His own clothes were soaking wet or he'd give them to her. He rubbed her arms.

"It's going to be all right," he soothed. "Just take one breath at a time."

But damn if she didn't sound worse.

Lance emerged from the shed. "Just fishing equipment in there. I'll be back. Sit tight."

"Hold on," a female voice called out. "You're not going anywhere."

Who the hell—Sharp turned and froze, fresh dread gathering in his gut.

A tall woman with a long ponytail stood ten feet away. She held a pistol like she knew how to handle it.

"Who are you?" Sharp asked, but he could already guess she was Stephen's sister. He supposed they *were* working together after all.

"Shut up and put your hands up," she said in a clipped voice.

"Sharp, meet Kim Holgersen"—Lance raised his hands—"Olivia's literary agent."

"I said shut up." Kim shifted her position so the gun also covered Lance. "Get those hands higher."

Sharp debated rushing her. He was wearing body armor. So was Lance. But Olivia was vulnerable if Kim started shooting. He moved in front of Olivia.

"Isn't that sweet? You're going to shield her with your body." Kim's voice dripped with disgust as she aimed at Olivia. "Both of you, toss your guns in the lake."

"Mine is already in the lake," Lance said, wiggling his empty hands in front of his face.

Sharp reached for his gun.

Kim stopped him. "Use your left hand."

Sharp pulled his weapon from its holster. With two fingers, he lobbed his gun into the shallow water at the edge of the lake. "Why are you doing this?"

"Confessions are stupid. Shut up." Kim turned to Lance. "Release my brother."

Lance walked to Stephen. Without a knife, he had to unlock the teeth to remove the zip ties. Stephen groaned and rolled onto his back.

"Get up, Stephen," Kim said. "Go get the van."

Stephen turned over onto his knees. "What are you going to do?" His voice was thick and slow. He wiped what Sharp assumed was blood from his face.

"Plan B." Kim blew out a hard breath. "Kill them all and dispose of their bodies far away from here. No one will ever link us to the murders."

Chapter Forty-Five

Lance turned his hand so Kim couldn't see the rock he'd picked up from the beach when he had released her brother. At some point, she had to lose her concentration. She intended to kill them all. He had nothing to lose by trying.

Had Morgan received his text? Had she called the police?

He couldn't depend on help arriving. He had to stop Kim and her brother. He was grateful Morgan wasn't here, about to be shot.

Stephen stumbled up the slope onto a trail that led into the woods. Lance had taken off his NVGs to go into the water, but the moon provided enough light on the beach for him to watch Stephen's form disappear into the woods. The buildings couldn't have been far from the water because a few minutes later, a white utility van appeared from around a bunch of trees. Stephen drove the vehicle onto the beach and stopped next to his sister. He stepped out of the vehicle. When he turned, the moon lit his face, which looked like raw meat. One eye was swollen almost shut. His nose had ballooned, and drying blood coated his chin. He was moving slowly, as if he didn't have much fight left in him. Had Lance broken one of his ribs too? He hoped so.

If Lance could take Kim and her gun out of the picture, Sharp would be able to handle the injured Stephen. Lance tightened his grip around the rock. The gun in her hands was a semiautomatic. If he missed, she could shoot them all in a couple of seconds.

Stephen opened the cargo doors of the van.

Kim gestured toward Sharp. "Now pick her up and put her in the van."

"No." Sharp planted his body-armor-clad self in front of Olivia. "You just said you were going to kill us all. I'm not going to make it easier for you."

With her gaze locked on Sharp, Kim lifted the gun and looked down the sight. "Are you volunteering to go first?"

Sharp didn't move. Lance whipped the rock at Kim with a vicious overhand. He was barely ten feet away. It struck her on the side of the face. Her head snapped around. She stumbled sideways, bobbling the gun. Lance lunged at her. Stephen tried to block him, but Lance knocked him aside with his shoulder and kicked him in the balls. Stephen hit the dirt like a sandbag.

Lance kept moving. Five feet. He almost had her.

A hand grabbed his ankle. He went down on his face in the dirt. Looking back, Lance saw Stephen, still lying on the ground and holding his boot with both hands. Lance kicked him in the face. "Let go!"

Fresh blood spurted. Stephen groaned and went limp.

Lance scrambled to one knee. Kim whipped the handgun around and pointed it at him. He rolled, trying to get out of the path of her aim, but there was no close cover.

A gunshot rang out over the woods. Lance froze. To his shock, so did Kim. She hadn't fired the shot. Who had?

"Stop!"

Lance knew that voice. They all turned their heads. Morgan stood about eight feet behind Kim, her own gun leveled at the literary agent's body. Relief, pride, and love all surged through his chest. Morgan still had his back, as always, despite the fact that Lance had deliberately removed her from the action.

"Put down the gun, or I *will* shoot you," Morgan said.

Kim didn't move for a few seconds. Was she considering not surrendering? Even if Morgan wasn't an excellent shot—which she was—Kim would be hard to miss at that range. Was Kim suicidal? Morgan had once shot a man in a similar situation. She was not a violent woman, unless someone she loved was threatened.

But Kim was desperate. She dropped to the ground and swung the gun 180 degrees—pointing it right back at Morgan.

Two shots rang out, almost simultaneously.

Morgan stumbled backward. Her hand went to her ribs. She'd been shot.

No!

His gaze swung back to Kim. She was scrambling to her feet and stumbling toward the woods. Her gun lay on the ground. Morgan missed?

"Kim!" Stephen shouted in a weak voice.

But Kim didn't even look back at her brother's pathetic call.

Ignoring Kim, Lance refocused on Morgan. She was holding her side and gasping. Was she bleeding? Panicking, he surged to his feet and started toward her. But she recovered before he could reach her. Then she did what he least expected: she sprinted right past him faster than he thought she could run.

"I've got Stephen!" Sharp yelled, heading for Kim's brother and collecting Kim's gun on the way.

Shocked, Lance lost a second before starting after Morgan. Kim had slowed, and Morgan caught her in a few strides. She reached forward and shoved Kim's shoulder. The agent tipped forward and face-planted, sliding in the weeds. Morgan was on her in a second, landing hard, then planting a knee in the agent's lower back.

Lance caught up as Morgan forced the agent's arms behind her. She glanced over her shoulder. "Do you have zip ties?"

"I do." Lance handed them over.

Morgan secured Kim's hands. Then she sat back on her heels, breathing hard.

Lance crouched next to her, shoving up the hem of her jacket. "Are you hurt?"

When his hands hit the body armor, he exhaled. "You're wearing your vest."

"You saw me put it on." Morgan took off her jacket and vest.

"I forgot." Lance had panicked.

She lifted the hem of her shirt. "I feel like I was hit with a hammer."

"You're going to have a big-ass bruise." Which Lance was grateful for.

"I'll take it." Morgan lowered her shirt.

Lance rolled Kim to her back. Blood bloomed from her shoulder. Morgan hadn't missed. They'd hit each other, but Morgan had been wearing a vest and Kim had not.

Wounded, Kim had run on sheer adrenaline. Lance patted her down for more weapons and found a folding knife in her jacket pocket. Taking it, he glanced back at Sharp, who had secured Stephen's hands. Stephen didn't look like he was going to do anything except maybe vomit. But Sharp checked his pockets and zip-tied his ankles together anyway, then returned to Olivia.

Lance hauled Kim to her feet and marched her back to the clearing. He sat her down.

"I'm bleeding," she complained.

With a sigh, Lance took the scarf Morgan wore to camouflage her pale face and tied it around Kim's shoulder.

"The police are on their way," Morgan said. "How is Olivia?"

"Not good." Sharp turned to her. Olivia's breathing was strained. She wheezed and whistled with each breath. He touched her face, and she opened her eyes. Olivia lifted a hand and reached for Sharp. He closed his fingers around hers as the sound of approaching sirens filled the woods.

Soon, four Redhaven police cars, a paramedic unit, and an ambulance were parked in the clearing next to the lake. Sharp climbed into the ambulance with Olivia. The paramedic had started treating her immediately with inhaled and IV medications and oxygen. Her color had already improved.

Lance put an arm around Morgan's shoulders. She leaned her head on his shoulder. They didn't speak at first. The physical contact was reassuring enough. The crisis had passed. No one had died—not even the Holgersens. Weariness seeped into Lance's bones. He was wet, cold, hungry, and utterly exhausted.

But his heart was light with elation and disbelief that they had found Olivia alive. Or maybe he was light-headed.

"I want to go home and sleep for a week," Morgan finally said.

"I hear you." Lance squeezed her arm. They hadn't slept much since the previous Thursday. "It's been a long four days."

"We're not going to get any sleep tonight, are we?" Morgan asked.

"Probably not." They had a long night of questioning ahead of them, but Lance didn't care. Everyone he cared about was alive, and that was all that mattered.

Chapter Forty-Six

Olivia reached for the water cup on her rolling bed tray.

Detective Stella Dane sat in the bedside chair, taking notes on a small notepad. "I can come back if you need a break."

"No." Olivia sipped. "I'm almost done. I want to finish." She wanted to put the whole incident behind her, but realistically, she knew that would never happen. She would carry the scars of her kidnapping forever.

Would she ever be able to be alone again? Sleep without nightmares?

She shuddered, wishing Lincoln were there. This was the first time he'd left her side since he'd found her the night before. He had been gone for twenty minutes, and she was missing him. She'd gone from being super independent to super dependent in five days.

Olivia had already detailed the events spanning from the night she was kidnapped to her escape and rescue. "I still can't believe my agent arranged my kidnapping as a publicity stunt. I knew she was having a tough time with her separation, and she'd been getting irritable about the book proposal I owed her, but still . . ."

"It is bizarre," Stella agreed. "You never had any clue as to how desperate she was?"

"No." Olivia thought about her last few conversations with Kim. "She did mention she was afraid she'd lose her condo, but we'd only worked together for a short time. I really don't know her that well."

Olivia thought she would eventually feel betrayed, but for now, she was grateful to be alive and afraid to be alone. Maybe after she'd processed the ordeal and spent a few hundred hours in therapy, she'd get around to being angry.

"We thought one of the killers you were investigating was innocent and the real guilty party didn't want his case reopened," Stella said.

"Will Cliff Franklin get a new trial?" Olivia asked.

"I doubt it. Joe has given us all kinds of details on the deaths of Cliff's five other victims. If the search teams find the bodies, we'll have evidence to back up his story. Joe didn't want to testify against his brother until his own neck was on the line. Now he won't shut up. Even if Cliff gets an appeal on the conviction for Brandi's death, he'll be facing five additional murder charges."

"That's a relief," Olivia said. "I knew I had to come forward with the information about the chain of evidence and let the legal system handle the fallout. I had already finished the book proposal, but something inside me just didn't want to submit it. Maybe I shouldn't be a journalist anymore."

"You're being too hard on yourself."

"It's not my job to form opinions or assume the roles of judge and jury. I'm supposed to report the truth."

"It's OK to be human and not want a killer set free to hurt other people." Stella tilted her head. "Did you ever think Erik Olander was innocent?"

"Only briefly in the beginning. His case was interesting, though. I suspected his parents helped him invent the intruder scenario to cover up his wife's murder."

Stella put away her pen and notepad. "I should let you rest, and I imagine Sharp is pacing the hallway outside the door."

Despite her trauma, Olivia smiled at the image.

Stella stood. "Are you going to be all right?"

Olivia thought about the nightmare she'd had that morning and how Lincoln had woken her and held her until she'd stopped shaking. "It isn't going to be easy, but eventually, I think I will."

*****

Sharp leaned against the wall in the hospital hallway outside Olivia's room. He was bone-tired after sitting up all night with her. Treatments overnight had greatly improved her breathing, but her sleep had been interrupted by nightmares.

Still, he would take this kind of tired any day over the last few days of thinking he'd never see her again.

Morgan strode down the hospital hallway. At her side, Lance carried a teddy bear holding a GET WELL balloon. They both looked as exhausted as Sharp felt. Morgan was pale, and Lance sported dark circles under his eyes. But they were holding hands and smiling.

Could he and Olivia be that happy together? Deep in his heart he knew the answer was yes.

"You two didn't get any sleep last night either?" Sharp asked as Morgan greeted him with a touch on his arm.

"The girls woke us at six." Morgan smiled wistfully. "Sleep is still a dream for us."

Lance grunted. "The kids don't want to hear any *we got in late* bullshit. I couldn't even get in the shower until after they left for school." But under his exhaustion, he looked pleased that Morgan's girls had missed him.

"We're clean and caffeinated," Morgan said. "It's the best we can hope for today."

"Is everything OK with Olivia?" Lance nodded toward the closed door.

"Stella is taking her statement," Sharp said. "Olivia's asthma is much better. They have her on multiple medications."

The door opened, and Stella stuck her head out. "Sharp, you can come back in now." She didn't seem surprised to see Morgan and Lance in the hallway. "You two might as well listen too. It'll save me from having to repeat myself."

Sharp led the way into the room. He listened for wheezing but heard none. He offered Morgan the chair next to the bed, but she shook her head. Sharp eased into it, his hand reaching for Olivia's. "You all right?"

She nodded. "Talking about it helps."

He squeezed her hand. She would need counseling, but she was tough. Before Stella had come, Olivia had told him everything she could remember about her kidnapping. Sharp pictured her trying to strangle Stephen with her drawstring and digging rocks out of the dirt floor to fill the toe of her sock. He couldn't believe she'd made two weapons out of her pajamas.

Lance set the teddy bear on the rolling tray. "How are you?"

"I'm going to be fine, thanks to you all," Olivia said.

Stella chimed in, "Kim has opted to exercise her right to remain silent. She literally has not said a single word since we arrested her. She stares at the wall in her cell. If I bring her into an interview room, she glares at me." A conspiratorial and slightly feral smile crossed Stella's face. "But her brother hasn't stopped talking. He's terrified she's going to try to hang most of the blame on him. We might have implied that she did."

"It probably helps that she was going to run away and leave him at the survival camp," Sharp added.

"It certainly does. He was angry and hurt she would betray him after all he had done for her. He spilled the whole plan. Kim asked him to kidnap Olivia and hold her for a long weekend." She paused for breath. "He was supposed to release her on Monday or Tuesday under the guise of wanting to hunt her down and kill her in the woods. The plan was for Stephen to let her escape. That all changed when Olivia saw his face. Once Olivia could identify Stephen, she had to die."

Olivia closed her eyes for a few seconds and swallowed. Her escape attempt had been her death sentence.

"Let me guess," Morgan said. "Kim's husband was suing her for half the value of the condo, and she needed money to buy him out."

"Yes." Stella nodded. "She'd also invested heavily in her brother's survival school, which failed. She had no cash. She needed to bring in a significant amount of money over the next six months. She had also grown increasingly aggressive in other deals, pushing publishers to get contracts signed, not bothering to negotiate terms but rushing to close—and get paid—instead. Kim was the one leaking information to the press. She thought the media attention generated by Olivia's kidnapping and courageous escape would make Olivia famous. Everything they did—from the anonymous call notifying the press of the bombing to pushing the car into the ravine—was all designed to keep Olivia's story in the news and increase publicity. The film company interested in her first book was then expected to make an offer that would drive up the value of Olivia's next book. Kim convinced her brother she could get a five-million-dollar contract on the book, at minimum, on top of the film deal. She speculated that movie studios would race to option the story of Olivia's kidnapping."

"That's crazy," Lance said.

"Yes," Stella agreed. "But she was desperate, and she went a little psychopathic when her husband left her. Apparently, she had supported him for the last ten years while he lost money in the real estate market. He repaid her by cheating on her with a twenty-year-old and then suing her for half their assets. The betrayal stung. Stephen said Kim's attachment to her condo had become obsessive."

"And her brother went along with the plan because he was in debt too?" Lance asked.

"Yes," Stella confirmed. "And he kept emphasizing that they never intended to hurt Olivia, just hold on to her for a few days. He acted as if being kidnapped wasn't a big deal."

"He'd better go to prison for a long time." Sharp blew out a hard, angry breath. "The DA better not offer him a sweet deal."

Stella held up a hand. "I wouldn't worry too much about that. The evidence against Stephen is overwhelming. The DA is playing hardball."

Good.

"What about Kennett Olander?" Lance asked.

Stella shrugged. "His death appears to be unrelated to Olivia's kidnapping. We suspect the LMS orchestrated his murder. The ATF and FBI are taking over the case." She didn't look upset. "They'll keep me informed, but based on the organization's size and history, I wouldn't count on Olander's murder being solved anytime soon. In an interesting turn of events, the ATF agent thinks Stephen Holgersen may have had some dealings with the LMS. A few suspected members were on Stephen's student roster."

"That's not so strange," Lance said. "He ran a survivalist school."

Stella turned to Olivia. "Call me if you have any questions or if you remember any other details."

"I will," Olivia said.

Stella left the room.

"Thank you so much." Olivia sniffed. "I wouldn't be here without all three of you."

"We're just happy you're all right." On the other side of the bed, Morgan patted Olivia's shoulder. "But we won't keep you. You need to rest. Call us if you need anything." Morgan's gaze shifted from Olivia to Sharp. "Either of you."

"Thanks." The offer made Sharp feel all mushy. Moisture filled his eyes. His emotions had been running high since they'd found Olivia. Exhaustion wasn't helping. He didn't have any family left, but he had the very best friends. "I hope you two are headed home for a nap."

"No." Lance shook his head. "Gianna is being discharged today. We're going upstairs to pick her up."

"That's great." Sharp stood and walked them to the door. "Thank you both. I don't know how I would have gotten through this without you."

Morgan kissed him on the cheek. "We'll always be there for you."

Lance gave him a one-armed hug and a manly back slap. "Call us later and give us an update."

"Will do." Sharp watched them walk out the door. Then he returned to his chair next to Olivia. He took her hand and rubbed the smooth skin with his thumb.

"You look tired, Lincoln," Olivia said. "You should go home and get some sleep too."

"I'm staying here with you." He lifted her hand to his mouth and kissed her knuckle. "I'll nap when you do."

"I won't pretend I don't feel safer with you next to me."

"Then that's exactly where I'll stay."

"Thank you." Olivia's voice was weak, but her smile was solid—and so was her grip on his hand. He had no idea where their relationship was going, but from now on, he wasn't holding back.

This was not the time for proclamations. They were both too strung out. When Sharp told her he loved her, he didn't want any negative energy in the air. Because he did love her. He knew it. His eyes met hers.

She knew it too, and maybe she loved him back.

But she'd been through a terrible ordeal. She needed to heal, physically and mentally, before he hit her with an emotional zinger. There was no rush.

Sharp wasn't going anywhere.

Chapter Forty-Seven

It was late afternoon when Morgan carried Gianna's bag from the car to the front porch. Her discharge had taken longer than expected. Hospitals seemed to exist in their own time zones.

Lance pushed ahead and opened the door. "Let me work crowd control."

Gianna followed them up the walk. "I'm fine. You don't have to control anyone."

But Morgan worried about the temporary dialysis access. A large patch of clear tape sealed the catheter to Gianna's chest, and Morgan didn't want the kids or dogs to pull at the short tube. Infection was a risk, and Gianna did not need more surgery.

They went inside. Mac had thought ahead and restrained the dogs. They barked and strained at the ends of their leashes. The girls met Gianna in the foyer with hugs.

Mia wiped her eyes. "I missed you."

"Me too." Ava hugged Gianna's leg. "So much."

Sophie jumped up and down. "Come see what we made you!" She grabbed Gianna's hand and pulled her into the kitchen. A long banner of taped-together paper read WELCOME HOME GIANNA in blocky blue crayon.

Gianna swiped her hands across her cheeks and hugged the three girls. "I missed you all too."

Sophie pushed her onto a stool. "Uncle Mac made chicken soup."

"You girls set out bowls and utensils." Mac went to the range and lifted the lid from a large pot. The smell of chicken soup flooded the kitchen.

Sophie fetched place mats and napkins. Mia counted spoons, and Ava set out bowls, one at a time. Grandpa shuffled into the kitchen with his cane.

"Morgan, I'll leave you to serve." Mac took off the apron he'd been wearing. "Stella will be home any minute." Mac ladled soup into a glass container and secured the lid. "I'm going home to have dinner with *my* girl."

"Thank you for everything, Mac." Morgan hugged him.

"Bye, Uncle Mac!" the girls shouted in unison.

"Wait till Stella and I have kids. There'll be plenty of time for payback." He kissed the girls and left.

Were Mac and Stella thinking about kids? They hadn't even mentioned getting married. Her sister didn't seem to be in a rush, but maybe Mac was trying to convince her.

Morgan put the thought aside and enjoyed dinner with her family. Afterward, the girls cleared the bowls, and Lance volunteered to do dishes. When Gianna protested, he shook his head. "You're on light duty for a while. Enjoy it."

Gianna sank back into her chair.

Morgan took advantage of the quiet. She cleared her throat. "So we decided to postpone the wedding."

"Why?" Gianna's voice rose.

Drying his hands on a dish towel, Lance crossed the room and stood next to Morgan's stool. They'd agreed to present a united front. Even though Olivia had been found, she was still severely traumatized, and Gianna was in rough physical shape. "We thought it would be better to wait until things settle down."

"No!" the girls shouted.

Sophie broke into tears. "Aren't you and Wance gonna get mawwied?" The speech impediment she'd outgrown months ago made a sudden reappearance. "I want Wance to be my daddy."

"We're still going to get married," Lance said. "We just might wait a little while."

"I don't see how we can pull a wedding together in a week and a half," Morgan began. "I haven't even thought about it. There are about twenty details I've let go. Olivia is still in the hospital—"

Gianna cut her off. "She'll be out in a day or so."

"Wouldn't it be better to put it off until you're feeling better?" Morgan asked.

"Absolutely not!" Gianna slid off her stool. "Where's my bag?" She found her backpack and brought it to the island. After pulling out her computer, she opened it. "Everything is done. I called the caterer from the hospital and gave them the final head count."

"You worked on the wedding planning from your hospital bed?" Morgan leaned back, overwhelmed.

"Yep." Gianna tilted her head. "It was better than staring at the ceiling. I'm all right, Morgan." She gestured to her chest. "This is just a minor setback. I'm still ten times healthier than when I moved in with you. This disease is my reality, but I won't let it keep me from living. And that includes going to your wedding."

The girls surrounded Morgan's chair.

"You hafta mawwy Wance." Sophie's eyes welled with tears.

Ava and Mia nodded.

Morgan and Lance shared a glance. He shrugged. "I want to marry you, and seriously, our lives will always be filled with chaos. If we wait for a quiet moment, it might never happen."

"I still have the final fitting for my dress." Morgan reached for her phone to check her calendar.

"It's on Friday, and you look like you've lost weight." Gianna frowned.

Grandpa passed Morgan the bread basket. "Use butter."

Warmth filled Morgan. "If you're sure it won't be a hardship . . ."

"Since you've put me on light duty, I'll definitely have time to review the final details." Gianna motioned to her laptop.

"OK, then. I guess we're getting married next week." Morgan smiled, joy filling her heart. Lance was right. Chaos was their hobby. Their lives were never going to be settled. But that was OK. She loved the chaos of family life.

The girls cheered and rushed to Lance for hugs. The rest of the evening was blissfully quiet. Morgan and Lance went to bed right after the kids and slept for ten straight hours.

Chapter Forty-Eight

JOHN H ROGERS
CAPT
US ARMY
IRAQ
NOV 14, 1982
JUL 10, 2015
BELOVED HUSBAND AND FATHER

Well, this is awkward.

A week later, Lance stared at the tombstone of Morgan's late husband.

Ava and Mia had wanted to visit their father and show him the dresses Morgan had bought them for the wedding. They wore matching blue dresses, shiny black shoes, and mini peacoats. Sophie had dressed in her zombie costume and yellow ladybug rain boots.

Morgan was busy with last-minute wedding preparations. Mac was grading papers, and Stella was tied up with the FBI. During the past week, the bodies of all five of Cliff Franklin's additional victims had been found. But for Lance, the case was over. Since all he had to do on Saturday was put on his suit and show up on time, he'd volunteered to escort the girls to the cemetery.

Ava was the only one of the three girls who remembered their father. She faced the headstone and smoothed the blue fabric of her poofy dress. "Mommy let me pick the color."

Mia stood next to her sister, but her attention was on Sophie, who twirled in a circle a few feet away. Her zombie costume was getting more ragged by the day. But she was happy. Mia moved off to spin in circles with her little sister.

Ava stopped fussing with her dress and looked up at Lance. The space between her brows furrowed into the vertical thinking-line she'd inherited from her mother. "Can Daddy really hear me?"

Angling his body so he could keep one eye on the younger girls, Lance crouched next to Ava. "What do you think?"

"I don't know." She turned back to the tombstone. "I want to talk to him, but it feels weird. He doesn't answer."

Lance carefully considered his response. "Do you remember the funeral?"

Ava's frown deepened. "A little. Soldiers shot guns. I covered my ears and cried. It was scary." She shivered.

"I'll bet it was." Lance wrapped an arm around her shoulders.

"Is he even here?" she asked, looking around.

If he told Ava her father was buried under the ground, she'd have nightmares for a week. But she asked to visit her father now and then. At seven, she was just beginning to understand the concept of death. Lance didn't want to take any comfort away that she received from her visits to the cemetery.

"Do you like coming here?"

She tilted her head, thinking. "Sometimes."

"Then you should come when you want to, but you can talk to your daddy anytime. You don't need to be here. Your daddy is wherever you are. He's always with you." Lance tapped the center of his own chest. "Right in here."

"Grandpa said he went to heaven."

"I'm sure he did."

What was she really asking? Was he flubbing this?

In the last six months, Lance had learned one good lesson regarding children. They were direct.

"Ava, what's wrong?" he asked.

Tears filled her eyes. Her lip quivered. "At school, Emily said my daddy would be mad at me because I'm happy I'm going to have you as a new daddy." She sniffed. "I don't want him to be mad at me."

Emily, Emily, Emily.

Why were kids so mean? How long had Ava been thinking about this?

"Emily is wrong," Lance said firmly. "Your daddy loves you, and he wants you to be happy. End of story."

Ava brightened. "You're sure?"

"Positive." Lance nodded.

Ava threw her arms around his neck. Then she skipped off to join her sisters, twirling in circles on the grass.

He faced the headstone again. *Now what?* Just leaving seemed wrong. If John hadn't died, Lance knew Morgan would still be married to—and in love with—him. Yet, Lance felt no jealousy toward the man who had once held Morgan's heart. Wherever John was, he was there without the woman he had loved, something Lance did not even want to imagine.

Lance bowed his head. "I'm sorry you died, John. I love your girls as if they were my own. I love Morgan too much for words, and I promise to take care of all of them. Nothing will be as important for the rest of my life."

With a lump in his throat the size of a softball, he turned away from the headstone, gathered the girls, and herded them toward the minivan. As he buckled seat belts and car seats, Lance felt as if he'd passed a very important parenthood test.

301

Chapter Forty-Nine

Morgan walked onto the sand at Scarlet Beach. Her grandfather's arm was looped through hers. In his other hand, he held his cane. He stubbornly refused to lean any weight on her. In front of them, rows of folding chairs faced the lake. The afternoon sun shimmered on the water.

Ava, Mia, and Sophie lined up in matching blue dresses. Ava was in love with the poof and lace and patent leather.

"Are you ready?" Stella asked. She wore a knee-length sheath dress the same shade as the girls' dresses. Morgan smoothed her own dress, a column of white silk that hugged her body to just below her knees.

Wait. Where are Sophie's shoes? Morgan smiled. It didn't matter. The afternoon was warm and sunny.

At the end of the aisle, Lance waited for her in his dark-blue suit. Sharp stood at his side, as always. Morgan spotted Gianna and Olivia in the front row. Olivia held an iPad so Lance's mother could watch the ceremony via video chat.

"Mommy, can I go?" Ava asked in a whisper loud enough to make all the guests smile.

Morgan nodded.

Ava walked down the aisle, tossing rose petals in front of her. Mia followed, her steps slow and measured, just like they'd practiced the day before. Sophie turned in circles and pelted the guests with flower petals.

Stella walked behind the girls to stand in front with the minister.

Morgan's gaze went back to Lance and stayed there. His eyes held hers as she walked down the aisle toward him. Grandpa sniffed as he patted Morgan and Lance both on the shoulders; then he went to his seat in the front row between Morgan's other sister, Peyton, and her brother, Ian. Stella took her place next to Morgan, and the girls clustered around their feet.

With three young kids, they'd opted for a short and sweet ceremony. The minister read the traditional opening, then said, "Lance and Morgan wrote their own vows."

Lance faced her. "I promise to be your lover, companion, and friend. I will be your partner in parenthood, your ally in conflict, and your accomplice in mischief. I will make sure you always have coffee in the morning and donuts on Saturday, and I will love you with all my heart for the rest of my life."

Morgan had expected to cry, but joy filled her as she squeezed Lance's hand. "I will never take you for granted. I promise to be your lover, your friend, your sidekick—and your lawyer when necessary. I will be forever grateful to be your wife. Today, I give you my hand. You already have my heart."

They said their *I do*s and exchanged rings. Before Morgan could blink, the minister proclaimed them man and wife, and Lance kissed her.

It seemed like a dream. Three years before, her life had been shattered. Now it was rebuilt, and her heart was full.

Lance lifted his head. His blue eyes sparkled with happiness—and maybe a tear—as he smiled and kissed her again. She wound her arms around his neck and held on.

The girls cheered.

Sophie pried them apart. "That's enough kissing."

"It's never enough kissing." Lance put Sophie on his back and scooped Mia and Ava into his arms. Music played and kids raced around the tent that had been set up on the beach for the tables and chairs. The girls were a little disappointed there was no bouncy castle or ponies, but Gianna had hired a face painter and organized some games for the kids.

Morgan dragged Gianna away from the children and shoved a plate of food into her hands. "Sit and eat. You need to conserve your strength."

"I'm feeling much better." But Gianna sat and forked pasta into her mouth.

Sharp tugged Olivia to the table. He turned his chair to face Gianna's. "So, I have some news for you. The day Olivia was released from the hospital, we went down to the transplant center and got tested. I don't know if they told you, but the whole family went. The center called yesterday. It seems I'm a match for you. There are still a bunch of tests I have to have, but as long as I pass, I can give you a kidney."

Gianna put down her fork. Tears flowed down her face. "I can't . . . I don't . . ."

Morgan's knees went weak. The family had been devastated to learn none of them were the right blood type, and Sharp hadn't said a word. She hadn't even known he'd gone to the center, not that it surprised her.

Sharp patted Gianna's arm. "It's OK. You don't have to say anything."

She threw her arms around his neck and hugged him hard.

Sharp froze for a few seconds, then returned the hug, patting her back. "I didn't mean to make you cry."

"I should say no." Gianna sniffed. "Taking your kidney feels selfish."

"Why the hell would you say no?" Sharp frowned. "I have two, and I only need one. It's basic math."

The decision was anything but basic.

Morgan's eyes brimmed with tears. She hadn't cried during her own wedding, but Sharp's generosity did her in.

"Thank you, Sharp," she said.

He nodded. "Friends help each other. It's what we do."

The rest of the reception flew by. Morgan held Lance's hand as they said goodbye to the guests.

The caterer shooed Morgan away from the tent when she attempted to organize the cleanup. The sun was setting as they loaded the girls into the minivan. The kids were exhausted. Sophie fell asleep on the drive home. Lance carried her to bed and changed her into her pajamas. Morgan helped Ava and Mia change and brush their teeth. Then she tucked them into bed.

"I'm going to bed too." Grandpa kissed Morgan and disappeared.

"And me." Gianna hugged them both and went to her room.

Morgan went into the kitchen in her wedding dress and bare feet.

Lance opened the fridge and took out a bottle of champagne and a container of leftover pizza. "I'm starving." He'd taken off his jacket and tie. The sleeves of his white dress shirt were rolled up.

"Me too. I didn't have time to eat anything at the wedding." She took a slice from the box and ate it cold.

Lance opened the champagne and poured two glasses. "Is this the right vintage for pizza?"

"Everything goes with pizza." Morgan lifted a glass. "To us."

"To us." Lance touched his glass to hers.

Morgan's heart overflowed with happiness. She felt almost giddy with it.

"It was a perfect day." Morgan sipped. Pizza and champagne were the perfect combination to end it.

"It was." Lance set his glass down. "I have something for you." He took an envelope from his jacket pocket and handed it to her.

She opened it. "It's a brochure for Italy."

He nodded. "That's where we're going. For eight days."

"Eight days? But the kids . . ."

Melinda Leigh

Lance held up a hand. "Peyton is staying here with the kids. She wants to spend some time with your grandfather anyway. She says she's missed him."

"Eight days in Italy." Morgan opened the brochure. "Rome, Florence, and Venice. It feels like a dream come true."

Her whole life felt like a dream come true.

She suddenly remembered her gift for him. She grabbed his hand and dragged him from the kitchen, through the living room, and into the den. "The space is a little tight right now, but we'll be getting new furniture when the addition is finished."

She had shoved the furniture against one wall to make room for a baby grand piano. Lance froze, disbelief in his eyes. "How?"

"I had it delivered today. Our neighbor let them in." Morgan felt her smile to her soul. "I worked really hard to make this a surprise."

"You did a great job. I had no idea."

"I wanted to show you how much I love you by giving you something that speaks to your heart."

"I love the piano." He wrapped an arm around her waist and pulled her closer. "But *you* speak to my heart. You are all I need."

Their lips met in a warm and unhurried kiss, the kind of kiss they could look forward to enjoying for the rest of their lives.

Morgan pulled away and smiled. "Are you going to try it?"

Lance set his champagne glass on the piano and sat down. He lightly touched a few keys, then began to play "Can't Help Falling in Love."

Morgan sat next to him, drank her champagne, and listened to his easy tenor.

He finished and turned to her, pressing his lips to hers again. "Thank you."

She kissed him back. "Promise to play for me often?"

"There isn't anything in the world I wouldn't do for you. I meant every word I said today. I will love you, heart and soul, for the rest of my life."

Morgan looped her arms around his neck and kissed him again. Lifting her mouth from his, she said, "Back atcha."

Lance pulled her onto his lap. "And now that we're alone, I can show you how much I love you."

Happiness shifted to heat, and Morgan whispered in his ear, "Maybe we should go to bed."

"I heard music," a small voice said. Oohs and aahs followed.

Morgan turned to see the girls standing in the doorway. She rested her forehead on Lance's shoulder. "It's my fault. I wanted you to play."

Lance was shaking with laughter. He kissed her nose and said two words: "Eight days."

"They're kissing again." Sophie shook her head. Rushing to them, she pushed Morgan aside and climbed onto the bench between her and Lance. "Let me play."

"And me."

Ava and Mia crowded Lance. Morgan slid off the piano bench to make room for the girls. Lance mouthed "sorry" over the kids' heads.

Morgan could wait. In two days, she'd have him all to herself for eight whole days. Then they'd have the rest of their lives together.

The kids would have to get used to lots of kissing.

Acknowledgments

It truly takes a team to publish a book. As always, credit goes to my agent, Jill Marsal, for nine years of unwavering support and great advice. I'm thankful for the entire team at Montlake Romance, especially my managing editor, Anh Schluep, and my developmental editor, Charlotte Herscher. Special thanks to Rayna Vause and Leanne Sparks, for help with various technical details, and to Kendra Elliot, for helping me push through those days when I need to write but don't want to.

About the Author

#1 Amazon Charts and *Wall Street Journal* bestselling author Melinda Leigh is a fully recovered banker. A lifelong lover of books, she started writing as a way to preserve her sanity when her youngest child entered first grade. During the next few years, she joined Romance Writers of America, learned a few things about writing a novel, and decided the process was way more fun than analyzing financial statements. Melinda's debut novel, *She Can Run*, was nominated for Best First Novel by the International Thriller Writers. She's also garnered Golden Leaf and Silver Falchion Awards, along with nominations for two RITAs and three Daphne du Maurier Awards. Her other novels include *She Can Tell*, *She Can Scream*, *She Can Hide*, *She Can Kill*, *Midnight Exposure*, *Midnight Sacrifice*, *Midnight Betrayal*, *Midnight Obsession*, *Hour of Need*, *Minutes to Kill*, *Seconds to Live*, *Say You're Sorry*, *Her Last Goodbye*, *Bones Don't Lie*, *What I've Done*, and *Secrets Never Die*. She holds a second-degree black belt in Kenpo karate; teaches women's self-defense; and lives in a messy house with her husband, two teenagers, a couple of dogs, and two rescue cats.